This book is dedicated to the version of me I left in 2019.

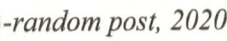 *-random post, 2020*

One day someone is going to ask you, 'What did you do during the quarantine?' What will you say? What will it say about you?

Preface

Looking back on the one of the times I read a social media post like that is probably the best place to begin. During a time when the world was in such turmoil social, spiritual, physical, economical, and racial... What was the *right* answer? We all were going through different things, there were to be a wide range of answers, but the questions seemed so unfair.

So, what does a person's actions during a nationwide shutdown even say about them? All whilst folks dying in the news, jobs shutting down, protests in the streets, riots in the streets, bodies in the streets, families are running out of basic supplies like toilet paper. Yet, some made it work. They were starting delivery companies, clothing companies, food trucks, restaurants, podcasts, online stores, and learning to invest. What was right or wrong? Everyone just did what was best for them at that time, I assume.

Even beyond just the basic pandemic struggles, had there been a thermostat in the ass of the country, it would have shown the temperature was at an unhealthy degree. The political climate was up daily, disrespectful campaign signs were everywhere, folks were really showing their asses on the news and social media. It was even hard to get along with neighbors and co-workers on the simplest of topics.

Laws and rules that had been taught, believed, and reinforced my whole life were being broken and debunked right in front of the entire country! You were almost wrong, ignorant, if you didn't start to question everything. The creators of the rules were the biggest breakers of them.

Many people, me included, were also dealing with deaths of our family members and loved ones, but due to the safety regulations that were imposed, we were unable to have proper funeral services. Newborns being born alone without visitors, some even pulled apart from their mothers until fully tested for the virus. Thousands of people were laid off or lost their jobs all together. Rent and mortgages were at an all-time high and comically the hardest for some was their own children home with them all day.

At minimum, even the most decent of people were fighting over chicken sandwiches and common household items. The reactions ranged from public execution of innocent folks to country leaders inciting riots. I recall my students referencing the foreshadowing of a movie where neighbors slaughter each other freely, and even the sales and low inventory on bullets showed even adults were stocking up on weaponry.

So, what was the *right* thing to do? It felt almost philosophical.

My first thought was against the authors of those types of posts and commenters who agreed, shaming others who were unable to persevere or thrive, due to hard times brought on by the pandemic, it seemed truly insensitive. However, as the quarantine continued and the question kept coming across my mind and social media feed, I began to subconsciously build a respectable response that would satisfy myself in the future. With that said, I do give credit to those posts, as it led me to *seek* growth. Otherwise, I may not have been so ambitious to achieve so much in the year of solitude.

It also deepened my vision while I people-watch and make observations. I paid attention to what others did, considering what it might say about them. Only out of curiosity, judging anyone for what they did to keep their sanity and spirits, during the unfamiliar transition of a worldwide pandemic, just didn't seem fair. But on social media, everyone had an opinion.

Yeah, in 2020 shit got real. It was not an easy time for the soft, nor a dry time for even the slightly sensitive.

Social media also made things more entertaining. Exposing the highly commendable philanthropic efforts in communities and organizations or displaying burning buildings on folks' LIVE feed whilst

4

vulgarities chanted in the background. News was spreading much quicker these days, so were opinions and perspectives that would have never been relevant otherwise. I won't even get into how the comment sections, could be breeding grounds for suicidal thoughts if a person accidentally cared too much.

There was a line drawn and people were choosing sides. All under magnifying glasses, cell phones, exposing alternate perspectives. It was such a strange lens to view humanity through.

It gave me time for introspection, with the extra downtime from no longer having to commute, not really conversing on social media, cooking my own meals at home, making my own coffee, and no longer having to bring my son to school... At some point I decided I wanted to make this new time count. All 1,440 minutes a day!

So, *what did I do during the pandemic?*

I can recall already feeling damaged and damn near defeated just months prior to the year even beginning. I was struggling with my own sense of existence and purpose, as I sat crying on the kitchen floor fresh from heartbreak. Retrospectively, it could have been an honest overreaction to an upcoming menstrual cycle and a strand of awaiting misfortunate, single-woman's chores that I now had to get used to doing. After another break up, that day I talked to myself, I realized it was time to get my shit together.

I lovingly refer to the knowledge I embarked upon, the seed, as my Self-Guided and Self-Paced: *Quarantine Education.* I consciously made a choice to simply learn more, to smarten up: mentally, physically, financially... and then inevitably spiritually.

I learned to take full accountability in becoming the person that I needed to be for things in my life to go as I want them to go. Despite personal or health issues, I also would need to learn to toughen up for whatever is destined to come next. No more sitting on the kitchen floor, being a victim to limits on my life from *any*one. The old way of being this idea of *me*, Acacia, was not working anymore, I tried it, I've witnessed it among others. It was time to plant new seeds and grow a new tree.

At first, I filled my free time with gathering knowledge. I learned the rules. All the ones I could find. I read over seventy good books twice on prominent topics such as self-help, positive thinking, visualization, manifestation, and finance management. The really good books I read over again, some up to five times! Found out what the pros were doing. Also, I read a great deal of the books that were heavy in financial literacy and wealth. As a takeaway, I invested in my ongoing business of five years by making it official, purchasing an LLC title along with a plethora of new technology. Spending more money on the business, in turn, made me more money, which was nice to add to the newly established savings account. Read a few more books and got brave enough to *play* around with some stocks.

The more books I read the more variety of perspectives I gained. The moments of insight and realization I gathered about systems, societies, and their structures was almost immeasurable. I was embarrassed that up until this point I'd only made time to read fictional worlds for pleasurable escapes and the school-issued nonfiction textbooks I skimmed just enough to pass the exams. Alone with my thoughts, I began to wonder if for years I stood idly by and allowed my own indoctrination by the *majority* my entire life.

Next, I spent hours upon hours watching hundreds of videos online, sorting through what was credible and what might not be, keeping the video speed on double to maximize time. The videos were on topics like history, governments, religion, and politics, which supplied enough knowledge for me to pass the certification exam to teach high school social sciences with my master's degree. This entitled me to an even bigger salary for the coming years. The knowledge was paying off and the blessings were pouring in, the fruits of the tree were starting to grow.

Due a partially funded grant, I was blessed to take more structured courses as well that were online, for nearly free from a very prestigious ivy league college. A school that a much younger version of me dreamed of attending, but society quickly had that was destroyed due to my lack of money, test scores, and ancestral blood. Yet, there I was every night, in my college apparel merch ordered in from some timely warehouse and attending ivy league college classes from my bed!

Inspired by all the reading, I got motivated to concentrate on my passion for writing, my thoughts were running wild. I had no choice but to begin taking my writing seriously again, dedicating 500 words per day on paper to myself. Short stories on current issues in humanity, events, and topics that I encountered firsthand, especially with dating, parenting, and teaching. I'd have six tabs open daily and so night, trying to get all the stories in writing and out of my head.

When writer's block would inevitably kick in, I'd transition to the much simpler curriculum development side of the business; creating worksheets and textbook pages that might one day change how we teach. Selling worksheets online to other educators, while creating content for curriculums I planned to one day package and sell.

More noticeably physically, I began a weight loss journey that has me down thirty-five pounds thus far! After years of doing it completely wrong, I learned the key was simply the small stuff, consistency and self-discipline. Adding a basic 30-minute fitness regime to my daily routine was key, making the daily disciplines as regular as brushing my teeth.

Maybe my favorite part was losing the fears that held me. Of course, I still have my Achilles' heel, but I had subconsciously developed this person inside myself that doesn't back down from shit she wants. Whatever it was, if I woke up thinking about running on the beach, exploring a theme park, mountain climbing, dancing at a nightclub, skating, taking karate lessons… whatever it was I did it. I would hear this enticing voice daring me to go out and try things, alone without distractions.

I started to call the annoying voice Dare-You, it was my voice yet seductive, I could tell the difference. In the beginning I'd argue with the voice because I wasn't willing to take her dares without my extreme hesitation, I'm only adventurous to a degree, but Dare-You always got me to do anything. And every time I did a dare, fully present and in the moment, I learned something new about myself. The more I stopped fearing things, the less I heard the Dare-You voice. I haven't heard it in a while, I suppose it's because I dropped most of my inhibitions, but anytime I feel the old me creeping back… I do hear that distinct voice whispering, 'I dare you'.

I began vlogging, posting bits of my workout online, it kept me consistent and accountable. Occasionally, I would post wise words, golden nuggets of knowledge I gathered in my studies for myself, with the notion that maybe there is someone out there in the world that can use me to elevate themselves. Or maybe the knowledge was for myself, advice I might need later in my own nearby future.

All in all, I felt rejuvenated as our country transitioned into our new sense of *normal*. I had not finished writing any of my many incomplete novels or textbooks, but I was working on them simultaneously, hoping one would be completed soon. My goal of reading 100 great books hadn't been met, but close to 70 in a short time was quite a feat for me. More importantly I gained lots of knowledge spiritually, mentally, and physically. I was just a few pounds away from my goal weight, despite a standstill with the numbers on the scale. I slowed down with ads as I didn't need the money from my LLC as much as I needed to write!

Not a picture-perfect ending, but all bills were finally all being paid on time and then some! I was dancing in front of every full-length mirror I passed, feeling strong enough to face the challenges that inevitably come up in all of our lives.

I was grateful and began to see little signs in my life as qualifiers to the affirmations, the new rules of life were working. My confidence was up, the knowledge I was gathering from the books was working. I attracted sporadic positive attention, compliments, and tokens of appreciation. These served as clues that the knowledge I was gaining from my Quarantine Education was factual and trying to lead me to something… or maybe someone.

Overall, I would be pleased to give my reply should the question ever be asked to me, 'What did you do during quarantine?' I'd gathered so much knowledge and had all the notes to prove it! But there's a difference between gathering knowledge and having the wisdom of when you use it.

Fears are barriers to what you want for your future!
Face them all.
Break them all.

@AcaciaIvy 2020

1

"Best friend? Hazel, wake up!" I was surprised she even picked up the video call, I tried to remain patient as she adjusted the phone. "Bitch, guess what I just got?!"

"What do you want?" Hazel groaned, barely awake as suspected. She's far from choosing to be a morning person, but she knows I have been keeping a hectic schedule due to some treacherous writer's block… and this just could not wait.

"Best friend! Get your ass up, go smoke something, do whatever you need to do because you are not gonna believe this," I cautioned her. "I still don't even believe it."

Hazel took a deep sigh, not in the mood for my antics. "Acacia Ivy, if you don't hurry up with this 4 something in the morning phone call…"

"Bitch you better relax, cause *somebody*, your very best friend, just got inboxed free V.I.P. tickets to the DeCreed show this weekend."

"No, you didn't."

"Yes hoe, I did! Backstage!" I yelled, then she yelled happily with me for a few moments, and we eventually regrouped. I knew my bestie would be happy.

I have always been a girl's girl, I pride myself on it, five of my closest friends are women from individual friendships of over ten or twenty years! Although different, the friends were just starting to merge, and I preferred hearing my own thoughts. At one point the friendships used to be so crucial to who I was as a person and the decisions I've made up to this point in life.

Just prior to the pandemic I would have dozens of secrets just dancing around my head daily, but with the physical social distance came a still lingering detachment. It was a gift and a curse, nice to finally hear my own thoughts without the interference. I have always bounced my ideas off my girls for counsel, but recently I'd been a little less vocal

9

about my personal life. Avoiding advice and becoming confident in my own voice and decision-making skills.

"Are you sure they are legit?" She made sure to clarify before getting too excited. DeCreed getting back together for a tour after the pandemic was mind blowing enough, but seeing them backstage for sure, seemed too good to be true. But it was, I'd been verifying the validity for twenty-five minutes and they were legit.

"Do you know who you are talking to?" I checked her. Since middle school I've been the one my friends call to find if, when, where, and with whom their boo is cheating. "Verified account and sent an email confirmation from the company email, biatch. Legit as they are going to be."

"Whose verified account did it come from?"

"You'll see one email address on the invite at the bottom that has the name Chris in it, but that's a very common name so who knows." I knew Hazel was going to be skeptical about the whole thing, who wouldn't be with the new influx of internet scams, so I sent the screenshots. "It's from the group's account, check your messages."

I escaped to my mom-cave and rolled up at my bar, while Hazel read through every screenshot I sent her. I smiled while listening to her 'oohs' and 'ahhs' coming from the other end of the phone. I acted as my own hype man as she was impressed.

"Chris is in DeCreed, maybe he has a thing for you." She told me. "But he is kinda short and he might even be married."

I sighed, "I'm good, a man is the last thing I need, especially someone else's lying ass husband."

"Stop selling yourself short, the married ones are so busy you hardly have to entertain him," Hazel joked.

Recently, we had been finding a sense of collateral bliss, going on dates and collecting trinkets of adoration from appreciative men, since the nationwide lockdown was finally over. These concert tickets are in the top 10 best freebies. The new trinkets were sadly proving to bring just as much, if not more, happiness than settling with an unprepared man, in a serious relationship.

Decades of women falling victim to lies, neglect, abuse, deception, and even contracting STDs (not me), had proven to not be worth the stress anymore. Of course, I've known many, many... MANY women who chose to settle or pick up way too much slack, but that wasn't me.

If I was ever going to fall for someone again and give him my full, unwavering love, I would need to see enough proof that he would complement me. It would have to be worth it.

Fast forward to now, a year of being single, Hazel and I were focusing on our own happiness, and it was going well!

Of course, I wanted a man to totally sweep me off my feet, but as for the time being Quarantine Education taught me to spoil myself and be responsible for my own happiness. I wasn't going to settle for shit anymore. I *intentionally* became the prize that the man that I desire would want.

I went on plenty of dates, keeping an open mind to many types! But I felt like a counselor. It got boring, I tried to make connections, but the chemistry was never there.

Instead, it became a game of just collecting cute trinkets and biographical data for what will probably one day be my doctoral thesis in Humanities or Psychology. At this point I had a myriad of unsolicited life stories, not to mention stories from my friends and associates just floating around in my head. I began storing their stories as some form of data in my mind.

In the past, even before college, I jokingly claimed to be writing one of my life's works, a book, a collection of short stories on my erratic dating life. Recently I'd been adding new ones and writing some of those old experiences into a journal. A collection of stories which were once only written on random notes, text message threads, and told orally in social settings.

I'd learned from my Quarantine Education that life was meant to be lived as a great experiment, that the mistakes were just data on the way to getting it right. Therefore, there were no bad experiences anymore, every experience was just gathering the fruits from the tree.

"Cay, these really are backstage passes to the show and to the private after party." Hazel sniffled; I could hear her ugly crying through the phone. "Bitch, backstage, we are meeting DeCreed that night, I promise you that. Do you know how bad I wanted to just afford to go to the concert after the deadbeat did me and the kids on Christmas?!"

Hazel started her own business during the quarantine, renting and setting up party supplies from oversized letters with balloons to bounce houses for children. She was just beginning to do well for herself, starting the party business was just the right thing for her lifestyle. The finances hadn't quite leveled out, but she would get there in time.

I couldn't help but to laugh, "I know you ain't crying over some tickets?"

"This is my fuckin dream Cay, you know I been praying for those, how are you not crying? I was just talking about seeing them! You cannot buy these tickets at the box office or online, these are backstage. Please don't be pranking me because I'm about to get the babysitter!"

"I promise. I think they sent me those tickets from when I used that new song you sent me for my video. So, it's only right that I offer the guest pass to you." I offered kindly, having a slight reputation of being a prankster at times.

"You think you have a choice?" She screamed at me. "Of course, you are taking me!"

"You know I'm bringing you," I said. "You are about to meet Scandal, Kenz, J-Main, Manuel, who else? Ummm, you are about to meet Chris... and whoever else is in the group!!!"

"Of course, you are bringing me, who else would you bring? A date?" She was wide awake with a giddy laugh, "They don't even allow men backstage at their shows."

"Well, if there's no men backstage then maybe those are not the tickets we need," I laughed. "I would not have even tried to bring a man to this show, I'm hoping there are going to be some fine men there! The whole concert lineup is decent, I'm sure a few will come out. Worse come to worse, maybe spin the block with an old college flame?"

Hazel sighed for me, "Well, while you are hanging out with the bottom of the barrel, with the broke and broken boys of college past... I'll be bagging up one of the DeCreed men."

"Those ones are just as broken."

"Sis, look at humanity, would you prefer broken and rich or broken and broke? Aren't you sick of the nightmares?" She paused with an over dramatic laugh, and I took a moment to reflect on a response. "We've been there, Acacia, we've done that, we're ready for something new. Let's move on from the mediocre dreamers who don't apply themselves and the needy boys who need you to do every meaningless chore for them as if you are their momma!"

My best friend was on her soapbox, but with joyful tears, for about ten minutes before we hung up.

Hazel and I appreciated that it had been years since we were single at the same time, probably not since we met back in high school. For the last ten months, we were living it up. We were traveling around the country, clubbing in new cities, partying on party boats, dancing at brunches, and whatever else came up.

We were truly enjoying our adult years these days, without trying to cater our entertainment and existence around husbands or my very long-term boyfriend. Of course, we still had our children to tend to, but our vision boards were all about enjoying life, and so far, many of the "to do" boxes were getting checked.

Occasionally dating new people, going to nice restaurants and making idle conversation, but so far nothing serious for either of us. Although, along with financial success and stability as a published writer, being an epic mother to my son, traveling the world, and finding a man that met my needs and wants was still on the list of goals as well.

*   *   *

As I looked around in the V.I.P. backstage at the DeCreed concert, I felt slightly cheap compared to the expensive name brands splattered all over the women in the section with us. I was wearing a simple little black bodycon dress that was available with 2-day delivery, with a pair of two-year old red pumps that I hesitantly splurged on for a past birthday. My jewelry, freshly cleaned to add that little sparkle to my outfit, along with my gently used red designer wristlet that completed the look.

Hazel wore a caramel brown catsuit that practically matched her skin tone and fit her thick curves like a sexy glove. She is typically two inches shorter than me, but tonight she wore six-inch designer print heels to match her designer print bag. As a pretty and sociable woman, Hazel fit right into the scene. She spoke with every staff member she could, getting every cent out of that push-up bra, trying to get us to meet the group. I admired how she moved about the crowd and stood firm in questionable moments.

The old version of me may have tried to follow her lead, but thankfully that wasn't me anymore.

I've never been backstage, so I didn't know what to expect, but it was more exciting than I had imagined it would be. I didn't expect to fit right in with the crowd, I never do, but I did not think I would feel like such an alien among the backstage. There was ass and titties shaking everywhere!

Of course, Hazel acted like a super fan, not as bad as most, but she is a hard-core fan, and I am not so much. I was more laid-back and reserved than the dozens of women screaming, jumping, and throwing their thongs and bras to the small meet-and-greet stage couches as some of DeCreed walked in.

Before the men came in, there was a familiar sense of sisterhood in the room. Women were helping each other get cute, laughing, and making small talk. As soon as DeCreed came in the same women were all excited that they were pushing and hitting each other. The whole scene turned me off from the line. How do they thrive in this? I could not believe how willing they were to embarrass themselves. The women were just hoping to be seen by the group. The lines for meeting and pictures were so long that women were giving peep shows to security workers to get closer to the front.

The men from DeCreed and their staff loved the attention and played right into it. Encouraging the once kind, but now desperate women and their scandalous behavior. Women were flashing up their shirts and dresses and twerking with bare ass exposed.

We couldn't see everything from our spot in the crowd, but no doubt from the sounds and cheering, the men were there for all the shenanigans. Enjoying and slapping on whatever they wanted, security guards included.

Women in line were also not shy about what freaky things they wanted to do to the members in the group. They were acting out pornography intros, kissing and touching each other, for the men while simultaneously chanting, "Sweet! Sweet! Sweet!" I recognized the chant from the ending of their popular song "Be My Sweetheart".

It was undomesticated! I will never hear that song the same after seeing the behavior of the women! This whole time I'd been singing that song I thought a *Sweetheart* was a good thing! Backstage I didn't know where to stand, where to look, I quickly wanted no parts of the bad bitch circus.

Yet a part of me realized that the average man would sell their family home to get the treatment DeCreed men were receiving. For a second, I questioned humanity for the thousandth time this year. Is this what people really want when the cell phones and inhibitions are gone? Is this what free will looks like? Everyone was just having a good time, I suppose. I took notes in my mental pad of life lessons.

Whether they were screaming it, wearing it, or holding up a sign; these women were letting the men know that their legs and mouths were open.

14

"Cay get up here!" Hazel called to me, as she strategically inched through the line, working her charm to get up to the front. "Hurry up, I'm making it up there!"

I waved my hand at her, silently applauding her carrying out her dream, but it just was not giving me peace. The closer we got to the front the freakier and funkier the line got! "Go ahead, I'll wait til everything dies down. I'm gonna try to see the show."

"They said we can't leave!" She reminded me, but quickly waved her hand back at me and went ahead on her mission to the front of the line.

Once I'd gotten far enough away, I looked back, had to be at least two hundred women lined up in the rows made within velvet rope, in the front of the line were a few couches: The DeCreed Meet and Greet. A few group members were on the couches waiting, it looked like they were deliberately choosing who they were meeting and greeting with from the crowd. It seemed like a contest where women were getting rewarded with a gift card, the rejected ones were just given a hug and walked out the exit by security!

Prior to the men coming in the room, while we were waiting in line, we spoke to other women who also received an invite through social media. Some admitted they weren't even fans of DeCreed, just pretty girls responding, looking for an opportunity! Exclusive backstage passes, that apparently not even spending money could have bought. The Meet and Greet was more exclusive of an invitation than I thought, we all were private-invite-only and yet still a decent amount of us were still left.

I forced myself to be in the moment, another goal for myself. To get out of my head, to stop overthinking every situation so much. There is truly no point, it was time to learn to go with the flow, be present and let my life be the great experiment I desire.

I turned to find a way out, but not too far for myself.

I preferred regular seats at this point, away from the others and in front of the music, but Hazel would be pissed, and I didn't really want to separate… with lack of news coverage on missing black people in the last year, I didn't feel it was safe to leave her alone.

Following the sound of the music, I crept around to an Authorized Personnel Only/NO TRESPASSING area to see if I could get a glimpse of the opening act's performance while Hazel fought to get through the line. I was crouched enjoying the art, kneeling by a blaring speaker, risking the loss of hearing, but it was a decent view to watch the concert. The singing

15

was the type that gives you goosebumps, the backstage pass invitation was cool, but I preferred to see the concert.

However, not even ten minutes into enjoying the act, a tall brown skinned man with a slightly pissed off face was tapping me on my shoulder. He had on all black with a black hat, along with his security clearance badge. The man was very muscular and would probably be cute if he didn't have such a mean facial expression.

I stood up, embarrassed.

"I am so sorry." I mouthed, backing slowly away from the stage and towards my "designated" section. I paused and held up my simple backstage pass, just as confidently as he held up his SECURITY pass, as if it equaled or excused me being in the unauthorized area.

The security guard wouldn't even give me enough eye contact for me to flirt my way out of trouble, nor did he say a thing. He used his index finger to motion for me to follow him.

The security guard did not look amused when I didn't budge, he adjusted the designer man purse that laid against his chest. "Follow me."

"Hey, Sir, I am sorry. I know the guy said don't leave the area, but I just couldn't see any of the show from backstage." I held up my pass again as I began to follow him, simultaneously trying not to be put out of the theater. "I got my ticket from someone in the group. I'll just go back over there with everyone else."

He looked at me, "You do talk white."

"What did you say to me?" I asked him.

"Let's go, don't tell me you're the hardheaded type," he said sternly, walking in his path quite swiftly.

"What is your name and who do you work for because the company as a unit is unprofessional and honestly just trashy?" I was insulted, but he wouldn't answer me, he only smiled as I followed him out trying to get a glimpse at the company name on his uniform.

I somehow had to inform Hazel I was getting kicked out, she might think something happened to me causing this to ruin her night. I looked in my purse for my phone then I remembered they took our phones from us at the backstage entrance, but we weren't going that direction.

Not sure how I forgot that after listening to Hazel rant about it for ten minutes, I agreed it was a ridiculous rule in the year we live in. However, she took it a little too far as usual, yelling at the security guards and demanding to speak with a supervisor. This man was probably happy to ruin our night by kicking me out.

16

"Hey, can I just run backstage right quick, I gotta tell my friend where I'm at and I gotta get my phone."

"I'll bring it to you, and I'll tell her." He said with little sincerity in his voice, he was aware of the dramatized scene made earlier. "I know exactly which one she is."

"Okay, I see we got off on the wrong foot. My best friend can be a bit self-righteous sometimes, but she's really cool when you get to know her. My name is Acacia." I tried to befriend the grumpy guard by extending my hand.

"Brilliant that you were named after wood." The security guard said with a laugh, I was slightly impressed he knew the word, as most people struggle just to pronounce uh-kay-shuh, but here he is minimizing my name to just a piece of wood. "Your parents must've known you were going to be hardheaded. Naming the child wood?"

"It's not just fucking wood, it's a flowering plant and so much more, do you know about acacias?" I corrected him as the insults seemed to be personal. He was annoying me intentionally.

"Did you say fucking?" He mimicked me, putting emphasis on the 'ing' sound, mocking me while keeping up his pace. "You're not from here, are you, my friend?"

"I'm not your friend." I said, "People use acacia to make all types of things: weight loss medicine, reduce cholesterol, even treat hemorrhoids! You should educate yourself instead of picking on people who are enjoying life. Nothing happened, a victimless crime!"

The big bad security guard had something to prove as he smirked at me, looking quite proud to be kicking me out of the show.

"There's rules around here lady, you know how that goes, right?" He asked condescendingly, as if he knew I was a self-proclaimed rule-follower. "You like rules."

"Yeah, ones that make sense, your shitty company just takes peoples phones and barks orders in hopes for blind submission. Make it make sense."

The big man nodded at me, for some reason he had an ah-ha moment, I could see it. "Things won't make sense when you don't know the goal."

"Did you know that about 4 million arrests in this country a year are for victimless crimes? There are more than 3 million people on parole or probation for victimless crimes today. Hundreds of thousands are still locked up. Did you know that one-third of incarcerated Americans are in for victimless crimes?" I reluctantly followed behind him, spouting off some recent research I learned during my high school debate class. A debate I'd been angrily overanalyzing, as the con-team only won by pointing out the pro-team was not wearing lotion! "You'd think a brother of the oppressed would care."

"This security company," he paused for a moment as we walked down the tunnel-like hall, he held up his company's symbol, a diamond shape with two intersecting lines above the words Bulwark Resilient Optimum Security, "hires convicted felons, provides tactical training, office training, weapon safety, then pays them way above fair wages for security services. The company also teaches financial literacy workshops to its staff and their families. The company was created to reduce the recidivism rate in my state, which we did by over 60% in just the first seven months. Most people just needed direction, knowledge, and focus. I'm very aware and active when it comes to what is happening to us."

"Moreover, this company," again pointing to his uniform's crest that I noticed was stitched onto his designer man-purse as well above the company acronym, "provides mentorship and necessities to the children of incarcerated parents. The donation program is led specifically by me, so I can assure you, we are helping the community. And it ain't by letting women hide backstage."

"I have a—-. That's awesome, all that they did," I humbled myself instead of making an excuse for my comment. Guess they weren't too shitty, it did give a little more insight as to why they weren't the most professional. I followed the probable felon and shut my mouth.

"Listen to this, in 2020, the owners forfeited their own salaries to accommodate for the loss of incomes due to the pandemic until they were positive that no one on staff lost health insurance or a paycheck. This company even dropped off plates, clothes, and face masks to homes with elderly folks and children who couldn't go out due to restrictions." He went on, "They work alongside DeCreed who sponsors an in-prison program that trains inmates in various trades as well."

He said nothing else and silently walked at a swift pace. I tried to reciprocate his silence and pace, but I couldn't help myself as I began stumbling while looking around in awe.

"Oh wow," I mumbled under my breath just seconds later as I started noticing we were not walking me in the direction to leave. In fact, he was walking me in the direction of the performers' dressing rooms.

As we walked down the hallway, I started seeing names of artists who were performing tonight. My mind was blown knowing I was in such proximity to them in the hall.

What in the entire fuck is going on, I thought to myself.

I followed that security guard as if I was a child and he was my parent guiding me through the mall. I was not sure where he was taking me, or what punishment you get for walking into the unauthorized area, but I was elated by the experience. Occasionally try to sneak glances into opening and closing doors of dressing rooms.

The security guard stopped in front of the door that was labeled **Manuel**.

Manuel from DeCreed? Arguably the lead singer in the group.

The security guard opened the door after a unique knock pattern, and I immediately locked eyes with Manuel…. from DeCreed! We both walked in, and he closed the door behind him. I was in a room with Manuel, his security, and his friend. There was some space between us, but Manuel's presence was so big it felt like he was directly in front of me. He was sitting on a couch beside a very light skinned black man with dirty blonde curly hair, about six feet away. Manuel looked directly at me, then back down at his phone.

"Manuel," I said to myself, but apparently not to myself. I felt my eyes getting watery, completely unwarranted and unexpected, because I truly don't know much about this man, other than that he's a celebrity. It was just the energy surrounding him that made me cry, I guess.

"Ooh no, no, no, don't cry now. You didn't even get in the line to meet him." The androgynously dressed light-skinned man with his face full of freckles forbade, as I wiped my happy tears from my cheek. The man stood up, probably about 6' 1", and handed the security guard some rolled-up cash from a man-purse almost identical to the first security guard. "Ugh, I'm an idiot, never bet against Buck."

Manuel looked up from his phone shaking his head at the security guard, Manuel had a gorgeous smile. His teeth were so flawless; the way his lips curved around them was so cute. Finer in person, I'd seen him in interviews, videos, and pictures… he was never *this* fine. His skin reminds me of my favorite candy bar so smooth and soft looking, yet with sexy bad boy tattoos placed sporadically.

"Yeah, yeah, everybody knows that already," Manuel said with an exaggerated sarcasm.

"Corbin, look she's crying? EmManuel, she thought I was putting her out the show!" Buck, the security guard, laughed at me as he informed the light skin man. The tears were more a mix of confusion, shock, and excitement, plus I am a sensitive person. However, I let Buck have his moment.

Corbin had lots of tattoos as well, yet he seemed secretarial, he naturally copied Manuel's posture and mannerisms. "Man, give me back my money."

"I said I would bring her in, nothing more, nothing less." Buck threw up his hands, then counted the cash he was handed for accuracy.

"Ignore them." Manuel told me, while getting up to hand me a box of tissues. "I told him he gotta stop fuckin with everybody, hope he didn't scare you."

"I'm not scared," I responded.

Buck was evidently comfortable with his job security as he egged Manuel on. "See, she's not scared Boss, she can handle it. Besides, you know I don't fuck with *just* anybody." He said in a sly voice to his boss, "Except the ones *you* don't give the pass to, it's rare that I get to do this with you."

"I know that's not a cubic zirconia on your ring finger?" Corbin asked me, staring at my left hand. I noticed him practically scanning me for viruses since I walked in, he was on a mission in search for any flaw or apparently discounted jewelry! "So, you got a man?"

"Let me see the ring," Manuel requested, but it sounded more like a demand.

"No, see what? Corbin shut up, what did I say? We don't even give a fuck about no nigga handing out cheap plastic rings," Buck snapped at Corbin. "Why would you even bring that up?"

I laughed slightly offended, quickly flashing my quaint little $135 ring that I forced myself to wait two pay periods before purchasing, just in case an emergency bill came up. "It's a commitment ring, I bought it for myself a while ago."

"A commitment to what?" Manuel asked, giving a rude look at his security. Buck held up his jacket to laugh an embarrassed chuckle.

"Myself." I responded. "I bought it to keep a promise to myself."

"But on the ring finger? That's kind of misleading, no?" Corbin said matter-of-factly with a laugh. "Personally, it's giving fake engagement ring to keep men away. Who hurt you?"

"It's not that, I just have a lot of other things going on right now. I don't want to be distracted; I'm committed to my goals." I mumbled looking at my little rose gold ring from the mall with its little cubic zirconia rock at the top. It's shaped like a heart, a reminder to be kind to myself, plus there was sentimental value in the timing of the purchase.

Corbin cringed; he seemed a little judgey. "You still haven't faced it."

"Okay, leave her alone." Manuel instructed, possibly sensing my embarrassment.

Buck still tried to hide his laughter, simmering down, he found it obnoxiously comical that a woman would purchase her own ring. "It's not bad, it's kinda cute." Then he tried to add a little more optimistically, "But some distractions put you on the right path you didn't know you needed to be on."

"Let's get out!" Corbin playfully pushed the security guard, Buck, out the door and winked at me as he closed it. I didn't know what to say to Manuel, alone. I preferred maybe Corbin; he seemed like a good buffer.

"You want them to stay?" Manuel asked, *did he read my mind?*

"No, I'm fine." I lied. *Was it that obvious that I was nervous?*

"I saw you out there earlier, I thought you were gonna get in line," he said, his tone somewhat disappointed. "I mean, I did send you tickets to come here, you could have said thanks. Gratitude is the birthplace of joy."

"The tickets were from *you*? Thank you. I am grateful, I wondered who sent them, I saw the name Chris, but I wasn't sure, such a common name." I was embarrassed as typically I was getting better at being grateful. "I'm surprised you even noticed me with that long ass line out there. It was wild in VIP, I had to get out of there. That's truly why I was by the stage, I felt kinda out of place, I didn't mean to be in the way." I rambled on to avoid an awkward silence, "And thank you again, for the tickets, I responded back online. My best friend loves you and DeCreed, me too."

He nodded with a smile. "Yeah, the backstage was wild. Probably why I don't send 'Very Important Person' passes." He paused. "I got a friend to help me do it, I really been wanting to meet you. I was surprised you weren't in line to meet me."

"Sorry, but thanks, that was nice of you." I smiled, feeling just a little more than astonished that I was here. "My best friend is still in that line waiting, she would love to meet you also."

"That same long line you wouldn't even stand in to meet me?" He joked. "Corbin got her, she's probably running through that line as we speak." He smiled that million dollar smile again, one that I'm sure made fans' panties wet, even I was even beginning to melt upon this second one. "Plus, I want to talk to you."

"Me?" I blushed, "I mean *you* are Manuel, in person, you are the one *everyone's* here to see. It feels like you grew up right on my tv, with me watching you. I'm sorry I didn't get in line to thank you; I hope I didn't offend you."

21

"It's okay, just nice to see you in person, too." He moved an expensive, patterned backpack from the couch so I'd have space to sit beside him, "You can sit. First, excuse me, do you mind me pulling you from the show? Buck told me where you were, I can get you a better seat than the spot by the speaker, that's not even safe."

"I don't mind at all." I gave him a friendly laugh and sat beside him, "I like the environment you all brought out. I live like an hour away, and I went to college in this city. I have a little phobia of crowded places, but I like this crowd you all brought out."

Manuel shrugged. "What can I say, we're peaceful souls who make peaceful music."

"True, I can agree with that. Your music has quite a vibe."

"So, you are a fan after all?"

"I am a fan, I'm here, just not a big-big fan, the line was super long! My friend is a huge fan." I told him, "Give me some credit! I have a ton of other shit I could, and probably should, be doing Mr. DeCreed. Like a lot."

He shook his head, "It's okay, you're not a big fan."

I rolled my eyes, "If you say so."

"Which famous niggas would you wait in line to meet?" Manuel paused to watch my reaction. He was sexy, wearing a sleeveless undershirt that showed the detailed stories written via hot ink on his muscular skin.

I wanted to look at them closer, I loved reading a sexy man's inked up body. And to make it worse, he must've just left the barber because his hair cut was screaming "fuck me".

There was no getting out of this question, he flexed a little as he eagerly anticipated hearing my answer.

I smirked, contemplating if I should play it safe. "Okay, so, frankly I'm just not a fan of *any* lines."

He made an unamused face, "C'mon, who would you wait in line for, don't bullshit me."

"Okay if I *had* to choose, since you're making me," I flashed my flirtatious smile and batted my eyes while I pretended to think of an answer, but I knew. "Hmmm, an artist to wait in line for would for sure be the group DavenPort… and probably Young Todd, I love him too, his music."

"Okay, just those two, I'm not a hater, but even if I was I couldn't, those are all great men. Waiting in line worthy. You saying DavenPort, shows me you got some real soul in you, I like that." He made such

22

strong eye contact it was beginning to feel almost like a competition of who'd break first, I was thankful for the lessons I once taught my public speaking class on mastering eye contact. "I would've waited in line to meet you. Just in case you were wondering, Acacia, Cay." He pronounced my name as if he were practicing speaking my name for the first time, "Can I call you Cay?"

"Yes, it's Cay, but Acacia's fine too." I nodded with an accidental girly giggle, I wanted to pinch myself to see if I was awake. He was such a natural flirt with his mannerisms and tone, *Manuel from DeCreed is flirting with me*, I wasn't sure how to take this. I liked the way he said my names.

Why does he know my name?

"You are extremely beautiful, you know that?" He commented after a pause. I wondered what he wanted from me, I smiled politely, but I didn't want to come off too impressed, too easy. "You stand out to me, that's rare because I meet a lot of women, you can imagine. Was that a little self-sabotaging to say to you? I hate when I do that, but either way, you're different from them. This is my attempt at a compliment."

"Thanks," I laughed nervously, blushing quickly remembering to be grateful for all things before rambling on through my nervousness. "Self-sabotaging? I assumed you have the most beautiful women just waiting on call for you. To be honest, I'm flustered to even be talking to you. My best friend is in love with you and DeCreed, I've been hearing about you for years. Now I'm here and you are talking to me, sitting beside me on a little couch, it's nostalgic. I sorta feel like I know you, but obviously I don't."

"Okay, two things. So first just relax, we're just talking, no pressure just be yourself. Second, stop talking about your friend, I want to talk about you." He said bluntly, "No disrespect of course. But I like you."

I nodded my head. "Okay."

"You know what? Let's get coffee before the afterparty. You're coming to the party, right? I'll talk to you later when we can relax a little more. Typically, I don't even talk much before my shows, but I just had to meet you." He told me, touching my hand as he stood up, putting the bookbag back in his spot. "I'll have Buck take you and Hazel to better seats. Just wait for me backstage after the show."

"Thank you," I said slowly.

He extended his arms for a hug, "Alright, don't just leave after, okay? I'll get you after the show."

"Sure, okay, I'll meet up with you after your show." I nodded slowly, after receiving the warmest hug I didn't know I needed. Then on cue as if he knew he'd be summoned, or maybe he was eavesdropping, Buck opened the door and led me back to where Hazel was waiting for me.

"Will we see you after the show?" Buck asked me softly on the way to where Hazel stood, somehow it seemed sketchy coming from him. I ignored him and hugged Hazel gleefully once we reached her.

"You should've stayed! Papi got me through the whole line!" Hazel loudly whispered in my ear, as she stood with Corbin by the V.I.P. table. "You were asleep, bitch!"

I was smiling so hard I couldn't even talk, I wanted to tell her everything, but she was too busy telling me about the line. I tried to focus, but I could barely believe what just happened. She followed beside Buck and me telling me about the haters watching her whilst still standing in line, Buck led us to some secluded balcony seats. Once he was out of earshot, I let out a squeal that could only be drowned out by the group that was ending the opening act.

"What's going on with you?" She asked.

"Oh my God! Hazel you will not believe where I just was. First, I was hiding trying to see the show and the security guard got me and brought me to the room with Manuel from DeCreed! Girl, he asked me to wait for him after the show. I don't even know how he knows me, and he knew of our names. He said he was the one that sent the tickets. I didn't even know what was happening!" I said in one breath. "I'm freaking the fuck out. He told me to wait for him after the show! He got us these seats on the balcony and said don't leave. What should I do?"

She squeezed my hands in excitement, "What do you mean, what should you do? We're staying!!! What do you mean? Why are you questioning it?"

"His security guard was a little sketchy," I mentioned, then I let out a sigh of relief, "I was also worried you'd be upset; you're obsessed with him!"

"Girl I'm literally obsessed with all of them in DeCreed, just bring me with you!" She joked. "Hell, I'll take one of them fine ass bodyguards!"

I guess at that time, Hazel's blessing was the confirmation I needed to know that it was OK to go forward and see what Manuel was about. It wasn't that I'm not a fan of his music, I just wasn't as big of a fan as Hazel. So naturally I would give Hazel *dibs* on the artists in the

24

group. However, he is undeniably attractive and interested in me, until this day, this hour, I never wondered whether I was interested in him.

From the moment the red curtain opened, the concert was going amazingly well. At certain parts, I felt like he was staring directly into my soul while he was on stage. I felt like I was a fifteen-year-old girl, giddy and eager to see my crush.

Hazel and I were seated in the ideal spot in the huge theater, in the top balcony, sitting stage left. Even better than where we were originally going to sit, amongst the other folks in the huge crowd. It was like we were in our own little room, able to see both the crowd and the show.

Throughout the performances all I did was imagine what it would be like to be in a serious romance with someone like Manuel. Lately I was resenting dating altogether, they were proving to be nothing but a waste of my time, I'm wondering with someone like him if it'd be different. Or the same games and nonsense.

Could I date someone like him? I'm a small-town teacher and he's an international celebrity. He practically updates his social media page with a new city or country weekly. I carefully plan out and save for my three yearly vacations.

Can I keep up?

Whenever he was on stage I studied him, I watched him in a different perspective than I had before meeting him. The way he moved, his presence was strong and highly attractive. His eye contact was seductive, it felt like he was looking in my eyes, and with every lyric it seemed he was serenading only me.

Every song flew by except one, "Dream", a radio classic the world couldn't help to know, the crowd sang every word. It went in slow motion; it was most likely the finale most were waiting for and probably the last song of the night. Looking from my balcony view I saw some dancing, couples holding each other, and fans crying. It's a heavy song, about allowing yourself to be whomever you want to be, a song that encourages listeners to imagine more for themselves. One of my favorites.

I imagined he was singing to only me. It began to even feel like he was.

In the most unexpected turn of events, from somewhere in the venue loud gunshots were being fired, possibly two or three, the screams got so loud that I could still hear them over a deafening tone that seemed to be coming from the speakers. People on the ground floor below us were

25

screaming and running in multiple directions. The stage was cleared before I even turned back around.

I thought back to the many Code Red training drills from work, the instructor's words going through my head: run, hide, and fight if necessary. Don't stay stationary. Locate the closest exits and safest route out. Be prepared to fight if necessary.

Hazel pulled me down to the floor with her, hiding low for a few long moments, when the balcony's entrance door swung open and a different security guard with the same company crest as the others on his chest came in.

The man had a similar height and physique as Buck and had that same rigid facial expression as when we first met. Yet, this new guy had slightly slanted eyes, a relatively wide nose, high cheekbones, and kempt loc'd up hair hanging down to his shoulders. In his rage he couldn't hide his slight accent, it sounded of Caribbean descent.

The security guard locked eyes with me as soon as he opened the door, almost disgusted to see us.

"Are you fuckin' serious?" He asked himself loudly, hitting himself upside his own head. "I knew it!"

"Hey, what's happening out there?" Hazel yelled to him.

"Follow me," He ordered, bringing us through a nearby exit. There was an SUV there waiting and he ushered us into it.

I looked at him confused, was this the end of the night? "Manuel asked me to wait for him."

The security pulled up his left sleeve, looking at his smart watch, "tell the driver where to go. EmManuel said goodbye," he put extra emphasis on the word goodbye as he looked into my eyes for confirmation that I got the message, I nodded, then slammed the door harshly.

Leaving us in the hands of another buff, potential ex con from the security company with a baseball cap embroidered with the company symbol. "Where are you going tonight ladies?"

I nodded, I'm sure with a stupid look on my face. So *that's it?* Concert over? Meeting him over? Over before it even got to start. I knew it was too good to be true.

"The Empress Suites Hotel, near the outlets," Hazel luckily took charge and told the driver, following the mean guard's orders, I was too disheveled. "I have my own king size bed."

The driver nodded with a straight face, paying no mind to Hazel's flirtatious advance on him.

I was nerve wrecked; I hadn't even let Hazel's hand go yet. "I can't believe that shit happened. And where are all these fine ass security guards coming from? They were not here when we were in college."

I was shocked and confused, the concert had such a positive vibe and atmosphere, I didn't imagine it ending like that at all. Manuel just said *goodbye*? That's it? I still wanted to talk to him, the more I watched him on stage tonight, the more I was really looking forward to speaking with him. Who knew if he was even staying in the city tonight.

I should've given him my phone number. He has my social media information to reach me if he truly wants to get back in touch, that's all I give most these days. Or should I say something to him? I was spiraling.

"You okay right?" Hazel asked, holding up our locked hands. "You just made it through your worst fear, you did a decent job. Breathe."

I nodded, giving her a half-ass smile while releasing my tight grip from her hand. Hazel assumed the anxious look on my face was from experiencing a shooting in a public venue, a long-time fear of mine. However, it was more the idea of no longer seeing Manuel, being rushed out of his life without a second thought, I'd been planning on what to say once we met up after the show!

"At least he said goodbye to you, I hope the rest of DeCreed is okay." Hazel muttered, looking out the window. "I did hear some girls backstage earlier talking about a fight might happen."

Oh shit, I didn't even think of if everyone was okay. I immediately took out my phone and scanned the internet for any information on the shooting.

No one was killed, but someone was shot in the abdomen and taken to the hospital. There were women fighting in the back of the auditorium.

It was all over social media, that the concert was shut down, DeCreed was unscathed and someone released their condolences statement. DeCreed also canceled their appearance at the afterparty where they were scheduled to meet fans, due to safety reasons.

It felt out of character sending a message to a verified celebrity account, but I sent Manuel a message. Not knowing if he would read it or not, but I couldn't get him off my mind and wanted to try before he left the state.

My private message to Manuel: *Hey sorry about your show, you did so great. Glad I met you.*

2

Hazel and I sat on the balcony of our hotel room, a requirement on all our girl's trips, enjoying the cool night's breeze blowing in from the nearby ocean.

"The further we get in these thirties the more I'm having fun just smoking on the porch in a onesie with a bottle. Instead of dancing in the hot ass clubs looking for somebody with potential, forced into some dusty man's conversation because he paid for a watered-down drink."

My best friend was elated, meeting some of her favorite artists, she felt on top of the world, and I was happy for her. She hadn't stopped dancing and recording videos for her followers since we got back.

Personally, I was struggling with my patience to still be grateful after the sudden change of plans, I had an intense feeling of wanting to see Manuel again, it was making me anxious. The way he dismissed me, it seemed so curt, almost rude compared to how nice he was when we met.

It'd been an hour and he still hadn't even opened my message. I wondered if he ran his own page or if it was one of his employees. He wasn't going to answer, but that's okay.

"I think we both did enough in our twenties to say that." I agreed, half-heartedly.

"Yes! Meeting DeCreed tonight was the boost I needed to let me know there's better men out there. I hugged up on almost all of them! I swear that I can pull one. Strong ass chest and arms! Shit, you even got to talk to Manuel one-on-one, in the fuckin' private dressing room, with his fine ass. I would've been on my knees back there, Honey!!!" A familiar version of Hazel was starting to show, her drinking brings the true ego out of her. "Real talk, I'm glad you two didn't meet up after the show. The more I thought about it, the more I think I *would* have been in my feelings seeing you with him."

I paused, annoyed at her because she has done similar things with men in our past. "You said it was cool to entertain him, so what changed?

Are you jealous? According to you, celebrity fantasy crush only, you said you liked *all* of them, the driver and the security guard got an invite. I'd almost swear you don't like to see me happy!"

"Wow, take it down a notch! You are mad? Here you go being so sensitive and defensive, it doesn't matter, we aren't even seeing him anymore! They canceled the party, he's probably gotten on a plane out of here already, and we are leaving for home in the morning." She deflected, overly casual, she shaped her thumbs and index fingers into a heart shape. "No need to get angry and argue. However, do consider this, how awkward would it be for you to be fucking a man who I fantasized about since middle school? You know all those posters I had on my walls for years."

"True," I agreed, yet pondering her faith in me as a friend. "Why do you think I would just be fucking on him?"

"Who wouldn't fuck on Manuel Eaton," she asked. "Wait, you thought he wanted to get to know you, me, anyone? My apologies Twin, he just wants to collect pussies the way we collect bags, he's a man just like the others you take notes on, you know that's what they all want! He's like every other nigga, Cay. To get the newest cutest pussy to walk next to them."

I stared at her blankly, as she threw some of my old words in my face.

"The only difference between Manuel and the men we've been dealing with, he can afford to buy a whole lot of the new cutest pussies in the store. He's still only been single for two years; you think he's thinking about settling with you?" She laughed at me, "Do you know how many bitches he gets a night?" She looked at her invisible watch, "I bet one is sucking his hard veiny dick; choking and gagging, thankful not to be breathing as we speak."

"Settling?" I asked, insulted. "Glad to know you see me as a *settle*."

"You know, I mean settling down." She rephrased trying to make me laugh, then began to make slurping sounds as she quite impressively deep-throated her phone as if it were a penis.

"You're immature," I told her with a side eye.

"Let's give you a quick tutor session, make sure you make the noises, they like that." She coached me. "And pretend you love the way it tastes, visualize your favorite treat and go to town Sis! Think about it, we could've been at the penthouse suite floor of a crème de la crème hotel, had you acted right."

The word *settling* kept repeating in my head as she spoke. Why would I think Manuel would be any different than all of the other men doing less than enough, in hopes of getting some sex. Manuel is handsome, sexy, hazelnut complexion, with a top-notch smile... plus rich! I was hoping that those qualities would make him better, but they probably only made him 10,000 times worse.

"Never know. Maybe he isn't like that stereotypical celebrity-whore, maybe he just wanted us to have a decent time." I bowed out the argument, but still had hope in the back of my mind.

"That man, all those men tonight, were looking for *toys*, Acacia! Playthings. I'm sure that is all he was going to ask you after the show, do you want to be his toy or not? Probably for the best that you got *cut*, stop overthinking it." She explained, laughing at my surprised face. "Did you hear his security guard, he said bye, that means you were cut."

"Really? Cut? No fuckin' way," My jaw dropped, I was surprised she felt it was *my* fault Manuel didn't see us after the show. The security guard was rude getting us out, but there was a shooting! It wasn't my fault we didn't meet back up.

I don't think I was cut.

"Don't feel bad, I mean it in a good way, you were truly meant to be the princess housewife-type. I know you saw what those women were doing! You are a prude at heart, you do not want anything to do with that life he's living!" She rubbed my shoulder gently, but I shrugged her off. "In all honesty and no disrespect, I have a better chance with those types than you, and I don't even think I'd touch any of them after all the whores we saw backstage!"

"I'm not a prude when I'm comfortable, bitch. I am a whole freak!" I laughed slightly abashed, then playfully took a twerk-break for my bestie holding onto the railing. She watched me with complete lack of faith, my best friend had no faith that I could get a man like Manuel.

"You won't even suck a dick that hasn't gone through your prude-pussy-inspection!" She laughed, "Head is part of sex now, just so you are aware. You must suck it!"

She was not necessarily lying. How long would it take him to get bored with trying to understand me sexually? I was far more work to get to than the girls we saw tonight.

"I would... if it's mine," I mumbled, unable to even convince myself that I too could have been a wild woman for a night.

"They are all for everybody. Wake up." She told me with sass, "Just have fun."

Have fun? After I failed the tryout? I got cut in the first round. "Didn't you say you got the cameraman's number, what's going on with that?"

"He's texting, we might meet up, but he's just a dreamer." She sighed. "I can tell by the way he's talking. Hopefully he's still out with some of the group and I can meet someone worthwhile. Or hell, maybe he knows how to scratch an itch. It's been long enough."

I considered using her cameraman connection to find out where Manuel would be tonight, but I didn't have much faith in the men Hazel finds.

"Yeah, I guess some of us don't even get an invitation to the tryouts." I retorted. "Did you at least win a gift card?"

She looked at me naively, "A gift card? Those were room keys getting handed out, Acacia!"

I shrugged. "Gross."

"Yeah, but bitch are you really that mad? Would you even be able to just go fuck a celebrity, Acacia? You wanna be Manuel's little sex toy? You don't know what kinda freaky shit them types are looking for and we know you barely passed H.O.E 101 in college. You are not even going to know how to respond in that situation." She laughed even after I stopped, evidently the liquor had kicked in. "Sorry I was not hating; I was being a real friend. Shit, it'd be a great way to break the *fifteen-year curse*. I'm cheering for you."

"Maybe I'm finally ready for my hoe phase," I admitted as I'd been considering spicing things up a little more anyway.

"He's NOT on the practice squad!" She hollered laughing as if I were funny enough to sell out arenas. "You were in some serious ass *baller* territory; Acacia Ivy are you not listening? MVP Baller territory at that, years in the league, undeniably. Even his biggest haters can only call him overrated... internationally great women would respectfully walk out on their husbands *tonight* to climb him. You should've shown him you were a great prospect."

"I thought I did."

She shook her head, "Women get his name, face, and symbols tattooed on their body. Just a few months ago his ex CoDéy got his name on her."

"I forgot they were together. Did he take her back?"

Hazel shrugged, "No, not publicly, but that's the type of shit even the baddest hoes will do for him. She posted it, then took it down after like seven hours, then screen recorded herself unblocking him. Got so many views, that single got so many streams, she's smart."

"Well, I just wanted to get to know him. Besides, his ex's music is fire, but she doesn't have anything to do with this!" I cut her off before she minimized my qualifications anymore, "he seems cool and maybe if he did think of me as more than just a booty call... who knows. I am more open sexually when I feel comfortable, trust me I know what I'm doing."

She sighed, with a chuckle. "He's not even your type, Manuel's the momma's boy type to the next level, and we know you swear you're done with them types. Or at least you wish you could be."

I snapped at her. "And I told you to stop mentioning that fake ass curse, it really annoys me when you guys do that!"

"I'm just being honest. Comfortable, to you, means with that same nigga, with that same sex you been getting forever. These things come in different lengths and widths, you never know what you are going to get, and you need to live and get experience for times like earlier!" She laughed, probably at me more than with me, as my sex life is commonly a joke amongst my close friends. "This is Manuel, so had you been at that afterparty, you would probably be hiding! You can't even handle the things he's gonna want that *thing* to do! Better put some benzocaine on the back of that tongue beforehand just in case."

"I get asked out on a date every day of my life. I get proposed to at least once a year by door-to-door salesmen who meet me in pajamas and a bonnet. I destroy families of men who fantasize but can't touch me with consent if they were crying." I ignored her, not about to get upset because I know who I am. "You of all people know I lost two gynos, from two different medical centers, because they wouldn't stop asking to take me out after my annuals. This *thing* is professionally Grade A, medical doctor recommended. Fuck you, him, and the practice squad. I don't need *him*."

"Oh, don't do all of that," She brushed me off with a smile. "I cursed that last doctor out, raised hell, I had the 9mm in my purse ready for him to say something stupid."

"Yes, a month before my delivery," I sighed remembering the fiasco.

"I'm not saying you're not great, Acacia, I've been your best friend for twenty years, I'm saying you don't use what you got to its full potential! I don't usually say anything, but you always leave a little easy money on every table." Hazel told me. "There's power in our little

32

pocketbooks… when we stop giving it to the wrong kind of man. And you just fucked up your biggest amount yet."

She hates my son's father; all of my friends do.

My friends were not completely wrong for getting a comedy kick out of my dating life. As much as I date and take men up on offers to share in a little piece of their world… they constantly drop the ball then beg for second and third chances to redo it again. I may or may not be hexed, according to my friends, we call it: the baby daddy curse. It's an ongoing joke, a fake conjuration, with my friend group that prevents me from either:

A. Dating a man that I like enough to want to give some coochie.

B. Giving a man some coochie and then almost immediately he absolutely turns me very far off in some way.

Whatever the case may be, A or B, however the new man disappoints me, it somehow always triggers me to allow my son's father back in my life. Hence the name of their ongoing joke, "baby daddy curse" that has prevented me from happiness for too many years of my life!

Luckily as I begin to acknowledge that there may be something wrong with me and I may need to truly get professional help for this… I have met other women who struggle with similar issues.

Hazel straightened up a little, realizing I was getting offended. "Well, while I do not necessarily applaud you considering doing hoe shit, we've definitely fucked men who've given us less than backstage passes. He could've thrown you a little something green or gold for memories, although I appreciate the free car ride saving sixty bucks getting back to the hotel." She laughed at herself. "I wish you would've got that rich ass sugar daddy."

"You know I'm not looking for a sugar daddy, and he's only like three years older than us." I retorted, feeling myself get more and more annoyed by her. I changed the subject to avoid a drunk confrontation. "We should've enjoyed this view more while we were in college."

"Oh, you don't have to look too hard to find that man's money, he *been* rich. I've heard so many rumors about them doing illegal ass favors." She gossiped. "Now you lucky he didn't have you over there getting turnt out like those other women, you are a moral woman!"

"Hazel, shut up," I told her. "I don't even care to hear your opinion."

"Opinion? I have followed DeCreed, including Manuel, for years. Now you are acting like you care about them or know him better than me!

Girl truly at this point go fuck him and the rest of the group if you want to, I don't even care anymore! If you can't find me in the middle of the night just know I'm out getting mine." Hazel was annoyed with me, in her typical condescending fashion, she held up her liquor and made an impromptu toast, "Death to the baby daddy curse!"

I turned up the music, I didn't want to talk about Manuel with her anymore. Not that I thought he was a realistic prospect, but this little situation reminded me of why I made it a rule to keep my friends out of my dating life. It was fun to fantasize about him at the concert, I didn't need her stomping on my fantasies, even if that's all it was going to be. I was fine with what it was.

We sat on the porch for about an hour before we decided to call it a night, a little after midnight. I didn't even wish her a good night before heading to my couch bed.

Just as I was beginning to feel comfy, doing my nightly reflection and goals checklist. I heard the notification for a text message from my phone. It was from an out-of-town number I didn't recognize.

404-123-MYOB

Come to the lobby

Lobby? Manuel? Had to be him, no one else knows I'm here. How did he get my number? The thought alone that it was him was the only motivation that could have gotten me up.

Luckily, I took the common area sofa bed, so it wasn't hard to leave the hotel room without Hazel hearing me. I contemplated telling her where I was going, but after hearing her comments after the show, I knew I didn't want to be persuaded by any other perspective than my own.

I wanted to speak with Manuel privately before letting Hazel know he was here. If it was even him.

I grabbed my hotel room key, phone, and purse, then approved of myself in the mirror on my way out the door.

"It is him!" I mumbled to myself with the lowest screech possible as I looked over the railing of the fourth floor down to the lobby.

It was Manuel, he was with Buck and another six-foot-tall man with locs, it was the rude one who got us out of the venue after the shooting. Locs still had the same asshole-demeanor as when he first saw Hazel and me earlier.

34

Manuel walked a few steps away from his staff when he saw me coming down the glass elevator, but they made it clear they were still very present.

I could feel a smile involuntarily stretching across my face as I walked closer to him. I'd be lying if I didn't say I was ecstatic to know I was still in the running for the team! *I knew I didn't get cut the first damn round.* I spent too long in conditioning to get cut that damn early, can't believe I almost psyched myself out, I will find joy in telling Hazel.

"Sorry about the concert," he said immediately, approaching me then giving me a hug.

"I should be sorry, my state did you all like that." I apologized also, "I'm glad you found me, I didn't think I'd see you again. Glad I get to tell you how dope you were in person!"

"I told you I'd meet up with you after the show. Why wouldn't I come find you?" He questioned, then moved on, "No worries. This is my state a little bit too. I lived here with my family for a short while, not too far from here."

I smiled at him, literally questioning everything I was doing in my head. What do you say to someone like this? "Cool."

"Yeah." He chuckled at me, getting a kick out of my nerves. "Do you mind coming to my hotel to hang out... or we can go out and sit by your pool?"

"Pool," I quickly picked the safest option.

"I have a really nice balcony," he tried to persuade me, but that only freaked me out more, alone on a balcony with a wealthy stranger.

"No thanks," I can write five horror scenarios with that setting alone.

"You sure?" He asked again, probably preferring to go back to his hotel. He only added the pool option because the face I made, fuck, he can tell I'm a prude. "Are you scared of me?"

"Not before you asked that," I flirtatiously joked, forcing myself to be a little braver in his presence. "Now I'm a little scared."

"I get it, a group of big niggas and you in a hotel probably sounds weird, but it ain't like that," He chuckled a little looking at his security team, who were having a low argument between themselves. "You don't have to be scared or nervous. There's a little family gathering happening at my suite, plenty of other men and women are there. You will find, I was raised to be a gentleman by a gentleman."

I side-eyed him, "I'm not going to your hotel tonight."

"Okay Acacia, can I just say it's hard for me to stop looking at you. I wouldn't let anything happen to you."

I blushed, "Thanks, that's sweet, but I'm not the *go to your hotel room* type of woman."

"Yo!" The rude, loc'd up security guard called out, rushing us in that same tone he dismissed me from the concert with, "Meet and greet."

Manuel took my hand and led us to the hotel's outdoor pool area. There weren't many people walking around the hotel common areas, but the ones that were around all did a double take when they noticed who Manuel was.

Manuel was more noticeable than I thought he would be to people of different cultures. He wore it very well, humble, but with apparent confidence.

"I get it, you are very safe. No pressure. So, how'd you feel about the show?" He asked, sitting at an outdoor picnic table, and patting for me to sit down beside him. I complied.

Buck and the ruder security guard were following us, but not close enough to hear our conversation. They seemed to be more into their own argument than what we were doing anyway.

"Everything tonight was very surreal, I felt foreign, I never been backstage or sat *that* close to a stage before," I told him gratefully, "No lie, we were sitting so close that I felt like you were looking right at me."

"I was," he confirmed my suspicion with a straight face, eyes locked in.

I was sure my face was turning red from his flattery; it would have been impossible for him not to see how enamored he was making me feel with his compliments. I loved it and disliked it at the same time, because it was hard to be casual with him. Reading his expressions, it was obvious he knew I was impressed.

However, I didn't want him to see how impressed I was, god forbid Hazel is right and he thinks I'm a toy.

"Okay, I'll just own it. You are here at my hotel," I put a hand on my head, then nervously moved it to my lap, "so, I'm a little nervous. I guess."

"Can I hold your hand?" He asked, I nodded, and he took my hand, massaging it softly in a comforting manner. "Just chill. Be soft, I'm not expecting anything from you. I wanted to see you. I want to talk to you. We can just talk about whatever you want, anything's fine."

"That incident, the shooting, that's one of my biggest fears, mass shootings." I changed the topic, searching for something with less pressure. "Thanks for getting us back to the hotel, that was nice."

"Of course, I am the one who invited you, my father would kill me if I didn't make sure you made it safely home. I tried to get you myself, but they started tripping." He made an ugly face in the direction of the security staff.

"Daddy's little man?" I asked him.

"More of a momma's boy." He told me and I felt my muscles tighten and apparently, I made a face, "What was that face about? You don't like a man who appreciates the woman who raised him?"

"No, that's not true." I shook my head, "I've just had some bad experiences with that type, there's gotta be balance. It helps when there is a present father, like you had I assume."

"Yeah, my dad was the ultimate father, all my parents are great people. I hate that the whole shooting happened. Personally, I really aim for peace, joy, shit like that around me. Trust me, I don't force it though, gotta let people learn their own way in this world."

"Yeah, it's sad that things like that happen."

Manuel said, "My youngest brother died in a shooting not long ago, it was over a football game."

"Sorry for your loss. My son plays football, those sports parents are intense. I won't even let him play in certain leagues, his father complains I baby him, but some of those folks are too intense. I probably do baby him a little." I admitted.

"You have one child, right?"

I nodded, a little surprised he knew. "You still had a great performance tonight, it was better than I expected with that view, but I knew it would be great."

He chuckled to himself, "You didn't think it would be great enough to stand in line?"

"Am I never going to live that down?" I ask. "It was a long ass line."

"I had him waiting to move you up to the front." He pointed in the direction of the guards. "That mean one, and he's a rule follower."

I put my hand on my forehead sarcastically, "Well, I didn't know that!"

"I kinda like it, you're not a big fan," he sucked his teeth. "Lowkey, that almost makes me want to fuck with you more."

"Want to *fuck* with me? What do you mean by *fuck* with me? You don't even know me *at all*." I thought out loud, partially offended, Hazel was right about him. "I'm not a toy, if that's what you think I am."

He laughed, acting taken aback, "Whoa, like hang out with you, get to know you. You feel like I think you're a toy?"

"Okay, my bad, but should I? I don't know your protocol with meeting people," I mumbled. "Or your intentions."

"I do want to have a fun time with you, but I do not think of you as a toy. Let me apologize, maybe I used a bad choice of words."

"No need, I think you used the words you believe. I mean, obviously you are famous, you are certainly very dope, but do you think you can just pick a random woman you *want* and go fuck them or something?"

"When did we start talking about fucking?" He asked me with an awkward laugh.

"Be real, you are not inviting me over just because you think I'm a nice person, Manuel. How many women do you invite to shows? And how many do you tell to stay after the show? And how many get you to come out to their hotel, or do they always take the option to go back to your hotel?" My conversation with Hazel was replaying my mind, I was being a little too aggressive, but she made honest points in her argument. "Then threesomes and orgies, or does it depend on the day? Y'all were playing with those V.I.P. women like they were naked dolls or hookers in a video game."

"And you are kinda being offensive," He sighed, but tried to make light of the situation. "I'm infamously known to be picky. Some even say I'm shallow, I know what I like. I'm not what you think."

My insecurities, being played for a fool in my past and others' shitty opinions, were all coming up against this seemingly innocent man. I could not shut up. "I'm sure. So how many ladies were waiting for you after *this* show tonight?"

Manuel stood up and looked over at his security team. Although it was a vague hand signal with a "look", it seemed even to me like a signal to go, and I quickly saw that it was. Manuel gave me a hug and kiss on the cheek.

"It was nice meeting you," he whispered in my ear. "I think you are dope as well."

"Damn, you're leaving?" I said softly, covering my mouth. "I should've shut up huh?"

38

"No, you don't have to shut up, I get it, you got trust issues with men. Probably rightfully so. But try to consider another perspective, that I don't think you're a toy, that I don't even like toys. When I was coming up, my dad didn't even let me and my brothers have toys." He recalled looking at me with his enchanting eyes.

"So, what did you do for fun?" I questioned.

"We had to play sports, read, make up games to bet on, or whatever was entertaining. Our dad felt toys were a waste of time, so instinctively I avoid shit that looks like toys. Big sports family." He spoke so casually; I could tell he is the type of man that is comfortable in all situations. "I hate wasting time."

I found his toyless story hard to believe, "So you're just out here keeping it in your pants? Not playing with any of the toys?"

He chuckled, with a more realistic look, "Okay, I won't lie, I've met millions of women who are toys and want to be toys, I'm almost an expert at recognizing them. I won't say I've been completely toy-free, but it's not what I was thinking of you." He confessed. "I knew right away you weren't a toy."

"Did you see your DeCreed *fans* and co-workers backstage? It smelled like, hot *vagina* back there! How can you blame me for being skeptical of your intentions?"

"I like the way you talk, you really are a teacher," He said with a laugh. "I believe you, backstage is a whole other animal, there's a lot of people in my camp. I get how it can look, but I was looking at you, did you see that? And I'm asking you to just have faith, go with the flow for once."

"Yeah, this time you may not have been with the toys." I mumbled and changed his lips to a frown.

"You are very tough, you gotta take down the walls you built for someone else. For us to vibe, you gotta let your guard down with me, be yourself, relax; let all that mean, tough shit go." He said in a serious tone. "You're good with me."

"So, I'm supposed to be comfortable going back to your room and being open with you? Not being alert about anything, day 1? How do you even expect that? I'm *mean and tough* because I'm skeptical about a man taking me back to his hotel?" I huffed rhetorically. "Is this what you believe and expect or is it reverse psychology? You're famous, yeah, but I don't know you and you leave as soon as things don't go your way?"

"You're right. What do you want to know to feel better? I will take questions if that'll help."

"Yes. Why should I just leave here with you?"

"Okay, first I haven't shown you a reason not to trust me. Second, I have a lot to lose. Too much to risk by doing something stupid. How *many* women? I've invited thousands of women to my shows over the years. I've told hundreds of women to stay after shows. It's been years since I've been to anyone else's hotel, it's forbidden and probably why those two are arguing. That one on the right, Garon, is meticulous with rules, he reports everything back to my manager."

I raised my eyebrows as we took a brief break of silence to hear the two men argue. "Can't you just fire him?"

"He doesn't work for me; he works for her." Manuel continued, "It's no big deal, Buck will handle him, we all bet you wouldn't come to me, so I had to take a chance. I prefer to leave right after my shows. I stayed because there are a few things I want to do here this weekend; one was to meet *you* in person." He told me.

I awkwardly smiled, unsure how to feel about what he said, "So why do that for me?"

His speaking voice is even somewhat melodic, "You glow, you stand out, your soul. Then your personality and your vision that I read on your business page, very dope. I like your ideas on changing to an integrative curriculum, I saw your plan for your own private school. A school where the students are the teachers and the teachers are, like, academic consultants? I hit the *like* button a few times, surprised you didn't see that. The system needs a change."

"Yeah, I have some ideas. You were on my business page?" I smirked with glee. My business page has very little traffic, and rightfully so, the promotion is very low on my list of things to do lately as my writer's block was even spreading into my academic content.

"Yes, ma'am, been waiting for you to upload another short story," he flashed that smile at me, then glanced at an incoming notification on his phone.

I shook my head, "I took them all down, they weren't me anymore. But I'll send you one."

"Send it to Sora Eaton, you'll see her email on almost all my pages. I bet she can help you do something with your work. Try it, if it's your dream."

I smiled at him and mumbled, "Thanks, it feels bigger than a dream."

"My car's ready, you want to come back with me or will we one day just meet again? I'm telling you, I have a jacuzzi on my balcony, if you don't want to mingle at the gathering with my associates. I'm even willing to break the rules and give you the address so you can text it to your friend in case you're scared."

Urgh.

I looked over at Buck, who seemed to never have his eyes off us for too long, he smirked at me. Buck probably sees this regularly, possibly even partakes in the festivities, his employer taking home random women, I'm sure there are hundreds of women a month. Hell, there were hundreds of women just tonight losing their damn minds over this man. I was not going to be just another one, I'm not a groupie, I convinced myself.

"I guess we'll just meet again," I extended my hand for Manuel to shake, but he only nodded and turned to walk with his security, down the hall and through the lobby. He left me hanging.

The idea that women have sex with these celebrity men just off the strength of money or their fame is wild to me. I couldn't do it. I was not going to do it. Stay overnight with a whole stranger in a big city like this? Not happening.

Hazel was right.

What made me even more upset with myself was that I wanted to still hang out with him. I didn't want him to go away.

I sat at the pool trying to decide how stupid I was for maybe three minutes before I got up and walked down the hall, through the lobby to see if I could still catch Manuel. Not exactly sure of my plan, but I couldn't just let him leave on that note. If he wasn't gone already, maybe he could come up to my suite?

He was gone. I walked around the parking lot area twice looking for him, but he was nowhere in sight.

I started to feel impulsive as I texted that number he'd contacted me from, maybe he could send the address to me after all. I could borrow Hazel's car to ride over to his hotel and be back before she gets up.

Manuel	
	Hey Sorry, I didn't mean to be a bitch, caught up in my thoughts
U are good, don't be sorry. I wasn't expecting anything from	

you, it was MY pleasure to meet you.
Promise You were perfect.
Gn

I want to come hang with you

No you don't

Yes, I do

No you don't stop teasing me.

Lol, stop playing. I really do.

Ok Garon is still there with you in front.
He'll bring u to me just don't talk to him

Wow, u knew to leave him. ok.

I took a chance.
I kinda like when you sassy it's cute.
U probably just afraid of change but don't wry I got u
I'm a real man, u don't have to baby me

I'm afraid of change? What an interesting analysis this man made in three hours of knowing me.

I looked over to the front lobby and could now see his security guard sitting watching his phone from the inside of the lobby.

Why did he leave his security guard? Was he that damn sure of himself that he knew I could change my mind. Fuck, how predictable am I? Am I just like everybody else? I wondered how long Garon was going to get paid to wait there.

42

I walked over to Garon and smiled stupidly, clutching my purse tight like a toddler with her security blanket. "Hey."

"You weren't supposed to be back." Garon replied with a look of such disappointment, you'd think he knew me in a former life.

We began walking to a luxury SUV that the valet was impressed with as they stood nearby taking selfies before scattering. Garon opened the back door for me. I could tell it was expensive just by how the doors opened in the opposite direction and had colored lights on the handles. The reclining, massaging back seats were two-tone leather, with lit up handles with colored bulbs that matched the light that lit up the elegant cocktail table trays.

I took a deep breath as I tried not to fit in during the awkward ride to Manuel. I tried to relax whenever I noticed Garon looking at me in his mirror. At some point in my Quarantine Education, I learned that the idea of "fitting in" is mental, we fit in where we want to fit in, and we don't fit in places we don't want to fit in. Supposedly it's all mental, although I wasn't fully sold on that theory, I liked to practice it when I felt out of place.

As we rode to meet up with Manuel, I wondered if Garon thought I was just some random backstage whore, gold digger, or a lady who dates lots of high caliber men. When I accidentally rolled my window down and couldn't get it back up, Garon rolled his eyes at me in the rear-view mirror, knowing full well the car was very techie! The way my nerves took over trying to roll it back up wasn't much smoother either. Why was I caring so much about what he thought of me?

Breathe, I reminded myself, feeling my mindfulness techniques about to take charge.

It was time to be different, take a risk, get out of the routine, I was waiting for this. It was time to be a little freer.

3

After a short fifteen-minute ride of silence Garon pulled up to the front of a massive hotel with no signage or name. Although he didn't seem to like me much, I could tell he was a genuine gentleman as he took the lead, waited for me, and held doors appropriately. However, Garon stayed silent with me from the car ride until we were let off the floor labeled PH, not even replying to all my "thank yous".

Penthouse, I thought to myself, slightly impressed, but expected from someone like Manuel.

As soon as the elevator doors opened Manuel was standing there alone, with his arms open to greet me. The lobby was a bright white with crystal accents galore, a very rich feel, it was fitting as a backdrop for him.

"Thank you for changing your mind, I really do appreciate you coming over here to see me." He took my hand eagerly after we hugged and walked me to his tinted glass suite. "I was waiting to do that."

Garon quickly walked past us and disappeared into a cloud of smoke that escaped once the doors were open, and the blaring music bounced off the lobby walls.

I got a little tight wondering what I was going to walk into. I have never been a party girl, although I tried, but especially not solo at a party. I should have had Hazel come with me, I regretted being so petty to have left her. She knows how to blend in on every occasion from royal to ratchet. I stand out like a sore thumb everywhere.

"You are tense, relax, I'm not going to leave you anywhere." Manuel told me, I noticed he was rubbing my hand softly. "Be soft Ms. A–," I almost thought he was going to call me by my last name, "Acacia."

"What's that even mean?" I asked. "Be soft?"

"You gotta stop being so tough, so rough, when you are with me, I want you to soften up." He instructed. "If you don't soften up, you won't be receptive."

"I like being tough," I mumbled, before repeating his lingo, "*Be soft,* sounds like something you say to your women so you can impress upon them."

"No, I don't think of it like that. Think of it like gardening, you trying to grow something beneficial, it would be useless on bad soil- that's hard or rocky, right? It's not going to grow; the soil isn't receptive. Only in good, soft soil can we grow. That's what I mean when I say *be soft*, be soft so that you are able to be receptive like the soil."

"Willing to consider new suggestions or ideas, receptive." I recited the definition to one of the ninth-grade curriculum vocabulary words. "I see where you're coming from."

He nodded his head at me. "You willing to accept some new ideas?" I gritted my teeth and slowly shook my head no. "This world got you real hurt. Just try."

"That's hard." I laughed at the irony at how hard it was just to be soft with someone again. "I'll soften up a little."

He extended his pinky out to me, "Let me just make this easy for you, give me 100% trust and if I hurt you, then you can go to being hard again. But for now, just be soft with me and I got you."

I laughed at the idea to just trust this man 100% based on... nothing? A pinky promise?

"You know what Manuel, I can't even imagine what it feels like to trust someone that much anymore."

"Losing your imagination is one of the worst things you can do, let's just do it." He raised his eyebrows at me, "Just pretend you know me, and I always do what I say I'm going to do or better. That no matter what it looks like, I always got your best interest at heart. Therefore, you gotta trust me."

"That's a lot of pretending." I told him with a sigh and a smile.

"I can deliver it on my end, if you do your part." He extended his pinky, "And cause you look like the loyal type, we are going old school pink promise, give me that pinky."

What do I have to lose? I fought with myself.

Myself?

"Okay." I heard my voice say to Manuel, intertwining my pinky with his, ready to take on a new risk. I believe I know where to find me if I got lost *again.*

Manuel opened the door to the penthouse and smoke escaped into the lobby once again. We entered a dimly lit, smoke filled room. I immediately noticed the lightly clothed dancers. A few people were playing dice, a couple groups had a card game going, liquor bottles lined the countertops and plastic cups were not being spared. No one really looked at me, and I didn't try to make eye contact with anyone either. I just followed Manuel, his grip guiding me through the small but slightly crowded gathering.

Everyone we walked past in the party called out to Manuel, and he would either speak back, dapped-up some of the men, and side-hugged a few ladies, but never let go of my hand. Not even when he stopped to talk to people. And they noticed, almost everyone noticed our hands, I kind of liked it.

I stopped for a second to watch a game of Spades being played, by two DeCreed members versus Corbin and an elderly man with two women on his lap.

"Don't act like you can play, if you can't." Manuel was asking me if I could play spades!

It'd been years since I had been fresh meat, forced to place a bet just to earn an unsupportive bra or just play a friendly game of Spades for hours to occupy my time with something other than reading. Funny how our present will always be intertwined with flashbacks of our own history.

The handsomely rich old man in front of me proudly showed me a losing hand that he for sure overbidded with by the looks of what was on his paper. He looked like the type that would cheat; I didn't put that past him. I'd even suspect the women on his lap were sent over as a decoy, I doubted they were genuinely interested in him or this card game.

"I can play," I leaned in and whispered to him, "but how slow this man is playing, we'd be here all night."

"This is Uncle Mo, he was in that special needs class so you should feel bad," Manuel introduced, pulling me over as he rubbed the very elderly man's shoulder. "He and my dad were very close. Mo played a very big part in making DeCreed who we—."

"Fuck you, it wasn't special needs, it was speech class." Uncle Mo caught fit eavesdropping, just after taking a hit from a huge blunt with a mini forest in it, the type you roll when it's not your weed. "What you mean *was* close, we *still* close. That's my best friend, now who is this mighty fine lady?"

"Uncle Mo, this is Acacia." Manuel introduced me.

"Okay, Ms. Acacia," Uncle Mo gave me the full once overlook, then he nodded his head in approval of my appearance, I assume. "I know you must be *somebody* cause my nephew ain't ever gonna bring me just *anybody.* I'm Mo, the one they call when it's time to lay down the law or

46

lead those fools out of trouble. You can ask their mothers. I'm so happy the tables done turned, now they come free me out of jail."

"Nice to meet you," I said to his Uncle who stood up using an oversized blinged-out pimp cane as a boost to stand and give me a hug. He hugged Manuel also before we walked away,

"We are heavy gamblers over here; you might fit in if you know what you are talking about. Can you play?"

"I can," I told him with sass, sensing a tone of doubt in his voice. I wanted to tell him how I got so professional, several months in jail gambling for chocolate bars and hot coco. Fortunately, I've learned the importance of timing, and this was not the time to tell him about that part of my past. "Can you play?"

"Definitely," Manuel responded with that smile, that smile he does, the one that makes women want to do grown up things with him. "I really need a partner."

He took my hand with that gentle squeeze and led me down a long, dimly lit, empty hall that was leading to a master bedroom. We walked until we were alone. Not even the security team was around, is this the tryout Hazel was telling me about? Second cuts, so to speak. I was more nervous than I realized I would be.

I had to remind myself to breath, relax. "True."

Manuel said. "You gotta see this balcony view too."

I nodded, pretending to act like this was regular that this rich famous man was walking me into his room!

"So, this is your life, penthouse suite parties? When do you get to be alone and relax or go visit family, your brothers, your women?" I wondered, feeling slightly empathetic that he had so many people around him like this.

"DeCreed is my family. No woman." He explained, "I'm used to being around my people, we know everyone here... but if *you* wanna be alone with me I do have a little island, I can take you to visit for a month or two."

I smirked, pretending to be unimpressed. *Does he own an actual island? I* should've done some internet searching before I got here.

"Come to the jacuzzi with me, I been waiting to get in all day," he said. "You smoke right?"

"Yeah," I typically would not smoke with strangers or on first dates, but I was not going to say that to him after I pinky-promised this man *100% trust.* Manuel opened another oversized door and walked me through the elegant, modern style bedroom.

"I could tell you do," he said, raising his eyebrows.

"What?" I playfully hit him as he laughed at me. "Do I look like it?"

He nodded at me, then shook his head. "No, I'm joking."

"Boy hush, I am a very discreet career woman." I hit him again, his body was firm, he probably works out daily. "The jacuzzi sounds like fun, I should've brought my bathing suit."

I thought back to cheap college dates sneaking in complex apartment hot tubs playing truth or dare with friends. Although it wouldn't be the first time naked in a jacuzzi, I was past that era in my life. No way he was going to get me to go skinny dipping.

"I got one here for you to wear." Manuel pointed back to the bed where a brand-new bikini was laid out probably for whichever lucky lady showed up tonight. Although the price tags on the bikini were high enough to cover my monthly bills, I was bothered about the suit. I almost preferred going in a bra and panties rather than wearing the suit for some random TBD-hoe. "I ordered that one because I know what compliments you… the colors. Meet me outside when you're dressed."

After a sigh of relief and scolding myself lightly for a lack of confidence, I got dressed and followed just a minute behind Manuel.

Separating the curtains to the balcony revealed a seductively lit, very wide balcony; beyond the balcony to the right was an ocean view, to the left a view of my familiar city that I'd never seen before.

On the balcony, was a charcuterie picnic setup, it was a small, but quite a variety, nonetheless. The table wore a white soft linen cloth with a beautiful silver table runner and crystal decor, on top of that sat an exquisite charcuterie spread. Behind the table was a friendly faced, short, thick black woman with the cutest cheeks and an apron that read, "Bites". Her logo on the apron was a cartoon that looked like her, if she had a makeup filter, taking a bite out of an appetizer. I assumed she was Ms. Bites.

The jacuzzi was in the middle of the balcony. Manuel got in first, then took my hand to guide me, looking for a reason to touch. I was not complaining.

It overlooked the pool and bar area where many folks below us were wrapping up their night or enjoying one of the few hotel fire pits. They looked so small beneath us, or maybe I just felt so big standing with Manuel and being up so high.

"Well, I was just telling my favorite client, before he rudely ran out of here to get you," Ms. Bites smiled facing me, but her eyes were too

48

busy fucking my date and the imprint of his body in the swim trunks, "that I won't stay out here with you two because I have to tend to my big table inside and I'm sure you want privacy. But I want to walk you through the menu one time and give your pallet a few suggestions before I go back inside. May I?"

"I'd appreciate that," I replied, but she could barely pretend to care about my presence.

Ms. Bites walked us through all the cheeses, meats, and fruits in her spread. By us, I mean Manuel, because he is the only person she cared to connect with throughout her whole spiel, I could have left that porch and she might not even notice.

Manuel started eating once she was done, he picked a cracker, pepper jack cheese, and a pepperoni. Ms. Bites flirtatiously says, "I can tell a lot about a man by what he picks for his first bite. So don't think I don't know what that means, Sir."

He raised his eyebrows at her and covered his eyes from her. I rolled my eyes, there's no way she knows anything about him from that.

"Let me take a picture of you with that bite for my social media page," she told him, taking a photo of just him and his overrated cheese cracker.

Before leaving Ms. Bites took a few pictures of her work on the picnic table. She was proud of herself and rightfully so because her elegant picnic was marvelous. Also, she was nice and knowledgeable with cheeses and blends with fruit. She waved goodbye and I could've sworn she blew Manuel a kiss as she exited silently.

"Does she come with the hotel?" I asked. "That spread over there is very impressive."

"No, she's a family acquaintance, slash possible investment, trying to help her with her small business she started in 2020." He told me. "So, tell me more about you, the career and the hobbies?"

I reminded him. "I'm a teacher, and I like to write, but I guess it's a hobby until I start making real money from it."

"Oh, yes, the writer." I sat beside him in what I must point out was the softest, most form-fitting bathing suit I've ever worn in my life. Plus, the shade of coral to match my light beige skin, famously (to those that know me) one of my favorite nail polish choices. "You have your own business; you should be proud to be a *writer and entrepreneur*. Claim it."

"Yes, you're right, I am a writer. Academic writing is selling well, it's just not my passion. I'm working on a template for a curriculum that gives teachers and students a different perspective of what the classroom environment can be. I'm trying to get it right and package it up before I really stamp my name on it." I explained, getting in on the opposite side of the jacuzzi, spilling my passion with a smile. "I mean, the educational stuff is just one realm I am into, but I want to write these stories that I'm hearing too."

"So do it, you seem to have enough ambition for it," he stated with ease. "Don't wait, get out there. Publish."

"I will." I assured him, "Some weeks I can't write, I'm so all over the place, soaking in humanity, taking notes in daily conversations, unable to stop smiling. Then I'll spend weeks being hyper focused on my goals, ready to build this education-physical-mental health community center, full of desire to give back. Then there are those long periods of time that I want to run away and live on an island far away from everyone and just reflect. Laugh, cry, and write."

"You can have all of that," he told me nonchalantly, but then a little excited. "Let's go to my island there for a few weeks and you can focus!"

"I was being sarcastic," I told him. "Can I tell you something?" He nodded so I continued, "I've been seeing things differently ever since the 2020 quarantine, I gained a lot of perspective that year, I found a key to life. Which was great at first because I got things to be near perfect, but then I outgrew my old definition of *perfect* and just lost who I thought I was. Now, I keep hearing these stories in my mind, but sometimes when I go to write them down, my mind gets cluttered or fogged. I have bits and pieces of stories in my phone. I feel like I'm uncovering something bigger than me at this point."

"So, you can hear stories in your mind? Experiences you've never had?" He asked, not looking at me completely psychotic like I imagined he would do immediately. "Or is it like a guiding voice? What were you smoking today?"

"Repetitively, passionately, storytelling voice. Something's foreign, but it feels like I'm right there experiencing it with them." I told him with a laugh, "I'm probably a little high, but I'm serious! What I think is that I've met so many great people that I just have their voice and their stories, plus my own experiences to discuss. Or maybe they were me in a past life. I don't know. And, at the chance of just sounding insane to a stranger, it's like I'm feeling some divine obligation to tell those stories. I just want to make sure I do it right."

"Okay, artist type shit, trying to get it out and sometimes you can't." Manuel applauded, not making fun of me anymore. "Don't feel like you need to wait for your product to be faultless before you present it. Too many people fail waiting, trying to present perfection. Let your art grow unapologetically, but humbly."

"Thanks for the advice, and not thinking I am insane."

"No, a little high, but I don't think you are insane Acacia. I think you are an artist who has a lot of work to do. An island vacation might help with writer's block, if you wanna try it I got you."

I breathed a sigh of relief, I hadn't told many people how intense my urge to write was these days or the random stories I'd been hearing, even Hazel only witnesses a small amount of my writer's anxiety.

"Maybe one day we can."

"When?" He asked impatiently.

I flipped him off, jokingly, "Don't rush me."

"I'm only saying that because we only live this life for however long we live this life. You don't want to get to the end of it and just be another voice, another collection of untold stories." He said sincerely.

I listened to him with admiration. "I am learning to embrace my artistic side; it's been a while. I gotta get my focus back."

His insight is very appreciated, but I know an island-vacation-murder-mystery-story or screenplay with a fine ass rich man setting when I hear it. There would be no island vacations anytime soon.

"Just do what makes you most happy, trust yourself, you're smart." He complimented; it was hard to look him in the face while the steam from the hot tub glistened on his sculpted chest. "Our time is priceless, with that said, thank you for spending it with me. I'm sure you could've been writing or something."

"Yeah, likewise," I got my eyes off his body enough to notice a familiar sight on the porch with us. "Is that a Sweet Acacia plant?"

He smiled at me, "So you really *can* tell?"

"I've seen and learned about acacias my whole life. My great grandfather with dementia lived with my family while I was in elementary school. He remembered some things mostly about my mom, but he didn't remember my name. My great grandpops also remembered how to play cards, he taught me to play very well," I told him as I waded over to the plant that sat beside the hot tub. "Anyway, whenever he would forget me, I'd introduce myself, then he'd give me random facts about acacia plants. I can basically make a few healing cures, wooden objects, and a couple sketchy sounding recipes." I laughed at the thought. "Did you bring that here for me?"

"Yeah, I heard you wanted to start an acacia healing garden."

"I do! I did, I think. I don't know, I just talk shit sometimes, it was a random idea." I explained, surprised he knew that, although it was one of my favorite ideas to visit. "I learned so much about them, that I always thought I would one day grow my own garden and invent a few cures. You know, save the world as a side hustle. Manuel, this is seriously one of the most thoughtful gifts I've ever got, thank you."

"You're always welcome. Guess what my Grandma Azalea used to say about women with names that are flowers?" Manuel asked.

"Azalea? Hmm… What would an Azalea say? We are pretty to look at, but have sharp thorns? We are sweet as we smell. We can grow in places more people think we never would. Even a tiny flower can have tough roots?" With each time I guessed, he shook his head no, eventually I don't think he really wanted me to guess anymore. "Be very gentle with us? Ohhh, is it that, if you like a flower, you pluck it, if you love it you care for it? She'll bring color to your world?"

"No to all of those." He slowly tilted his head at me, "You've thought about that question?"

"Well, I get a lot of flower pick up lines, no one has ever brought me acacias though," I responded with a smile. "Plus, I took a botany class during the pandemic, for really no reason. The professor made a lot of flower jokes."

"Well, let me tell you what she said, 'before planting a flower, you must learn how she grows, then make sure you plant her somewhere that will allow her to grow properly,' It's the first thing I thought of when I heard your name." He recalled. "She also would tell me, 'flowers need sun', anytime she needed a vacation. I think flower names are deep, Acacia Ivy, he practiced my first and middle name. If I were ever blessed to have a daughter, I'd give her a flower name."

"Your grandma was probably right, I felt like I was planted in the wrong spaces for a long time." I admitted, watching him stare at me through my peripheral vision, how can I want to kiss him and wade away from him nervously at the same time. "I've been replanting myself though, growing much better."

"Let me see if you know the answer to this, when is the second-best time to plant a seed?" Manuel asked me softly.

I knew this quote; I'd heard it somewhere for sure. "Now."

I turned to face him, and he did it, he kissed me. And it was so different than I anticipated. The chemistry was so strong between us that I felt a shock rush through me when our lips touched, but a positive shock, it felt right. How'd he know I wanted him to kiss me? I've never been a big kisser, almost to where I despise it, but kissing Manuel felt comforting. He was impressive, it didn't feel awkward or forced.

He was an even better listener. I watched as he listened attentively every time I talked. I appreciated his interest. I felt myself getting comfortable enough to take out my sativa pre roll from the dispensary and smoke with him.

"I came prepared," I showed him my pre-roll.

"You're a real girl scout," he mocked me sarcastically, he handed me the thickest blunt I've ever seen. "Try this."

I shook my head no, concurrently nodding proudly of my scout experience. "Yes, I was a girl scout for 2 years! However, I am overly cautious about a lot of things. Like smoking, I don't smoke just anything, especially already rolled up!"

"Don't forget, with me? 100% trust. Don't switch up on me and don't get scared, I won't let anything happen to you. My dad owned a security company since I was born, everything around me, secure as fuck. When you're with me, you are safe. But smoke your own, I won't pressure you, I get it." He reminded me, flickering his lighter, then pointed at the acacia plant again. "What's that right there by the root?"

I looked over at where he was pointing, I reached over and grabbed the box behind the plant, and pulled it out, it was long, and gift wrapped. "What's this?"

"Open it," he had a smile on his face as he watched me open the box. I opened the wrapper and opened the lid of a blue box to reveal a rose gold watch with diamond gems surrounding the face and all the way around the band. The watch looked like it carried its own insurance plan.

"Oh my god, wow, this is a lot," I gasped, shocked to even be holding such a gaudy, that appeared to be an expensive piece of jewelry. "You got this for me?"

His smile softened as he tried to read my facial expression, I was in shock. "It's gonna be nice on you, try it on. You don't like it?"

"Of course, I like it, it's so pretty," I nodded, at a loss for words. "I'm just much simpler than this… Wow. You did not have to get me this."

"I know that, but it's gonna look perfect on you. You are not *simple*, put it on." He softly told me, looking into my eyes in his naturally seductive manner.

"Why are you trickin' on me, Sir?" I asked him, jokingly, my eyes locked on the glistening diamonds.

"It's ok, I got it." He said casually, leaning back in the jacuzzi bubbles.

As impressed as I was inside, I didn't want him to think that there was a price tag associated with entering my body and I didn't know the right way to announce that. "I hope you don't think you can buy me."

Manuel laughed out loud genuinely, "Damn, as if not waiting in the line wasn't insulting, but you think I gotta buy women too?"

I shrugged, "Why would you buy this expensive ass watch for a stranger?"

Manuel stood up and helped me unpackage the watch, "I wouldn't call you a stranger, I did some research on you. I like you. No bullshit, the more I learn about you the more I believe you are invaluable Acacia. I'm glad you're here.

"Okay, let me recap, you invited me to your show, got me an acacia plant, put this lovely, expensive watch with it… we're on the balcony in a hot tub with a romantic ass balcony picnic. Are you trying to make me your girlfriend or something? I don't want to assume, but is that what's happening?"

"Do you know what an asset is, English teacher?"

I summarized a quick definition, "Something that is used to generate value, in some kind of way."

"My dad taught me that when you see someone as an asset, you invest in them. Especially a great woman." Manuel took the watch out of the box and spun it with his fingers, it glistened dangerously. "I don't really do girlfriend-titles-obligations, my schedule is too stupid to try to keep up with the expectations. I'm more of the free will type, do what you want, and I'll see where we can fit into each other's lives. I do like you, Acacia, I do *want* to be your…something. Friend? Whatever we want that word to mean to us, we can talk about."

"Friend… for me, just means friend," I nodded, unsure of his angle. "I'm cool with that, I just wanted to be sure we were on the same page, friend. I was just saying I need some new friends."

"So, what are you looking for?" He asked.

Shrugging my shoulders I told him the truth, "I don't know, but I need it to be something different than I've ever felt before."

54

I let him put the watch on me, right beside my smart watch. He loved it, his eyes lit up when I twirled my arm left and right, the diamonds were striking.

"You like it?" He asked as I nodded eagerly.

"Yes, I love it, thank you." However, it was the time on the watch's face that caught me off guard.
"Oh no, time flew by!"

I jumped out of the hot tub to get my purse and phone, I had to text Hazel, it'd been over two hours since I left the room.

She would kill me if she woke up and I was missing. She was probably going to kill me either way since I didn't wake her in the first place.

Yet to my surprise, when I got to my bag my phone wasn't in it.

"Garon has your phone." Manuel said casually after I came back outside and looked around for my phone, he'd notified him on his own watch. "I let him know you need it."

"*What the fuck* why would you guys go through my bag? You can't let me know you are gonna check my bag? You invited me here!" More annoyed they went through my things without permission than anything else.

Garon walked onto the deck, with my phone, he looked reluctant to hand it to me. Yet handed it over as Manuel nodded an agitated, "ok" at him, then Garon went back inside.

He was not even pretending to want me around.

Manuel didn't seem bothered by my line of questioning; I suppose he was used to it. "I have security, Acacia. I told you there were some rules that come with being around me."

"Okay, well what are all these rules, let me know them all? The damn charcuterie lady had her phone, no one stopped her. I have to trust you though?" I mumbled, sarcastically.

"Well, when are you gonna start?" He asked, getting out of the jacuzzi, walking over to me and the astonishing view of the ocean. "Just trust me. Stop worrying about little shit and relax, I'm right here. I want to get to know you and show you a good time. At the same time, you're right, I should've let you know upfront about the phone, sorry."

I cracked a smile, lightening up a little bit with his nonchalant apology. He was taking the imagination-trust exercise to heart. "Okay, thanks."

"Thanks for understanding and not getting upset. I'll apologize in advance, my team is hypervigilant about me, it's my reality." He held my waist, and slowly began to lead us in slow dancing to "Can You Stand the Rain" by New Edition for a few moments. "This is one of my favorite songs, my dad used to play it often on rainy days. Back before internet playlists." Manuel informed me as if I too weren't from the 80's, he began to sing gently, "Sunny days everybody loves them. Let's have an enjoyable time, don't be mad at me."

I wasn't used to getting apologies or thanks at all in my previous relationship, especially ones that felt so sincere. He kept dancing with me. It made accepting his apology more rewarding, and hearing that he was thankful for my understanding, made me want to be more understanding with him.

Ugh! But where's the line before stupidity again?

"Let me call and tell Hazel where I am. She's going to be worried if she gets up and I'm not around. We are driving back in the morn—"

"No, stay with me," he cut me off, twirling me with one hand. "Tonight, the weekend."

"What?" I questioned but continued to let him lead. "I have papers to grade tonight."

"Give them a participation grade," he shrugged, "You know other teachers do it."

"You sound like a high schooler. They need constructive feedback, not participation points, don't get me started on that!" I explained, "How will the work get better if they are only getting participation grades?"

"It's all pointless, you know, and they know. AI is writing the work, then grading the work," Manuel told me, and he was not completely wrong, the students were getting very clever with technology. However, I didn't believe it was pointless, this youth may be all we have to sustain a world one day if it were to crumble.

I loved the way he stood so sure of himself every time he spoke or even breathed. I'm highly attracted to a confident man, but Manuel's confidence was stronger and more assuring than being in the presence of almost anyone I have ever met. He speaks without reservation, not only as if he has no fear of rejection, but as if he's certain to receive the perfect "yes".

He went back into singing and talking intermittently, "I'll do whatever needs to be done, I want you to stay here for the rest of the weekend with me." He explained between the lyrics, "Come out with me tonight. I want to get to know you while I'm here."

56

"I have a job, Manuel. And a child, do you even know I'm a mother?" I asked him. "I can't just stay here with you on a whim, my life isn't like yours. Do you have children? To be honest, I know very little about your personal life."

"No, no children." He said to appease me, but I could tell he wasn't giving up that easily. "It's cool, no pressure, but if you want to stay, you know that we could get all of that figured out. You don't want to always do the work, you gotta enjoy the harvest too. Live."

"What?! I do *live* Manuel, just because I'm not going to stay the weekend with a stranger does not mean I don't *live*. Are you seriously trying to use reverse psychology on me?" I shook my head with a childish laugh, but seriously considering he was right. "I'm not your usual, dumb groupie."

"No, and I don't think you are dumb, not usual. You are way too tough to be *my* usual." Manuel told me, then got back into singing the lyrics, "Will you be there for me?"

His singing voice was nostalgically angelic, hearing him in concert tonight was remarkable, but so close in person was breathtaking for me. Although I appreciated my tickets were free, I understood why the tickets were so expensive… for this voice I may even have stood in line to meet him. "I'm not too tough, I just don't have the same freedom in my life as you."

"That's a choice… yours to make. It's your life." Manuel kept his arms around me as he started to sway side to side to the music from his penthouse. As he sang, he'd occasionally pause and look in my eyes. I kept turning away from him to hide my big smile and keep from giggling!

Yet, I almost despised how casual he acted around me, as if he wasn't Manuel! As if he were just another man. He isn't. I began to rethink the proposal, a weekend with a superstar. Am I crazy not to take it?

"This view is phenomenal," I said, trying to get out of my head, be present. "I didn't know there was a place where we are able to see both the city and ocean."

"I want you to see so much more, but you're leaving." He said with a pathetic shrug.

"Of course, you do," I snickered, partially wanting to stay the other part thinking I'd end up in some underground trafficking ring in the next 48 hours. "What do you want to show me?"

"Outer space."

I rolled my eyes, not going there. "I don't want to leave, just not sure."

"Oh woman, just be soft, I promise you're gonna have fun with me. I got a couple errands to run tonight, then I'll take you on a date tomorrow. You'll love it. It'll be something different." He informed me of the plan with a smile, embedding my name within the lyrics. "Can you stand the rain, Acacia?"

"I used to, but now I don't want to. I stood in a lot of rain for people I loved, like a lot of downpours. Even hail at times." I told him. "The *rain* back in 1988 was bad news in the media, the newspaper; the rain y'all men are putting us through is self-inflicted! Controlling your own image in the media and still fuckin' up, I'm done saving folks from themself. I'm over standing in the rain, I want the double rainbows, and butterflies."

"What if I buy you a sturdy-heavy duty umbrella? It'll be cute too," he added, possibly sarcastically. "An impenetrable umbrella with a matching designer rain jacket.

"That is one of my class's vocabulary words, impenetrable." My easily distracted teacher-brain blurted out. "But no thanks on the umbrella and jacket rain combo."

"How do you want a double rainbow with no rain?" Manuel sighed, "That's a problem, that soil is just gonna be dry with no rain." He thought out loud.

"Ain't nothing dry." I retorted back at him, and we both laughed.

"Nothing, huh?" He nodded his head making a sexy look at me. "I'm just saying, every relationship is going to have rain, no matter who is at fault for it. The seasons will always change, 4.5 billion years in and that hasn't changed on Earth. Bad weather is inevitable in everyone's world. You have to decide who you are willing to stand in the rain with, and what kind of protection is he providing you for life's storms."

"I've been through plenty of rain, Manuel. I'm tired of it. Now I run from the storms very well." I told him, trying to keep our metaphor alive. "I prefer just going inside and locking myself into one of my labs of creative solitude."

He made a serious face, "Don't be scared of rain, you should know that, Acacia Ivy. You do need it to grow."

"Not scared, just happier not dealing with it and I don't *have* to. I do very well on my own."

"That's when you miss life, miss experiencing all the miraculous shit… You're going to miss the benefits of the rain," he preached.

58

I repeated his words in my mind, *"be soft"*, he was starting to make some sense. Closing the door to myself wasn't truly the best option, but it was safe for *me*. The *me* I found not too long ago after lots of years being torn down, confused, unsure, and waking up at night trying to figure out if I even loved myself.

I feel good now. Great! Better than I have since I was 18. I'd finally found my meaning for life again, I was revived! Consequently, it was easier to keep people I am unsure about away, then to allow them to disorient me.

"Are you okay? You wanna go inside to the party? We can just go play cards. No pressure."

The DJ was doing a great job and I was not nervous about the party, but leaving the balcony would mean not having Manuel to myself. And I was feeling a little stingy with him.

"No." I loved looking in his eyes, "I'm fine out here with you."

"You know, I felt your pulse increase when we walked in, you don't really trust me yet." He moved a little closer to me.

"I do." I assured him. It wasn't full trust, but he was getting more than most people get.

"Say it again?"

"I do?"

He licked his upper lip, to my voice. "That does sound kinda sexy coming from you, but nah."

He was seductive without even trying, so his flirtation was intimidating. I slowly walked to the other side of the balcony and flashed a flirtatious smile at him. *I do.*

"I want you to be comfortable, I only want to get to know you as a person. I'm not trying to fuck you or play with you like a toy, as you call it. I don't expect anything from you, and I **don't** want you to do anything that you don't want to do. Just stay with me, let's have fun and I'll bring you home after." He assured me joining at the city side of the porch, and taking my left hand, then with a smile he also let me know.

It was a very enticing offer, a weekend of fun with a fine ass rich man, no strings attached. No expectations for sex. Although sex, if we got to that point, wouldn't be the end of the world, maybe I could break the curse.

I nodded *yes* to the offer; I am staying the weekend with a stranger.

Manuel finished with his disclaimer, "Now if you try to fuck me, I'll only say no maybe three times then I'm gonna give in. It's gonna be hard for me to say no to you, I can already tell. I'll make sure you get back safe and sound."

"Okay. I'll stay, but I gotta go call Hazel or she'll be paranoid."

He shook my hand to solidify the deal then kissed it like a gentleman in one of those chivalrous movies.

"I really like your energy, but I knew I would." He told me sincerely, before closing the sliding glass door to give me privacy.

I took a soft, but deep breath, knowing Hazel for the last decade and a half of my life, I knew what she was going to say. However, I decided when I left my ex that this is my life to live and anyone who got in the way of that was not going to win. Even Hazel.

I spent too many years living for other people's opinions.

"Hey," I said to her voicemail, thank God, she did not pick up. Typically, I'd send a text, but I knew she'd need to at least hear my voice to believe I was okay. I talked in a low voice. "It's Cay, I'm with Manuel at his hotel, I'm fine… like very fine. He's cool. You can head back home in the morning without me, he's going to bring me back home. I'll call you tomorrow. Please don't worry about me, Tré's with Hayden, so no worries."

I stood admiring the view of the ocean and posed just about to take a selfie for my own memories.

Just then Garon popped his head out the glass door, "No pictures. No videos."

Of myself???

I went ahead and put the contraband in Garon's extended palm.

"You take your job very seriously," I pointed out, and he closed the door.

Garon had a familiar look that I couldn't exactly pinpoint what it was, maybe a little reminder of the asshole bouncers outside the nightclubs when I was a teenager. I sensed something familiar in him, I determined that I was not his cup of tea, and he wasn't mine either. The realization of someone constantly being around, especially with that boring personality, seemed a bit annoying.

When else would I see a view like this or sleep in a suite of this luxury style? I had no choice but to take it all in now, since the photography ban. The quality of the hotel was obvious in everything from the paint on the wall to the light fixtures. I was no slouch when it came to hotels, but the elegance and futuristic feeling in his suite was impressive.

From where I was standing on the balcony, I could discreetly see Manuel in the attached bathroom, he was brushing his teeth. I stepped off

60

to the side so he wouldn't notice me watching. I admired him, he was very handsome, possibly even more so now when he wasn't talking so much.

After he finished brushing, I watched Manuel turn on the shower and remove his swim trunks. His lower body was just as impressive as the defined muscles on his upper body.

I spun around quickly when he turned around and almost noticed me, but I had seen enough that I was very pleased. I took another sneak peek through the crystal-clear glass, Manuel was looking directly at me this time, he motioned for me to come to him when we locked eyes.

I tried to coach myself to not be timid, but I am not usually this woman, I don't go into bathrooms with a naked man after knowing him for four hours. I'm a serial monogamous! I ultimately regretted skipping my hoe phase, who was I even trying to impress. Yeah, I've had decades of great sex, but it was with mainly one person who knew me inside and out.

This was different.

He is not the practice squad, Hazel's words replayed in my head, motivating fake confidence.

I entered the bathroom through the balcony entrance, I tried to keep my eyes on his eyes, but I couldn't help but notice the rest of him. When I locked the door that led from the balcony the glass door frosted over for privacy, I played with the lock and frosting glass a couple times.

"So, you kept it unlocked on purpose?" I asked him. I was not disappointed but remained very composed and told myself not to act too giddy.

"Wanted to see if you would look," he shrugged. "Take a shower with me."

I admit, I was feeling irrationally safe or maybe just felt the urge to do something different than I normally would. For some reason I believed him when he said he wasn't looking for a toy, so I accepted the invitation by slipping off my pricey swimsuit and getting in the shower with him.

Both leafless, fully exposed. The vulnerability was seductive.

"How are you even doper in person?" He asked, "So balanced."

"Thanks, I guess," I replied bashfully, stepping into the water with him, feeling sexy tonight. Rejoicing that Hazel influenced me not to order another round of biscuits for dinner earlier.

"So, what really made you change your mind about coming out here to be with me tonight?"

I shrugged, determining how honest I felt like being with him, I went full honesty. "I didn't want to let my fear of letting new people in, make me lose the opportunity to know *you*. Guess I was afraid you might get the wrong idea of me if I gave in so quickly. Like I'm just one of those women at your show, throwing myself at you desperately."

He smirked, taking his eyes off mine to look at my body. "When I look at you, I don't think you are desperate or the type to throw yourself. You didn't find me Acacia, I wanted you here, I'm the one throwing myself at you, if anything."

"You always get what you want, huh?" I asked him, looking deeply into his eyes.

Nudity hasn't been a problem to me in quite some time. Spending months in county jail for beating a sideline you caught with your man will have you get over that shyness rather quickly. I've showered in front of over 600 people minimum. Not that I was a very modest person when it came to my body prior to that. However somehow here with Manuel, I did feel just a tad self-conscious.

"I'm glad you came; it means a lot to me. I really don't do this either, even if you don't believe me." He assured me with a smile, his eyes locked in on mine. "I mostly like to be alone, I'm kind of an extroverted introvert."

I looked at him doubtfully, "Sure."

"You don't believe people much, do you?" He asked. "Some connections drain your energy and some help you charge. I don't like to be drained so I stay to myself. But you bring energy, I'm attracted."

"Okay, stop throwing yourself at me," I joked. "I'm glad I came."

I liked looking into Manuel's eyes, I didn't get that intense feeling to look away, instead I wanted to investigate them deeper. Like his soul was trying to tell me a secret.

The water flowed down the muscle cuts in his body like little rivers, his medium length hair was starting to curl, his body was glistening. He somehow looked bigger in person, more muscular, yet more approachable than I predicted.

I stepped closer to him, standing at 5' 5" and he was almost a foot taller. I put my hands on the sides of his beard and tiptoed to kiss him under the water. He kissed me back, putting his hands on my back, then sliding them down to my ass.

I accidentally giggled at myself out loud.

"What?" he asked, moving only two centimeters away, enough for us to breathe.

62

"I usually hate kissing," I happily confessed, empowered as I felt like I was someone else leaning back in to put my tongue in his mouth. It felt enticing to kiss him.

Was I doing a good job? I am so out of practice! I fought to keep my negative self-talk and doubts out of my head. It does nothing for you, Acacia, I reminded myself.

He lifted me up and I wrapped my legs around his wet naked body. "I'm not your usual type."

I stopped overthinking it and relaxed.

Kissing him felt natural, he let me lead for just a moment, then his tongue took over. He leaned my back against the shower wall for support as he kept me in the air, hands under my butt. I could feel him getting hard against my thigh, so I loosened up and pulled back a bit.

I did not want it to go any further. I did not want to sleep with this man on Day 1. No matter how fine or rich he is.

Feeling my resistance he put me down, then kissed me on the lips. He took a step back to ease my discomfort, then he handed me his soap and loofah. "Can you do my back?"

"Sure, *friend*," I said sarcastically.

I gratefully obliged, rubbing the soap into a lather, then soaping him. In silence I read images on his smooth skin like a book as I lathered him up with soap on his back and arms. There were names, script, and many different images. The historian in me played hieroglyph ologist, in hopes to decode who he is inside.

"I see you like to look at my tattoos," He told me, as I also had begun to trace a few of them with my fingers.

"Yeah, I like to learn about people that way, tattoos tell stories."

"Some tell stories, others hide them." He smiled warily, "What do mine say to you?"

"So far, they are telling me you are a family man, you love music, you are bossy, hmmm..." I pointed to the one of a man with angel wings with a recent death date and messy signature above some motivational lyrics. "Is this for your brother that passed?"

"Yes, my little brother, Ryū, that was my nigga." Manuel told me with a hint of sadness, but so much love. "No lie Acacia, I still haven't been the same since he got killed, but I am way better than I was at first. We would talk almost every day, even when he moved, he still always checked on me."

"Sounds like it was an important relationship, I can only imagine it was a struggle for you to lose him," I pouted my lip for him. "Was he your closest brother?"

"We are all very close, it's almost a vital bond between us, how me and my brothers just have built so much around each other. Not so much as we got older, Ryū moved away years ago, he met somebody, Lyra, and they wanted their son to have a normal life." Manuel said to me.

"Is that what you would want to do one day?" I asked. "Leave all this glamor and hang out with us simple folks, normal, as you say."

Manuel didn't even have to think about it, he raised his eyebrows and shook his head no. "I love it here, even when it's hard. Matter of fact, when it's hard, I try to find out how I can profit from the problem. But everybody doesn't share the same perspective, we all see things differently, he just wanted the wife and kids."

We were facing each other, I held his hands, "How'd you get to a better place? You seem so happy."

"A huge part was spending time with his son." Manuel told me, "Getting to know my nephew better was a big key. I don't have any kids so it was my first time having one around me a lot, before that I would only see him about twice a year."

I understood the need to shift focus to avoid falling deeper into a depressive state.

"Take this perspective," Manuel said, "we should all be so happy to die focusing on the things that we want in our life. We all die from something, and happiness is in the journey not at that finish line. My brother was a great husband, dad, and brother. I believe he died happy."

I tried to get the lesson, "So the key to happiness is to be resiliently focused and progressing on something that is meaningful to you?"

"Maybe," Manuel said, "Plus, I don't know anyone that didn't love him."

"Sounds like you?"

He shook his head no, "Not like me, I never had what he had."

"Well, it seems everybody loves you, to me. I know you see how people look at you, you must be able to feel their eyes at this point." I rolled my eyes flirtatiously. "You're pretty humble."

"Quality over quantity, when it comes to love," Manuel shifted the conversation, directing my attention to another tattoo. He dragged my hand across a collage on his chest, "Feel this?"

64

Where he ran my hand over was covering a lot of scar tissue.

"Yes. What happened to you?" I asked, I was impressed, they were disguised so well no one would ever see how cut up his skin was. I simultaneously winced painfully, rubbing all the welted skin on his flesh.

"Everybody doesn't love me, Acacia, but I don't care to talk about haters or folks with bad taste, they'll always be there. I'm fine now." He brushed it off.

I touched him again gently, "You can talk to me, if you ever want. I'm an expert at keeping secrets."

"Bet." He said but gave me no secrets.

Then we just used his body art as a non-chronological timeline of his life, as I asked him questions about the different images and symbols on his body. He told me short versions of life stories and walked me down a very comical, lighthearted memory lane. He wasn't ready to tell me more about his hidden scars, or anything else too deep for that matter, but I enjoyed what he did tell me.

Most of his stories were funny, I never would have guessed he had such a comical side. A few other tattoos were for lost relatives and close friends, dates, and even places. None were as big as the one for his little brother. He had symbols and art for just about all his family. Of course, the DeCreed symbol as well.

Manuel laughed to himself, he said he was reminiscing on wild endeavors of he and his brothers as children. Manuel said no matter how stupid the ideas were, they could always find at least one brother to help carry out their mission. I loved the way they believed in each other, even if they didn't necessarily agree with each other, they supported one another.

We talked in the shower for about thirty minutes more then decided to get out, my fingers had wrinkles.

"I want to make a couple of stops tonight and I want you to come with me." He informed me as he used a towel, and I dried off in the suite's techie body dryer. "You cool with that, right?"

I nodded. Curious as to what and where Manuel's celebrity errands would take us.

On his king-sized bed was a navy-blue strapless dress with beige and gold designer branded, strappy heels. Beside the woman's ensemble was a soft oversized women's tuxedo-style coat that was dark khaki color with gold gaudy embellishments. His outfit, a navy-blue designer cotton shirt with dark khaki pants.

"I like to match while we're out," Manuel told me, explaining the outfits before I even had a chance to ask.

It was for sure cute, exactly my size, and the price tags were so outrageous that I hoped he got them at a much more discounted sale price. Everything fits like a glove. He has a talent for measuring up his type, I joked to myself, loving the soft satin dress on my body. The shoes being the right size and height was just pure luck. Not too tall, but a comfortably cute height, since I'd be standing beside Manuel all night.

Once we were dressed, he came behind me with a diamond cut-Cuban link necklace and clasped it around my neck. It was the same style as the one he wore, but smaller and without his symbol. It was gorgeous. It fit and fell around my neck at just the right spot against my collar bone.

"All this for errands?" I questioned.

"Yes," he assured me, leading me out a side door. "Just a few stops."

The door led us directly to the lobby Garon and I used to come into the penthouse suite.

"So, there was a private door?" I asked matter-of-factly. "Why didn't you just use this door to let me in earlier?"

He smiled at me, "I like checking your pulse, wanting to see how you act in different scenes."

I shook my head, "You like to play around a lot, huh?"

"No," he lied, kissing my forehead with his soft plush lips. "I like getting to know you."

"Did I pass?" I asked.

"We're still here," He shrugged as Garon held the door to the elevator open for us and Buck waited silently inside.

4

"The afterparty wasn't canceled?" I asked when we arrived at the back entrance of a very familiar nightclub from my early adult years, three bouncers were waiting to receive us outside. "I used to go to this club in college, the drinks were so overpriced we would be walking around with melted ice more often than we had liquor."

"Do you mean water?" He asked.

"It was melted ice!" I told him, realizing it was just water. "So, is this a performance type of thing?"

"No, the actual location was canceled, but the promoter found this spot closer to the college. We are just making a short appearance. Unless you are feeling nostalgic and want to have melted ice." He told me, raising his eyebrow. "I'm kidding, you can get as many drinks as you want."

I hit him; I was surprised by how playful he was. "Shut up, that was like fifteen years ago, I can afford drinks without you here, thank you."

We went in through a back door, then another one that led us directly upstairs to the VIP section. Kenz, Scandal, and Rich, from DeCreed were in the section; each man with no less than three women sitting either on them, beside them, or directly behind them giving them a massage.

Upon greeting each one of the men with an elaborate handshake, Manuel introduced me to them as *his lady Acacia.* I was falling in love with the way my name sounded on his lips. Manuel's group members responded with a half hug or smile. They did not introduce the women they were with to me or Manuel. I gave everyone a small smile as I followed Manuel, I recognized one girl from earlier backstage at the concert, I only remembered her because she was so pretty.

The club was packed, people were taking so many pictures in our direction that I couldn't help but feel a little self-conscious with every gesture I made. The waitresses came nonstop with unlimited bottle service, they kept the pour so heavy, I had only had 1 drink and I could feel the liquor. Manuel had about three bottles of water.

After two drinks and a few dances I started to notice I was tipsy. The club was crowded, and much too loud for a conversation, but for no more than five minutes, with me in his arms and his eyes constantly locked onto mine I swear everyone disappeared.

To have said not a single word, it felt like our souls were talking to each other. Maybe it was in my head but at times it seemed like Manuel could hear my inner thoughts. He was so responsive to unspoken needs.

"Let's go sit down," he told me, walking me to a sofa.

"You don't ever drink?" I yelled to him over the music.

"No, I don't." He shook his head, "I'm going to go over and thank the fans for coming, are you okay right here?"

I nodded, trying to play off my intoxication level, I was tipsy. "I'm doing very okay."

I wondered if being with someone who did not need alcohol to have an enjoyable time was important to him.

He kissed my cheek and politely excused himself and left to speak to his fans from the mic at the DJ booth. He walked to the mic so boldly, but unnecessarily humble for someone with so much admiration.

Manuel stood holding the mic for about 2 minutes, just alternating between smiling and posing, the women were freaking out! Screaming, yelling, crying! He hadn't even spoken yet!

"Listen, thank you, thank you, thank you! As a thank you and an apology, DeCreed and I bought the bar, drinks are on us the rest of the night! Grab whatever you want: champagne, vodka, tequila, wine. Y'all have the best time!" Manuel announced. "Tip the staff, remember the more you give in this world, the more you get back! Peace!"

The fans yelled his lyrics along with the DJ's outro song, the fans screamed "I love you", and one lady fainted when he touched her hand. He was so gentle with his fans; he took pictures and shook hands as his hyper vigilant security stood behind him on either side just in case.

I noticed the change in Manuel's persona on the microphone, he was different than when he and I were alone. Same commanding, magnetic vibe, but the approach was much more vibrant and larger-than-life when he was in the spotlight. The strong, silent vibe he gave me when we were alone was much more mellow, although both were mixed with just the right amount of sexy and charisma.

From my peripheral I noticed a small group of women; they had just received 7 bottles of liquor with sparklers from the bar. The group were dancing on the couches and recording very happy videos of themselves. I noticed occasionally though some of the women kept looking at me, finally one was brave enough to approach me.

"Hello, I missed your name, who are you?" The sexy lady with a see-through leopard print bodysuit asked me once she was close, I recognized her from when we first arrived.

"Acacia, I'm a friend of Manuel's." I yelled over the loud music. She somehow was able to hear me, this was her scene, it was clear her heels were six inches taller than mine, yet she looked so much more comfortable walking than I did.

She reminded me how much I never even enjoyed nightclubs.

"(Saying) friend of Manuel is crazy, do you mean *fuck* friend?" She asked in the politest way I imagine someone could ask a lady in a nightclub if they are someone's fuck friend.

"No," I quickly replied, trying to keep my smile, "not like *that*."

"Sweets, he barely does friends." She smiled sinisterly at me and chuckled, "He does *not* do female friends. No, no, you gotta be a little more than *friend* to be around here."

I shrugged. "Acquaintance?"

Leopard Lady reached out to shake my hand as she shook her head, she was complimenting me, she even added two snaps. Being here with Manuel was a big deal, and for reasons I'm sure I'd never understand, she wanted me to know that she knew I was here.

"Whoa! Did he buy you that too? My *best* friend wanted this exact watch." She asked, impressed, pointing at my diamond watch, which I noticed was blinging out of control against the club's lighting as soon as we walked in.

"Thanks, it was a gift." I told her modestly, covering the watch to tone down its shine.

She playfully held my hand and turned it side to side to flaunt it, "No, bitch when you start fuckin' a rich nigga you gotta act like it! Hold the wrist up and let these hoes know!"

"I'm not—," I stopped myself and just smiled, let her think I was fucking him if she wants to.

Is she an ex? I wondered.

Manuel started walking back toward us and she huffed, she wanted to talk more. I smiled at him as he came and took my hand, he made an unfriendly face at the Leopard Lady, then smiled back at me. He pretended to tell me a secret, but instead kissed and sucked on my ear under his concealed hand. I couldn't help but giggle as the sexy Leopard Lady walked away with her tea.

"That was cute, you are a very kind person passing out free drinks," I told him when he was close enough to hear. "Although I had to dance on these same floors with *melted ice*, my 21-year-old self, thanks you."

"Walk with me, gonna go wash my hands, that mic was filthy."

I followed Manuel into a private room behind the V.I.P section, through a very incognito tinted sliding glass door. In fact, the whole section was behind a glass, we could see the whole dance floor, but they couldn't see us.

Manuel walked over to the restroom areas as I headed to the bar for another drink.

The music from the DJ booth was still audible and very loud in the private back room. So, after I grabbed my drink I hit the smaller dance floor to dance solo like a few others were doing. Manuel came over after watching me for one song, he slowly began to dance behind me to the music.

Mid song he stopped me to kiss me on the dance floor, a couple of his associates saw us, I blushed but didn't hesitate to join. I didn't know we were going public.

The private room in the club wasn't much to look at, same half ass decor as the main floor ten years ago, but it was behind the tinted glass of the VIP section. It had privacy, which is all I cared about, Manuel and I were able to dance and relax without the fans being right in his face snapping pictures. The others in the private room appeared to be minding their business as well.

All the years I went to this club, and I never knew about this room. The private space was nice. If more clubs were like this, private, maybe I'd be more inclined to go.

I looked around, no one seemed to be watching. I was excited, he moved around so effortlessly that it gave me a strange sense of comfort and security. He found cute ways to touch me without being creepy or overzealous.

As the chemistry was growing, we were slow dancing face to face, and I just couldn't help wanting him. I found myself grinding on his

70

pants as I danced, mischievously enjoying feeling his erection grow against my body, he was making me wet. And blame the liquor, I wanted him to know it.

I stealthily took his hand and encouraged him to feel between my bare legs, he didn't object.

"Damn, is it always like that?" he asked softly, referring to the wetness he felt inside of me, he rubbed my clit in between his index and middle finger as I closed my eyes from the rush. "You're supposed to be the good one."

I laughed, letting his hand explore for a few more seconds before gently pushing his hand away. "I am the good one."

I tried to relax my hormones as he sang his slow song in my ear as the DJ played it on the speaker. But my vagina had a whole pulse throbbing inside of it for him. The sexual frustration was going to make me explode, what was he doing to me?

I put the alcohol down.

Only a little while later Garon came onto the dance floor and whispered in Manuel's ear, whatever he said, it was time to go. It'd been years since I danced with a man on the dancefloor, song after song like no one was watching, the time felt irrelevant.

I looked at my watch and was shocked at how long I was awake much less the amount of energy I still had!

Manuel and I were all over each other once we got into the back of the SUV. Typically, I'm a stickler for safety and a seatbelt, but on this ride I sat sideways on Manuel's lap. He held my back for support as we sporadically kissed, and he let me suck on his tasty neck. We flirted and whispered much about nothing for about thirty minutes, had we been at the hotel I would've no doubt caved into my sexual desires.

"Next stop is to the studio, stay awake." Manuel filled me in as we rode down the interstate in the back of a very impressive SUV. I wasn't tired, but he felt nice to lay on.

"This watch is impressive, I got a lot of compliments, thank you." I told him. "I've never had anything this expensive in my life, it feels weird. I feel like I don't deserve it, I guess."

"No, you earned it alright," Buck said, eavesdropping from the front seat.

Manuel kicked Buck's chair, "Shut up and mind your business."

"This ain't no rental, Bruh," Garon called looking through the rearview mirror. It seemed like he was purposely finding reasons to pick at Manuel about. "Get y'all feet off my $300,000 seats."

"Fuck your seats," Manuel snapped back at him, as I took my feet off the seats apologetically. "Buck, did I buy this ride for him?"

Buck looked tired, he had his eyes closed and his chair far back, but he wasn't sleeping. "I ain't your Corbin, Nigga. I got my own to count."

"No bitch, you didn't buy this, although I will send you a bill." Garon quipped back, I took my feet back off the seat, but Manuel left his one foot in place.

Everyone was getting more relaxed around me, talking a little more candidly. Manuel's very relaxed attitude with his employees was much different than I'd expect a professional to be, but I like that they were all able to be themselves.

"Send me the bill Garon, I'll pay it twice!" Manuel added as he put my legs back on the seats with his and whispered to me, "Fuck his seats, I like when you relax. The studio is fun, you'll like it."

"He already doesn't like me," I whispered back to Manuel. "And this is a luxury ass car."

"Trust me, he likes you," Manuel laughed out loud, but I shook my head no, "Or he will. Give it time."

"I didn't know cars were that expensive." I commented.

He nodded, "Hell yeah, vehicles can get very expensive, Garon collects them as a hobby, he has a whole parking lot about an acre or so full of vehicles, so don't worry about him or this car. Do you want a car? You said you like this?"

I shook my head, "I wouldn't even want a car this expensive. Such a target on yourself."

"Well, the windows are bulletproof, but I'll keep that in mind," Manuel nodded with a smile. "What is your dream car?"

"I really like the one I have," I told him, was he hinting at buying me a car? I shifted the subject. "Are you making a new song tonight?"

He shook his hand side-to-side indicating yes and no, "I want you to hear a hit I worked on, I think you'll like it. I almost finished it yesterday, but something happened to it."

Garon pulled up in front of a huge dark gray family-style home with a wrap-around porch; there is a very wide semi-circle driveway that made for more parking. The parking area was full, but he let us out along with Buck at the front walkway.

Still feeling a buzz from the drinks earlier in the night as well as sexual frustration from making out in the backseat of a SUV like a teenager, I held onto Manuel's forearm and rested my head on his arm as we walked up to the house.

He kissed me on my forehead, "You sleepy, you don't need to wait in the truck, right?"

"No," I responded, enjoying the feeling of lust in the dark early hours of morning and not wanting to hang out with his security.

The studio's security guard opened the door, he sported a visible gun on himself, but showed favor as soon as he saw who was at the door. He looked honored just to see Buck and Manuel.

"Your wife got those clothes for the baby?" Buck asked the security guard who nodded and hugged him. He hugged Manuel as well and he nodded his head at me when I passed by beside them.

The home was transformed to a music studio, from the bedrooms transformed into recording rooms to the living room having a built-in desk as the centerpiece of the lobby. Whoever owned this was no slouch, the carpentry work was top notch, I've been to shady looking studios, yet this work was exquisite.

As stunning as it was to look at, it isn't somewhere I would go alone. Not my scene at all. I stayed close to Manuel, he liked to hold my hand.

It was hard for me to think this was an actual lifestyle, a profitable business as well. The lights were low as well, dimly lit with fluorescent bulbs. There were quite a few women walking around in the lobby area, some were working, and others seemed to just be hanging out. Of course, there were men and boys hanging around, too. There was a stationary fog lingering around from the smokers.

I followed behind Manuel as he led Buck and me into one of the studio rooms. There were only about four people in the room. I recognized Chris from the group, he seemed so business minded on television and media, but even more so in person. As I would soon find out, his leadership qualities were on full display as he called many of the calls in the studio.

"No women-," Chris started to say in my direction.

Manuel cut him off before he could even finish. "She's good."

"What? Is this work?" Chris made a repulsive face at Manuel, "You know-."

Manuel cut Chris off again, "You are wasting time, let's go. She's fine in here with me."

Chris didn't want me to be in there, but he didn't persist; he let me in. They got straight to business.

Two younger men in the studio were with Chris, possibly interns. One was more of a do-boy, jokester nature; he got water, weed, sweat rags, and whatever else the workers needed. Each time he did something for the men or was given a directive, he made a slick comment to his friend. The other youth was quick with taking the more technical directions, more focused.

Manuel was in the booth most of the time, he had to redo the verse to the track he wanted me to hear. Chris tried to explain why it was erased, but Manuel just shrugged off the explanation. I noticed he didn't fret or get upset much about anything.

I mostly sat on the sofa and watched Manuel make music through the glass while Buck, Chris, and the others orchestrated his music with the tech equipment. One young man would cue the music, Manuel rapped from inside the enclosed booth. Chris would mumble something to Buck then Buck would call it out to Manuel through the headphones about what to fix.

Apparently Buck was not *just* a security guard. He had an ear for music and Manuel trusted him. It gave me a little more respect for the security guard.

Manuel was a sight to watch, he was passionate about his music, but still remained lighthearted and comical the whole time. He interacted with me, pointing at me, blowing an occasional kiss. I realized I no longer needed to use my imagination to pretend I was comfortable, his energy was magnetic, it made me feel good.

It didn't take long to record the verse, each time they recorded him they gave criticism, and he corrected it. For just the short while we were in the session I could feel my attraction for him grow. He looked at me a lot while he was working, so much that by the end of the session I was lip syncing his whole verse.

Watching him work was sexy, if he was trying to impress me, it was working. When he finished with the verse Chris and Buck went into the booth with Manuel, this time they turned the microphone off so we couldn't hear.

Whatever they were saying to Manuel, it was clear he was not on their side of the conversation. Chris seemed to be lecturing Manuel, Manuel visibly was growing annoyed. Buck was making light of the conversation, laughing at seemingly tense moments. He occasionally looked at me, not sure if he was just being weird or if they were talking about me.

With nothing better to do I began to casually eavesdrop into the hormonal male bullshit that young guys converse about. I'd made eye contact with guys a few times in the studio, but we hadn't spoken at all since hello.

"We did him a favor by deleting that verse, this shit sounds way better than the one he put down yesterday." The tech savvy young man gloated, but looked shameful when we made eye contact. They seemed a little diffident.

The jokester, who did very little important work, looked pleased at himself when he looked over at me, "Pure facts! Do you sing?"

"Me?" I repeated, realizing that was an obvious question as we were all alone in this room.

"Yeah, I'm looking for a female artist for a couple tracks. I make music too."

"No," I said with a smile, wishing I could sing and enjoy such an opportunity. "Unfortunately, I've never been able to really sing, I can lip sync."

"What can you do?" He asked, looking me down then back up, "Can you dance, shake that ass? I need a lead dancer for my music video also, and you look like a lead."

"No," I snapped at him defensively.

"What did you just say to her?" Manuel asked the jokester, I didn't realize the men had come out of the booth and joined us back in the main room. Manuel looked ready to hit the guy and Buck always looked like he was up for whatever Manuel wanted to do.

If Manuel is as loving as he said he is, I knew he would not hurt the kids.

The boys now looked terrifyingly embarrassed, I felt nervous for him as well, they were barely 21. Chris looked reluctant at the men, possibly hoping that they'd have something redeeming to say.

"Don't I always tell you to shut up, you are way smarter when you close your damn mouth." Chris snapped at the boys.

"I just asked if she could sing," he tried to respond, before Buck cut him off.

"You lying too? You see who she's with, why would anyone need you? *You* don't even know who you are yet." Buck spoke with his hands as he talked, intimidating them as he stepped closer to him. "What do you even have to offer yourself?"

"Nothing, yet. I'm work-working on some stuff," he responded with a stutter, very cautiously. "Sorry, sorry, Manuel. Buck. Sorry, and also, I didn't mean no disrespect mam."

"Then what did you mean?" Manuel asked, he wanted to punish those boys so badly. "Because it felt like disrespect, and I hate that shit."

I was starting to feel uncomfortable as Buck looked at Manuel, waiting for the word just to escalate the situation to another level. The young man braced himself, standing with the bad sense he was getting ready to take a punch. It wouldn't have been worth it to fight back as the young men stood without a chance against either of them.

"They were just talking, they were kidding. They're just immature." I spoke up, locking eyes with Manuel, but stepping closer to his security who seemed more upset than Manuel. I wanted him to stop this staring contest before it escalated, say something to spare the young men from whatever Buck does to men who are disrespectful. "Everything is fine."

"Let's go. Check ya boy, Chris," Manuel told Chris. Manuel turned to the young engineer, "I like your work, could've taught you some things, but your friend is a fool, you won't learn with him around."

"I did-," The fool began to talk again, but when Manuel made eye contact with him it was as if his lips were glued together.

"Be careful who you hang out with, you become them." Manuel finished his thought, and we turned to leave.

As we headed out, I watched to make sure Buck was following behind us. I felt secondhand embarrassment for the hormonal, foolish apprentice, but quickly followed behind Manuel.

"You were too lenient." Buck said bluntly.

"It's important to have a little grace on the youth, one day that'll hopefully translate to patience when they have to take care of us." I winked at him and shared a little of my philosophy. "I think they were only joking around."

"Well, the next one who tries to be funny you don't get to spare, you just handed out your one Pass." Buck told me, scooting in front of us to lead the way. "EmManuel, let her know the rules, she only gets one!"

"He's right," Manuel nodded to appease Buck, but pulled me close and whispered with a sweet smile, "You get more than one pass, nobody sticks to that rule."

I raised my eyebrows, then followed behind them. Not sure if they were serious.

As we went down the hall to exit the studio of course every person greeted or gawked at Manuel, he had his arm around me, it felt comfortable, the perfect fit around my shoulders. We noticed a group of people were formed in a circle, I struggled to see who was at the center.

"Ho-ly shit!" I stopped abruptly and held my chest. Staring in disbelief, I whispered loudly to Manuel, "Do you see who that is?"

"You wanna meet him?" Manuel asked casually, but with a huge smile.

I felt tears building up in my eyes. "Yes, are you serious? You know I love him. Manuel, I'm about to pass out."

"I'll carry you if you fall," Manuel laughed at me and gave my shoulder a gentle squeeze, he held up his finger to get the artist's attention. "Ay yo! Todd!"

My favorite living artist turned around, immediately stopping his conversation once he saw Manuel.

"Yo! Mi familia!" Young Todd called back, grabbing Manuel up in a hug. "You were right, the studio looks great, the best renovation I have seen in a long time."

"You know what they say, if you want something done right." Manuel said with a sigh, "I won't hold you, but I have to introduce a big fan of yours, this is Acacia."

"She's not yours?" Young Todd finally made eye contact with me once we were introduced, smiling at me and shaking my hand. I blushed so hard that my face hurt.

Although I will always cherish this moment, millions of people would want to be in my shoes right now, I couldn't ignore what my intrusive thoughts were wondering. The *Young* Todd was not at all the way I imagined him to look, the irony was in his *old* face. He was not as tall as I thought he was, nor as attractive in person, to be honest almost sickly. I somehow never noticed, but he even smiles in a way to cover his spotted teeth that weren't very white at all. Todd's face had excoriations and his skin a leathery texture, it wasn't uncommon side effects for the drugs that he raps about.

"No, not a *big* one." Manuel said, winking at my frozen face.

"You know all my songs?" Young Todd asked me.

I smiled sheepishly, "Not all, but a lot. You are a literary lyrical genius. I've loved you and your music for decades. Thank you for your resilience in staying in the fight."

Staring at Young Todd, an artist that helped me find the words to speak when I could not find the words myself numerous times. He stood there in front of me and looked me in the eyes with a smile.

"The toughest fight is the one in ya head," Young Todd quoted himself. Then stood in front of us and began performing a few lyrics and then pointed at me to pick up where he left off on the song. Typically, I would not be in the lobby of a business rapping, but I heard Dare-You's voice and didn't even consider backing down. Young Todd and I rapped two of his songs, not the popular ones, and a few onlookers joined in, but really it was just Todd and me.

"Okay, she seems legit," Todd told Manuel after pulling me in for a sisterly hug. "It was nice to meet you. Be careful around him, everything he touch gets better. Fuck around get too great!" He gave me a hug and continued to lean in as if telling a secret. "Seriously, he's realest nigga I know. He got a real soul. I'd give him as much as I'd give my brother… on my momma side."

"You know it's the ones on the daddy side that hit different," Buck told him, as he hugged Young Todd bye as well. I noticed that many of the important people, including Young Todd, gave Buck just as much respect as Manuel, they treated him as if he was just as supreme.

Todd hugged Manuel for just a few seconds longer than the rest of us, it was evident that he truly admired Manuel, he waved at me one more time as we went separate ways.

"I can see you're tired, wanna go back to my hotel or can you handle one more stop?" Manuel asked as we left.

"I can handle it," I assured him.

I got in the car and sat silently, in awe, all the screams I wanted to let out couldn't even escape my frozen lips. I didn't even talk because I was so happy, so astonished. Did Manuel just get Young Todd's blessing for me?

Am I awake?

Manuel squeezed my hand, then smiled at me, "Are you okay?"

"I'm just amazed, star struck. From everything, but I'm okay." I squeezed his hand back to let him know I was fine. "Did you plan that, him being there?"

He shrugged, "He records there a lot."

The car ride was quiet, occasionally I would look up and notice Garon or Buck looking at me in one of their mirrors. Why did they not like me? They were very well paid, evidently a much higher salary than me, he treated them well. Do they not want to see Manuel happy?

78

I put my feet on the $300,000 seats on the ride home, Garon wasn't going to like me either way. Manuel likes me, I told myself again, getting comfortable. It didn't matter what they thought.

Manuel massaged my hand, just like he did earlier, it reminded me of his presence. That I could *be soft*. I laid my head on his lap and accidentally drifted asleep until I felt the vehicle stop.

5

"Next stop is the office. We won't be staying long." Manuel said once the car stopped in front of a business plaza and the guys started getting out.

I looked at the time, it was way too early for most ordinary people, but I heard many geniuses have a strange sense of time and abnormal sleep schedules. I for sure got genius vibes from Manuel. I could see he did things much different from most people I know.

I put on a smile for good faith and followed him out the door as he led me by hand. We walked in front of a building labeled Finance Office, from where we stood we could see a light on in the back.

"Who left the light on?" Buck vigilantly asked Garon at the same time we noticed someone creeping around in the shadow. Within a second they went from walking behind us to pushing past us with their weapons already pulled out of their matching man bags.

"Don't worry, they're just going to check out the building." Manuel assured me, I must've looked scared because he started rubbing on my hand again, I forced a smile.

"It's Mãe Mãe!" Garon yelled out to us, and we came inside, he had a little pep in his step as we walked down the hall to where the security guards went. I could already hear Garon snitching as we walked toward the light, "Welcome to the longest *Meet and Greet* I ever saw!"

"You can meet Mãe Mãe, she's really smart, and a good teacher. My mom will love you." Manuel looked at me gleefully as I responded with a fake smile, he had no idea how much I detest the initial meet-the-mom hello.

We walked through the finance building that was decorated with framed posters, plaques, and awards along the wall. Although it was clear we were in a business office, it was very glamorous with chandeliers, pure white decor, gold accents, and tall bookshelves that matched the leather furniture.

A petite olive-skinned, freckle-faced, and curly-haired woman was yelling at Buck and Garon by the time Manuel and I stood at the doorway of her large office. She had a nasal accent and intermittently rambled in another language. I could make out a few words from a 9th grade foreign language class, it sounded like Portuguese.

"You call the office first if you don't know! I almost blew off your brain! You wanna die again!" She hit Buck with her house shoe but lit up with a huge grin when she saw Manuel standing at the door. "Who was in charge of these two?"

"Me, Mãe Mãe. I'm sorry, it was completely my fault." Manuel opened his arms to pick up the little woman as she screeched gleefully in his arms, completely losing her attitude by the time he put her down. "Why are you here so late? I don't like that."

"Oh, my filho!!! It's okay, I was waiting for the venue to get back to me with some numbers."

Manuel shook his head, frustrated, "No you shouldn't still be here for that. We can get somebody to do that. Garon, let Corbin know what's going on and he needs to get somebody or himself over here. I'm so embarrassed to have my mother working at 3 in the morning."

Garon raised his eyebrows at Manuel. "Who are you talking to?"

"It's okay, Corbin knows, we are having some issues with the legal side." She tried to calm everyone down, but Garon left the office anyway. "Mum is taking care of it, a união faz a força!"

"Stronger together? No, you're gonna hit him, too Mãe Mãe?" Buck threw his hands in the air as if to throw a fit, "Take ya shoe back off and hit him, too! EmManuel said it was his fault, but you hit me with that hard ass little shoe three times. You ain't *my* mother."

"Get out! Get out! Garon, come get him, and I want fifty!" Mãe Mãe was aggressive, she somehow found enough strength to push Buck out of the door and closed it shut. "He always drives me crazy, what a baby! I didn't know you were staying in town. Is this the one, is this her?"

Manuel laughed and nodded, the gorgeous woman looked at me for the first time in my eyes and smiled. "Yes, you are so covert, this is Acacia."

I reached out my hand and she pulled me in for a strong, but short hug. "Nice to meet you."

"I am Mãe Mãe, or Terra, EmManuel's favorite mother." She claimed with a cute dance, as he nodded with no hesitation. "That's because I'm the one who takes care of all his finances."

"No Mãe Mãe, that's not why. Besides, Corbin is in charge of banking, not you anymore." Manuel told her.

"Yes I trained him all last year and he is doing well, but I will always help when he calls. He doesn't keep as orderly as me, EmManuel." She brushed Manuel off and looked at me, "So let me see all that lavish jewelry I saw on the account! Because somebody has been shopping lately!"

Manuel sighed, "Mãe Mãe, please stop."

She held my hand as I showed her the new watch. "Yes, yes, yes! This is just right for you, just as gorgeous!"

"Thank you," I said, admiring her zest. "You are very beautiful."

Mãe Mãe flirtatiously posed a few times, giving me a few angles. "Thank you. And in case you are wondering, my son knows how to take care of a woman. I promise you that Acacia, we raised him right."

"He has been very amazing," I told her, quite nervously as I have never met someone's mother on our first semi-date. "You did a great job raising him."

Manuel put his arm around me and kissed my cheek. His Mãe Mãe smiled.

"It was not easy," she admitted. "How do you train up the child that creates his own world?"

I smiled and shrugged; I could hardly get my son to keep his room clean two weeks out of the month. "How?"

"Is there anything I can do for you while I'm here? We're about to head out." Manuel tried to get us out of there, but she ignored him and continued talking to me.

"You support, support, support until he gets it right and has everything that he wants in life. He has always had so much love, plus he was a good child." She waved her hands in the air. "It's the love of having family and a team that makes the difference, you'll see. Was Jenny and Sora able to get you a passport?"

"Mãe Mãe we don't have much time to talk, we just left the studio. We only stopped by to get this paperwork, so Ma doesn't lose her mind." Manuel interrupted her going over into a filing cabinet, grabbing out an envelope and putting it in his pocket. Mãe Mãe seemed like she wanted him to stay, but understood he needed to leave as she gave him a hug and a kiss. "We will see you soon, I love you, thank you for everything. I'm going to call Sora and see how it went in the morning."

She started quickly scrolling around on her phone. "Just wait, I wanted to show her some photos of you that haven't been stolen yet!"

"No, Mãe, this isn't a good time."

"Fine, it was nice to meet you Acacia, can't wait to see you again." She gave me the same tight momma bear hug and kiss that she gave her son, before we headed out the door, she handed me a business card. "Take my business card, just in case you need to speak to me sooner."

As we left, he reached out and took my hand as we walked back out.

"What did she mean by getting me a passport?" I asked him before we got into the car with his security guards waiting for us.

He swayed his hand to the side, brushing it off. "We take a lot of trips."

*   *   *

"I want my phone," I told Manuel as the elevator arrived at the penthouse floor. Hopefully we were going to relax, but I couldn't get past missing my phone! I'd been continuously checking for it, then reminding myself that I was not *allowed* to have it, which was starting to drive me insane.

Manuel sighed, frustrated. "Why?"

At the same time Garon said, "No."

Probably sarcastically, but Buck's response was, "Give it to her."

"What the fuck do you mean *why* and *no*? I'm grown as fuck." I snapped back at them just as rudely. Buck laughed.

"Sorry," Manuel responded respectfully, hopefully aware that he was being a jerk. "I should have said, do you need it for a specific reason, or do you just want to have it on you?"

I shrugged, not sure why this was even a group conversation. "Do you think I'm going to take pictures of you or scam you or something, because I won't take pictures or record anything. Plus, I can turn off my location for you, I just like having my phone."

"There's your fuckin' millennials, Garon," Buck said smugly, I questioned how much older they could possibly be, it for sure wasn't much.

Garon shrugged, "Grown children."

"Always want to be in the photo, but don't want to add shit to the picture." Buck said as if he were decades older than me.

"What?" I questioned Buck. "Add to what? I just want my phone."

"You can't have your phone on you around me, Acacia. If you need it for something particular, that's different, that's fine." Manuel told me, more sternly than he'd spoken to me before, holding open the Master suite entrance of the penthouse as we all stopped at the door. "Sometimes you just have to trust me on things that don't make the most sense to you."

Him and this *trust* again. I sighed, looking into his eyes, which made me calm down and breathe. "Fine, I get it, I don't *need* it on me, but just give it to me for a minute. I like to check on things."

"Give me the phone," he told his security team who stood watching the scene unfold.

Garon was pissed and made sure to show it by sighing, dramatically, but I secretly smirked and turned around. I wanted to have him fired. Then I went inside the master bedroom with Manuel following me, he shut the door behind just him and I.

He handed me my phone, he didn't seem mad, just blank faced, he went straight into the bathroom without a word. This time when in the restroom he locked the door and the glass frosted over for privacy.

Damn. Was he that paranoid? Maybe he didn't hang out with non-DeCreed affiliated folks much. I needed a full list of these *rules* he refers to.

I tried to be understanding of both sides, Manuel is famous, he doesn't know me, and has an image to protect. His image is his paycheck. I can respect it, but I'm still human as well! And I'm an invited guest. As he has noted several times, I didn't get in the line to meet Manuel, he wanted to meet me.

I questioned if I could even handle a lifestyle like this... I don't like to be controlled. Also, I'm quite a "phone person", would he expect me to change that?

I stop, smell the flowers, then take pictures of them for memories. Now to date someone who doesn't *allow* phones when I'm with him. It's like he wanted me to just focus on him or had zero trust in me as a person. Then to mention he seems to have 24-hour security always watching us, which is insane!

I scrolled through the meaningless nothing on my phone for a few minutes, more concerned if anyone was looking for me. No one was looking for me, no one of priority. Random followers from social media,

84

comments from family, group chat gossip... I didn't need my phone, he was right.

"I'm done with my phone security!" I called out, sarcastically, not sure if anyone even heard or cared. I whispered in a sing-song voice, "Come get it before I take a selfie."

No one came. Bathroom door locked; I was too timid to knock.

I peeked out the Master Suite door to the living area to see if the party was over. Only five men were left in the living room area of the suite. I recognized each of them from yesterday's various adventures. Among them were Buck, Corbin, and Garon. They were loudly confronting each other about something, but when I opened the door, all voices fell silent, and everyone was looking in my direction.

I gently closed the door back and went out to the balcony to enjoy the view. The sun was about to come up and the city would wake up soon. Yet even without much sleep I somehow felt wide awake.

I opened a new blank document on my phone and began to write about how I felt since meeting Manuel. I didn't want to forget this feeling. Besides, I've learned never to resist my urges to write, at bare minimum I'll jot down key words.

Manuel opened the bathroom door to the balcony, smelling delicious and looking fresh.

"My writer's block is gone!" I exclaimed proudly when he saw me writing.

Manuel raised his eyebrows at me, "I see."

"Look, the sun is coming up soon, it'll come from right behind the water. If you stare it can be almost blinding," I told him, looking down at the soft wet sand beginning to sparkle under the light. I could imagine it on my toes with the soft wind blowing in my hair.

"Wanna walk on the beach?" He asked.

"That's funny, I was just thinking that," I said with a smile, he smiled back. "Of course."

I quickly freshened up, brushing my teeth with a dental hygiene travel set, then put on a soft form fitting sundress that sat on the countertop.

Manuel was waiting for me at the suite door with a couple of pink acacias he must've picked out from one of the many bouquets.

"Guessing my favorite flower was easy, but tell me how you know my sizes in everything?" I asked Manuel, putting on my matching designer sandals as he held the door open to exit. "Or am I just your standard size for women?"

"You think I have a standard size for women?" He laughed, seeming truly surprised, gently tugging my hair as I walked by him. "I like hearing what you think, although I am seeing you have little faith in me being a great man."

I shrugged, "No, no, I'm impressed. You're doing a divine job finding clothes that fit me."

"I'll tell your stylist she has her job back," he winked at me, leading me into the elevator.

"Then you knew I was gonna spend the weekend with you?" I questioned, wondering if this was just too easy for him. "

"I wanted you to say yes, so that is what I prepared for. I always prepare for whatever I want, then it comes to me." He admitted, looking into my eyes. "I'm grateful in advance, now I'm grateful that you decided to stay."

"Me too," I kissed his soft lips, sucking in the bottom lip to get a taste. "I think I am starting to get a crush on you."

He licked my taste off his bottom lip and looked deep into my eyes when I stepped back, "Oh you gonna love it over here, but we're gonna be patient. We're on your time."

I laughed, truthfully a little reluctant because I secretly wished he would try to do something a little more risqué. But he was right, I wasn't ready. However, remaining a lady I took a step closer and held his arm until we got to the sandy beach.

"Would you ever want to have a daughter?" Manuel asked me.

I shrugged, but slightly making a face that screamed NO. "That's not how it works, you don't pick who you want. But I don't think so, it's barely like anyone stays together these days, not trying to end up a single parent again."

As much as I was embracing my single and free lifestyle, there was no denying Manuel had me feeling butterflies. And there were two times I thought about what he would look like holding a baby, and three times I practiced writing our names together in cursive with sand. He made me feel comfortable, safe, and secure! And as an attractive, educated, and financially secure woman dating today, it gets difficult to find a man that provides enough comfort for me to soften like this.

We walked the beach while the sun came up; barefoot, together, me on his back, and even had a decent race! Manuel asked me questions about my job and my passions, most were followed up questions from things on my social media pages. He seemed really interested in me, he was checking all the boxes, which I also thought was cute.

"You ask very particular questions," I told Manuel after about an hour of answering questions and discussing my family. "What do you really know about me?"

"I told you, I didn't just pick your name out of a hat, I saw things in you that I really like, you stand out to me Acacia. You're *extravagant* in such a simple way, it intrigues me just staring at you to be completely honest. But I'm simple, yet *extravagant* too. We could have some fun together for sure."

I loved that I stood out to him, and I probably should've been more curious as to why, but I was happy just to stand out.

"Ouch!" I yelled, stumbling over a piece of wood that was covered with sand. "Shit!"

We sat down in the sand so he could nurse my foot. He handed me the acacias while he checked out my foot. He found a cup and got some water to rinse off my foot for a full inspection.

"How bad does it look, Doctor?" I joked, it didn't hurt enough for him to be doing all that he was, but his attention to detail was cute.

He knew I was messing around, "I just want to make sure there was no splinter, not sure what kind of wood that is that you stepped on. I know a thing or two about artisan work now, let me see it."

"Did you know your security guard just asked if I was named after wood, too?" I told him, putting one of the acacia flowers on the wood board and carrying it down to the shoreline. "What do you say, we let this acacia go free and explore the world?"

Manuel nodded and so I helped the board and flower float off.

"Is that what this Acacia wants to do?" He asked, pointing at me. "Be free, go on the ocean or in the air to places you've never been. Meet different cultures, write about how they live their lives? Hear ancestral secrets from natives of your origin country? Go to international monuments and statues that you saw in those textbooks you studied? I can do all of that with you. Now."

We paused as we watched the acacia flower and the wood float off into the gentle water.

"Ahem," I cleared my throat, that was a lot to hear from a new friend.

"Just tell me when you're ready to finally be free. Because the worst thing that could happen is you procrastinate and never free yourself. Which means all those stories you hear in your mind, those characters, your talent, that all dies with you. Instead of being the art you were supposed to use it for. You have to get to the point of freedom in your life."

"I am free."

He shook his head with a half-smile, "You want me to show you what free feels like?"

"Manuel… Can we go on a first date…first? I guess I'm a little old school." I teased as we sat down on the sand and watched the ocean.

"I got our first date all setup for you, I'm taking you to dinner tonight then, if you want, I was thinking you can accompany me to an awards show?" Manuel softly said into my ear, I was sitting in between his legs with my head laying back on his chest, relaxing deeply, but that question woke me up. An award show? "We won't be completely alone, but it will be fun and probably different."

"Wow. First date?" I asked him, shocked at the big invite. "I mean, will you not feel like I'm in the way? The cameras? It doesn't have to be that *extravagant*, I was kidding."

"You're not in my way and I want you to experience it with me. Unless you don't want someone to see you on camera?" He asked nonchalantly. "I've been to hundreds of award shows, so I often skip 'em, but if you want to go, I think that will be fun for us."

I smiled at the thought of being at an elegant, televised awards show, especially with someone like Manuel. His attraction to me seemed surreal, not that I have low self-esteem, I just didn't think he would be so into someone like me this much.

"Okay," I clenched my teeth in disbelief, "I'm gonna be nervous. Wait, I don't have any clothes for that here."

"You will be fine, I got everything ready to go." He guaranteed. "It's all mental, you know psychology, don't you?"

"Yes, smartass," I smirked at him, "doesn't mean I don't have feelings, suppressing them often makes you feel worse in the long run."

"Would you say that for all emotions?" He wondered genuinely.

"I'd say so. When we let our feelings run their course unapologetically, they usually don't last as long as we think they will. It's okay to be human, it's okay to feel things. Minimizing your feelings, ignoring them, is only growing the problem." I paused, "You seem like you want to say something?"

"I went through a hard time when my brother died, I didn't expect it to be so soon for him. I lost my motivation; I was in a very fucked up place. Felt extremely sad and pointless. That was a first for me."

"So, what did you do?"

"It was 2020, what did anyone do at that time? I just needed to sit still, see nature, and be grateful. Looking back now, being stuck in quarantine kind of helped me sit still. I mean we were all kinda forced to sit down."

"We were forced to take a break from the real world. I hope you were able to get counseling also," I sympathized. "I know it was hard to get support, for most people."

"I did get help. To be honest the grievance counselors weren't who helped me. It was getting close to Ryū's son that helped me, working with him on homework. The boy was struggling in English and Science, so I brushed up on those. We hooped, fished. I got close to him during quarantine, he helped me refocus."

I knew the feeling of joy that he spoke of children can be rejuvenating when you pair them with a passion and a purpose.

Manuel continued, "My nephew helped readjust my perspective on life, in a time where I didn't give a fuck about anymore. I felt bored with life, he reminded me that I have so much more to do. He's a great little man, I guess I had to be outside of my routine."

"Kids will do that!" I agreed happily, "I love working with children, they keep me energized for sure."

"I love your energy." He complimented me. "You help the students with their energy as well... I mean, I'm sure you do. We get what we put out."

"I try to." I confessed. "They need adults who try to understand them."

He wrapped his arms around me and held me on the beach for about ten more minutes before we decided to head back toward the hotel to get some rest.

"Can I ask you a question?" Manuel asked as we walked back to the hotel, I nodded yes. "Do you believe in curses?"

"Why did you ask that?" I responded after a moment of wondering very skeptically, defensively. Somehow Manuel seemed to ask questions that were perfectly segueing to private or discrete details about me.

"I just wanted to see what you thought about them," he casually replied.

I laughed, "I believe they have as much power as we give them."

"My family knows I have a curse, me and all my brothers, my dad's line, hell I think it's six generations back." He revealed to me, I could not tell if he was serious or joking around. "It's true too."

"Some say the same about me," I confessed, reluctantly unable to close my mouth. "But I don't buy it completely."

"What is it?" He asked, overly eager.

I shook my head, "No, it's stupid and I don't even like the people who know it to say it!"

"I'll tell you mine, if you tell me yours." He began to skip flat rocks on top of the ocean getting approximately seven skips per rock. I attempted to join him, but skipping rocks was not my thing. "My great great grandfather was cursed by his first baby's mom; she was an island lady. When she was six months pregnant with his first and only daughter, she walked in on him with another woman and the two women fought. Somehow in the fight she lost the baby and she put a curse on him and all his sons. None of us, since before he lost his baby, can have a daughter."

"Are you sure?" I questioned, intrigued. "Kinda sounds like they are just bullshitting you."

Manuel stood behind me and I relaxed as he positioned me in a more successful way to skip the rocks. I did five back-to-back!

"It's no bullshit, since the incident there's been six times a doctor gave the wrong gender prediction, well into the pregnancies by ultrasound and blood testing. I know these doctors ain't what they used to be, but six times? The pregnant mothers would have all symptoms of girl-baby pregnancies: craving sweets and dairy, getting acne, high heart rate, extra morning sickness… baby still comes out a male."

My jaw dropped, "Wow! That's kinda wild. Do you believe it?"

"I guess, my dad and grandfather couldn't have girls, and they all tried. Multiple women, every ethnicity." He said, "My older brother has like 8 boys, my baby brother had 1. Now tell me yours."

"Why do I feel I just got tricked in some way?" I ask. Then finally managed to make a rock skip three times! I did it a few more times to change the subject. "I'm good at this!"

"You are a fast learner." Then he looked at me. "Come on, tell me yours."

"Maybe if you fall in love, you can break it, have yourself a little baby girl." I told him partially joking, we were standing so close to each other that I could feel his heartbeat and mine synching. I didn't want to tell him.

"My dad believed that the men of my grandfather would only be happy if they were able to find someone that gave them a daughter. But he also said to have a daughter they'd need to find someone that first made them happy," he redirected. "Your turn Acacia, please."

"Okay so, it isn't as well grounded in scientific research as yours, maybe it's just a mental thing, *but* bad relationship chemistry or experiences with a new person pushes me back to my ex." I paused for a reaction, then continued. "For example, one summer I dated three different men and coincidentally each of their cars broke down in some way either on the date, after the date, or before. It wasn't that they didn't have cars that turned me off, it was the way each of them handled their situations. Ironic shit like that always happens to me."

Manuel raised his eyebrows at me. "Where are you meeting these people?"

"Shut up," I chuckled, "They were nice. But this is what I have been going through for years! I am just unable to connect intimately with men. As soon as I start getting close to them something always happens. I just shut down, I don't want to kiss, touch, or anything. I just want to go back." I admitted.

"Back?" Manuel asked for clarification.

"Like, back to... what's comfortable for me."

He side-eyed me, and said rather frankly, "Let me be sure I understand this, the *curse* is... you still fuckin your ex? Your child's father?"

I stalled, surely by his simple response Manuel didn't understand the intensity of my dilemma. "I have tried to date other men and it does not work out. It only gets worse and worse!"

"Because of the car problems?" He asked sarcastically.

I took a deep breath, "No, but it is always something. A crazy ex, an insecure mother, forcing religion, being overly possessive, you name it, I've met him. And ran far away."

"You didn't run far, just go be with him. You think I didn't see my mother didn't go through this, that, back-and-forth with my father." He seemed to empathize somewhat, but he didn't understand. "If he's where your heart is, listen to it. You gotta learn to trust that voice in your head when you are feeding it the right things, it leads you to your destiny."

"It's not like that, the voice in my head isn't saying for me to go back." I told him, "I don't want to be with him anymore, too much history. It's telling me to keep going forward."

"Do you love him?" He asked me, I didn't want to lie, I shrugged. "Try again, you never know."

I was getting pissed he'd recommend another man have me after all that he said thus far, I couldn't tell if he was gaslighting me to see if I still wanted my ex?

"It's not like that Manuel, because I'll always love a lot of people, but not like you are thinking. How much do you think a person should have to take before they finally get up and leave, taking a chance at finding something that's better for their well-being? I do love him, you're right. He was my best friend, he knows me, I'm comfortable with him, but I know I deserve more."

"I got you," he told me, seeming a little more understanding. "So, you date, give other guys a chance?"

"Way too much," I lightened up and laughed, recalling a very recent bad date.

"It sounds like you just had a lot of lames with bad experiences and sex." As understanding as I was when Manuel told me about his fairy tale curse, he seemed almost disappointed upon hearing mine. "That's not a curse, that sounds more like baby daddy privilege."

"No, jackass, I'm not out here fucking these dates." I hit him on his (very tight) chest. "And they weren't *lame*, I just feel no romantic connection."

"You didn't *connect* cause they ain't it, nothing to connect with." He laughed at me.

"Okay so there were a few slightly lames," I admitted partially defending the few dozens of bad dates, "But practically anything can turn me off, I'm picky! I don't think they were all lame! I just didn't connect with them. What is this baby daddy privilege?"

He stretched his arms up and in a funny voice of a stereotypical know-it-all explained, "I've gathered about 70 lives worth of evidence, I've been here a long time and I have seen a lot of this. Baby daddy privilege is all the shit your baby daddy can do and you still gotta deal with him, he still gets access to you, if you are both relatively decent parents, for the sake of your child. I don't have children, but I've met many. And watched this amongst my own parents."

"Was your dad a good father?"

"My dad was the best there ever was," he informed me with a smile. "A father to the whole neighborhood. With so many brothers we always were in a large group, my dad was a father to many."

I raised my eyebrows, "How many baby moms did you say he had again?"

"He took care of his children and valued our mothers. Still till this day, I have five mothers and I keep in touch with them all," Manuel smirked at me. "Anyway, my dad used his baby daddy privilege to the fullest, my moms probably forgave him 77 times a year! It's baby daddy privilege, I'm telling you."

I rolled my eyes; his theory had some truth and flaws. "That's only true with some folks. I know too many women who won't even let their children's fathers in the house, much less in their undergarments. I just like being comfortable."

"Comfortable?" He questioned with a nod as I rolled my eyes, "Yeah those men are sleep, they dropped the ball somewhere."

"Who knows, you may be on to something," I couldn't help but laugh as I joined in his silly sarcasm, though considering his ridiculous privilege theory did have some truth. "I don't know how you remember all those lives you've lived, but I'm impressed and will keep this in mind."

"You're not cursed at all, Acacia. We all have privileges, just gotta use them in the correct way." He kissed me, "You're a special person, I bet you just need someone on your level to connect with."

I hit him, playfully and accepted a sweet kiss on my lips. "Whatever, maybe so."

"I'm glad you are here with me, connecting, I think we will be just fine." Manuel predicted. "Is there anything you are looking for exactly?"

I nodded, but paused, questioning my own heart's mixed desires lately. "I'm still trying to learn what it is again."

"Keep me around, I'll help you figure it out." He assured me, playing with my fingers.

6

Back at the hotel I was hoping to take a quick little nap, but the penthouse looked like an office by the time we got back. People were working on a variety of different things. When Manuel walked in with me on his back, Corbin helped me down and pulled Manuel into a side discussion regarding some paperwork.

A group of three ladies were sitting at a table filling out paperwork. Five men were sitting on the couch and around the living room. Two women were cooking in the kitchen, another was setting the table. Uncle Mo was sitting at the bar with a lady and two men.

The hotel was not as romantic as it was last night. It was turned into more of a business office now.

Uncle Mo waved me over when we caught eyes, I walked over to him with a smile.

"How is my future niece in law?"

"You're moving fast, huh?" I clenched my teeth sarcastically, "I'm very good."

"Well, he didn't add your city to the tour for nothing, and we all followed him here." Uncle Mo said with a smile, "Remember there's ups and downs, it won't always be easy, but none of it is too hard for us to handle. You'll never need more than you have, have trust in yourself and be kind to yourself. Go 'head with that little one."

"I will," I promised, turning around to see who Uncle Mo was pointing at. Behind me was a young, cute face on a perky young woman.

"I'm Manuel's favorite cousin, Jenny," then the young woman extended her hand to me. "I think this whole date is a horrible idea, but you are fine, and I got a stunning outfit picked for you tonight!"

Apparently, my signing up to go to the awards show with Manuel meant I would be spending the afternoon with Jenny, his mom's niece and aspiring celebrity fashion designer. Her personality was loud and vibrant with extra sass. She looked like she was in her late twenties, with a cute bubbly personality when interacting with the staff.

Manuel gave her a side eye, as I smiled, somewhat in agreement. A televised awards show with a stranger did seem like an extreme first date.

"Can you do this, Jenny?" He snapped.

"I said I'm going to do it, Manuel. C'mon Princess, your frog's gonna fire me again!" She grabbed her oversized bag and started for the door while mentioning, "You don't even know how many times I've been terminated this month."

Manuel pulled me back into the Master bedroom and pressed the door close with my body. He treated my lips like delicious strawberries, first with his eyes then with his tongue. He followed his teasing with a slow, intense kiss..

"Jenny's gonna get you something to wear. You'll have your phone, and you can text me if you need me. Garon will be with you guys, too." He explained, between sucking on my lip.

"Do we really need him?" I asked, kissing his soft mouth in between words.

"I like knowing you're safe, and it's safest with him." He assured me, allowing me to kiss him as he talked, "But you gotta stop kissing me if you are going to go."

"Okay, okay," I giggled while kissing him one last time. Every touch from Manuel was the ideal pressure, aggressive but not rough, gentle but not too soft.

Manuel put something in my back pocket, I took it out, it was a metal credit card.

"Just in case you see something you like," He told me. I put it on the nightstand and shook my head.

"I don't want your card."

"Let's go Princess!" I cringed being the princess that Jenny yelled to from the other side of the suite, Manuel made that same mean face he makes when she's present, apparently Jenny was not one of his favorite staff.

"Let me know if I need to fire her, she's only here for *you*."

"She's not scared of you," I smiled at him softly. "I like her."

"I like you." He kissed my lips twice, "I don't even want you to leave, but go get ready for tonight. I have to do a little work, or I would've come with you too."

I let him give me one last long kiss as he snuck the credit card from off the nightstand and into my purse. Being with Manuel, with his family and staff, I did feel like I was getting some exclusive royal treatment.

"You sure you're fine without me, right?" Manuel triple checked before leaving me, I nodded, and he kissed me on the forehead, handing me my phone and closing my door.

"I ain't gonna scare her too much, child!" Jenny called to him as she got into the passenger seat of Garon's SUV and slammed the door after calling out to him one last time. "She's gonna be flawless, don't worry!"

I took a deep breath from the backseat as we started to drive away from the hotel. Missing him already.

"I'm going to make her fuckin flawless, but I could literally put her in dog shit, and he'd be up her ass!" Jenny said to Garon with an attitude as we drove off, "Yall couldn't have figured something out to say to him? We're just going to act like everything is fine?"

"Don't talk to me in front of her, Jenny." Garon snapped. I'm sure my face looked staggered to see Garon talk openly with a negative tone towards me. I was partially hoping it was in my imagination that he didn't like me.

Jenny looked at me in the backseat. "I have no problem with you Cay, Emmanuel just does too much sometimes and it's not always the preferred way to do shit for business. *None* of us have a problem with you."

"Should I not go to the awards show? I don't want to screw anything up for him either." I asked, feeling slightly concerned, I did not want to overstep any boundaries.

"You see what the fuck you doing?" Garon swore at her.

"Hell no crazy lady!" She snapped at me. "Do not cancel on him and do not tell him I said any of this, at all. Like, nothing. Y'all go out there, dance, and have fun. Manuel does whatever Manuel wants and if someone gets in his way then he's going to just find another way. Or create one."

Garon snapped at her, "Jenny shut up." She rolled her eyes and turned to look forward. "Don't you two have shit to look at on your phones?"

I decided to just ignore them, Manuel told me to trust him, and I was just beginning to like the carefree feeling of trusting him. Even if it wasn't necessarily *reality*. I guess reality was getting boring after all.

96

Garon was somewhat right, my phone had plenty of notifications to keep me busy.

My son's father texted me asking for half our son's football fees which are due in two weeks. My mother texted, just seeing how the concert went. And of course, Hazel, whose message I was reluctant to open since I was sure she was pissed with me.

Hazel	
Nooooo Did you seriously leave me and go with them??!! Got your vm. Is everything okay still??!!	
	Sorry it kinda just happened, I'm great. They took my phone again, yes I'm good
He doesn't want to get exposed!! Find a way to get a picture bitch! Maybe we can make some money lol	
	I met his mother! And she was nice, I think she liked me.
WTF?? Red flag. That's too soon.	
	He bought me some nice things. Right now I'm going shopping with his "stylist" cousin

Well I guess get everything you can since he can pay for the pussy!!

I don't think it's like that
He introduced me to YOUNG TODD last night

Of course, u think there's still GOOD men out here.
Young Todd was in town too?

Girl apparently!
I didn't even know either, we ran into him on the way out the studio

That's VERY DAMN convenient Cay! He's trynna fuck uuuuuuu

See that's why I didn't really want to bring you for real, I told you, that negative shit ruins the mood

Damn, sorry. Just don't be stupid.
Did you fuck him last night?

"Hello, hello, here she is Mademoiselle!" Jenny called out to an older island woman who stood behind a sewing machine as she and I walked into the back of the boutique. "Show me the pieces I had you put to the side last Sunday."

"You are prettier in person, have you liked the pieces Jenny picked for you so far?" Mademoiselle asked me, walking me to the back of her shop. After she greeted Jenny, Garon, and even me with a big hug and kiss. "I'm Raven, Manuel's Mimi."

The boutique was an average looking shop from the outside, but inside it was luxurious, it was clear she'd invested a lot of money into the aesthetics of her shop. The shop was locked up when we arrived, but Jenny had a key, and we went right in.

The front of the boutique had women and men's elegant fashion, but we walked straight to the back. There was a large chandelier strategically placed over a low center stage. There was a large open fitting area with mirrors surrounding us in an octagon shape. It looked more like a bridal fitting than a first date dress.

"Nice to meet you," I nodded in regard to her question. "Yes, thank you for the clothes. Everything has been so perfect. That dress, last night, had a perfect hold on me up top like no other! Thank you."

"Thanks. I create everything by hand," Mimi smiled at my compliment.

"Your work is great. So many women at the afterparty were staring at the dress," I told her, and she looked shocked at the feedback.

She spun around with excitement, "Oooh EmManuel is going back to after parties again, Jenny. Did you hear that? He told *me* no more. Garon, were you there?"

"Yes, Mimi, we were there with him, he was only there for a short time."

Garon gave me a mean look and Jenny shook her head vigorously at my direction as if to say *stop talking*. So, I stopped talking.

"I bet Ma knew where he was, but not me, Mimi is the last to know anything." Mimi Raven huffed around, muttering to herself when she realized there were secrets behind her back. I tried to determine her relationship with Manuel, she seemed too young to be a grandmother, but definitely too old to be an ex. "He should not be at after parties yet."

The shop was an exclusive boutique, Mademoiselle Mimi went behind a curtain, and Jenny gathered different sewing tools as I stood on a small stage in the middle of the fitting room. They walked back and forth with different parts and pieces; they gave me minor directions as they treated me like a doll.

In the end I had a long sleeve, sequin, rose gold gown with a deep v-cut neckline. The dress landed at my lower thigh in the front then dragged slightly in the back. It was the prettiest one in the shop.

There was a smaller gown hanging beside mine, I assumed it was the second option for me if this didn't fit. Thankfully I didn't need it as it was mostly just made of mesh and strategically placed sequins, it sparkled on a full-figured mannequin. It was extremely sexy but left very little to the imagination. I was glad that she didn't ask me to try it on. That was a dress I could only wear after a week of healthy eating, running an extra mile per day, and if I had the confidence to show that much skin.

"Let me get you a necklace, it's the exact match," Mimi jumped up to grab a piece behind her shelf.

"No," Jenny said, "Manuel has her jewelry. He ordered it and I'm not arguing with him again about colors and tones."

"When he was young, Manuel would come to me to pick out his clothes for everything. When he needed certain tailored or customized things, I started to sew, so I could make it for him. Then I began making clothes for others. Many friends of EmManuel purchase my clothes now." Mimi bragged humbly. "It's cause my boy that I have what I have."

"That's significant, I'm sure he's grateful for you." I complimented her success.

"I am so grateful for him, but yet, where is he? He hasn't come by, instead he sends a woman and Little Jenny?" Mademoiselle threw her hands up in the air sarcastically, "Is he too busy for *me?* Is he in love this time? Or just throwing away my pieces? Do you love each other?"

I clenched my teeth and looked at her blankly, never knowing how to answer these overprotective mothers.

"Mimi, we gotta go, we're not having this conversation." Garon saved me, collecting things we would need to bring back.

"Auntie, this is why he doesn't tell you stuff, you do too much every time!" Jenny shrugged Mimi's tantrum off. "Why are you being so dramatic?"

"Fuckory! He's just like their dad! I can see it and I don't like it." Mimi told her with her island accent, hitting Garon in the forehead as she walked by. "I'm not dealing with another one of Him! No one barely ever saw that man's face… he was always going. Now when is the last time I saw my EmManuel?"

I took a deep breath at the conversation and the fast pace of the *relationship* I felt I was now in, but not in. We just met 48 hours ago. When did he have time to *special order* jewelry and why?

"Auntie, just pack it all up please. Including that matching clutch. He's paying for it, don't act like you are just giving it away for free. You are being so dramatic in front of his date." Jenny told her, rolling her eyes in my direction. "Stay out of his business, you already know how he is."

"Stay out his business? Stay out his business, you all say this to me, but his *business* is in my business, and yet I cannot know his business?" Auntie Mademoiselle Mimi seemed irritated, and her accent

100

was trying to come out as she paced between her dressing room and showroom floor. It seemed it was not the first time they kept her out of the loop nor the first time she's made the complaint. "It's not about the cost, these pieces take time and patience. I want them to go with righteous people."

"Did he not buy you the shop, Auntie?" Jenny snapped at Mimi, "Who cares who the clothes go to, they're just clothes. As long as you are making the money!"

"That's why your pieces don't sell, Jenny. You don't care about them," Mimi told Jenny. She pointed at Jenny's clothing line that was in the back of her shop.

Jenny walked over and grabbed one of her pieces, "No they don't sell because you only get old customers in here and what I make is for bad bitches! But my cousin won't get me a damn shop so I can show him! Urgh!"

"Jenny, shut up." Garon stood up, getting annoyed with the bickering. "Don't blame anyone else when you haven't done the work, you haven't put in the grind, and you know it. You get little, because you do little. Get better and stop waiting with your fuckin' handout for a gift."

Jenny squinted her eyes at the security guard and his harsh words about her, "I do a whole lot of work!"

"Then why you still blaming other folks for where you are lacking at?" Garon asked. "Get off your social media bullshit and read some books. Learn some shit." Garon strangely shot a look at me, "Perfectionists are just as bad as procrastinators, self-preservation will kill your destiny."

"Stop it Garon!" Mimi looked deep into my eyes with her light brown eyes, "EmManuel bought me the store because I raised him and all the boys like they were my very own! He knows my quality, but even more important he knows my effort. I raised him. Treat them all like my own blood Acacia!" She explained, then with a hushed tone leaned in to say, "He bought me the shop because he believes in me, he's a great man, EmManuel loves me more than the son I birthed at times."

Garon nodded, "I'm just saying, follow the rules or do it on your own and be a real failure til you grow."

"Actually, I read that failure doesn't get to be decided by others," I rebutted Garon's comment, "What you do and who you feel you are becoming is what determines if you are a success or failure. Just make sure you learn something new everyday Jenny."

Jenny looked at her watch, then at me with a smile. "We're kinda early, let's go get lunch?"

"Sure." I smiled back at her then at Mimi. "Thanks for everything, it was so nice to meet you."

"We're going next door, let me know if you need anything Auntie. I love you. I love you. I'm sorry for arguing with you, but you know how he is, and you know I can't talk about his personal life to you." Jenny apologized, giving her aunt a hug and kiss. "Your sons' gonna grab everything for tonight."

Garon pulled Jenny by her arm and continued to speak as if I were a child in the room, "Remember the rules while y'all over there, Jenny."

Mimi quickly accepted Jenny's apology and sent us both off with a mom-hug.

When we were out of earshot I asked, "Is that Manuel's stepmother?"

Jenny only laughed, then looked around the restaurant. "Sure, between us, we can say that she's one of them."

"What's the deal with Garon?" I asked her, looking behind my shoulders to be sure he was still nowhere around. "I feel like he's always around."

"Garon was raised differently. Taught to be annoying."

As we walked next door to a Japanese restaurant, I decided I would pick Jenny's brain for whatever information I could get about Manuel. She seemed most informed and easier to talk to than either of the security guards.

"Manuel takes care of his family, like buying her that boutique?" I stated, proud to see my new crush is a philanthropist as well.

"EmManuel takes care of everybody, whether or not they ask, he's going to be there," Jenny stated. "He is a giver, he's *too much* of a giver. He got that from our moms' side cause his dad would give, but he doesn't play, that's why all the rules matter to them." She explained. "So anyway, we're all thankful for Corbin's sense with the numbers or EmManuel would be lost."

"Corbin's his accountant," I raised my eyebrows at her, "Manuel's bad with money?"

"Money? Do you people really think he still cares about money?" She laughed, "No, you see how he lives, don't you get it? The numbers don't mean anything to him, EmManuel will be wealthy forever. Him, his dad, the family... they are owed a million favors, they have all the grace they need to be carried for generations. My Uncle was a networking and manifesting genius, he taught his family that same mindset."

I listened intensively, searching for an imperfection in Mr. Flawless, but Jenny didn't give me much. No one did. Jenny may have given me more evidence that he might be even more admirable than I thought.

"Their dad's high clientele security company brought in the start of connections for all the brothers, but especially EmManuel. No one took off like him." She told me, "He got his dad's brain and his mom's heart. He can help find the good in anybody, and I mean *anybody*. You seem unsure if you like him."

I smiled, "I do like him, I mean for as much as I can like someone I just met, he makes me feel like I knew him longer. He seems so sure about everything."

"He is sure about everything." She quickly responded. "That's why can't no one talk to him or tell him nothing half the time. Like don't bring distractions to work."

Jenny was outspoken, but even still I could tell she was trying to be a little reserved. She wanted me to know I was a distraction.

"Oh, has he always been like that?" I inquired, wanting to learn as much as I could from her. "Or was that something that happened after he got famous?"

"That's who he is, that's who he's always been. I swear he has all the answers," she proclaimed. "He does not make a mistake. Everything he gives out comes back doubled or more."

"Sounds lucky," I remarked.

"It's not luck, it's like a law." She rolled her eyes, "A lot of the time, the people who EmManuel helps don't typically seem to deserve it, but he changes people's lives, he's valuable. That's why he has had so much surveillance on him his whole life."

I was sure Jenny was not following the rules Garon gave her, because she spoke without reservation, she wasn't a rule-follower. "I get it, I'm sure people would take advantage of him if not."

"You know CoDéy, right? He made her everything that she is, she was literally a whole different person before EmManuel and DeCreed, the world wouldn't recognize the old her. And you see the type of songs she's putting out!" She rolled her eyes with passion, "Buck is to blame for that one though, he was her security damn near 24-7 back then. He should've known she wasn't any good."

"Why?" I wondered.

She shrugged, "Look at her, look at what she did. When it comes to celebrity relationships the celebrity has to be so careful that the non-celebrity has no malicious intent against them or that could hurt their brand."

"Are you and his team worried that's what I'm doing? Are you guys worried about me using him or hurting his reputation?" I questioned, referring to the evident awkwardness of the staff towards me.

"Nobody's worried about you, Acacia Ivy, 5'5", 145 lbs." She spoke of me so condescendingly. "School teacher, single mother of star athlete, several side gigs, first and youngest black adjunct professor to join the program. Just the typical sweetheart... I mean Princess, you prefer that right?"

"Who told you I prefer Princess?" I asked her, evidently, she'd done her research. "And that's a lot of information, where do you get all that?"

"Lucky guesses, apparently even you think you're his *usual type*." She said sarcastically mimicking my earlier conversation with Manuel. Overprotective baby cousin, I get it, been there. "As if he even has time for any of this."

"Wanna get some drinks?" I asked her, hoping she'd loosen up and give me more information, or at least try to get to like me. I couldn't tell if she wanted to tell me more or wanted me to just change the conversation.

"No drinks," She shook her head, "We're on the clock tonight. At the afterparty I'm sure he'll give you all the shots and joy you can handle."

"So, what more do you know about me?" I asked.

"Maybe everything, do you think we'd let you around him if we didn't know just about everything about you?" She shrugged. "You're not just on some everyday *date*, Acacia Ivy, you are out with EmManuel Eaton... from DeCreed, didn't you check his net worth? You at least know his minimum. Go see how much he gets for coming out of the house just to do a feature, and here he is running around town with you. Nothing he does might seem *normal*, if you choose to stay around you will see that normal is over."

I nodded, repeating my choices, "So choose to be normal or more?"

"More comes with more work." She paused and with a softer voice, "And you don't have to choose him just because he wants you. If he's too much you can go, but once you're in it's harder to leave."

104

For the first time ever, I was relieved to see Garon, although he still did not seem excited by me in the least. He walked into the restaurant holding a plastic bag with a few outfits for tonight's show.

"Y'all ready?" He asked, turning to leave before getting a response.

We got up from the table and followed behind Garon.

I didn't feel like Jenny was trying to scare me away, but maybe she wanted to let me know she could scare me if she wanted to. I didn't take anything she said to offense, I liked her a little less, but I got it. She was protecting her older cousin. And possibly trying to help warn me.

I would probably have done the same.

Manuel texted me and I immediately refocused on him, a breath of fresh air and warm feelings, he was the cure to the distracting background noises.

Manuel	
Are you happy?	
	Yes, the dress is so pretty. I will be happier when I see you
ur almost here. I got something for you.	
	You don't have to keep getting me things
Don't start. I'll see you in a few minutes.	
	Will we be alone tonight?
Yes	
	I wanna get to know more about u Thanks for everything
you're welcome. don't worry it will just be us	

7

While we were gone a sexy chestnut skin woman, Stephanie MUA, as her toolbox read, had turned one of the Penthouse bathrooms into a very cozy beauty parlor for me. She had everything ready to go for my hair, makeup section for my face, and even a little color for the smallest chip she pointed out on my nail that I hadn't even noticed was there.

Stephanie's toolbox had lots of stickers on it, one was "Black Owned", I loved Manuel even more for not just talking the talk, but actively supporting the community. In my recent google searches I learned a lot more about ongoing philanthropy and dreams for the community.

As a side note, he seemed to give away almost more money yearly than the internet said he was worth. That didn't make sense to me, but not much about his world did.

Whenever I would give Stephanie my preference on my hair, she did a nice job of accommodating me, but silently. Her silence made working with her uncomfortable, but she was doing a great job. While in front of the mirror I probably spent more time studying her than the work she was doing on me.

As she curled my hair she hummed and intermittently sang a song that sounded familiar, I just couldn't place it. Her voice was melodically sweet; however, her lack of conversation began to feel intentional as she spoke with everyone else who came around.

As a little experiment, I attempted to ask her a question, but she just continued to sing her song. She spoke to Jenny when she would wander in and out of the bathroom to give the stylist a direction or put jewelry on me. When Buck was looking for a restroom Stephanie spoke to him. It was definitely just me she was not responding to.

When Manuel would occasionally come into the makeshift beauty parlor to talk to me or just smile and stare; I began to watch as she was staring at him with her desperate eyes. Those eyes were just begging for

106

him to look at her. He didn't. Not sure how he noticed her staring, but it became hard for me not to.

Instead of going to the internet to put the negative review about this lady's personal makeup artist page like I wanted to, I texted Hazel back to entertain my boredom.

Hazel	
??? Lol! Answer me whore!	
	No, I didn't fuck him! He said he's not even going to try so you really are WRONG about him
Okay Sis, I love you, be safe. Have fun and don't let him treat you like shit just because he got coins. PERIOD!	
	Thanks, I will, right now I'm dealing with a weird ass hair stylist
Get used to it if you wanna be around him	

Once my hair was done Stephanie hummed around the large bathroom gathering utensils, from the looks of it, preparing for the makeup portion of my session.

"She's attractive," I said to Manuel, feeding into my stupid subconscious thoughts, the moment Stephanie stepped out of the bathroom. "Kinda envious that she got to be here alone with you while I was out shopping."

"Don't be envious of anyone," he instructed.

"I was exaggerating, I'm not, but she is very attractive," I smirked. "A weaker man might have given in had she thrown herself at him in such a romantic hotel with a sexy view."

"Is that what you are choosing to think about?" He crouched down to my eye level in the chair and kissed my lips softly. "I can have just about any woman I want and I'm only wanting to be with you."

"But what if she threw herself at you, you wouldn't do it?" I asked him playfully, reading that he did not want to answer my question, I squeezed his hand and looked him in the eyes. "C'mon Mr. Trust, you can answer, I honestly think a little jealousy is healthy."

"What's your intent? To make yourself angry?" He asked me. "Your type doesn't wanna hear the real truth."

"My type? I'm not a type," I winked at him.

"In that case, I have already been with Steph before, she's not my type." He let me know, then after just a pause and with a straight face responded. "Jealousy isn't healthy."

The sexy, yet unprofessional and slutty, stylist came back into the room, humming that same song as she began to put foundation on her brush. It dawned on me now that the song she was humming was a popular DeCreed love song, one that Hazel would often play a few years ago. The words:

Don't tell em anything, they'll just say it's lust.
We don't gotta call it anything, we know us.

I felt my face get hot, I felt humiliated, that song was about her!

I could not take the aggravation. When she turned around to go into her toolbox I stood up and left the bathroom. It was hard enough keeping track of the staff and family wandering around us prior to us even having a first date, but to have exes wandering around too was a bit much for me.

I closed the master suite door and started to look for my things. I felt stupid. How many of the other women around the suite or in his daily life will we run into that he just so casually had sex with?

Manuel came into the room behind me and gently closed the door. He stood quietly watching me pace around the room, looking for the items I came over with which were nowhere to be found.

"So, I thought you said you weren't a type?" After watching for a few moments Manuel said, breaking the silence with a light laugh. "No, but really I'm sorry, Acacia, did I fuck up that bad?"

I ignored him looking under the bed for my shoes I came with. "Yes, have you seen my shoes?"

108

"Just wear your new shoes. Are you really going to leave?"

"What do you think? Making me look stupid in front of your ex? While she's humming your platinum song you wrote to her!" I snapped. "While she's getting me ready to… what? Fuck you next, do you think this is funny?"

"We are not fucking," he told me with the tiniest laugh. "You don't look stupid; you look so beautiful."

"Well, I'm leaving. Go fuck your ex she clearly wants more."

"Ex-what?" He replied, laughing. "She wasn't singing to me, and that song is not about her. Even if she was my ex, I didn't write that song. She's not my ex, I've been with her a few times *with* my ex."

"So why the fuck would you hire her to do my hair and makeup if you are interested in me? Is that why you hired her?" I snapped at him, "That is so messy, I'm not into the sister-wives thing."

"She's just a superior makeup artist who was able to work for me, for *you*, on short notice, that's all." He told me, imprisoning my hands in his, with that gentle touch. "I'm more than interested in you, you're not leaving over this. Be soft, Acacia, please."

"*This* is what's normal in your world, just sleeping around with whoever? No heads up?" I judged him immediately, then released my hands. "Did you fuck that woman with the leopard outfit last night, too? She had a lot of questions about us. Or what about Bites?"

"*Who*?" He asked, bombarded.

"Oh, you *know* Bites. I had to stand there watching her trying to fuck you with her eyes right in front of me. Bites, the damn charcuterie bitch."

"Oh. Why would it matter?" He looked at me quizzically, "Was she rude to you?"

My chin dropped open and I snatched my hands away, "Ooh my goodness, you really did fuck Bites, too! Can you please let me know before you have me smiling in these women's faces who still want you, that's common courtesy. Obviously, they are not going to *like* me when they still want you!"

I paced his hotel room some more, repeating the story to myself softly out loud for clarification, because evidently, I was the only one that thought this whole situation was weird!

"I don't care what they think, *everyone* is here because I like you. I got my whole office staff relocated down here working the weekend, and you worried about her?" He told me, then stuck his head out the door and called out. "Jenny, get Stephanie out, send somebody else for makeup."

109

"Wait, don't fire her!" I snapped at him then groaned, realizing my spiral may be a little bit over dramatic and untimely. Also, a clear indication to the hoe that I was jealous of her!

Manuel was somewhat right, they were here to cater to me, I had no need to feel inferior to her or the charcuterie hoe. Not to mention I have a strong passion for supporting female and black owned businesses. The makeup artist and the charcuterie women of the world deserve love too.

On top of all that it'd be hard to get a makeup artist in such a short time.

"What do you want from me?" Manuel asked, closing the door back a little too hard. "You asked if I would have sex with her, I told you the truth. You don't want her doing your makeup and hair, I'm having her go! Now it's, *don't fire her*? Why do you play so many games? Is everything a puzzle with you?"

I raised my eyebrows at him, "You've got to be kidding me. This is my fault?"

He shook his head gently, "No, there is no fault, I'm trying to be logical with you. I'm trying to get to know you, but you like to create new challenges for me to get through. How many levels do I have to get through to win?"

"A lot." I mumbled, caving into his eyes.

He kissed me, I didn't kiss him back. "You can be upset, but don't leave. Just talk to me, I'm great at fixing stuff."

"Can you communicate with me as well? And don't hire more of *them* for me." I calmed down and let him kiss me a few more times as an apology. "You can stay out of the bathroom."

I played off my frustration as I left the bedroom, entering again back into my private salon with the slutty stylist. "Thanks for waiting."

Stephanie smiled at my apology, then spoke for the first time to me once the door was closed. "Yeah, I figured you must've just found out about us. Our history." She giggled like he was inside of her at this second. "Feels like... hmmm. Just a few days ago."

I nodded nonchalantly as we got back to work.

"He doesn't like to talk much about himself, most things about Manuel come from what other people witnessed. I once heard someone say, 'Manuel is the breath of fresh air that we take for granted when it's gone', so don't sleep, I can help if you have questions." She said with an exaggerated sigh. "Strong, silent type, I guess. But he's a really good man, not too many people get to be around him. Exemplary sex."

I remained as straight faced as possible, so she'd know I was not interested in her conversation. But apparently my awareness of her sexual relationship with our mutual friend was the key to her opening her mouth.

"There's little things you should know when you are dealing with Manuel though," she started to tell me, but I quickly cut her off.

"No disrespect, but me and you aren't even on the same level when it comes to dealing with Manuel." I put her in her place. "Not even close."

She chuckled to herself, as she got back to beating my face, "Lady, if you only knew how many faces of makeup that I've done for Manuel."

"Wow, *all* those faces *and* you still fucked him?" I asked sarcastically.

"Yes, fuck him very well." She said without shame. "You know what I learned from watching Manuel? Don't take anything in this life personally, most people are just trying to survive their existence. And you won't succeed at your personal goals if you take everyone else's ignorance to heart. His ex-didn't get that."

As if reading my mind, a half-dressed Garon came into my makeshift salon and got the slutty stylist out by her forearm. He was wearing a muscle shirt, with surprisingly more muscle than I expected, just the right attire for putting out the garbage.

Not saying a word, Jenny quickly came in and finished my makeup, then put finishing touches on my hair.

I just sat in the chair silently, surprised by the childish encounter, it felt as if I was just slapped in the face.

"You're going to be so fine on the red carpet, I got your face. Don't worry about that stupid bitch, I never liked her." Jenny assured me, tweaking my eyelashes. She was gentler during this interaction, she probably felt second-hand embarrassment for me after the encounter with the stylist. "Just stay cute on that jet because I am not flying up there to fix this again."

"Flying?" I asked.

"Yes! The show isn't down here, Acacia, gotta fly outer space to see the stars." She informed me sarcastically. "The ride is less than two hours, then you can enjoy the stank air of one of your bucket list cities."

I looked at her skeptically, how does she know my bucket list cities?

There was a knock on the bathroom door, then a woman a couple inches shorter than me with yellowish-brown colored skin, a high bridged

111

nose and eyes with an epicanthic fold. She was wearing an elegant business suit and red heels came in and closed the door behind her. No doubt she was Manuel's mother from the way she looked at me. She was less friendly looking than Mimi and Mãe Mãe for sure, but it seemed more cultural than rude. She had the same face as the one I saw on Manuel's tattoo, his younger brother's.

"Acacia?" She asked, giving me a gentle smile as I nodded yes. "I'm EmManuel's Mum, Sora, it's so good to meet you! Sidebar, I'm also his lawyer, but I was told I can only be Mum for now."

Manuel's father had a type himself, yet it wasn't a physical appearance, the women weren't even the same ethnicities, somehow, they all radiated almost a spiritual energy in common. Where did he find so many elite level women, women who make plans then execute them for their family and how was he able to convince them to have children with him!

"Nice to meet you," I extended my hand to her, she had soft hands and a strong handshake. "That's so cool how your family all works together."

"It's either cool or crazy, imagine having to be a parent for life instead of 18 years." Sora took a deep breath, "As a mother, I always support him, but as his lawyer I want to tie him to a chair and force him to sit down. Especially now without his brother here to check up on him for me." She sighed, "EmManuel has always been remarkable, so luckily trusting him comes easy."

"Well, I heard you are awesome at everything you do," I could honestly say.

"I'm his favorite," she said confidently. "I save his behind when he fucks up so bad that not his brothers or other mothers can't save him."

I cringed, "How often is that?"

"I like you Acacia, you ask the right questions." She shrugged, "It was my pleasure to meet you. Don't take it easy on him, you hear me?"

Mum, Sora, gave me a huge hug and kissed my hand to not mess up my makeup, she was so gentle!

"Yes." I agreed. "Nice to meet you as well."

I noticed she was barefoot as she is sashaying her little hips out of the bathroom and down the hall, past Manuel and his security staff, hitting all four of them in the forehead.

"She's readddyyy." Jenny sang out to the guys.

8

Jenny had us looking cute and comfy, we wore matching gray sweatpants with cool gray tennis shoes, white snapback caps and white form fitted shirts.

I felt like such a trophy with him, as random people took pictures of us on our walk through the hangar to the jet, secretly unsure of how I even became the prize. Occasionally Manuel waved at his fans, smiled for a couple photos, but no autographs. Garon also made sure we didn't stop for too long.

When we first walked onto the jet, I couldn't help but let out a squeal. And although his workers looked at me like a child, Manuel seemed to find intrinsic joy every time he amazed me. I would catch him glancing at me for a reaction anytime I was happy.

Once I caught on, I tried to play it cool, but he indeed was very impressive. Hence the squeal stepping into the upscale chartered jet plane. Being with Manuel felt like being around royalty, the scenery and the way most people catered to his every need with just a gesture. Yet very much knowing who he is, he was still humble.

"I have never done anything like this before," I told Manuel, looking out the window of the private flight to our first date. "Honestly, I have never even been in first class."

"You might be too bougie for that already," he smiled at me from across the little table that separated us, he seemed to genuinely enjoy my happiness.

"Look at this leather, it's so smooth." I loudly whispered.

The rich, eggshell leather seats swiveled and had armrests, as well as reclined and warmed! The oval shaped window beside me was so large it was as if we were floating through the sky.

I was facing a small booth and sofa set further away, that's where Manuel's team were seated, they seemed to be gambling. Along the side of the jet was a long couch, two people slept there.

113

"You look like a flying pro," Manuel lied as I got excited about everything. "Nobody can tell it's the first time."

"Do you always fly like this?" I asked.

He nodded, yes. "There's always so many people with me, Corbin worked it out number wise that it's better for us to fly like this. Granted it doesn't have to be this luxury, but I like doing this stuff with people I love."

The turbulence had me holding onto the table for stability, I was so far from a pro. He reached his hands across the small table and held mine. He squeezed it, *be soft*, I heard his voice in my mind.

I could feel myself falling for him.

"I am still that stereotypical little kid that looks up in the sky and envisions where the people in these little planes are off to. Now I'm here, barely handling the wind." I told Manuel, embarrassed. The lights on the jet dimmed and the lights on the floor lit up. "Did you ever wonder where people on planes were going when you were younger?"

He shook his head no with a laugh, "The opposite, I'm always the one in the sky. Ever since I was little, my brothers and I spent lots of time with my dad on business trips. He had us on paperwork as his business partners and had us working like business partners. He wanted us to know how to run things when he left. And then eventually I was on my own flights doing my music business."

"No childhood? That suck." I tried to empathize, although a rich childhood did not seem so bad either.

Manuel shook his head to disagree, "It was my dad's idea, it wasn't bad, just different. Me and my brothers were made for it. He's a methodical man, from choosing our mothers to the way he taught us to love. We all should love so freely."

"Well, it seems his plan worked, you are successful, and you seem loving to everyone, from fans to staff."

"And you, too?" He flirted, I bashfully looked down. "I'm not completely successful yet, but I'm patient. Come sit with me." Manuel patted the seat beside him once the pilot told us we could move around the aircraft. I obliged and got closer to him; I wasn't facing his staff anymore which was a plus. "I'm glad you're coming with me to the awards, it'll be nice to go with you. Thank you for coming."

He thanks *me* for coming.

Manuel was so infatuated with me; it just didn't make sense. What did I do to make him like me, dare I believe, love me, this much? I asked myself again for the third time.

"I'm still not grasping that I'm here." I admitted to him. "I'm here *with* you, look at how many people were just standing outside and hoping to just see you, just to take a picture, begging for an autograph. That's so wild that you touched so many people through your work."

He laughed, "So have you."

"Ya, but that's different." I shook my head at him, then opened his window that he closed as soon as we arrived. "It's so beautiful, look outside."

"I'd rather look at you," he kissed my cheek, "You are glowing."

"Stop." I told him seriously. "It makes me self-conscious when you keep complimenting me. But thank you."

Manuel whispered in my ear, "Get used to it, I'm not going to stop. Guess I'm just a really big fan."

I imagined what life would be like to be around Manuel regularly. Flying here and there. Going to fancy dinners and parties. Having exclusive access to venues and high-end events. Wearing the best of the best designs, some even created just for me. It would take some getting used to, but I did not hate it.

As his friend? Seemed a little strange, no relationship mess, according to him. I even somewhat liked the flexibility in the relationship.

I laid my head high up on his chest, snuggled right under his neck to get closer to his uniquely tailored fragrance and appreciated the moment. 40,000 feet high in the sky, feeling and looking amazing, with a man that many women daydream about.

I looked over and Manuel's eyes were closed, getting some rest, which was my cue to do the same. He stroked up and down my leg as I drifted off to sleep, giving my conscious mind a much-needed break.

I had all sweet dreams, but then there was a bad vibe, a dark shadow that woke me up abruptly. I could feel we were safely back on the ground.

Garon was the first face I saw coming out of my slumber. He was standing over us, and he had my phone in his hand. He was holding it out, showing it to Manuel, who seemed to be just a little ahead of me on waking up.

"My son's father is calling?" I asked, getting a glimpse of the caller id on my phone. I reached out my hand, but Garon didn't hand me my phone until Manuel nodded at him. Meanwhile I side-eyed him as I missed the call, only to see the notification that I'd missed six calls from him.

I raised my eyebrows, but kept my mouth closed. Garon already hates me.

I reluctantly called Hayden Sr. back. Six missed calls are never a positive sign, especially when they are from your ex who you have a child with.

"Hey sorry, what's up," I said once he picked up the phone. We'd been separated for almost a year and could barely have a decent adult conversation with each other. I was just hoping for some decency and cordiality on the phone, because I was not ready for Manuel to know about my relationship issues with my ex yet.

Manuel stayed seated beside me while everyone else prepared for our departure from the jet, gathering items and bags with the others. Garon remained close as well, I'm sure the thought of me with a phone just gave him anxiety.

"Sorry? What's up?" Hayden snapped, he was pissed, I should've just hung up right then. "I've been fuckin' calling you, emailing you, texting you, and you saying, *What's up sorry*? Are you fuckin' dead Acacia?! I sent the request for half the money, two days ago, you haven't even responded to that."

I softened my voice in hopes that he would do the same, I didn't want anyone to hear the conversation, but with the little bit of space we were in I didn't have much to work with.

"I was busy, is this an emergency? Is everything okay with Tré, do you need something else? I'll send it." I said as politely as I could under the circumstances, but he was pissed about way more than money, I could hear it in his voice.

Plus, I know he doesn't need my money.

After fourteen years you learn a lot about a person, especially when you've seen them at different stages of life. Even when we've hated each other, we've been able to call upon each other.

Arguably he's been simultaneously my worst and best friend for the last decade and a half. In small doses the dynamic of our chemistry could probably save lives, but for large extended periods of time, it starts explosions. Yet and still, after fourteen years there's no denying our bond, as toxic as it can get.

"I cannot get shit done with *our* son without your signature, so I need you to stop going out of town with Hazel playing *backstage groupies* and get back home to fill out this paperwork for your son!" He shouted, this time I could tell that Manuel and Garon heard him because they were both staring at me. "I don't even understand half this paperwork he's bringing in here and I'm hearing you're out of town again?"

Manuel put his hand out for the phone. He looked calm, but upset, his patience wore thin as he bent his fingers gesturing for my phone, he could hear Hayden yelling at me.

"Hayden," I tried to imitate the patience, it'd been months since baby daddy's last screaming fit, and I got better at not snapping back at him or stooping to his level from my Quarantine Education. Plainly Hayden was bothered by hearing I was out of town and of course to him this means I'm with a man, he's the jealous type, but I don't ever give him anything to be jealous about. "Nothing is due this week from his paperwork. I know what's going on, I will be by your house to handle this when I get back. I'll do it."

"Hoe, when the fuck is that gonna be?!" Hayden cut me off angrily, trying to spark a fire that he knows will ignite an ugly bomb I try to hide inside of me.

I saw Manuel's arm still extended out through my peripheral, wanting my phone, but shook my head no.

Manuel nodded "yes", reaching to take my phone out of my hand, but I leaned away and hung up the call before he could get to it. Hayden was still yelling as I turned my phone off.

"So, then you're cool with how he speaks to you?" Manuel asked me, he looked like he'd just watched me be beaten.

"No, but he's my son's father and I can't have you making things worse. I will talk to him," I told him, trying to deescalate the situation, but he wasn't buying it. "You don't understand, and you can't complicate that for me right now. We just met. And he can get kinda crazy."

"Who's crazy?" Buck asked aggressively, from somewhere in the plane.

"Nobody, she doesn't know crazy." Garon shook his head at me. "She hasn't seen shit for real."

"Acacia, we aren't playing that. There ain't no pass on that." Buck called to me; I dropped my head into my hands wishing the conversation would end. "EmManuel, I know he didn't hit her?"

I mumbled, "Can we not do this?"

"That's comfortable?" Manuel gently took the phone back and handed it to Garon who left us alone to pack up and head out. He empathetically kissed me on my head.

I sighed, embarrassed. "Sorry, he can be annoying. But I have to deal with him for three more years, at the least."

"Stop saying sorry. You don't have to be sorry for no one else's behavior towards you," he assured me. "Don't let him talk to you like that, you ain't dealing with that no more. Either hang up or give it to me, nothing he gotta say is that important. And if it was, he wouldn't disrespect you to say it."

"My son is doing really well with football and his father's really excited; it's just coming out wrong. They really bonded throughout his first season this year, but he's stressed. Experiencing being a full-time parent. Trying to manage his schedule and Tré's schedule." I tried to rationalize, but he only shook his head at me.

We got off the jet with everyone else and got into one of the golf carts that took us to the front. Garon rode with us, but in the front.

"Long as you are okay," Manuel said with caution.

"He's a great father to our son, just not good for or with me."

Manuel shook his head, "Not talking to you like that, especially in front of Tre. Don't listen to that, Cay, don't let anyone talk to you like that. I don't care who it is. If you don't know what to say to them, call me."

"Can we not talk about this anymore," I mumbled, embarrassed to be lectured. Especially in front of his asshole security guard.

Manuel kissed my forehead, "You deserve everything great and nothing less, especially when I'm right here." He thinks so highly of me. *Everything great and nothing less,* if he only knew everything about me, he'd probably think differently.

"I don't have it all together, please don't think that. My ex and I take turns, alternating weeks with Tré for the last three months, we split the costs for his needs, and it's finally been working out for us."

"You let me know when you get tired of the way that situation is *working out,*" he let me know. "Is this his week with Tré coming up now?"

"Yeah." I replied.

"Come stay with me for the week, take off work, call out sick." He invited me. "I can be free too, so we can do whatever you wanna do. Anything you can imagine."

I laughed nervously, but genuinely flattered by such an invitation. Anything? "I'm *not* free at all. I still have a life, work, bills, and my student organization has a big presentation to prepare for. Plus, next week is spring break, maybe we can make a plan to meet up for that coming week. I'll be with Tré, but I can get away for a bit."

"I don't want to wait, honestly. What if I pay you double your salary for the week, take a week off work." Manuel bear-hugged me from the back, hands around my waist, and playfully kissed me repeatedly. I got a feeling that this was not his first time offering a woman this version of PTO.

"You're for real? This works in your world?" I laughed, looking into his very serious light brown eyes.

"Just stay with me, it doesn't have to be here, you can choose any state, hell any country. Do you have your passport?" I shook my head no. "That's okay, we'll get it, I just want to spend more time with you." He glanced at Garon who seemed to always be watching, almost lip reading if you ask me, "I want you away from everyone."

Manuel's eyes were cheerfully looking at me for the only answer I believed he would accept.

"Choose any state?" I shook my head laughing, disturbed yet intrigued at the proposition he made. "You're not paying me to hang out with you. But I will check to see if I can get my classes covered this week though."

"Is that a yes?" Even he was surprised.

I nodded, surprising even myself. "Yeah, I'll figure it out and plus it'd be nice to get to know you more."

9

Manuel kept his promise and we got to go to dinner alone. No family. No security. No staff, he even drove.

He looked at me as he spoke sternly. "Okay, so listen, I have a rule when you ride with me: don't tell me how to drive. That means don't say stop, slow down, *you can't go that way…* just sit back and trust me. I'm letting you know in advance, because it's a pet peeve when people tell me how to drive."

I looked at him wide-eyed, immediately missing the comfort of Garon's bulletproof car!

Yet, maybe a little more I wanted to go on an adventure with him.

I snuggled up closely against him on the ride, ignoring the low arm rest that divided us. I found myself being clingier to him since we landed in this new city, it was unfamiliar to me, but he was beginning to feel like a cozy comfort blanket. My left arm intertwined with his right tightly as he weaved through traffic effortlessly.

For whatever reason I didn't want to admit it to myself, it was feeling more than a crush, Manuel was turning me on. Every time I looked at him I got excited. It wasn't how the doors to his fancy sports car opened in the totally wrong direction, or how fast he sped weaving through traffic flawlessly. It wasn't even how his biceps poked out of his arms as he gripped the steering wheel. I was liking him, as a person, I was really feeling him.

"You're quiet. Why do you ask people about me? But when we're alone you don't ask much." Manuel inquired as he drove us to the restaurant. "You'd rather ask Jenny or staff about me, like you can't just ask me."

Didn't know they were reporting back on me.

"I like to hear other perspectives," I told him. "For me, knowledge is peace, the more I know the more I find peace. I can't only learn about you, from you."

120

I like to think of myself as a natural inquirer, gathering research from many sources.

"I don't want you to feel like you need to ask anyone questions about me. Trust me."

"It doesn't mean I do not trust you," I told him, "I like hearing others' perspectives also, especially those people who know you."

"Just ask me, I'll answer unbiasedly, as honestly as possible. I want you to hear from me, not them, I want you to know me outside of as a musician." Manuel responded, pulling into a restaurant with a huge purple water fountain in the center of the driveway. "The seafood here is really fresh and they season their steaks very well, the best steak and lobster in the city."

"My favorites." I told him, as he held my hand and looked into my eyes, I felt an unexpected feeling of comfort. "I'm interested in getting to know you, outside of you as a musician also. I have lots of questions."

Once the valet opened our doors, we were taken into the well-lit, beautiful foyer made of all glass. There weren't many people in the restaurant, which made it easy for us to get through to our reservation. As he spoke to the hostess, I went to check out the gigantic aquarium.

In the center of the room was an oversized aquarium with beautiful fish swimming aimlessly between the up and down escalators. For a moment I felt bad for them, trapped in their limited society without much room for growth. Sometimes I didn't feel much different than they probably felt.

The hostess and Manuel came over and we were led up the escalators to the second-floor balcony seating, which was empty of other patrons, very private. The live jazz band played on the stage downstairs; we could see them from our table.

He picked an impressive date spot, very romantic vibes.

"It's so quiet in here," I said softly to him.

He smiled at me, "Because the restaurant is closed."

"This restaurant is closed. Why?" I asked, trying to figure out which holiday it could have been.

"For you." He told me as we scooted into a semi-circular booth.

Manuel put his hand on top of mine, interlocking our fingers. The menus we received were customized before printed highlighting the special for us, on the front it read "Happy First Date Acacia and Manuel". It was one of those cheesy little things he did that made me smile.

The menus weren't even necessary because the staff brought over different appetizers and salads nonstop since we sat down, apparently he pre-ordered a little of everything.

The waitresses couldn't help but gawk and drool over him being there, they tried to be secretive, but I wouldn't be surprised if they slid him their number. I felt no need to hate or get mad at their drooling, hell they probably had posters of this man on their dorm walls. Besides him never taking his eyes off me, kept me very secure in my position tonight.

"I can't believe you chose to still wear *that* watch," he commented, rehashing a comical argument that took place at the new hotel, when I left the diamond watch for the more productive smart watch option.

I laughed at him, sticking to my same points, "I gotta finish counting my steps. Plus, I might lose a diamond or get robbed!"

"You really think I would let something happen to you?"

"No, I'm sure there's a man with a hidden purse hiding somewhere. I'm just saying!" I tried to rationalize, knowing that I should not because there was no reason I felt not worthy enough to wear valuable things. "Leave me alone, you're gonna get used to hearing no."

"You're gonna get used to nice gifts," he reminded me. I agreed that I would wear my smart watch to dinner and my yearly-salary-watch to the awards show tonight.

"It's a beautiful watch, I'm going to be so excited to wear it. Thank you again."

"So go ahead with these *lots* of questions. What's on your mind?" He asked. "Let's get you comfortable."

"How did you meet me?" I wanted to know, too many details were coming up with loose ends. "I thought at first, you saw my fitness team tag me in something with a DeCreed song, but then you mentioned my business page. So, what was it? How did I come to your attention?"

He smiled, "I saw you got an award, minority Samaritan? Then that led me to a lecture you did over at the museum, and it brought me to you, you know how the social media spiral goes. I went to your page, saw your business page, and saw that you used a DeCreed song... I knew I had a little chance. I figured you were a fan, so I invited you out to the show."

One of the many times when my ex and I split, I had to get a second job hosting history museum tours and giving lectures on social science topics. "That's ironic, I always felt that job was keeping me from meeting men."

He nodded, "Next question."

"Women? Are there any other women that you are currently like *this* with? Dates, jewelry…plants?" I asked. "I know we just met, so I'm not going to be upset, just wondering. I don't know what to expect anymore."

"Like *this?* No," he turned my cheek to kiss my lips. "Just you. You never saw me with anyone else, other than CoDéy. I'm very cautious of who I have around me, Acacia. And it's not cause I'm hiding anything, I am focused on what I'm going to leave behind, not many things can pull me away from that."

Why me? I asked first to myself, then out loud. "Why me?"

"Honestly, something is pulling me towards you," he said, sitting up. "I'm in tune with my ability to see radiance in people and I can't explain what I see, but I can see it. And feel it, too. Everything I did for you was already before the concert. Then when I saw you in person, you walked into my dressing room. I saw an invisible glow around you, as inescapable as a forcefield. You're a magnet."

I could feel emotional tears beginning to form in my eyes, he used his thumbs as a swale, blocking the water before I could fuck up my makeup. I never heard anyone talk to me like that before, not even myself.

"How'd you know I would be mutually interested?" I joked the heavy mood off.

"Not tryna sound boastful, but no, people rarely say no to me." He boasted, wrapping his arm around my waist. I couldn't help but love the way our body's connected, we were practically two puzzle pieces.

Sticking with his concept of full 100% openness questions, I took a deep breath and asked one I'd been dreading, "Will CoDéy be there tonight, I'm a little nervous?"

He nodded, unphased by my question, like he knew she would come up. "Most likely, she was nominated."

I winced at the idea of his super model, actress ex-girlfriend seeing me with him tonight, on our first date. She's gorgeous with a model figure, I am probably more of a fan of her recent work than his, I hoped it wouldn't be awkward.

"I don't want her, Cay. Me and CoDéy have been apart for about 2 years now." He assured me. "Is that what you are worried about?"

"I wouldn't say I'm worried, I just want to know ahead of time what's going on. What to expect," I paused. "We're moving very fast *for me*, and I told you, the more I know about something the safer I feel."

Plus, she's rich, famous, and gorgeous, I thought to myself. "Why did you break up?."

"She's where she wanted to be, I don't want her. I still care for her as a person, but that's it, I had to walk away." He confirmed. "I don't overthink anything. You have to trust yourself and anything that your energy tells you to walk away from."

"But don't you still miss her sometimes?" I asked, he made an aggravated face with that question, he could probably tell I was projecting my own relationship issues.

He sighed fighting patience with my insecurity, "Reminisce and smile at old memories, yes. Miss her or feel any longing for that bullshit? No. Staying in that suffering of *missing* people, just holds you back from the celebrations in front of you. I'm bringing you tonight because I want to be around *you* and have fun with *you*."

I kissed him as a thank you for his compliance and patience with me and my questions. Many in my past have quickly shut down or brushed off my slightly intrusive nature. He was keeping his promise of safety in allowing me to *be soft*, and it felt genuinely okay to be soft with him now. I like it.

No more questions about CoDéy, I made a mental note. However, it didn't stop me from wondering how she might react to seeing another woman with him.

According to my earlier short internet search on the way back to the hotel, Manuel and CoDéy were very public with each other, but he has never gone public with any other person since then or before her. Although there were some interesting rumors.

CoDéy has dated quite a few other mildly popular celebrities publicly in the last two years. Not hating on her whatsoever, I believe we should feel free to be ourselves as long as we aren't hurting anyone. And she is gorgeous so I'm sure she gets offers constantly. CoDéy's the tall, legs-type with flawless almond colored skin. Rumor has it that she wasn't born with her current boobs or ass, but I couldn't care less, she looks amazing. She kept her hair changing colors and styles, but always cute!

"You've been famous most of your life, so have you dated anyone else in the celebrity-realm?" I asked.

"I don't believe in relationships the way most do. CoDéy was my only official for real." He shrugged, "I never really have the time to invest like that."

Two waitresses walked over, giggling, one held a gift wrapped 8-inch-long box and she set it down in front of me. The three of them took a step back but remained close enough to see.

I smiled a big grin at both them and Manuel, then slowly opened the gift. A diamond necklace and bracelet.

"Since I could tell the watch wasn't your thing," he finessed, as if he didn't have the jewelry already chosen before the watch fight.

"You are a lot, like, too much." I whispered to him, and for some reason got teary-eyed again. He quickly saved my make up yet again with his fingers. "Sorry I'm not typically a crier, I don't know why I keep crying. Thanks."

"You're fine," he whispered. "People cry around me a lot."

I held up my hair as he clasped the gaudy rose gold diamond necklace around my neck and then clasped the matching tennis bracelet. "Thank you, Manuel, this is my favorite metal. I might not take this off."

"You gonna wear that to work and not worry about getting robbed?" Manuel asked.

"It matches my ring. I'd wear it to work, look at it! Probably cost the same as my rent." I shrugged, then saw my ring was not on my finger anymore. I tried to recall when I last had it.

"It for sure costs more than a few months of your rent." He corrected me kindly. "I don't think it really goes with that ring. What's wrong?"

"I can't find my ring," I told him, looking through my bag. "I had it on this morning."

"Are you sure?" He said, "Maybe you left it at the hotel."

"Yes I'm sure, I was scared to take it off and leave it… but it kept slipping." I thought back to when we were skipping rocks and I had to keep adjusting it. I put my hand on my forehead. "I think I might've dropped it when we were skipping rocks."

He bit his bottom lip, I'm not sure if he was trying to hold back a laugh, but he tried to be sweet. "We can just get a new one, I'll send somebody to… the mall? Right? They sell it in a mall?"

"I can replace it, thank you. Just so you know, you cannot buy me, I'm not that type."

"I know that attitude turns me on a little," he said softly, accepting my philosophy as a challenge.

I liked the way he looked at me, I couldn't help but to smile whenever we made eye contact. I laughed, blew him kisses, teasing him as I slid over in our booth, so he'd want to move closer.

"I got it." He told me. "I'm not trying to buy you, but I do like to spoil you. Money doesn't control me; people can't abuse me through it, and I wouldn't do that to anyone. It's just a tool, I can just go get more, anyone can when they know how to get it. Don't believe the numbers on the internet, those aren't right."

I nodded. Did he see my search history?

Earlier when I was out I remember searching Manuel's net worth (among other minor facts) on the internet, not because I want him for his money, but how is he able to afford so many things, people, businesses? I was curious.

His net worth was more than I could imagine spending in this lifetime. His yearly salary was more than I'd seen in my entire life.

"You said you don't believe in relationships?" I asked him, not forgetting his comment. "But I remember you were engaged. So why the change?"

"Engaged to do what? I bought a ring for someone who wanted a ring. What anyone else chooses to interpret is completely up to them and not my business. She knew what it was." Manuel spoke casually about a ring the world knew was over a million dollars, I looked at him as if he were speaking baby talk. "You people and these symbols you idolize are still funny to me."

"Engaged to be married?" I shot back obviously.

"Guess not," he shrugged, "What is a ring to you?"

"Well to me, and most people on Earth, that ring is a promise to make the biggest commitment and be devoted to someone you want to spend the rest of your life with. It's a beautiful symbol that has no ending, it never stops."

"It means whatever you want it to mean," he said with his familiar smart aleck smile. "I believe in alignment; being on the same page with respectful understanding. Lining things up properly so that they can flow. I have connections, bonds, but titles are irrelevant when the bond is there."

"So instead of a true love, you prefer an open relationship?" I asked frankly.

"Not *instead* of love, all I have is love," he told me, "I can see myself loving some, you, more than most. I just don't prefer titles, no boxes to be confined in. You live your life, and I live my life. No regrets or expectations, do what makes you happy and if we are in sync, we'll continue to align."

"And if or when we're not in sync?" I asked.

He shrugged, "Go do what makes you happy. I just want someone in my life who is genuine, wants to enjoy life and have fun with me."

"So basically, you just want to do whomever and whatever you want to do, and get to keep coming back?" I asked, shocked that he was presenting such a tacky idea to me.

"Why would we *not* do what we want in our lives? I don't want anything bad, do you? It's mutual, I want you to have everything, too." He seemingly invited me to his relationship mantra. "By the way, I had Corbin send the money to your account. Let me know if he was cheap."

I checked the incoming payments to my mobile banking app; he sent way too much for one week.

Manuel had a way of making his words replay in my mind. Was being without a title the best way to go these days, it did seem more freeing. Not having to answer to someone, but still having someone who cares about me, might not be so bad. The current situation of looking for a serious man wasn't working much better.

"I told you not to send me anything, I don't want you to pay me to be here." I told him seriously, it seemed too weird.

"Donate it." He brushed it off, "or use it for your son. I bet he is a great kid."

"Tré really is wonderful, he was my whole world for so long, and now he barely tells me what's on his mind. It's been a big transition starting with sharing time with his father." I smiled genuinely. "It has turned out to be a blessing, he gets to have a man in his life more and I am starting to get more time to focus on my thing. Plus, I'm glad I met you; I would have said no if I had my son at home."

"So, you are glad you met me?" He asked, gloating.

"I don't know, some of your ways of life are throwing me off. But I'm more than glad that I came," I nodded, blushing. "I feel like I'm dreaming a little."

"Maybe you are. What else do you dream about?" He asked me, looking into my eyes with intent. "What are your dreams, what do you want? You can have anything, just tell me what it is you want."

I leaned back, away from Manuel, "You are not going to buy me."

"I told you, stop saying that I just like making you smile." He spoke with a serious face. "Plus, it's mine, I can do what I want with it. So, show me your goals, where do you keep them?"

"My head, I also have a vision board at home." I shrugged, "You want me to tell you like my weight goal?"

"You should start writing down everything you want for yourself, all your goals, so you know what you are aiming for." He instructed. "Even if you don't want to tell me what you want, write it down somewhere. And make them the most fun and challenging things you can dream, like the song."

"Okay, I can't believe you just referenced lyrics from your own song, but I will take the advice. I read that in a book, just never got around to doing it. And trust me, I'm smiling, you don't need to get me anything else." I leaned back in for a kiss. "Being around you is making my heart feel very happy."

Although the food was delicious, we hardly ate. The music was so nice, he even danced with me for two songs. Manuel wasn't shy or socially awkward, he was having fun and being a little silly with me. I didn't think he'd be so down to earth!

Most of the time at dinner we just found cute ways to touch each other, kiss each other, and then very seldomly we fed each other a bit. Which I preferred since I planned on looking as snatched as possible in my tailored gown tonight.

10

"The parties after the awards are big, especially if they win, which they will, Manuel said they are winning something. Your afterparty dress will be hung in his closet and the heels are in there as well." Jenny explained sharply into my ear bud, running me through the last-minute details as Garon indiscreetly watched me use my phone in the rearview mirror. "There are some flats in the purse, but Bitch if you wuss out on me tonight I will bully you, keep the heels on. Don't answer any questions from them nosey ass people either, they are vultures just looking for someone else's business. Just stay cute and quiet. Even and especially those red-carpet hoes, don't even make eye contact with them zombies. Got it?"

"Red carpet zombie hoes?" I asked.

"Yes, the hoes without a ticket who will be trying to get into the show, asking you all your business. Manuel is giving them a lot to talk about today, so they will try, but don't talk to them," she explained. "You're smart, you'll figure it out. Oh, and remember to have fun, enjoy the experience."

"I got it, thanks," I told her, scrolling through my phone to see what all I missed before my phone went back to Garon's phone jail. "Bye Jenny."

Hazel

What's going on???
Anything new??
I'm living through you, give me details when u can.

OMG I'm going to the award show tonight bitch!
And CoDéy will probably be there.

Whaattt?????
She's a whole queen!

Definitely! I would ask her to sign something if he wasn't here! Girl this man has me dressed in diamonds!

FML!!! You the luckiest hoe ever, just fuck him already!!! He paid for the pussy at this point!

Girl he's not even trying to

Maybe he's gay?

He isn't gay

Think about it he does have some red flags

Who doesn't. I don't think he's gay.
He did tell me I'm too hard☐☐♀☐

Probably cause you too hard to manipulate?

It ain't like that, I'll hit you up later. Going to the show!

I also got a chance to respond to Tré, who as of recently was impossible to get ahold of or get a phone location on due to… whatever new excuses he could come up with day by day.

Tré	
Mom wyd? Can I call you?	
	Hello, my son, I've been calling you! I'm busy right now! I am going to an awards show! I will call you in the morning. I love you XOXOXO
	Watch tv and see if you see me!

Buck sighed before unlocking the doors for us, "Y'all ready to go hang out at the planetarium?"

"Planetarium?" I whispered to Manuel with excitement, I loved a good astronomy exhibit.

"He's talking about the fake stars, you nerd," Manuel laughed as he took my hand when men in black tuxes opened the door for us. "Let's go, keep your phone on you."

I smiled, clutching my phone even more stirred up, "Hmm, does this mean you trust me now?"

"You think you'd be here if I didn't trust you already?" He said as he kissed me right in time for the photographers to start snapping pictures rabidly.

Manuel and I walked up the red carpets alongside a large group of people affiliated with DeCreed, the carpets led to a huge fancy theater, on the sides were vloggers, news reporters, and tabloid reporters with so many questions. For the most part I only smiled and held his hand as we moved through the crowd. I overheard him tell one interviewer that I was his *special friend*… and I liked the sound of that.

Our seats were not too close, but close enough to see everything. There were plenty of people I didn't recognize at all, so I didn't stand out among the celebrity guests like a sore thumb as much as I thought I might.

We also didn't do much mingling around, we just whispered to each other as we people watched. Many people came to him, but he handled it so nicely. I tried not to appear starstruck, but seeing so many people I grew up watching on tv was exciting. Manuel sarcastically played along when I would whisper to him a celebrity sighting. Many of the people of a lesser popularity rank than him.

"I think you're my favorite one," I told him.

"Not enough to stand in line for though right?" He reminded me.

"Right," I joked back. "I would stand in a very long line for you now that I know you."

He responded with a soft kiss. "That's all I wanted."

"Hey Manuel," we both looked up, two rows ahead of us was CoDéy. She wore a familiar sparkling silver and red sequin ombre gown that showed her completely naked body underneath. She didn't need it as excellent as her body looked, but it had sequins covering all the private parts for modesty. The diamonds she wore in her ears sparkled, dancing from her ears down to where they stopped at her shoulders. She wore bright red lipstick, and her makeup was flawless.

She was sitting next to a big man who looked like a football player, and two other ladies who did not turn around.

"Hi CoDéy," Manuel said reluctantly. She looked at me, when he noticed he made the introduction. "This is *my*... Acacia."

"Hi, I admire your work, you're so great." I complimented her genuinely across the row with what I'm sure was the stupidest grin on my face.

She only responded with a nod and slightly sassy stare, then sat down as the lights were beginning to dim and the ceremony began.

DeCreed won three awards, they were a large group of people, more than I'd even realized. Manuel walked to the stage with his group of men each time they won; they moved in such sync with each other. As if they all were very intent on their purpose.

Each time Manuel made an acceptance speech, he thanked his parents, the members of his team, and all of his supporters. Then they'd go backstage for a short while, then he'd come back to sit with me, he glanced at me often as if to check on me.

I took in the experience. As I watched others in the theater, trying to remain casual, but seeing some people that I would never have imagined seeing in person was making my heart smile. And most

132

appeared happy to see Manuel with me, as we collected lots of smiles, waves, and winks.

CoDéy won an award as well. As shocked as she pretended to be for the cameras in her face, she knew she deserved that. From young girls to old women, her songs were blasting all over the country, singing and gyrating to her music for the whole summer! CoDéy walked up only with her male friend, but he stood far off to the side as she accepted her award.

Buck got up and headed out the auditorium doors, which seemed to concern Manuel, his demeanor subtly changed to more vigilant. Looking side to side occasionally with his foot quietly tapping on the carpet; Buck's presence seemed to have the same significance as a toddler's missing security blanket. I grabbed his hand, so he'd remember I was here for him too.

CoDéy had a long list of thank yous, she included Manuel and his camp in them. I smiled at him, I thought it was nice she still thanked him even though they were not together.

"Hey, let's get out of here," Manuel whispered to me a few seconds before the end of CoDéy's speech.

The last two artists left to perform weren't anyone I cared to see; besides I decided over an hour ago that I would rather just be alone somewhere getting to know more about Manuel. As cool as the environment was, he had my attention and he'd already won the awards that he was nominated for.

I thought it seemed a little rude to leave while she was speaking, but Manuel looked ready to go. We silently got up, and I followed behind him down the aisle toward the exit elevators. "I have to go to the restroom."

"They have a restroom in the lounge, we can go there on the way out." Manuel told me as we entered the large elevator, he pushed the button for the first floor. "Come over and kiss me while I have you alone for 30 seconds."

"I did read that orgasms are more intense when you have to pee," I informed him flirtatiously, walking over and giving him a big kiss.

Manuel leaned over and pushed every button on the elevator panel, "Let's get some more time."

I giggled as he came over to my side of the elevator and we kissed. Sadly, we were quickly interrupted at the next level when three people joined us, one familiar face and two other ladies with her. The first thing they did was congratulate Manuel, one is an aspiring solo artist in the industry, but from my students I heard her career wasn't doing so well due to her recent content. Manuel spoke politely with them as he held me close, by his tone and body language I could see he wasn't a fan of hers.

Once we were off the elevator he took me to an elite lounge where there were open bars, hor'devours, and very important people. There were artists and actors casually walking around the lounge conversing! From artists I pirated music from in high school to the common faced reality television types, many went out of their way to come over to speak to Manuel.

Manuel introduced me with almost every hello. It was cool seeing him interact with his peers. Peers that on any average day in the street I might walk over to and ask for an autograph. But I played it cool as he walked me to the restroom.

Immediately upon entering the restroom I recognized CoDéy standing at the sink, for someone who won an award she did not look very cheerful. She stood just a few feet in front of me, adjusting her eyelash. I had to walk past her to get to the stall.

"Hey, congratulations, CoDéy!" I said with a friendly smile, she didn't even look up at me once. "You looked great on stage tonight."

"Yeah, it's funny how some people can't even sit through a speech. And my dress was almost late, now I get why. People who fuck around with my time vex me," she said with a smirk, then paused, "What's your name again?"

"Acacia," I told her, enunciating slowly because no one ever gets in on the first try.

She was shorter than I thought, and with the bathroom lighting I could see she was wearing a lot of makeup. Still beautiful nonetheless but humbling for me to see it wasn't as natural as it appeared in the media.

"You're here with my fiancé right?" She paused, looking at her hand lovingly. "I mean, ex-fiancé, thanks to me really... that heavy ass engagement ring had my poor ring finger sore all the time. I had to drop him and that rock for my own security and sanity. But you can enjoy."

She's a bitch?

"Are you talking about Manuel? Fuck that cheater, CoDéy! All the money and time you busted your ass in the studio last year, don't let him steal this moment. What did my psychic tell you? You will become a tree producing nothing but fruit sis! You are winning right now, don't throw this away for no man." One of her friend's advised from the bathroom stall.

"Yes, we're definitely talking about my main." CoDéy laughed, brushing off her friend and stretching out the word fiancé whenever she said it. "So y'all dating?"

I nodded awkwardly, "Well, I'm here with him tonight."

"What do you *do,* you look like you have a real... *job*?" she asked frankly. "Like a J-O-B."

Her friend chuckled, "Like, just over broke."

"I'm a teacher," I took Manuel's suggestion and claimed my future as well. "Also, a writer, entrepreneur, and as of recently, curriculum developer."

"Sounds boring," the eyelash flunky trying to help CoDéy commented.

"Well, I was waiting to see who the chosen one was going to be," she said, sarcastically while glancing at me up and down, frustrating her friend who struggled with the lash.

The friend glanced at me for a second, "You think this is her?"

"Hell, they are holding hands, kissing in public, in the club with his hand on her pussy," she snapped at her friend for questioning her. Then looked back at me, "And y'all in public at a televised event? *Where I am*, that's called bold."

"There's no disrespect, sorry if it came off that way," I told her honestly, almost in disbelief that she was being so immature, especially when she was here with someone else as well.

Feeling uncomfortable with their disposition, I walked in the bathroom stall, but CoDéy continued to speak from the other side of my stained-glass door.

"Nah, he's being disrespectful, can't expect anything from you. You're cute though, and you look smart. He did say I was not intelligent enough for him, complaining about my lyrics, when clearly we see he had the money to hire a writer for me. Yet, my project was always getting pushed back." She said, "He also said that I didn't seem very motherly. You look like a mom, you a single mom?"

"Trust, he couldn't have afforded me having to work with you. Yup, I am smart, he really loves that." I responded, gloating sarcastically, she wasn't very bright and probably didn't get the insult. "I do have a son as well. But like I was saying, we are just getting to know each other."

"Just be careful with him, he's not exactly what he seems." She warned, sounding slightly genuine. "You have to be cautious with him. The same people he has serving you now will turn on you for him in a second. Watch your own back."

"You think he's dangerous?" I asked her, coming out of my stall.

"Him?" She thought about it for a second, "He's not as squeaky clean as he has so many believing, but he sure will make it look that way. And so will everyone around him. He's the golden child, he can do no wrong, and if he does... they'll cover it up."

"Oh, he's not the paradisiacal man they think!" Her friend said, pointing to a slightly noticeable stain on CoDéy's dress. "Look at this blood on her hand designed dress."

"Can't you read between the lines, or did you just sign up for the sparkly lights?" CoDéy told me, "Buck punched my date on the right side of his head, blood leaking out of that man's ear. Just now walked right backstage. No one said anything. Security is everywhere, even the police. It's Manuel, damn near everyone getting something from his pocket."

"That wasn't no punch he did, he had a blade or something in his hand." CoDéy's friend interjected, "Her date is on the way to the hospital as we speak. Manuel got him a police escort and everything."

"The worst thing that'll happen to them is Mimi is going to slap both of them for ruining my clothes!"

That was the dress I saw at the shop beside mine, we brought that dress with us? "Mimi made my dress, too."

"I bet she did, she's just as part of the brainwashing as the jewelry. Grant your wishes, then siphon your life and energy from you." CoDéy shook her head as if she felt a little sorry for me. "He's got tons of mommy issues."

I wasn't sure about her, "Well thanks for the heads up."

She sighed, "I really can't say too much because all the walls around Manuel talk. One day you are wearing a million-dollar engagement ring on a video call then you notice he's been flying your personal stylist in private once you notice her luggage behind him on the call."

Was she talking about Stephanie? Was Stephanie CoDéy's stylist?

CoDéy went back to fixing her makeup with her female companion, carrying on as if I were already gone.

"Nice to meet you." I said, leaving the restroom, not sure of exactly how I should take the newfound information from his ex.

Manuel was outside the restroom holding his three awards and taking a photo with a fan, when he saw me and came over.

"You ready to go celebrate?" He had a huge smile, and a kiss for me. "Almost time for the afterparty, gotta make some room or buy a new trophy case."

136

"Congratulations, I'm happy for you." I told him, once he moved his lips and let me breathe. I tried to warn him we had company coming behind him, but I was too late, "CoDéy is–."

CoDéy had come out of the restroom with her two friends, the one I saw correcting her lash and my old friend, Leopard Lady, from the nightclub afterparty. "Manuel, I'm proud of you too... Babe."

"Thanks." He replied, he ignored her when she opened up her arms for a hug, he only shook his head and held my hand pulling me to the exit. CoDéy made a pissed off face at me.

"Did you know your security guard punched her date?" I whispered to Manuel as we walked away.

He shrugged, brushing it off slightly, "Yeah, I talked to him about it."

Be humble enough to learn, but smart enough not to become a follower.

@AcaciaIvy2020

11

When Jenny said there was no party like a DeCreed party, she was right. It was more elegant than I expected for sure, but somehow with an equal amount of *hood*.

The location was a huge pristine white building. I overheard some of the guests in the pool area say it is labeled as a palace that cost in the likes of 45.5 million dollars. I bet the architect never imagined the home filled with loud bass and provocative lyrics from Hip Hop music, with a marijuana cloud surrounding his structure. There was a huge ice sculpture in the shape of the DeCreed symbol in the backyard as a backdrop to a big, heated pool surrounded by a lazy river. There were bartenders and very sexy cocktail waitresses walking around serving drinks in G-string bathing suits with heels. More impressive were the naked, but body painted women swinging from aerial silks in the grand living room.

I kept my celeb sighting reactions to a minimum of absolute zero, for it was too intimate of a party to be a fangirl, but there were a few familiar faces there. Manuel made sure to introduce me to everyone he spoke with, and they all seemed so loving to him.

I found it interesting that in almost all of Manuel's relationships and interactions that I've been watching, everyone treated him like a true king. Spoke to him with gratitude and admiration, even those people relatively just as wealthy spoke with high regard, and Manuel handled it most humbly. He treated people the same, whether they were fans or famous.

Most people at the party were in the DeCreed family, only a small handful of others were from other labels or organizations.

He proved his words to be true, I let him lead, gave him close to 100% trust, and he made sure I was happy.

Although it was obvious I was tagging along with Manuel, he didn't make me feel that way. He kept me in the loop with inside jokes and in any conversation I may have gotten lost in, he cleared up. We mixed and mingled with small groups for a little over an hour, then he took me on the dance floor, and we danced for about five songs.

"This place is so gorgeous, that theater and that gym will be in my future home. And did you notice that the aquarium glass is on the other wall of the pool?" I asked as we took a walk around the palace.

He smiled at me, "Yes I did."

"I want that in my house one day."

"What else do you want?" He asked attentively, he really wanted to know.

I shook my head at him, "Stop trying to buy me."

He gave me an aggravated look, but he knew I was playing.

Chris came by asking to borrow Manuel for a little, they left me in the *safe* hands of the DeCreed wives and girlfriends in the meantime. Christina, Chris' wife, and about five other ladies he left me with referred to their circle as the Sweethearts.

"Y'all look so cute together," Christina told me, once the introductions were done and the men were gone, they left us to discuss business in another room. "The chemistry is clear between you. You'll find that it's hard to stand out when your literal purpose is to be in the background."

"Standing in the background is how Christina does it, but all sweethearts aren't the same." Tania, a Sweetheart that introduced herself as an influencer said.

Christina shrugged, "I'm the sweetest Sweetheart, current interim President until Ma says otherwise."

I smiled at her, they all stared at me. "Sweetheart, that's a song! Is the song a dedication to your group?

"Of course, it is," someone quickly snapped at me, I couldn't tell who said it.

"How long have you been together?" A Sweetheart named Val asked.

I didn't *want* to tell them much, but I reminded myself of my goal to make more of an effort to build relationships with women. I needed to step out of the box and make new friends as an adult, build connections with women who are more like minded with me. Who better to start with then the ladies of the DeCreed men, it'd be worthwhile for me to get in with them if Manuel and I were to get serious.

"I wouldn't say we're *together*; we're just getting to know each other." I answered humbly, however by the looks on their faces it wasn't a sufficient answer. They wanted more information. "I used to love that song, Sweethearts."

"Ok, but you must *know* each other in some way," Val walked around me dramatically, eyeing me up and down as the ladies tracked us with their eyes. "Do you know where you are, Bay-bae? Not just anybody gets in here. This is a DeCreed party; we are damn near one step away from Chateau Eaton."

Christina shook her head, "This isn't even close to the chateau."

"Well, no one gets in whose 'no one', Especially not with Manuel. He's making it obvious he's feeling you; everybody can see it. He brought you to the show, too and rumors of an afterparty?" One named Drea added, she had enough jewelry to purchase an apartment building, "And you shopping with Mimi, got matching clothes, too. Very Manuel."

"Thanks, I like him, he's a good vibe." I agreed neutrally, remembering Jenny's warning not to answer too many questions, not sure if these women were potential friends or frienemies. I was sensing a little bit of both, but that could've just been my old emotion, paranoia, visiting me.

"Of course, you like him," one name Desirae, who seemed intent on being a snob added. "Everybody likes all of them, but not just anybody deserves to walk right in. None of us walked right in. Everyone must follow the rules that come with being with them."

Drea nodded, softening the tone of Desirae's message to me, "We are all happy he has someone, but there's rules and processes for a reason. We gotta follow them to keep the systems running smoothly."

They sounded like they'd gone to an orientation or training on how to date DeCreed members. Although hearing the rules would be intriguing, I would decline signing up for any more structural systems designed to control me or interfere with my thoughts.

"He just *deserves* a good woman." Christina redirected the group to be more positive. "Don't let anything scare you away from him, the haters will come, and you stick by him. No matter what they say." Christina added, looking at the others for confirmation. "Are you in love?"

I smiled politely at all of them, not wanting to be anyone's argument topic. I redirected them to talk about themselves. "It's still early, although it feels kinda fast, but I'm enjoying getting to know him, so far so good. Any advice on these kinds of relationships?"

"Oh, fast is gonna seem like an understatement, they're different. You're gonna go through some bullshit, so hold on tight and keep your patience."

140

"Get a side nigga, but don't fuck the opps unless you are 100% done, he'll never respect you again." A sweetheart warned me. "Most opps aren't respecting you either."

"Don't fuck with the bros either, it's almost impossible to come back from that. And don't leave, that's not going to help him or you, it's going to hurt your pocketbook if anything."

"And it's not always going to get you a new bag," Val chimed in with her advice. "Don't try to fight the groupies either, you will just look dumb, just keep up with all your gyno appointments. That's my advice after five years of this."

"Vanessa, that's so gross," Christina laughed. "Don't tell her that."

"Or you could be in denial like Christina and the other Sweethearts here," Vanessa joked. "Believe any of what he says at your own risk." Vanessa paused before singing lyrics to Sweetheart. "You can be my sweet, sweet, sweet, sweet, sweet."

"Or can you spell it S-U-I-T-E, cause as the non-delusional know, the remix wasn't for us!" Val leaned in to say.

"There's another group called the Suite Hearts. Basic ass bitches who will meet DeCreed in any city, any time, to fuck any hole in a timely manner."

"That's a myth!" Christina screamed loudly, Val just shrugged, she believed it. "The Suite Hearts are a myth, the only people that can see them are the ones who want to see them. They are as real as angels and ghosts, my husband shares everything with me, and he's never met a Suite Heart."

Val raised her eyebrows, "And you've never met a ghost, but you know they exist."

"I'm more of the, believe in angels type." Christina told us.

"Tell the angel in the hospital, a Suite Heart, in the last city with a hole in her stomach." Vanessa mumbled, holding up both her hands to me. "Not that I encourage violence. In fact, I say, let the dirty girls do the dirty work. I welcome the angels, the ghosts, and the Suite Hearts! Less work for me."

It was a Suite Heart who got hurt at the concert, how sad.

I immediately thought of how disgusting the men were acting backstage at the concert. Those were the Sweethearts' boyfriends and husbands they were fighting and shooting other women over? The same men who were groping women and getting danced on by women in G-strings and body paint. Why did they sign up for that?

"Don't say that Vanessa. Whether or not the Suite Hearts exists," Desirae shrugged innocently, "Every one of us Sweethearts has got a groupie, side chick, or second- or third-family story. And my philosophy is, if the comeback apology is 10 times louder than the bitch, he can come back home."

"Don't feel obligated to adopt hers," Drea interjected. "You'll see how these hoes will throw themselves at your man, they are tempting at times. They're only human."

"It seems slightly unfair to only blame the women who are living in this fantasy your husbands have lured them into. If your men are having sex with them, the men are more guilty than the women." But their faces I could see I wasn't making a good impression on my new *friends*. "You don't agree?"

A few of the ladies looked dumbfounded, "Our husbands must portray an image to pay the bills, it's not personal, it's music. The groupies and desperate women looking to get ahead off scamming someone else's man, need to realize that."

I shook my head, as bad as I wanted to stay on the Sweethearts good side, I didn't see it the same way. "Were you not backstage before that concert? I was shocked by the way both the women *and* the men were behaving! The men weren't acting, they were encouraging it."

"*She's* allowed backstage before shows!" Drea said with a sarcastic laugh, hitting Christina on the shoulder.

"You were backstage?" Christina asked me, I nodded slowly wishing I didn't talk so damn much. "You really shouldn't be backstage before shows, Acacia, it's a big rule around here. The CEO doesn't allow it."

"Okay, well Manuel called me back there. I didn't really know the rules or that there were rules," I said, unnecessarily embarrassed as I have only known this man a day.

Vanessa shrugged, "Manuel is gonna do whatever he wants, everyone knows that."

Thankfully the intimidating Sweethearts backed off me and reminisced with stories about run-ins with groupies and fights with side chicks. I listened half entertained, the other half concerned that maybe this was not the life for me after all. The women were damn near flawless in their own ways, yet they didn't seem to really care that their men were most likely not loyal to them.

Manuel didn't seem as wild as their men, although many fans consider him as the lead artist, he was more chill than most of the others

142

in his group. I may be wrong; he did not seem to seek attention like some of the other men were doing. But what if he did? Would I be sitting here like the Sweethearts?

It seemed through their stories that the Sweethearts lived in a different world than me, with infinite opportunities and fun just for being in their relationships. The world they were playing in came with its own rules that all the Sweethearts were playing by; they were expecting me to play by them too. Some directives, mantras, and affirmations to survive as the lovers of DeCreed men were slowly slipping out as the liquors kicked into the Sweethearts' system.

I believed a few of the ladies were a little jealous, more than they were upset that I broke a couple rules. Some of the women were not going to like me no matter what I said or did, I studied those types of people, I knew how to work them. First, try to understand them. Second, smile like a friend as you hand them the rope to figuratively hang themselves.

I questioned if dating a man like this would be worth the stories the ladies told me. It was glamorous and I was impressed by the name brands they wore, the nice things they had were attractive, but was it worth being submissive to someone you know isn't exclusive or honest with you?

Considering my own dating roster, it wasn't too much worse than what I was doing in my own life. On a much smaller scale.

"So, is Stephanie styling you?" The shadiest of the women, by the name of Tamara asked. I saw Christina give her a look on my behalf, but a few of them chuckled. She shrugged with a devious, bitchy grin at the other ladies.

"Don't be messy, Tamara." Christina told her.

Drea teased, "Tamara was a Suite Heart before she was one of us."

"Suite Hearts and Sweethearts, pronounced the same way and getting the same dick and the same green ass dollars that y'all can't trace back to them. I was not one of them, but I do not knock their hustle. They're not as dumb as you think." I noticed that Tamara is comfortable in her role as the group's biggest bitch. "Stephanie played the cards she got dealt."

"I believe she got let go," I told Tamara nonchalantly. "Was she a friend of yours?"

"Canceling Stephanie?" Desirae was surprised. "Highly doubt that."

Messy Tamara looked shocked, then retorted. "Manuel would never."

"Hey, hey, hey, you never know, they are breaking rules already." Vanessa winked at me. "Have you been to the Chateau?"

"What's that?" I asked finally.

Desirae chimed back in, "That's a no, but Steph has."

"Look, I'm not in any competition for him. I'm just getting to know him?"

Drea shrugged, "What's more to know?"

"Well, just so you know, once you are done with him, you're done with us, too. It's not to be a bitch, it could happen to any of us, and it's a conflict of interest to the group." Tamara informed me of another rule, "If you leave him or he leaves you, you get a grace period to get him back, then you're on your own."

"I'll remember not to get too close to you guys," I joked, but no one laughed, apparently the truth behind that joke was too real for some. "I gotta run to the restroom, I'll be back."

I excused myself politely, Jenny was right, they are vultures.

Christina followed behind me as I walked to the restroom, "Don't worry about anything those girls said, they barely like themselves or the men that are cheating on them. I spent the whole last year trying to unite the Sweethearts, we are a work in progress, but you'll fit right in."

I raised my eyebrows with a forced smile, "I don't think I want to."

"Trust me, you are gonna love it on this side. My only advice to you is never just take anyone else's advice, it is not universal advice is only someone else's perspective. Just be always real with you and do what's best for you." She said with deep eyes, "You will be just fine, and you call me if you need anything."

"Has Chris ever cheated?" I asked, she nodded her head without a hint of shame.

"No one is perfect, not me and not you," she said to me. "There's more to a person than the mistakes they make, do not expect flawlessness from man. Stop overthinking and come back to the table when you're done."

"I don't think they want me back over there either," I admitted. "I keep breaking rules that I don't know exist."

"We are all protective of the group, it's nothing personal. If anything, they might be a little jealous of how he is treating you, everyone sees you glowing, plus you are breaking all the damn rules. Besides most of them were CoDéy's army for years, you have big shoes to fill, and it'll take time. They don't really like the rules either, although they help minimize distractions."

"No one ever likes the rules." It seemed like Manuel's exciting world had just as many rules as mine. Switching one group's crumbling laws for another's just felt like a lateral move that I was not up to embracing. "When do I get to see what I'm signing up for?"

"I'll fill you in on everything, but I am glad he met you. You seem like a lovely woman, and he deserves that." Then she leaned in and whispered, "Don't worry about the rules too much."

She tapped her phone against mine and it vibrated, her contact information transferred over to my phone, and she sashayed off back in the direction of the Sweethearts.

I sighed, recognizing that creating and breaking the rules just might be another part of life.

After using the bathroom, I took a small tour around the party, grabbed a couple appetizers, and hoped to bump into Manuel as I roamed around. Although I didn't see him, getting a glimpse at the other party guests was just as impressive as the venue and decor itself.

Inevitably my walk around the party somehow led me back outside by the pool with the Sweethearts group. If Manuel and I did become more than just friends, these were probably going to be my new friends. I determined I should try to make and build connections with them.

However, this time as I got close to the Sweetheart's table I saw CoDéy was now sitting with them. It was too late to bust a U-turn, I had to keep walking over to their section. She looked relaxed, like she was having a good time, she even had a drink.

I flashed my friendly smile at everyone upon approaching them. This time I was met with much less eye contact from the other ladies.

"Hey, he brought you *here* too!" CoDéy called out to me surprised, I wondered where her poor date went after being assaulted as she partied here with his assailant.

"Hey CoDéy," I remarked, putting on a nice smile.

"What's your name again?" She asked after a dramatic pause, but she knew.

I shook my head, before turning away I told her. "It doesn't even matter."

"You are absolutely right, you don't matter." She agreed loudly, a few of the wives and girlfriends chuckled at her, most just sitting in the awkward silence. They seemed to like her in their group, or relatively respected her, I'm sure she was practically a founding member.

I was the outsider at this point, I didn't want to look like a bitch and walk away, but I knew that was the right thing to do. I was not going to fight over this man I just met!

I eyed her up and down before turning around to retreat. It was hard to believe that I really used to like this woman as an artist, I truly admired her work and here she was disrespecting me because I was dating her ex-fiancé.

"CoDéy, I sincerely don't have a problem with you." I told her, making eye contact with her in hopes she could see I was not an enemy.

"You should though, Acacia, I'm a mother fuckin' problem, Groupie!" She shot at me; she could tell that bothered me. "You think you're the first or the last? The ladies were over here trying to figure out if you are a Suite Heart, but I told them you would barely cut it as a Suite Heart."

Groupie? Suite heart? I thought. I didn't even chase him! He found me!

"Chill CoDéy," Drea tried to hush her.

The other women and wives were silently watching for my reaction, holding back laughs from the looks on a few faces. Christina even watched me quietly, but she looked empathetic towards me. They all probably thought I'm just a groupie.

"Not my problem, Hun." I reminded her, walking back into the palace and finding a seat at the indoor bar.

That direct line I had to my peace was not picking up, I let CoDéy get under my skin.

My smartwatch would have monitored my breathing and walked me through a mindfulness breathing technique had I been wearing it. Unfortunately, I wore the yearly salary of a 20-year veteran teacher on my wrist instead. Therefore, I sought for liquor to clear my head.

Although I was not going to drink tonight, I walked to the bar once I decided a small drink would help take the edge off. I was feeling very uptight, and I didn't want to let her ruin my mood.

I took a few deep breaths then texted Manuel.

Manuel	
	Hey. Where are you? I'm ready to go back to the hotel.

I told myself I'd give him five minutes to respond before I ordered a rideshare out of here. CoDéy pissed me off. Why would she even come to his party when she's not with him anymore? Why would she not go to her own celebration?

Honestly, it wouldn't be so bad that she was here if she wasn't being such a bitch. I really did love her music; she was practically my whole playlist several months back.

I cautiously sat down at the bar beside a man who had his head face down, hoodie up, presumably asleep based on my years of teaching adolescents. There weren't many seats left or to begin with, and he seemed harmless as he was asleep. Although there was a slight odor, it wasn't unbearable.

"Mind if I sit here?" I asked the back of the man's head; I think he groaned yes. "Thanks Sleepyhead."

In front of Sleepyhead was a shot and a whimsically colored drink.

I looked at my phone for Manuel's response, nothing.

"You picked an extremely great seat, what can I get for you?" The bartender asked, she had on a corset, fishnet thigh tights and a G-string that was practically invisible against her thickness.

As a straight woman I couldn't keep my eyes off how stunning she was, I quickly thought about Manuel being around *these* types of women daily and sighed. Beautiful, voluptuous in all the right places, way more seductive than me (and I read that book six times!) Of course, Manuel wouldn't want to be in a serious relationship, he keeps his options open because look at his options!

I kicked the thought out of my mind, a difficult strategy I was learning to be disciplined at but gave up and ordered a drink.

"I'll have a mai tai," I told her.

The bartender was pointing to the sleeping man beside me trying to mouth something, but I didn't understand what she was trying to say. She had a smile on her face, so I just awkwardly smiled back. Once she walked away I noticed that she was pointing at the intoxicated man's designer wallet that had fallen from his pocket.

"Gonna give you an extra heavy pour, look–," she talked in code, pointing again, there was even more cash on the floor.

I clenched my teeth at her, "Wow, that's a lot."

"Wanna split it?" She asked, fixing my drink in front of me with an extra strong pour. I looked down at the money and shook my head no, she seemed disappointed.

So *those* are the kind of women Manuel's around? Maybe he does want something real after all, getaway from the shady people. I convinced myself.

I got down and picked up all the cash and the wallet and tried to get it back together for the stranger. The amount of cash was almost too thick to fit, I knew it wasn't going to fold. I tapped Sleepyhead a couple times to get his attention, but he was too fucked up, I sat it in front of him on the bar as I took out my own money to leave her a tip on my own drink.

The bartender shook her head disappointed at me as she left me with my drink, I tipped her and checked my phone for a response from Manuel. Nothing.

I turned to leave but felt bad knowing poor Sleepyhead would probably be getting his cash stolen any minute.

"Sleepyhead, I'm putting your wallet under your arm, it fell on the floor." I tried to tell him over the loud music. I propped his wallet under his right elbow with the overflowing money facing inward so no one would see it.

As soon as I lifted his arm, Sleepy Head, Young Todd turned around and looked me right in the face.

"Oh my, Sleepy Todd?" I jumped when he turned. "Sorry! I was putting your wallet under you; it probably fell when you were sleeping. I didn't know that was you!"

"Acacia," Young Todd said, trying to sober himself for a moment, he had a horrible stench of alcohol mixed in with breath every time he talked. "I love your name, that's how I remembered you. It's heavenly."

"Thank you," I mumbled, trying to hold my breath. "You know, I saw there were couches back behind the restroom area if you want to lay down."

He laughed, touching my shoulder, the odor from his mouth lingered even when his mouth was closed. "I fuckin spewed puke on that couch, that's why I came back over here."

I nodded, "I see. Do you need me to find or call anyone to come get you?"

"No, no, no, I'm good. Got a thick-thick one coming to pick me up any second and if she doesn't come I'll call my wife, don't worry about me, concern though little mama. You are a good person; I can tell you work with children cause your heart ain't too fucked up yet. These people out here are savage little mama, most of them ain't real. I promise."

The irony of expecting people to be real with you, when you yourself aren't even real to the person you vowed to love, the old me might've said. "Well take care of yourself."

"You're a teacher right? It's different from when I was in school." He struggled just to move his head to look me up and down. "I wish my teachers looked like you, I probably would've gone to class, and finished high school just so I can see you after prom night."

"Gross, nothing is more disgusting to me than having a sexual relationship with someone attended a prom." I made a puzzled face at him, this is not who I thought he was, it's not the image he portrays in his music, online, or through his philanthropic efforts! I was lowkey disgusted. Cheating on his spouse and jokes about pedophilia, how was he my favorite anything? He was just a character playing a role.

"Manuel is the undeniable truth, even the ones who hate him admire that, everything is verifiable," he mumbled, drooling on his arm, his eyelids involuntarily shutting as he spoke. Yet somehow, like most people I'd been talking to recently, something in his presence still perked up as he spoke about his friend. "He'll do you right, you don't gotta worry. I know I'll make somebody's mama cry if they son try him. He's one of my 20 percent."

"It's good to have real friends," I told him.

"Friends? Fuck friends! You got more to fear from your friends than your enemies, hire your enemies, they'll keep it honest. Everybody out here is screaming 'Keep it 100' and they always sitting in the 80-percenters section. Don't support you or your business, looking for a free ticket, close to the stage or on stage, to impress people they don't even know or don't care about them. Buck taught me who we are is completely our choice, we get to decide every day who we want to be, people decide how they treat you. Everything is a choice." Young Todd seemed very troubled with his drunk thoughts. "Yet, Manuel says it's the ignorance that they choose, therefore forgive, not to take it personal, as if we can't blame them cause they can only keep it as real as they choose to know. Well, I'm blaming everyone for their actions."

"True," I mumbled, not sure how I now feel about my once idolized Young Todd.

Young Todd put his cup next to mine, comparing the drinks. "Acacia, I mean they will sell you out for less than what I make in one day at a show. Be careful of your friends, love your family."

"Have you happened to see him? Manuel, I was looking for him." I tried to change the subject.

Young Todd rambled on, while my favorite artist slurred his words. I still respected who he was as a person. "Manuel ain't never been in nobody 80 percent, he's not fake, I'll tell you that. That 80 they will get you jammed up, turn their back on you or have ulterior motives. Lil Sis, they'll even steal from you. Do you know how many times I've been robbed by somebody I would've given it to if they just asked me?"

I shook my head no, poor drunk Young Todd.

"Too many. Manuel's a 20-percenter. Listen to this, I got robbed 8 hours before a show and you know what Manuel did? This man had me wearing more jewelry than was even stolen by the time I got on stage. Not just me, ask anyone about what he's done for them. That man's in everybody 20 percent, he keeps it real."

"That seems to be everyone's gist. How'd you get the percentages?" I inquired.

He smiled, shining a little gold in his mouth, and before dropping his head back down, in a sober voice he whispered, "I can see spirits, and every time there are ten people, I always see 8 evil spirits and two light spirits. The light ones lead you to the right paths."

"Oh, wow. Well, it was nice to see you again," I told Young Todd as I waved goodbye and took just a few steps away.

"Double shots!" CoDéy called out loudly to the bartender, interrupting my thoughts from the other side of the bar. "One for me and one for me and Manuel's new *friend*, Acacia!"

"No thanks," I declined abruptly, she was not my kind of friend.

"My ex-fiancé won't let you drink tonight?" She laughed, "I remember those damn days, fighting for my free will or just a little sense of being ordinary. He pretends to support your independent decisions, then silently judges you as you fail in front of him, just waiting for you to beg for his help. Undercover control freak, if you let him be. Now I drink whenever the fuck I want to, shamelessly. And put out tracks, whenever I want to, too!"

"Well, that's not really my problem nor my business." I held up my drink and politely declined, "I'm just not interested in more drinks."

"Oh, you feel like you're in paradise right now. Of course, you're not interested. Your ignorant ass doesn't even realize how dangerous the power that man is. But keep that same energy when you find out, Sis. Don't be one of those bitches that call after the warning."

"I'm not your *sis*, CoDéy, and I do not want to talk to you, nor get any advice from you about Manuel. I tried to be nice to you, but you made it very clear that you don't want me around. So, drop it. Cause at this point I honestly don't even want you around me." I watched her face get eviler as I attempted to hurt her feelings. "So, let's do our own thing... separately. Like you and Manuel."

"You'll see just how separate we are, silly ass groupie. Hell, if you're even around him long enough," she told me. "Maybe I'll let you fuck us."

She took both shots she ordered, then laughed at me in an overly dramatic fashion.

"Girl, bye." I mumbled to myself, taking a deep gulp, pretending not to be phased by this childish brat!

She stumbled when leaving with her shots. A random man, possibly a waiter, walked by and tried to help her balance, but she pushed him off angrily. "Don't touch me! What the hell is wrong with you? Why would you think you could touch me!"

The helpful man just held up both hands, claiming his innocence, but she had chosen him as the object of her aggression.

"Who even are you? Do not touch me!" She yelled at him, he ignored CoDéy. She looked at the bartender who'd been watching all along. "Get me another drink, what the fuck."

"I can't." The bartender told her. "I'm not serving you any more alcohol."

CoDéy looked at the bartender with that same mean look, then used her forearm to sweep a small collection of glasses from the bar to the floor. Glasses crashed loudly and liquids splashed to the floor. She laughed upon hearing the glass smash.

One of the security guards came over and stood close to CoDéy cautiously. I recognized him from yesterday at the penthouse back home and the studio session I went to with Manuel.

"Get Manuel," CoDéy told the security guard.

"CoDéy, what are you doing? CoDéy?" He asked her, hoping she'd snap out of her drunken episode. "Don't do this here, you know how it's going to end up."

I stood by a fast asleep Young Todd and watched her turn into a spoiled witch.

"Is everybody here going to hate me and choose Manuel's side, because that's what y'all did." She yelled at him matter of factly, then knocked down more empty glasses and drinks on the other side of the bar. "You all said I was *family*, but I ain't heard from any of you in months, you all chose him because of who he is. Somebody go get Manuel now!"

Buck walked over to her quickly and grabbed her, pulling her towards the door. She was super light, hell I could probably carry her myself, but he slung her over his shoulder with force.

I was so intensely watching the drama that I accidentally picked up Young Todd's drink, I didn't notice until I felt a wretched burn in my throat after my big chug. I was disgusted as I cringed and put his drink back down.

"Don't touch me, Nate!" She screamed at Buck, punching at him with hard blows. "This is your damn fault. Go get Him!" She demanded Buck. Buck stood with his arms bear hugging CoDéy's thighs as she continued to fight.

I wondered how many times in the past he had to remove her from an unfavorable position in such a manner.

Manuel came from behind me and took my hand, cool and calm as usual. "Sorry I just got your messages, let's go. I just got your message. I didn't know she was here being an idiot."

"It's fine." I replied, grabbing my clutch and following behind as he led me through the crowd. "That was Young Todd at the bar, asleep, did you see him? He was pretty drunk."

"He'll be okay, they'll get him home." He shook his head but assured me of my favorite artist's safety. "None of this is fine. We're supposed to be on a date, they were talking business, you had to see Todd and CoDéy. I don't want you around this on a date, our first date, I should've picked something else."

We walked to the truck, but with Buck having the keys we ended up waiting outside the vehicle for a while before he would make it over to us.

"Thank you for coming with me to the award show and this, I really was not planning on coming. I haven't been to any of these over a few years, it hasn't been fun in a while, but you make me want to get up. I needed to meet you."

"I would never even have dreamed of being there, sitting with you and all DeCreed." I was flattered, "So no need to thank me."

"You must've dreamed it, or it wouldn't happen," he told me with a smile. "Everybody likes you, too. They all see what I see, even the ones who don't want to admit it. You're invaluable."

"Wow they definitely don't act like they like me." I laughed, recalling the Sweethearts sideways comments, not to mention the horrible looks from his security staff since I've been around.

"Todd likes you," he said with a slight laugh. "You're *favorite*."

I clenched my teeth and shook my head, "I'm a little upset that I saw him today, he was not who I believed he was, not even close. Kinda ruined it for me."

"Damn, but whose fault is that? Yours? The fans. Idolizing people who are not any different than yourself, treating them like gods." He asked, "He's human. He's an artist. Don't be too tough on him, don't judge, you don't know what it takes to produce that art in a world like his. Lesser men would have faked their death years ago just to run from some of what he's been through."

"You're right, I don't mean to judge," I admitted shamefully. "He was drunk, but he said he'd kill for you. That's radical. A person would feel that strongly about you."

"A lot of people tell me they'll kill for me, that they want to be my shooters. The fact that Young Todd told you that is proof that I'd never even ask him to. I'd never ask any of them to, I don't have to ask, that's not even what I'd want." He smirked with his shrug. "But some men I give them a job, pay them very well."

"That's impressive." I considered a world where people were willing to risk their life for me.

He tilted his head, "Why does that impress you?"

"Todd's a big deal, is the love reciprocal? Would you die for Todd, and these other guys that say that?" I asked rhetorically.

He side-eyed me, lifted me up and sat me on the hood of the SUV. Stalling with his response, Manuel paused then tasted my lips with a couple quick kisses. He kept his hands on my waist, slowly massaging my waist.

"You'd be surprised what I would die for," he started to tell me before getting interrupted.

"No love for me, Manuel?" CoDéy asked, walking belligerently toward us, Buck was close at her heels, but not stopping her. "I'll share with her. Because you didn't say shit to me all night! Nothing, not even a *sincere* congratulations. Of all people you know how hard I was working for this moment. Because yooouuu," she slurred, "told me I was not ready

153

to release an album yet! You said I wasn't ready, that I need more work to get to the top, but I won and I'm winning!"

I hopped off the car just in case she tried anything, I'd been in enough fights to know you don't want to start off in a vulnerable position. Manuel held my hand tight and turned around glaring at her.

"Congratulations CoDéy." He told her, then sternly looked at his staff who stood right by her. "Give me the key."

Buck unlocked the door, but CoDéy stood in front of the door Manuel was going to get into.

"I need to talk to you about something first Manuel." CoDéy spoke to him as if we all weren't watching.

"We don't have anything to talk about, move." He said, his voice was stern and angry with her, as if she was a teenage child. In contrast, when she spoke to him she spoke in a meek voice, but yelled loudly when she wanted the small forming audience to hear.

"Talk to me Manuel." She whispered, then yelled and pushed him on his chest when he began shaking his head, "Talk to me!"

Manuel looked at Buck who seemed too relaxed in his level of security in this situation. Then Buck physically picked her up and moved her out the way from the door, but he let her go so quickly. Manuel opened the backdoor for me, then he followed behind me, however CoDéy was back and standing in front of the door so it would not close.

"We're gonna talk. You're gonna talk to me!" She told Manuel, she had tears from her face, and she was practically bright red. "Did you see me tonight? They know who *I* am, Manuel? You said I wasn't ready but look: award winning! Without you! I told you I do not *need* you. You aren't the only way!"

"Buck get us out of here now, now." Manuel said, pushing CoDéy toward Buck, slamming the door barely missing her hand. It was silent other than the muffled commotion on the outside of the vehicle. "Sorry, this is how our date is going."

I nodded at his apology and tried to make light of the situation. "I am not judging."

"Déy, you gotta go home, you want me to get you a ride?" We could hear Buck ask her softly on the other side of the door. He was trying to get her away, but he was nice to her!

Garon would have had her out of here by now.

"Talk to me, Manuel!" She screamed at Manuel's tinted window, looking right past Buck, slamming her fist on the locked door. "Get out the car. Please get out of the car!"

154

I looked at Manuel, his expression was still slightly unbothered, but I could tell he cared about her. Even if not in a romantic way, he still cared.

"I do not mind if you go talk to her," I assured him softly. "Don't ignore her for me. That's someone you were with for years, I get it."

"You don't get it," he told me. "I don't want her. She gets like this often, it means nothing now, I'm fine. We're leaving, I'm tired of protecting her from herself."

I nodded. Trying not to take sides, not judge, he seemed to be sure it was what he wanted to do. Since I was so new to the situation, I wanted to remain unbiased, but there for him.

Manuel opened the door and said very sternly, "Buck, let's go now or stay with her."

"You think that bitch is gonna make me jealous, Manuel? Is that why you brought her here? You think she can be *me?*" She laughed drunkenly. Then yelled at him, "Keep trying! You cannot just simply remake *me*, your fraud! You cannot just find some random *groupie* and make her *ME!*"

I was not fighting her over a man that I am on a first date with! I didn't even want to defend myself, I felt embarrassed for Manuel and even CoDéy. Almost half the party was outside awkwardly watching the scene CoDéy caused.

I've been the hurt ex before, I've honestly done worse than this, but why CoDéy? She is so beautiful, has everything that almost any girl could ever want, but making a fool of herself in front of all these people at who-knows-when in the morning, on the front driveway of a 45-million-dollar palace.

I wondered what truly happened between them, it had to be more than just her not wanting to be with him anymore. Something did not add up.

"Buck, let's go now!" Manuel snapped.

"I'm not leaving her out here!" Buck snapped back at him, more sharply than I would have imagined an employee, then tossed him a set of keys.

"Good, stay with her." Manuel said sarcastically as he got out of the car, then opened the front door to drive.

CoDéy grabbed Manuel's shirt, swallowing her tears muttered, "You can't just fuckin' talk to me Manuel? Why all this?"

I noticed Christina and a few of the ladies from the Sweethearts group were in the crowd that had gathered, no one stepped up to get their friend. Instead, her sweethearts and other people were looking at CoDéy like she was crazy. Not that she seemed to care.

"Open your eyes, look at yourself, have some fuckin' discretion. I don't want to talk to you, CoDéy. I don't want anything to do with you, for real." Manuel snarled at her.

"Calm down," I whispered to him from the back seat, trying my best not to get myself involved, but I felt he was antagonizing her. "Don't make it worse."

He looked back at me sharply, as if I was on her side. "I'm pissed. I'm trying not to snap."

"Oh, just shut up and *be soft*, Bitch!" CoDéy barked at ME, then slapped Manuel. "You haven't trained the new one how to act?"

WTF is happening in my life right now, I questioned.

Manuel's face turned red with anger as soon as she spoke to me, but the slap added injury to insult. Buck immediately stood in between them, she just glared at Manuel's face, happy to have struck an emotional and physical cord.

Where the hell was Garon when I needed him!

"You're a demon." Manuel said to her harshly, but not raising his voice, I wasn't sure which one Buck was holding back at this point. "Leave me alone before you make this worse for yourself."

She didn't care that hair makeup was streaked with tears or even that the tears were still coming. She sounded sincerely sad for a complete bitch. "I seriously only won for you, Manuel. You can't even be happy for me? Come over."

"I don't give a single fuck about you winning," he told her, enunciating every word so deeply, like a knife cutting into her.

CoDéy quickly responded by spitting right in his face, those left in the crowd, "ahhhhed" in unison, she stared into his eyes, half looking like she wanted to hit him, the other half as if she wanted him to kiss her.

"I will fuckin' cancel her Buck get her away from this car," he told him, low enough for just us close to hear.

"Looks like you're choosing, Manuel." She muttered to him softly as Buck finally showed some authority in getting her out the way. "You promised you wouldn't go, what would I expect from the son of an opportunistic prostitute." She looked at me and yelled loud enough for the entire crowd to head. "He made me get an abortion! Did he tell you that?"

"You are DONE!" Manuel told her, looking back and forth between her and the crowd of his friends. "She's done. You will never get a hit again!"

Manuel slammed the driver's side door and got the car going immediately, pulling out of the driveway.

We drove in silence for about ten minutes. I didn't even know where to start, but I knew I needed to start a conversation, or I would regret it.

"So, all that *be soft* talk was bullshit, you're just training me for something? You and her?" I asked, finally deciding on some words to break the long silence. "But that is like your *thing.*"

"Can we not talk right now?" He told me rather sharply, after a heavy sigh.

"Well, then take me home." I told him, just as sharp from the backseat. He asked if I wanted to come to the front, but I shook my head no. "Can we go to the airport? There's nothing in the hotel that's even mine."

He drove for another few minutes then pulled over into a reasonably lit, empty parking lot and put his head down onto the steering wheel. "Is there any way we can please just talk about this tomorrow?" He mumbled.

"I won't be here tomorrow. I'm leaving. I want to go home." I told him, slurring my words. The liquor had kicked in and mixed themselves up with my emotions.

He shook his head, "I told you not to worry about her and now you are leaving."

"And you were dead ass wrong, because look what happened tonight? I am embarrassed to be in that situation! I don't think you two are done at all." I told him. "When's the last time you fucked her?"

"What? I don't keep track of shit like that," He said casually, then forced a laugh. "When's the last time you fucked your baby daddy?"

I shook my head, "He's not trying to humiliate you or throw a big dramatic scene at a party! I don't even know you enough to be going through this weird shit."

"What more do you want to know about me?" He told me sincerely. "I will answer all of your questions, I promise, just not tonight."

"You couldn't have told me she's crazy in love with you and going to immediately hate me?" I shook my head, not willing to wait til tomorrow. "I feel like you lied to me, I just want to go home."

"I didn't lie, were you drinking in there?" He asked, probably noticing the signs of my inebriation as my own head was starting to feel dizzy.

157

I put my forehead into my palms then plopped them on my lap and cried to him, with real tears and boogers. "She was such a bitch to me! I liked her. I like so many of her songs, now my playlist is fucked. She was on my streaming service Top 10 artists last year! CoDéy hates me and I have to hate her too?!" I yelled into my hands, and he rubbed my back trying not to laugh at my drunken stupor. I was coherent enough to be aware, but too drunk to stop talking. "I feel very dizzy."

"I'm sorry that whole thing happened. She was just drunk; I think you might be too." He told me gently, opening the door beside me. "Let's get you some sleep. I'll take you to the airport first thing in the morning."

"Do I have rap beef?" I asked Manuel, wiping my eyes with a sigh.

"No, you're not a rapper, Acacia." He shook his head and smiled warmly at me, but I wasn't falling for it.

"Just take me to the airp—," Manuel grabbed my hair just in time for me to vomit out the door. He rubbed my back and sang softly to me for five minutes as I threw up hanging out the door. I don't even know if he was saying any lyrics, but his voice soothed me.

"Damn. What did you drink?" he told me. "We'll go to the airport first thing in the morning."

I rubbed my throbbing head, "I can get my own flight home. I accidently drank Todd's drink."

"You'll be asleep any second now if you had that. You are stubborn as fuck, that's going to get you in trouble, and you always want to leave. Why do you keep running?" He sighed, sliding into the back with me.

"I don't want to be around you right now." I said, snuggling against him as my eyelids began to droop, I'd been questioning my own sobriety for a flight home as well.

"Yes you do," he flirted, he was right.

We were going on another day of practically no sleep that was starting to take a toll on me, my yawning was uncontrollable, my head was pounding, and my eyelids were heavy. Manuel looked just as vibrant as he did the first day we met, he slept less than me!

I struggled to open my eyes, yawning. "I'm done being soft for you. You said as soon *as I feel like I can't trust you* then I could stop."

I drifted in and out of sleep, barely able to speak or lift my head as he stroked my hair.

"You really can trust me, but you do not want to. You want to find something wrong with me so you can run."

158

"Hmm, run?" I groaned, looking out the window, it was starting to rain, and it was probably too late to catch a flight tonight.

"Yeah, run to whatever is *comfortable*. I'm gonna go back to the hotel, okay?" He asked me, I finally just gave in with a nod. "You don't have to be so hard, Acacia."

"Yeah we know, you prefer your women soft." I mumbled, assuring him that I was aware of his preference.

"You are right, I do." He shrugged unashamed.

"Easier to manipulate?" I antagonized, but then unfortunately looked over into his deep hazel eyes, and felt my heart soften for him again.

"No. Contrary to what you want to believe about me, I am known to be extremely picky when it comes to women. I'm very intentional, it takes a lot to attract me in that way." He leaned over to kiss my forehead. "I just like my woman to be a woman."

"Now you're telling me how to be a woman?" I rolled my eyes reflecting on my night.

"No, just relax," he confirmed. "I'm attracted to feminine energy."

I was too tired to even argue, I leaned my head against the window and drifted off.

12

It was early Sunday morning, and I was at an even worse sleep
deficit. At some point after I fell asleep Manuel drove us back to the
hotel.

According to the clock I'd slept for less than an hour, but I woke
up sweating. In my dream was CoDéy, she was following me down a hall
yelling *"Be soft, Bitch"* repeatedly at me. I tried to stop walking back, but
something in that terrible dreamland wouldn't let me control my feet. And
her voice wasn't hers, it sounded like mine.

In the background I saw Buck and Garon staring at me, but not
helping me at all. Corbin was looking at receipts angrily. Jenny was
running alongside me handing me different clothing items and telling me
tidbits of information that I needed to know for a successful night. Behind
all of them I see people taking pictures, not all of them were fans of
Manuel, none of them seemed to be fans of me. I remembered looking
around, but not being able to find Manuel anywhere.

"Where were you?" I asked abruptly, waking up to Manuel
stroking my damp hair.

"You good?" He asked me when my eyes opened, he looked
concerned, I must've been tossing around in my sleep.

"I'm okay," I told him, realizing I was still half in my dream.
"Did we get to the hotel yet?"

He nodded, helping me get out of the car. "Yeah, we're here.
What were you dreaming about just now? You said, *'Where was I?'"*

I shook my head, "Just... Waiting for you to come back."

"Is this your version of being transparent?" He asked, rhetorically.

I shook my head, carrying my purse as we walked into the hotel.
"You are one to talk about fuckin' transparency. *Be soft bitch?*" I imitated
his ex.

"She shouldn't have said that to you." He admitted, "But it's just my vocabulary, I guess I wasn't completely clear, don't take it for more than it is."

The elevator once again took us to our secure top floor in which he used his key access to get to. I walked a few feet behind Manuel and kept conversation to a minimum.

I wanted him to realize that he was not my favorite person right now, I made it clear every time we locked eyes. I sat on the far side of the bed and scrolled through my phone, he was not getting this phone back, I thought to myself.

Manuel came and sat beside me on the bed. "Things in my life aren't usually like how you saw this weekend. I'm hoping that it didn't push you too far away."

Wow, an apology, I was too easily impressed.

"Well, it did push me away," I told him, "You gave me the impression that you were someone I could feel safe with, put me in a position to trust you, then led me straight to a damn dragon... with no preparation. Looking stupid."

Manuel slowly nodded his head, but remained silent, so I continued.

"You said, ask me anything, have faith in me, give 100% truth and then didn't give it to me in return." I reminded him, but he cut me off.

"Trust, not 100% truth." He mumbled. "No one gives you that."

"What does that even mean?" I asked, offended by the trickery.

"They're not the same." He clarified. "Trust and truth are not the same thing."

I was starting to notice that Manuel was even more of a strategic person than I first realized, "So no one can get 100% truth from you."

"From anyone, you probably aren't even that truthful with yourself. I told you; you can ask me anything and I told you to give me 100% of your trust. I did not say I was going to give you 100% truth; I cannot tell you everything." He explained. "But I'm not going to lie to you, and you can trust that you are safe with me. Even if you didn't feel safe, you were."

Silence.

He gestured with his hand, inviting me to bathe with him. I declined with a simple shake of my head.

"You can try to trust me, Cay. I won't let nothing happen to you, don't push away from me." He assured me, leaving me alone on the bed and walked into the bathroom. "You can come in if you want."

Even the strangest concepts made more sense coming from him, I don't know why, maybe I'm just foolish. I still wanted to run away, but I chose not to overthink the situation. Go with the flow.

As the weekend was winding down I remembered a few emails I needed to write and send. Recalling that there was an office center on our way into the hotel I peeked into the bathroom to let Manuel know I was going to step out for a few minutes.

"Hey, I'm going down to the lobby, I need a computer to return a few emails."

"No, Cay." Manuel poked his head out the curtain, he looked concerned, apparently hypervigilance was a normal feeling for him. "Can you just use my tablet? I don't want you to leave the room alone."

The infinite times I've walked alone in hotels over the last thirty years, wouldn't have been enough for Manuel to be comfortable with me leaving.

I compromised since he seemed genuinely concerned rather than just controlling, "Sure, I'll use it."

Buttnaked and a little wet, Manuel came out of the bathroom and signed into his tablet, then left me to work.

I ignored my desire to see more of Manuel's bare, very tempting body and focused. Getting right to work checking my emails and responding to those who needed a response, as an entrepreneur I take my clients seriously and on most occasions wouldn't get distracted. But Manuel as a distraction wasn't the worst thing at all.

Unavoidably, in the midst of my working, I couldn't help but notice several notifications pop-up on Manuel's tablet. It turned out that Manuel's cellphone was also connected with his tablet, therefore the same things I would be able to see on his phone, I was able to see through the unlocked tablet in my hand.

I felt guilty when I saw an emotional message from a friend thanking him. I stuck my head into the bathroom to be sure he was okay with me seeing these things.

"Hey, your messages are showing up on this tablet, is that okay?" I warned him.

"It's cool, I don't have anything to hide from you." He let me know. "I trust you."

I huffed overly dramatically at him and left the bathroom.

He was very charming.

With timing being on my side another notification popped up and it was from CoDéy, but I was scared that if I clicked it he'd know I was

162

going through his things. Even if he didn't mind, it was weird for him to *know* I read it!

Instead of clicking her message, I satisfied my curiosity by clicking on some previously opened messages from others, skimming through them. Most were vague or boring: about music, events, shows, and more work. I checked to see what apps he had logged in, the typical socials. I rummaged through his messages to see if there were any open doors lingering, but there was nothing that felt concerning, a lot of women throwing themselves at him only to be left on *read* or altogether unopened. Mainly just more music, events, and work.

His social media private messages were surprisingly dry, unread or left open. Even the "recently deleted" had no action. Good sign.

There were still those, now four, notifications by CoDéy's name, she was as exciting as the phone search was going to get. But of course, I felt like I couldn't open those messages without being obvious, so the excitement was in the mystery.

In my short search, there weren't even any hoes that could make me nervous. Not that many do, but I like to be aware of the competition in all cases. I didn't see CoDéy as much competition anymore, mainly because his interaction with her in person seemed very toxic. And I don't think that's his true type... but I was curious!

I quickly checked his recently searched people, a few sexy women were among his search history, including myself! He had been watching me for a while, and often.

I wanted to call Hazel to let her know he passed the socials and phone check! Not too many men out here get high scores on the surprise phone check these days.

Manuel's self-control, in a world of women who would love to just breathe the same air as him, turned me on. I love a man that knows his worth and wasn't just sleeping with just anyone and everyone.

I decided that I would forgive him for the whole scenario at the party. At the awards show, when I saw him on stage I got so turned on that I'd decided that tonight I would sleep with him. Of course, that got recanted after CoDéy embarrassed all of us at the DeCreed afterparty.

But now... At this moment, passing a simple smart phone check, it felt like a good sign to again consummate the weekend rendezvous. Challenge the so-called curse.

I quickly glanced in the mirror to get any smudged makeup out the way, then sprayed a little perfume on my neck. I took a deep breath, then started for the bathroom door.

Just when I was about to push the door open, I heard another notification sound coming from the unlocked tablet. Call it intuition, it sent me back over to the device, curious to see who it could be, but more surprised to find out it was Manuel himself in a conversation from the bathroom. He had responded to CoDéy from his cell phone, which cleared out the notification icon by her name, meaning I was also able to read her messages.

I could still hear Manuel in the shower singing his 80's R&B, even louder than the radio, so I felt comfortable enough to snoop.

CoDéy

Call me back please.

Do u want everyone in the whole fuckn world to know what you made me do.

I hate how much I love you Emmanuel. Please call me so we can talk, I need to see you.

U was right. The baby was a mistake. Can u call me.

I'm gonna get help, please don't be done

I been done.

U said you would never abandon me

Shit. I'm unnecessarily nosey. He's not so bad.

I closed the tablet, this time purposefully locking myself out of it, I didn't need to see anything else. I was going through this man's private

164

messages, and we barely know each other. Manuel is a good guy, searching for flaws wasn't going to show me what I wanted to see.

I went into the bathroom, feeling guilty.

"Hey," I called to him through the white curtain as he sang Can You Stand the Rain, "This really is your favorite song, huh."

"It's a coincidence or a sign I guess. My playlist is on shuffle." He revealed his upper body and face from out the curtain, "Hey Princess, come in the water."

"Eww don't call me that." I told him, rolling my eyes, but undressed and obliged.

"So, who gets to call you Princess?" Manuel twirled me around slowly to dramatically admire my body, then ran his fingers tracing through the vine of acacias on my back, but he stopped to point at my princess-crown tattoo, "I guess it's time for your tattoo stories."

"He's not alive anymore, he was one of my closest childhood friends," I took a gulp of air as I told Manuel, not loving how deep this *first* tattoo story could get. "He died in a car accident, someone at the funeral told me he was going too fast."

"Mmmmm, hence your fear of speed," he connected.

"Literally, ever since." I smiled as he figured me out, I knew he was a good listener.

"You must've really loved him to get a tattoo, right?"

"Yes, I did, but as a friend. And people didn't get that, even he and I didn't really get it at one point. At least I didn't." Reminiscing on such a strange time in my life. "Honestly, I've had a lot of amazing people in my life. I should have way more tattoos."

Manuel cautiously joked, "I hope I'm not competing with a bunch of amazing dead niggas."

"No, there's no competition. Timing, you ever notice how it all works together, with the way people come in and out of our lives. I've learned to just be grateful for the time that I'm here with whomever the stellar people I get to love might be." I got back on track with the conversation," This childhood friend who would call me Princess, was there for me through a low point in my life, he showed me another side of humanity. And I needed that connection."

"So now no one can call you princess cause *he* died? What was the low point?" Manuel asked, looking inquisitive.

"No, it's not the death per say, and I really don't mind if someone calls me that. The story is kinda deep and I don't want to kill the mood." I warned him by making a disgusted face, but he looked unphased like he wanted to hear. "You wanna hear a bad story?"

"Of course, I wanna learn things about you, Cay." He assured me, with a friendly smile as he lathered me up with soap.

Something I never feel had me comfortable enough to dig up my trauma with Manuel, so I began.

I braced my gut, "When I was a teenager, I went to visit my family. I was at a convenience store, and I ran into a person who was a family friend. He used to hang at the family house a lot, while at the store he kept saying how he ran into the *family's little princess*. He was an adult, but not way older than me. He told me he'd give me a ride back to the family house, save me from a walk, but somehow we had to stop by his mom's house. She wasn't home, no one was there, but he said she wanted to see me, so we sat on the couch to wait. Then he started being really playful and touchy, he kept calling me Princess, saying how much he admired me since I was a young girl. Bringing up memories he had of me growing up. I felt awkward and tried to make up excuses to go, but he just rebutted each one. I stupidly just stayed, thinking up different excuses.

"Next thing I knew he was on top of me and taking off clothes, things were happening so fast. Sucking on my neck, kissing me, licking me. I kept moving away, but not pushing him off hard enough, then I felt the tears on my face, and I stopped fighting it. He just kept telling me how I was a princess, and he was not going to hurt me, just would not shut up. Then I gave up, he took my virginity in a second. I had so much resentment because of that for a long time."

Manuel looked angry; I could tell he was not expecting such a story. "How'd you get out?"

"After like two minutes, the house phone saved me," I responded, with a slight smile recalling the experience, but Manuel wasn't smiling. "The house phone kept ringing and I kept telling him to answer it, at first he wouldn't. But after the phone rang about four more times, he got up to take it off the hook for silence and I got up, grabbed my stuff and dressed as much as possible as I ran out the back door. He followed behind me down the first set of stairs, saying he would just take me home, but I ran down the stairs and didn't stop until I made it back to my family's house. I remember my own cell phone ringing as I was putting on clothes walking down the street."

"You didn't tell your family?" He asked.

I shook my head quickly, "I wanted to pretend it didn't happen so bad. I prayed he didn't make me bleed, but he did. He was my first, technically, I guess."

"Is he dead?" Manuel asked bluntly.

I shrugged, "I stopped going back home for a while after that, never saw him again. I don't think he's dead, if he is, it's not because of me. I already forgave him, plus I never told anyone except this friend who is gone what happened. He happened to call me while I was running down the street after the whole thing happened. I made him promise he wouldn't tell anyone."

"Wow, you probably just want me to be cool with it, too?" Manuel asked with an annoyed sigh. "Buck told you; you only get one pass."

"Oh, don't act like that, we are just sharing stories, don't make me feel like I can't share things with you. Besides, you said no one really follows that rule." I reminded him of our conversation in the studio. "There was a condom, he didn't cum, and it was probably only two minutes of penetration before I was able to get up and run out of that apartment. I didn't want to make it a big deal, and honestly I felt like it was my fault for falling for it."

Manuel made an empathetic face at me and wiped the warm slow tears from my face.

"So anyway, back to the tattoo, anytime my friend wanted me to do something for him he would call me Princess, as a joke. From the slightest thing like borrowing a pencil to convincing me to commit misdemeanors like skipping school to go sneaker shopping. *Princess* was a joke between us, especially when I was upset at him, he'd use it to butter me up. Then it just somehow became my nickname between us," I chuckled awkwardly. "It made light of the situation. Which for me, at that time, was what I felt I needed. He was the only one I was comfortable enough to talk to about it. In his way, he taught me not to be "*princessed*" into submission. When he died, I got the tattoo. Memorializing the friendship, the lessons."

Manuel could hardly look at me, he put his face under the water, possibly to hide a tear. "I'm kinda pissed. You think people should get a pass for hurting other people?"

"No, what do you mean a pass? This was almost two decades ago and it's not the first or the worst thing that's happened to me. I'm not anyone's victim. There have been professors, police officers, fake ass friends, supervisors, you name it. Trust me, I've forgiven those situations,

167

I don't know why I'm even crying. The thought of me still being a victim just disgusts me." I assured him, hoping he wouldn't try to rehash it. "I like this feeling of being free, don't make it a *thing*."

I loved how well he listened as I spoke, we had real chemistry, it was more than just words. He let me initiate a kiss when I gripped his face downward toward mine.

I *wanted* him, in just one weekend, I wanted him. How did this happen?

"How'd you get past that?"

"It made me sexually awkward for a while, maybe even still, sometimes I get uncomfortable. While he was on top of me I got this depleted gut feeling that sometimes will come back to this day, I can't forget it if I tried, immediate turnoff. It helped me learn not to be naive." I told him, truly looking on the bright side.

"I get it." Manuel told me. "You built walls."

"I guess. Intimacy is difficult, but I'm learning." I took a huge sigh, that may have been a breakthrough. "Between two therapists in the last fifteen years that was the most I ever told anyone about that."

He looked at me with a little pity in his eyes, "I'm glad you told me, but I'm sorry it happened, all of it. If you ever feel uncomfortable with me, be sure to tell me. I want transparency, I want you to be open all the time, even if you think it's going to hurt me. I'm so strong, don't worry. Why didn't you tell your family when you got home?"

"The boys would've probably killed him, I was preventing a possible murder in my young mind. Plus, the night before I overheard some of the older women in my family gossiping, they felt my clothes were too provocative, that I was basically just asking to be assaulted by the way I dressed." I shook my head recalling my hurt teenage feelings as I stood silently in the hall listening to them talk about me. "I was ashamed and wore jean pants and a t-shirt the next day. Ironically, that was the day that I got... *betrayed*."

Manuel looked truly upset for once. "On behalf of real men everywhere, sorry some slip through the cracks. Want me to make a phone call."

"What?" I snapped. "No, that secret is like twenty years old, what are you talking about, a phone call?"

"Look, you're crying, you're still hurt."

"Stop that, seriously. I don't approve, but I forgive, I prefer not to carry the pain of what others do and did. Hurt people, hurt people, and what folks do say more about them than anyone else. I would've spent my

168

entire life being these fools' victim if I broke anytime someone hurt me, right? So, I just learn and keep growing. Trust, I love this version of me who you are meeting today, I'm much better." I felt relieved telling him my story, but I didn't like it made him vengeful. "Resentment harms the owner, I learned that, and honestly I am good."

"Yeah, okay you created a system of walls to protect you, but you don't have to be so overprotective as you are."

"Connections can be nerve wrecking for me sometimes, but I am working on it. I just take the walls down slowly."

"Don't be scared... of anything, promise."

"I can't promise that," I admitted. "Even here with you, you know who *you* are, that can be intimidating."

"Please don't be intimidated by me, I love how you are. Let's make a safe word, in case you can't find the words to tell me something," Manuel suggested after a few moments of looking at each other in silence. "If you feel uncomfortable or intimidated with anything...whatever is happening. No questions asked, just say the word and I got you."

"I like that," I blushed, slightly embarrassed that I told Manuel such a personal story on the first weekend we've known each other. *How did he get that out of me?* "Hmm, what's our safe word? And don't give me a word you've used with some other woman!"

"My brothers' and I have what we call a kill-switch, a word that kinda means truce. I've never cared about a woman enough to give her a safe word, and no one's ever asked for one," he told me. "You can pick, what makes you feel safe?"

"Maybe an umbrella? Since you like being in the rain so much."

"I like it, umbrella." He recited to himself, watching my eyes as I watched the water run down his broad shoulders. "What means *go*?"

"Everything else." I turned around and flirted back with a kiss, we could not keep our hands to ourselves at this point, I was loving the chemistry between us.

Manuel was the epitome of the man I didn't know I was longing for; he was enchanting. He's very fine, caring, confident, considerate, proactive, and successful; literally what I've been waiting for. His timing is spot on, and our chemistry was in sync to have just met each other this weekend! The little things we have in common, our interests and similarities from philanthropy to our taste in food.

But here I was overthinking if I could measure up to his expectations.

Constantly I fought the need to overanalyze what was going on, I was having a very good time, and that was all that mattered. Right? If he doesn't call me back after this week, then at least the time was worth it!

I turned facing Manuel, weaving my arms through his and gently clawing his back with my nails, he let his hands slide down to my butt. We kissed under the warm water, sucking on each other's lips and tongue for a few moments. I let my hands make their way around his chest, up and down the smooth bumps of his abs, but stopping at the top of his pubic hair when he grasped my hands to a halt.

I looked into his eyes and Manuel was staring back at me with his sexy eyes.

I asked him flirtatiously. "Umbrella?"

"Me? No, but aren't you scared of the curse? Is this what you want?" He asked me softly as I gently touched him sexually for the first time, looking at it for confirmation.

There would be no need for *umbrella* tonight.

Lying to myself I shook my head, "No, I don't even really believe the curse."

He let my hands finish their journey down to his erection. I knew for sure I could tell Hazel he is not gay!

I didn't take my eyes off his, but I could feel in my two hands why he was so confident in himself. I massaged him with both hands slowly while he leaned down to kiss on my lips, I sucked his bottom lip gently, but aggressive enough to give a preview of what was soon to come.

Manuel lifted me up from under my butt and leaned me against the wall for support as he passionately practically sucked off my lips.

I was ready for us to take this to the bed, "Let's go in the room, I don't want to be in here… not for the first time."

"Okay, whatever makes you feel more comfortable."

Manuel put me down and kissed me some more. He started to kiss my neck, then my breast, I leaned back against the shower wall to stay balanced. He got down on his knees and slowly began to kiss up my thighs until he got perfectly between them as water ran down my body.

Manuel spread my legs apart and began to kiss my lower lips, then let his tongue enter between them. He started sucking slowly on my clit, a sweet tease, I played with his hair as I closed my eyes and let him do his thing. It felt so good with every touch, my knees kept wanting to give out as he ate me out in my standing position. Securely using his hands to help me stay balanced.

170

About a minute before I could no longer stand he got up, wrapping his arms around me from the back as we stood under the water for a minute before turning it off. Then he handed me a towel as I followed him out of the shower.

"I didn't think we were gonna get to this point and we really don't have to, I meant that," he dried himself off, looking for me to give him a signal to call the whole thing off. I wasn't going to, but I thought about it as I half ass dried my body.

"I want this." I assured him then he quickly picked me up again before I was even dry.

"I'm still wet!" I laughed, then sucked on his neck as he securely held me in his arms.

"I want you like that," he teased carrying me out of the bathroom.

Unfortunately, we didn't get to the bed, I barely got two steps out the doorway of the bathroom. As soon as Manuel went to make the second step he turned and put me back down, practically pushing me back into the bathroom.

I could still see Manuel, staring in the direction of the door with a disgusted look on his face, he took a step up, probably an attempt to block my view. Fortunately, I could see from the dresser mirror's reflection, some of what was happening in the bedroom.

At the door was a short, brown skinned woman with Garon standing there looking at us. Her face looked somewhat familiar, but I couldn't pinpoint it.

"EmManuel, are you back in high school? Bringing girls to your room?" The woman asked abruptly.

"Ma, you are really trippin' right now," Manuel shook his head, not bothering to cover up although he was completely naked in front of this woman, *Ma*, and his security guard. "Why are you in my hotel room? Why did you bring her here?"

Manuel looked dumbfounded, but somehow not very surprised, like a teenager who just got caught sneaking out. He didn't look at me at all, although they couldn't see me I am sure I looked more embarrassed than he did.

"Send your friend home and come out to Corbin's room please, we need to talk," she instructed him, turning around and heading out of the room, Garon followed her.

Once he walked over to the closed door and added the extra lock. I got out of the restroom and sat on the bed, fixing my towel, watching him as he shuffled around to put on some basketball shorts and shoes.

"Was that your mother?" I asked shamefully partially hoping that wasn't who she was, but he nodded his head yes, then shook his head no, but didn't speak. "Transparency please?! You just pushed me into the bathroom to hide me from some woman."

"I'm so sorry, are you okay?" He asked, snapping out of his surprised, teenage boy trance, "Everything is fine, its business, she runs the business. I have to go talk to her though, to handle something."

I nodded, "That's not your sugar mama, wife, or something bizarre, right?"

"Bizarre? I promise you have nothing to worry about. I'm single, that's Ma, she's my oldest brother's mother, I'll explain later." He assured me, then handed me his tablet after unlocking an easy code to remember. Feel free to do some work, just try not to fall asleep. I'll make it up to you when I get back."

I nodded, "As long as you are going to make it up to me."

"Promise," he kissed me, then threw on a white shirt and headed outside behind his staff.

They were very overprotective of Manuel's whereabouts. He didn't strike me as the type to have a momager, I began to fear he may be a whole new-next level momma's boy afterall. It would make sense having so many moms.

I know very little about this man and here I am waiting in an expensive hotel suite performing pre-sex Kegel exercises preparing to fuck him.

Momager probably even heard us in the bathroom?

How embarrassing. Visuals of my exes' smug mothers who chastised me danced around in my head, taunting me with their fingers pointing.

I needed to learn more about this man and maybe even his moms.

Against my better judgment or listening to my intuition I decided to learn more about Manuel. First, I searched his name again on the internet and read a few basic facts, nothing too crazy popped up that I hadn't heard before. He has no children, had a relationship for a few years that ended almost two years ago, awards, charities, and his events were all there.

Wondering what Manuel might've said about me, I searched my name in the text search bar.

172

I typed in "Cay", over 20 mentions of me. There were mostly messages from Jenny that mentioned me, all size or style related. She was so particular when talking about me that it was uncomfortable to see these messages were dated weeks before I'd even been invited to the concert.

Why was he so interested in me before he even knew me?

Getting over the cringiness of the thought I searched for my whole name, "Acacia ", over 200 mentions. I clicked the notepad icon, which held more than half of the mentions found. It was no mistake, I kept scrolling up a notepad document that highlighted my name probably over and over. It was titled Acacia Ivy.

The top of the document was my basic information: birthday, favorites, birthplace, family, address, and things of that nature. As I let my finger scroll I landed on other key information about myself, it was like reading a sketchy biography that I didn't know was written about me.

I saw my old jobs, colleges, and even grade schools that I went to. There were pictures of me in the file, mostly from social media, but with date stamps, most of the screenshots were months old.

There were lists that read titles such as: likes, hates, favorites, interests, fav foods; and each title corresponded with a list of about 5- 7 things that were correct! Random opinionated comments strangely with redacted names. My favorite artist's name was highlighted, with a date beside it, the same date we went to the studio and happened to run into him. I scrolled over to see my medical history, which freaked me out, it read my major surgeries, one that was literally highlighted happened to be an abortion in college. There was a column of words with question marks: Patience? Self-control? Cursed?

There was information about past relationships and encounters with asshole men, all of them. Abuse, fights, heartbreaks, assaults… he knew more about me than I care to remember. Even dirt on me, seeing my mug shot was probably the most embarrassing, I would've preferred to tell him about that myself.

Some things about my son as well, mostly football related. And our parental custody schedule.

I scrolled down to the icing on the cake: @CorBEatn. A man I thought was a social media *friend* who'd been writing to me for months with just emojis, positive compliments, affirmations, or small talk. Most of his social media feed was restaurant reviews and dishes that he made, he seemed harmless. I've always responded back out of politeness, just as I do with any of my followers, but I quickly pieced it together.

On Manuel's device were screenshots of the short message exchanges between I and @CorBEatn, from *his* phone perspective. I scrolled quickly as I was beginning to feel intense anxiety. I checked out his profile, but it was just a few memes. Manuel is @CorBEatn? We've been talking every day for months.

I felt so... lied to, spied on, even violated. I got off the bed and began to get dressed, I did not want to be in this room when he got back.

A white lie or two during dating to mitigate a later conversation is one thing, but it is a whole other thing to stalk someone and manipulate them into believing you have common interests by researching through fake social media pages!

"Why go through all that?" I spoke out loud, but to myself. "You are fuckin' rich."

I scrolled quicker, not sure of how much time I had, seeing the extended vertical scroll bar indicating a very long document. So much was written in the file, the colors I like that he bought for me, the foods we ate this weekend, the music I like, the different charities I support... it was all there.

I skimmed, but there was a lot of information to see. The document didn't appear to end, though some information and receipts were frivolous. I could not reach an end!

"He knows everything about me," I whispered, a tear falling from my face again, was he some sick stalker. What was I supposed to do?

No wonder it seemed he was moving so fast; he's already been dating me in his mind.

I shared the document to myself after I quickly got dressed, I knew I had to save this for me to read closer later. When the document was shared, it alerted Manuel's watch, on the dresser, which was connected to his phone... which I was sure he had on him even in the shower.

Manuel knows I saw the document.

I quickly put my shoes on, grabbed anything around the room that was "mine", and headed to the door. This wasn't my first time running away like this.

Manuel beat me to opening it from the other side just as I was going for the handle. He'd been at least speed walking, his breathing heavier than normal and he even had a couple beads of sweat formed on his forehead. But even in his urgent state he didn't seem nervous or worried in his demeanor, at most he was just skeptical of me.

174

I took three steps back from him, I began to feel my chest panting. He closed the door once he got into the room. I wanted it open.

"Okay, so let me explain what that was before you decide to leave," he started before I even had a chance to speak, he walked towards me, but I continued to move away. "It's just for safety–."

"You fuckin' stalked me? I know what it was, @CorBEatn, you are a fuckin stalker! You ask me for transparency after you literally stalked me from my medical history down to sports stats on my son!" I snapped, cutting him off, walking to the door with my hand out between us. "Who do you and your security think you are, the fuckin' President of the fuckin' country? And there were other emails and phone numbers that that information was shared to, so who the fuck else has access to my damn personal records, Manuel?"

He sighed, but responded openly, reminding me of how I would scold Tré at home. He took a step back as I inched closer to the door. "My security teams. Staff. Jenny, of course. It's to be cautious."

"@CorBEatn?" I asked. "You were talking to me, spying from a fake account?"

"Not spying! I just really wanted to talk to you one day, so I used my brother's food account. I wasn't planning on talking to you so much, but you were so sweet and always responded back. It was nice hearing from you every day, I felt like that was enough, I wasn't even going to try to meet you back when that started." He told me, "I just couldn't tell you who I was, I wasn't trying to trick you. I'm sorry."

"That was not all for safety! My fuckin' abortion in college effects your safety around me too? Did that make you feel comfortable with me, we share an experience? This isn't just about your safety." I questioned, unsure of how much more he knew, I rambled on. I was past feeling the effects of the alcohol, I was fully awake for this conversation. "My credit score, my records from school, and my favorite foods are going to help secure your safety how?"

"I told you I researched you, maybe not just for security but for risks… financial-risks, health-risks, mental-risks, whatever is to my well-being my team is going to find out. It's just another rule. What kind of investment are you, liability or asset? They look at *everything*, I loved *everything* about you, that's why I'm here," he tried to explain, his face painfully respecting the space between us. "That's never happened, it's always the opposite, that's probably why I feel so close to you."

"I'm sick of all the rules all the time! What about how I feel? I have no choice then to be… audited? These people know private shit about me Manuel. I see why some of them didn't like me, they only knew random things about me." I couldn't help but wonder what Garon saw in my life file that made him dislike me so much. "Why couldn't we meet each other normally?"

"Normally? What is normal? Search me, Cay, anything you want to know, just look it up," he said calmly.

"Can I ask you a question, were you just acting like you were surprised to make things seem authentic?" I wondered out loud, running back the memories of this weekend; how he knew exactly what to say to make me happy and what would make me smile. Between stalking my social media and digging into some deep files, I realized I no longer knew how much of this *relationship* was real. "You knew about what happened to me, didn't you?"

His eyes somehow told me 'yes', because his mouth didn't move. "I just didn't know if you forgave him." He told me. "Please stop crying. Don't leave just because you are uncomfortable, I know it seems weird. I can explain more if you stay. Trust me."

"No, you learn things authentically or at the very least be honest about what you do know. I can't trust you anymore." I scoffed, shaking my head, the absent tears left nothing but true anger behind. "Your team can all rest assured I will not cause any safety concerns for them anymore. I'm done with this whole thing; I have a life in the real world with real people who know the real me. I don't need your world and all these stupid new rules."

"We can learn about each other; I want us to learn about each other. I want you to learn who I really am, but it's not just easy, so you can't just run. Let's go away for a couple days, talk and spend time together." He expressed seemingly genuine, almost enough to make me feel sorry for his weird, famous ass.

"Why? You told me you won't tell me the whole truth, so who would I be getting to know now? Another one of your representatives?" I began heading out the door but left him with my final thought. "You *ask* me for something that you can't even *give* me and then expect me to be cool with this stalking shit. I'm *good*, do not follow me, do not check on me, and do not worry about me."

"I'm the same person I said I was every time. Are you seriously that mad that you are leaving?" He asked, calmer than when he first arrived in the room. "Stop being afraid every time something is uncomfortable and get some self-control."

"This is so wild; you are turning this around on me?" I raised my voice, then opened the door to leave, not caring who might hear. "Who the hell dates like this?"

"Please stop yelling," he said, frustrated and backing up from me. "Everything I know about you made me fall for you, Acacia, I don't want you to leave."

I paused. Then I left. I left him standing in the doorway.

As I made my way out the building I ordered a ride to the airport using an app as I fought the urge to blink and let the tears fall. Each time I pressed a button on my phone more tears blurred my vision, until they were so heavy they just fell onto the screen.

Hazel	
	You were right. I got a flight home tonight. text you when I land.

When the rideshare vehicle arrived, I looked back one more time to see if he was going to come down. Manuel did not follow me.

It looked like someone was following the rideshare vehicle, but I may just have been paranoid. While I was headed to the airport, I blocked Manuel from all the ways he'd contacted me previously. There was an emailed ticket sent to my phone for a first-class ticket home on an airline that I prefer. I let my pride go and accepted the ticket as closure.

I wanted to pretend this didn't happen… the last part, or maybe the whole interaction. For now, I just wanted to go to the comfort of home and refocus on what matters most.

I put my shades on during the flight so I could get my tears out before the plane landed back home.

 Don't focus on the problem, focus on solutions.

@AcaciaIvy 2020

13

As we came to a stop at my gated community, I rolled down the back window of the rideshare vehicle to show my face to the security officer on duty, Carlos, who greeted me with a smile.

"Miss, Miss, flowers came, but I told them you didn't approve any deliveries… like you said to me last time," Carlos told me, proud that he remembered my request, meanwhile showing me a receipt of some sort.

Manuel got me flowers. More closure? How uncreative, I thought as I nodded at Carlos, too tired to even prepare a flower vase after such an eventful weekend.

"Thanks," I told him, not surprised that Manuel was able to deliver the flowers to my house before I was even able to arrive. Creepy, overachieving ass. "I don't need them, give them to the front office."

"Okay, I'll leave them in the office for you." He handed me the card, there was a message that I didn't even bother to read but dropped it in my purse. Water under the bridge, no need to dwell on it.

All I wanted was my bed, but while in bed he's all I thought about. Trying to convince myself that I didn't overreact. That I didn't run away for no reason. My soul felt so deceived after seeing the file on me, along with the fake social media page. It was too weird.

If it were basic information it would not seem so bad, but the lists, images, and family information was not normal. Then the dummy social media account that reached out to me every day. Manuel tricked me!

I did nothing wrong, no need to overanalyze, stress, or to find a deeper meaning, only room for a clean break. I knew what to do, out of sight and completely out of mind. My cut off game has been perfected to a tee at this point!

The fact that he's written, featured, or affiliated with one in every five songs that come on the radio, popping up on the most random podcasts, and always on some social media gossip could interfere with keeping him out of mind. Yet, I really knew I could just let the whole thing go… it was Manuel that had different plans.

My Monday

Although Corbin had deposited more than enough money for me to take a week (month) off work, I decided to go anyway. I knew it'd be better for me to get out of the house and stay busy rather than sitting around in my feelings. Keeping Manuel off my mind by being at work would be the best way to do that.

Or so I thought.

My day started off as a normal Monday, which is never boring, especially when I have to pass about two hundred people just to get into my classroom to start my day. I was starting to feel happy, I tried to think positive and be grateful for just the adventure. Occasionally I'd start feeling resentful and I'd have to refocus, but the students kept my mind occupied.

My classroom is a safe place for me, for the last decade it's been my home away from home. Working with young people, trying to find relatively meaningful ways to teach concepts, is my element. I was glad to be at work rather than home overthinking.

However, it was a little harder to speak without an occasional voice crack. No matter how hard I tried to not think about him, *I missed Manuel and wanted to talk to him.*

Between my first and second class I got a phone call from the main office that I have a flower delivery. Touché Manuel, finding a new way to deliver the flowers, I thought to myself.

"I'll send my teacher's aide to pick it up, thanks." I told the secretary on my classroom phone.

"Can you send your whole class, it's a lot of flowers," she explained with a chuckle.

"What?" I asked dumbfounded.

I could hear laughter in the office, "Yes ma'am, possibly more, should we get another class to help, or can you each make two trips? There are flower vans unloading outside with what someone said are all acacia flowers."

"Oh my," I shocked myself, letting out a loud laugh.

"From what the third delivery guy said, and from what it looks like, they're from different companies," the secretary explained. "Someone is really trying hard to get your attention."

The secretary was correct, he is a try-hard, as it turned out that Manuel ordered all the acacia flowers and plants he could find in my area. A front office staff member was able to cover the remainder of my classes while I redirected the deliveries to my house.

On each of the cards he had them print or write: Save the World Acacia. It was cute, seeing he listened to me.

When I got back to work, a few of my coworkers and students had lots of questions of where the flowers came from, of course there was some speculation and a few rumors, but I just pleaded the fifth.

I kept a couple acacias in my classroom and handed a few of them out to my students and coworkers. He was right, I liked sharing my blessings.

Hazel	
	Omg He sent me an acacia garden
Keep his ass blocked until you tell me what happened	
	I'm not unblocking him. They are just so pretty.
Fuck him.	
	Lol. Girl Bye, come over tomorrow and help me plant these

My Tuesday

As creative as the flowers were, Manuel remained blocked on every account. Hazel planned to come over after work to help me plant my new acacia garden, discuss my weekend, and have some adult beverages.

Tuesday still had some folks lingering questions from Monday, but other than that it seemed like it was a normal day. However, in the afternoon right before lunch I started receiving packages to my classroom, items from my Amazon classroom wish list which is posted on my classroom website.

"Can you put them on the side table," I instructed the maintenance worker, after his fourth trip to my classroom by third period. He seemed to be getting a little pissed that someone made him bitch-boy mail carrier with my packages.

Manuel bought the entire list. From the silly things I put on my wish list to the $100 individual student tablets.

The students wanted me to open the boxes, but I was overwhelmed with caution more than joy. Did I want to accept these gifts? There for the students, not really for me. I remained indecisive as more boxes came in.

My coworkers in the office could not stop asking where everything was coming from. With the amount of classroom interruptions, I couldn't blame them. Manuel was being very extra for sure.

"What are you doing?" I snapped at Manuel when he picked up the phone after the first ring.

I'd waited until my classroom was empty then shut off the lights to avoid any lunchtime visitors. As bad as I tried not to talk to him, I needed him to stop drawing attention to me. It was uncomfortable.

"Unblock me from your phone please," he requested, "Video call me. I need to see you; I want to talk."

"I don't want to talk to you, just stop sending stuff to me."

"I'm not gonna stop til you hear me out, I'll call you tonight," he pleaded. "Will you listen to me?"

"I have other plans tonight," I told him, intentionally remaining vague.

He sighed, "Baby daddy curse kicked in?"

"Don't flatter yourself." I told him before hanging up.

I was truly in need of some feminine energy as well as someone I could trust to vent about my Manuel-the-stalker-dilemma. By the time Hazel arrived at my house, I was pacing the yard, going back and forth with what's "normal". I regretted going through his tablet.

I struggled with the urge to protect *my stalker* from my best-friend's harsh opinion, but I had to tell her everything. The entire situation was driving me insane, the urge to unblock him was beginning to grow quickly.

As soon as she got there she poured me a drink and I began to vent, from the moment I left the Empress Suites to 7 different flower delivery companies he sent to my job.

"Hazel he stalked me," I told her after I thoroughly explained every detail of how amazing my time was with him, to give both sides. "He had shit about my past that I forgot about on purpose. It was so disturbing! He asked me about the curse, because he knew there was one! That's so embarrassing, and other people's names were on the recipient list of the document. Probably his security staff's reason for hating me so much!"

Hazel stayed silent the entire story; I could barely read her facial expressions on anything.

"So, he took you on a private jet to another city to party with him, and you left him because he ran a damn background check on you behind your back? He's a fuckin' celebrity, Cay, you need to get your damn grown woman panties on to fuck with him… and pray you are able to keep him! Look at this beautiful jewelry." She held up my gifts.

182

"You're being biased because he has money, he had his staff research me to get me to like him! Not just for safety." I yelled at her and sighed, surprised she didn't agree. "You should've been there; it didn't feel like just a background check."

"I wasn't there because you left me," she snapped at me.

"You're right, I'm sorry," I dropped my head. "The document was just creepy."

"Did you tell him about your book?" She asked evasively. "Have you told any of the men you date about any of your books?"

"Shut up!" I was shocked that she'd even compare my research on dating to Manuel stalking me on a computer document. "I date them, and they turn to research, I don't research them so that they'll date me!"

She rolled her eyes, "Oh Acacia you know you aren't going to settle with any of the filler dates you go on. You know they'll all be just *research* in the end."

"Bullshit, you know I've actually liked some of them!" I retorted. "They just fuck it up, don't turn this around."

"You're just scared of dating a man of his *caliber* and now *you* are going to fuck it up. If he did all that research, maybe he does like you!" She shrugged. "Either way, what are you losing in this by entertaining him? He is intentionally going out of his way to give you everything you want."

I couldn't believe she was suggesting this, I wasn't going to do it, but I needed clarification, "So use him?"

"Acacia, call it what you like. I don't think you should use him, but if he wants to get to know you and spends money whilst doing it then stop fighting it! We've gone back to broke niggas who've given us less." She reminded me. "He's rich, he wanted to make sure you weren't a crazy person before meeting you, just go back and enjoy it."

"I guess that's one way to look at it." I took a deep breath and tried to understand the perspective of my best friend.

Maybe it wasn't as weird as I thought, I once thought online dating was weird, and it's probably the number one way to meet people for relationships. Times evolve.

"How many men have we entertained who have done literally nothing for us." She asked, I agreed with a slight nod. "Okay well, he may have hired folks to learn about you, maybe he really wanted to make a good impression. He did a lot of research, many don't do shit, literally they just wing it."

I laughed at her, "You're right, something just seems off, I don't think I want to be with someone like that."

"Have you ever been with someone like *that*?" She asked, then took the liberty of answering her own question. "No. You've been with one stupid ass type forever, he's hella different."

"I felt so violated reading that Hazel." I told her, remembering my private business on that document. "But maybe you're right. Maybe I just can't handle that type."

"Wish it was me," she winked and stuck out her tongue. "I know exactly what I'd do."

My Wednesday

Waking up to the view of my acacia garden made me feel happy inside. My vision of having my morning tea in my own garden was happening, thanks to Manuel. I wondered if he listened to me and remembered I wanted the garden, or if it was just someone who worked for him, doing their job.

I tried to revisit his document that I shared to myself, but the entire thing was erased. I wanted to be reminded of what he knew, there were some notes on the side, words and quotes, from what I could recall he was talking to someone in them. But what did it say?

I jumped back into my out of sight, out of mind mantra. I stayed present in the moment at work to keep busy, but Manuel wasn't going to be forgotten and neither was his number one fan.

Before the first period bell, Hazel tagged me in a picture of us posing together at her sorority sister's Dream Man vision board/manifestation party not too long ago. She convinced me to go to the event instead of sitting home sulking in my writer's block.

It turned out to be an entertaining girl's night in! Quite a few of the ladies had just read a book on how to obtain their dream man, the ladies were completely sold that this was a vital step in the process. And their energy was contagious because even many of us who hadn't read the book were taking the Dream Man Vision Board seriously. I was skeptical, but played along, I didn't even think my own dream man existed anymore.

On the invitation we were advised to bring our own magazines and art supplies, along with anything else we might want to put on our board. We had small talk and cut out keywords, characteristics, and details that we want from our dream man. I only brought gold markers, but was able to mooch some black empowerment stickers, positive affirmation quotes, and leftover stickers from others. Many women took it more seriously and brought full body pictures of the exact men they were trying to bring into their lives, from celebrities to their boss! Hazel was particular with her board using mostly muscular men, but in my true English teacher fashion, I chose to avoid pictures and be particular about the words I choose.

My poster is sitting on the floor of my desk at my home office. I was supposed to hang it up, but I hadn't found a place for it yet.

A few of the words jumped out as soon as I opened the photo: Protector, Entrepreneur, Giving, Creative, Benevolent, Traveler, Listener, Reputable, Comforting, Sincere, Responsive, and Astounding.

Weren't those qualities of Manuel? In the short time I spent with him I saw all of that! Or was this just a honeymoon stage. It's been over a decade since I've even liked someone!

I brushed it off and made it through the first period without completely overthinking how I acted to Manuel.

The bookkeeper and my principal urgently pulled me from my second period class and informed me that the Psychology Club, which I manage, which has been fund raising in hopes to take the students on an international field trip, just received a five thousand three hundred fifty-dollar anonymous donation. The remaining amount from the club's online donation fundraiser.

With the amount of time, I'd spent praying that the funds would get raised for the club's account, I knew that we would eventually get the money. However, I didn't expect it to be that soon or easy, betting 100% that Manuel was my club's anonymous donor.

I smiled and pretended to be shocked, but both my boss and the club president could see that I was not surprised. However, I refused to drop any hints or names on who the anonymous donor might be.

I called Manuel on my way home from work, and truly couldn't find it in myself to be mad at him anymore. Although I stayed silent, remembering that the more you listen the more a person will tell you what is really on their heart.

"Hello, Acacia?" Manuel picked up barely after two rings, hearing his voice made me sensitive immediately, like a great Gospel song. "Did somebody steal Cay's phone? Did somebody steal Cay?" He continued to be goofy as I remained silent, enjoying the silly side of him. "If this is a ransom… I promise you ain't asking for enough, I'll pay it seven times, whatever it is. I don't care. I just want her back. I miss her smile, that energy."

His voice was calming for me, even when he was being silly, I couldn't help but smile.

"Ms. Acacia? I can hear your breathing, it's definitely you," he sighed appreciatively, "I'm sorry you feel like you can't talk to me right now, but you can always talk to me. And I'm sorry that you felt that I wasn't being real with you."

"You weren't but thank you for the donation to my students." I told him, "I accept your apology."

"You're very welcome, I can hear you smiling," he said, we simultaneously exhaled in a moment of silence. "Did you unblock me yet?"

186

"Maybe," I flirted, before hanging up with just a quick salutation.

"Unblock me, Cay."

"Bye." I told him before I hung up.

My Thursday

My phone chimed about four text message notifications before I even opened my eyes.

Tré	
Mom! Are you up yet? Mom? I won tickets to go to the pro bowl please take me this weekend I just need a ride!!!	
	From school?
Idk, it says I won them	
	That's crazy, could be a scam. Aren't those so expensive?
FREE TICKETS mother, from the league relax. I'll see if I can get dad to give me some money for a flight if u say I can go	
	We'll talk

Tré winning a trip to the one place he's been wanting to go for a few months was a bit ironic, and had Manuel written all over it. Especially since he did not enter in any contest to win the tickets!

I called Manuel, this time no answer.

Manuel	
	Do NOT bring my son into this

Manuel called me back, but through a video call, I didn't mean to, but instinctively I answered it, "What's going on? What are you talking about?"

I hid from the camera as I responded but checked him out in bed. He had no shirt on, but the covers were draped over him. "Tickets to the Pro Bowl, Manuel?"

"What about the pro bowl, Cay? Do you want tickets? I'll get you them, just say it." He replied dumbfoundedly, by the looks of it he was just getting up and unaware of what I was talking about. "Is everything good with Tré?"

"Did you send him tickets?" I asked Manuel, then retracted, I was paranoid. "Never mind, sorry, Tré *magically* got some tickets to the Pro Bowl, and I thought you sent them. You can have anyone you want, why are you doing so much for me?"

"Remember when you told me you keep hearing those voices telling you stories and what to do. I hear them too, most great people will, but a voice inside of you only matters if you listen to it. The voice I'm hearing is telling me not to give up on you." He said softly, then in his sexy assertive manner made a request. "Show me your face, please, Acacia."

I peeked into the camera a little, "This was a misunderstanding, sorry if I woke you up."

"Don't hang up, you just like fighting with me," Manuel paused for a moment, then asked. "Let's bring him to the game, I'll meet you guys there."

188

"No, I'm not sure about that just yet," I told him immediately, getting out of the camera, although just watching him made me want to see him in person. "You don't get to just do that: make everything captivating and get access to me again."

"Why not? I can hear you smiling." He flirted, "You are telling me you don't want to come visit me?"

I laughed, "I do *not* like how much I want to see you."

"I'll get a hotel right down the street from the game, I'll even make sure he can meet some of the players too." He offered. "I got a group of young men who I sponsor to go every year, he can hang with them, it's been a few years since I've joined them anyway."

"Stop that shit, Manuel! You can't fuckin *buy* me into your life! Especially through my child!" I snapped on him. "I said I'm not sure, you act so hardheaded."

Manuel started to get frustrated himself, raising his voice at me, "I'm not trying to *buy* you, I just want to see you! You act so hard-hearted."

"Yeah, you know all my mistakes right?" I shot back fighting the resistance to *be soft* for him. Knowing I'd love to just cuddle with him, I consciously eased up, not wanting to push him away too much.

"Nothing you've ever done has been a mistake," He sighed, impatiently. "I just want to spend time with you, but you make it impossible."

"Don't try to turn this around on me! Oh, you know what you did, going behind my back. Using some @CorBEatn to talk to me? You purposely booked Young Todd to be there that night because you knew I worshiped him, and now I can barely listen to his music without feeling sorry for him." I told him. "I'm going to get off the phone, I have work."

"Okay, okay, Cay! Yes I did go too far, but if it meant anything, I wasn't just trying to fuck you or buy you, you watch too much television. I simply like you," He promised. "I'm not a bad guy, if you would let me show you something different than you're used to you'll see that."

"I don't think you're a bad person at all."

"Can you just let me fly you out there?" He asked politely, then ended it with, "Please, I'll show your son a great time and I want to take you to one of my favorite places."

My son was doing so well in football since he tried out and made the team, it brought him and his father closer together as they are both passionate about football. When a key player was injured, Tré was ready and able to break records and grow fast his freshman year. Doing something like this with him would probably mean a lot to him.

"Let me talk to Tré about it." I said, considering this weekend getaway could be fun for the both of us, or absolutely awkward. "Honestly Manuel, I've never brought a man around my son before, especially not a man I'm dating, it's very new."

I could hear the smile in his voice, "So we're dating again. I like that."

"Shut up." I told him playfully. "I don't know what this is, but I'm gonna talk to him."

"When are you gonna talk to him?" Manuel asked eagerly, stepping out of his patient demeanor.

"He comes home tomorrow after school; I'll see what he thinks and let you know." I warned him.

"Okay," he agreed. "Tell him over dinner, I'll send you two to a nice restaurant, then I'll fly out after."

"Don't start to plan the trip Manuel, let me talk to him first, then I'll let you know. He might not be ready for that yet."

"You'll come. Can I send the car to take you two to dinner tomorrow? I want to make a good pre-first impression."

"Yes, you can send us to dinner, but that's it. Don't show up, let me do the rest my way please."

I called and briefly spoke with my ex, Hayden, asking if he wanted to take Tré to the pro bowl or if he has plans for the weekend. I didn't think he would, but I wanted to give him a chance to attend. Being that it was out of state I wasn't surprised he passed on the tickets.

Although Hayden and I have separated many times before and I've dated plenty during the time I was single... This would be the first time Tré was going to meet a man that I was dating. I take pride in dating in silence.

His father, on the other hand, has brought several women around throughout Tré's life, and our son seemed fine with it. I was hoping for that same grace. Although Tré doesn't get very close to his dad's women, neither does his dad for that matter, but it never seemed to bother him.

For me, this was a big deal, and if it was going to happen I wanted to be sure Tré felt somewhat comfortable before taking a vacation with the new man.

My Friday

All I could think about at work was having to tell my son I am dating and how he might take it.

Coming home to my fourteen, almost fifteen, year old little-big man is a blast from the past every other Friday. Alternating weeks had its pros, but the cons were missing Tré's company.

Throughout me and my ex's fifteen-year relationship we were probably 70% together, 30% apart. There were a lot of "breaks" for mom and dad, but Tre always lived with me and would visit with dad.

Until this year he has been my consistent, daily reminder that I have a reason to breathe, entertaining Tré was my top hobby for a long time. And not that that has changed completely, but every other week I get to explore other interests than being Tré's mother. Since he's been going back and forth between the houses now, finding and reinventing myself has become my second favorite hobby.

When I opened the door to my house my son's presence was immediately apparent. Starting halfway up the hall that led to Tré's room, there was a trail that consisted of: cardboard box pieces, red athletic socks, random black cord, packing debris, and a hair tie.

"Excuse me, my house did not look like this when I left Hayden the Third!" I called out to him, walking down to his room as I gathered the miscellaneous crap. "Why is all this stuff on my damn floor, Boy?"

"Perhaps it is gravity holding these things down to the floor, my sweet, patient mom." He said back to me as I approached his room, kicking the newly accumulated clothes pile all the way to his doorway. "How was your day?"

"You are too damn big and grown for this dirtiness, I know you don't do this at Dad's." I said to him, "What does your dad say about that?"

"He yells, clean this shit up!" Tré imitated and dodged me as I tried to slap his mouth for using profanity in my presence. He slightly removed his video game headset, gave me a quick strong hug and kiss, and got right back to his virtual game.

My son stood about a foot taller than me, 6' 5" and every time I see him it seems he's only getting bigger.

"Thank you so much, I don't even know how you did it, but you are the best mother." He told me sincerely. "I told Dad you got this, and he thinks I edited the picture!"

I raised my eyebrows but embraced the compliment. "Thank you. We have plans for dinner tonight, so wear something nice and be ready by 5:00 my love. And clean that shit up!"

"Aww Mom!" He groaned, "Why would you get me *this* then say we gotta leave in an hour!" Tré called out. "It took thirty minutes just to set the whole thing up."

"What are you talking about?" I asked him, looking at a brand-new gaming system in my living room, I assumed it was just one of Tré's. "That gaming equipment was here when you got here?"

"What?" Tré asked, he could not hear me with the headset on, fully appearing to kick someone's ass in the virtual world. "I'll get clean

192

and dressed, I'll be ready so quick I promise. How did you get this, it's not out?"

I shrugged. "Magic."

I left Tré alone to drool over his new gaming system in his room while I got ready for our mother-son date. Where I would have to tell him about Manuel.

Manuel	
	Sooooo R u just gonna try to buy him or can I introduce you first?
Buy him? It was free! That's not even his.	
Its mine for when I come visit you, he can play with it.	
	Good luck getting it back now
Text me as soon as you tell him y'all coming.	
Can't wait to meet you at the airport	
	IF we come, then that'll be perfect
You are coming.	
I never meet anyone at the airport. You're special af	
	Don't forget it!

Promptly at 5:00 Tré and I were picked up right outside the house by a man in a familiar B.R.O. security shirt, although referred to himself as a chauffeur. He was the guy who drove Hazel and I to the hotel.

The restaurant was a local exclusive with a beautiful view and it wasn't too far from my home, but somehow I'd never noticed it. Tucked away by palm trees and right in front of the ocean. Tré looked impressed, but he also looked very nervous, as bougie as I am, this restaurant was another level for the average Friday night dinner with mom.

"Is something wrong that I should know about? How much was that driver?" Tré asked me, when we were sitting down at an ocean view table on the second floor. "Why are you doing all this tonight, did something bad happen?"

"Okay, no, I started dating someone… he makes music, he's famous." I was stuttering on my words, "It's still new, but he wants us to join him on a short vacation… tonight. To the Pro bowl."

"Wait, since when are you dating?" He whisper-yelled, my son was apparently not very observant, as I was dating for months. "What about Dad?"

"Tré, me and your dad haven't been together for almost a year, this last time, what are you talking about?" I asked, surprised he still held onto the dream of a two-parent home.

"But I thought sometimes you two still—." He stopped his sentence short and shrugged. "You always just go back to him; I thought you were going to do that again."

"Wow!" I exclaimed, unaware. "I don't want to keep going back and forth with Dad. I was not planning on doing that even if I didn't meet Manuel."

"Manuel?" My son repeated with a tiny smile. "That's why you were at the awards show."

"Yes, Manuel."

"From DeCreed?" Tré asked with a smile. "I like him."

194

"Me too," I smiled back at Tré, "He wants to meet you… tonight. We can fly out there and sit with him for the Pro bowl game tomorrow. Do you want to go?"

He nodded casually, but the smile on his face said it all, he was sold.

Now with Tré being unbothered by the news of me dating, I felt I could relax a little more. However, I wondered how my son would respond if it were just some regular dude, with a 9-5 job. I almost despised Manuel's celebrity privilege.

"Are you sure you are okay being around me and a man?" I asked and he confirmed with a yes.

I texted Manuel, trying to contain my smile from Tré.

Manuel	
	It's a YES
Knew u wouldn't let me down.	
	Would u have let me?
U couldn't if u wanted to. Can't wait to see you at the hangar	

Tré and I had much needed catching up to do for the rest of the dinner. Tré shared stories with me about his school, friends, and things that he was learning living with his dad more. I told him about meeting Manuel and going backstage, meeting my favorite artist in the studio, favorite childhood music group, and a few of the beautiful scenes. I was sure to leave out the sexy details.

When the security-chauffeur came back to the front of the restaurant he had a chummy, familiar passenger beside him.

"Girl you are a stubborn ass bitch, huh?! I thought I was bad!" Jenny laughed as Tré and I got into the vehicle. She leaned back and gave me a hug. "Corbin was about to make me call you if Manuel threw away any more money!"

"Jenny!" I laughed, surprised to see her, her energy was contagious. "What are you doing here?"

"Don't ruin the magic, Sis. How was this driver?" She asked, looking at him up and down.

"I'm the chauffeur, but you're always driving me crazy." The driver joked with her.

Jenny stopped noticing my son, "Hi, you must be Hayden the Third, also known as Tré?"

Tré reached out his hand to Jenny for a handshake, but she pulled him right in for a hug across the seat as well. "My family calls me Tré."

"Tré, I'm basically your mom's fairy godmother, as far as my boss is concerned, so I guess I'm like your great-fairy-godmother. Better than family," she tried to explain. "So, if you need something you just let me know, if you don't see me, you can ask Marcus."

The chauffeur-security guard, Marcus and Jenny seemed very close, they bantered back and forth entertaining Tré and I with stories from their childhood for about thirty minutes. He was an old family friend who grew up with Manuel, and some of the others from DeCreed as well.

"I didn't know you were my fairy godmother," I quietly told Jenny, sitting up close to her as the guys got into a sports conversation. "I would've had so many more requests."

"I'm sure you see Manuel will give you anything right now, what do you want? Just tell him." She said, raising a brow. "He has a private jet and driver on standby to fly you to him ASAP."

196

"Wait, where are you going?" I asked, noticing we were going away from the direction of my house.

"Straight to the jet darling," Marcus told me. "That's where I'm getting paid to go, no exceptions. I heard you might argue about it, so I came with facts: we are eleven minutes south of the airport, your house is thirty minutes south from here, it would make no sense to go further south when we need to be going north. Everything you need will be there."

"No, because I *need* to go home and pack, so does my son, and I need to get the house ready," I began to ramble, annoyed.

"Pack what? Everything is there. Did you say get the house ready? What does it need?" Marcus reiterated with a laugh, then reached down and grabbed a bag, handing it to Tré. "Here's a gift, someone said you'll like this."

"EmManuel has everything, trust me I was shopping for a month for *this* weekend. You have everything you two will need and more." Jenny smiled at Tre as he opened his gift. "Or the house. Cause we're going to see the All Stars!"

Tré's smile sealed the deal as he held up a football jersey. It must've been impressive because he was very impressed.

"Did you just say you've been shopping for a month? We didn't decide this until today." I asked, realizing that she was preparing for a month for something that was just decided a little over an hour ago and was only even on the table since yesterday. Manuel just plans for everyone to do as he pleases. "Wow this was just another one of his plans?"

"Damn girl you *are* so hard at times!" Jenny snapped at me.

I seemed to be the villain so much in this world he was bringing me into. "Why? How is it me?"

"Stop being so tough on him, Acacia. He likes you and he is trying to be sweet. He can be obnoxiously extra at times, but don't punish him for it. He's a hard worker, it's good to see him spending on something involving his happiness." She shot me a harsh look, then glanced at Tré. "We'll talk alone later this weekend; I'll steal you for coffee on Sunday

197

morning. There's things Manuel won't say because he doesn't want to hurt others, but I will. Just don't be so tough on him."

"Okay, talking over breakfast on Sunday sounds good." I looked at her, dropping the subject, she seemed to have a good perspective on Manuel. Maybe I am too hard.

I sat the rest of the way in silence, in my own head, convincing myself to just enjoy the weekend and not to overthink it.

Tré tried to play it cool, being on a jet for the first time. However, every time I looked at his eyes they sparkled with excitement. Occasionally he would point out something in the aircraft, it reminded me of when he was younger and we'd go on adventures together around town, exploring new surroundings. The older he got the less exciting our adventures became; he was getting older.

The jet took longer to take off than the one Manuel and I took last time. The chauffeur-security guard was beginning to get annoyed waiting for something, but Jenny snapped at him, and he quickly walked away from us.

A few moments later a beautiful, disheveled woman in her late twenties came onto the jet. She was slightly out of breath, but with an energetic toddler struggling to get out of her hand, her lack of breath was understandable.

"Sorry I'm so late!" She sighed, hugging Jenny, then looking at me with a friendly smile. "Thanks for letting me tag along, we missed our flight when we got lost at the theme park! I had to leave the nannie back at the theme park! Could not find her anywhere and I have her phone here in the baby bag!"

"You left her?" I asked, surprised.

"Yes, but EmManuel sent some security to find her, and held this flight for me. I just had to make it tonight, my husband was about ready to kill me. We'll find a sitter when we get to the city." She tried to settle herself in, but the screaming toddler was giving her a hard time. "I need a drink."

I laughed, remembering those days with Tré at theme parks, luckily I never had to leave anyone behind. "It is difficult but remember it's only for a short time that they are that small, enjoy that time while you can. I can't get him to go to theme parks with just me alone anymore."

"I really do, I just can't wait til his dad can retire and come along with us, he's so busy that it takes the nostalgia out of family trips." She told me, "But, God forbid his little boy's not there to show the world how great of a dad he is. Meanwhile I haven't been able to piss or reapply makeup, since we mysteriously lost my nannie-niece-in-law this morning."

"Yes, get it." I extended my hand to her, "I'm Acacia, this is my son, Tré. If you need to use the restroom, do your makeup, or just relax, your son can hang out with us. I love children and he's really good with them too."

"Thanks! Well, let's order some drinks before my nerves kick in." She suggested getting the flight attendant our drink order.

The tired momma, who called herself Kiki, was very fun to be around!

"If I talk too much, let me know, it's how I cope with my fear of heights. I have to stay busy, or I start to panic," Kiki explained. "I spent the whole pandemic overcoming that fear so that I can spend more time visiting with my husband. It worked, and the liquor helps."

Kiki used the flight to fill me in on some top spots we needed to visit and even some of the festivities that we might be interested in. She and I drank a whole bottle of liquor, it was her favorite. She said she was a little surprised to see they had such a rare brand on the flight.

Kiki's recent studies on facing her fear of flying paid off. She knew some cool insider tips on how to have a fun flight. First she hooked up her phone to the speaker and let Tré be the DJ for the ride. Then she got the flight attendant to bring us out the *Secret Sky Menu* and we had more treats to choose from.

Her toddler took a liking to Tré, and they ended up tossing a nerf football throughout the fight. Everything Tré did was hilarious to the little toddler, I could see their friendship was a nice break for Kiki.

Once we landed and were ready to go, a tipsy Kiki and her son hugged both Tré and I.

"Thanks again for making room for us at the last minute. Maybe we can meet up for dinner tomorrow before we leave the city, with the men of course," she winked at me. "If the men haven't booked up our entire weekend for us."

I nodded genuinely, she seemed like a cool person, nice enough to hang out with in a new city on a double date. Kiki digitally tapped her business card to my phone, and I received her contact information. We hugged again then she headed out the jet behind her son, as I straightened up my area in the cabin.

Jenny ushered Tré out the jet behind Kiki, giving my shoulders a tight squeeze as she stood by me, like a giddy toddler. She was up to something.

14

Manuel was waiting to meet us as soon as we landed, he waited near the bottom of the airstair with a small group of people, who were welcoming Kiki and her son. I watched him from the tinted window, admiring how extraordinary of a man he is, almost questioning my own ability to keep him enamored with me.

Manuel finding joy in trying to amaze me was beginning to become very cute, not because of the price tags attached to his gifts, but the thought behind them. The attention to detail could be breathtaking at times, for example how Tré got shocked so much that he stopped walking and stood as still as a statue at the top of the stairs. He was staring at the group of people on the ground who stood with Manuel.

"Come down the steps, I'll introduce you," I whispered to Tré. Taking the lead down the steps as Tré slowly followed me down the steps.

Kiki and her child were both reuniting at the bottom of the airstair with a man who stood with Manuel. The baby was so happy to see his dad, he jumped right in his arms.

"Mom… do you know who that is?" Tré asked, seemingly referring to the man standing beside Manuel, with broad shoulders and a signature hairstyle that was starting to look very familiar.

"Oh, shit. Is that the football player you always talk about?" I asked him, trying to bring a name to the familiar face and haircut. "Manuel is too much."

Jenny chuckled from beside us, "It damn sure is Swift. Come meet him Tré." She jogged down the airstair, holding Tré's hand, to begin introductions. "He's your favorite, I bet, right?"

I locked my eyes with Manuel's sweet eyes as we walked down the stairs, shaking my head, but smiling from ear to ear. He did it again.

He walked up the stairs to meet us halfway and whispered to me, "Don't be mad."

"I am not mad at all," I whispered, giving him a quick kiss because I was so happy for Tré, but then I joked. "You are such a manipulator, trying to win over my teenager."

"No, no, what can I say? Like you, I happen to have a lot of great people in my life." He shrugged.

"I see you do," I nodded in agreement, continuing to whisper. "What happened to the nanny?"

He laughed with a shrug. "I'm sure she's enjoying herself."

Manuel and I stood back as Jenny introduced Tré to his favorite athlete, Kiki's fiancé and the toddler's dad. Kiki bragged to Swift about how Tré was so helpful by playing with her son.

"Thanks for helping with Jr., I got a special seat for you at the brunch I'm hosting tomorrow," Swift told Tré. "I bet Junior recognized that jersey you are wearing and knew you had good sense. Want me to sign it?"

Tré nodded eagerly, "Yes please."

"They had your liquor on flight, right?" Manuel asked Kiki.

"Yes, you know I drank it all." She playfully hit Manuel then organized us all in a photo. "Let Tré and Swift get one alone, also, get a picture together with everyone." Kiki organized a few photos before we went our separate ways. "If you need anything while you're down here call me."

Once they were gone I took a deep breath and began my own introductions.

"Tré, this is Manuel; Manuel, this is my son, Tré." Standing between them as they shook hands, Manuel pulled Tré in for a little hug.

"Thanks for coming over here this weekend," Manuel told him, "I'm glad you could join me."

Tré nodded, "Thanks for inviting me, no one is going to believe I'm really here this weekend! I'm trying to enjoy it, but I don't even believe it yet. I can't believe that it was Swift's family on that jet with us! I can't even believe I was on a private jet at all! I'm so glad they lost their nanny in the theme park!"

"Yeah, things can happen like that," Manuel touched my cheek.

"It makes sense why they had her favorite liquor on the flight, even though she joined at the last minute," I whispered to Manuel. "And what happened to the nanny?"

"Yeah, my pleasure, it worked out great. We gotta busy day tomorrow, try to get a good sleep." Manuel told us both as Tré walked ahead with Marcus and Jenny. Then whispered to me, "She's fine, she was just hanging out with one of my workers. Nothing weird."

Even from behind him I could see that Tré was wearing a big smile. We all walked together in the direction of the deeply tinted black SUV, Garon was standing outside of it at the driver's window.

Oh, great, I thought, my favorite security guard was still around.

"I got stuff for us to do alone, tomorrow night." Manuel told me when Tré was out of earshot. "I really can't wait to make up for last weekend."

"You better." I flirted back, sneaking a kiss on those soft lips, those lips that I missed.

"Were you in there getting drunk with Kiki?" He asked, I responded with a smile and shrug. "Your tongue tastes... strong."

Almost as soon as we got into the SUV Tré and Jenny both fell asleep in the middle row against their windows. Manuel and I were in the far back, purposefully. Marcus was in the front seat with Garon, it was nice to hear Garon talk like a normal person.

Manuel pulled me closer to him, "Thank you for coming."

203

I kissed him passionately, playing with his lips with my tongue, and combing his softly textured beard with my fingers. Occasionally glancing at Tré, hoping he wouldn't wake up.

"I'm taking you somewhere special, but lowkey tomorrow night." He whispered. "Tré can hang with the team, or security and Jenny… I just need you to myself."

"That sounds like something I would love to do," I mumbled, not letting my lips off his, slightly aggressive.

Not sure if it was the liquor or the anger that I was feeling toward him the past week, but Manuel was running through my mind like crazy… somehow that rage had turned into sexual frustration. I was pissed that he was still lying to me, but my body language was translating completely wrong. My body wanted him. Badly.

"Good because I want to show you the world." he asked as I sucked on his neck and squeezed on the hand he was using to keep me from straddling his lap. "You need to trust me."

"You, me, and the word trust have a conflicting relationship right now," I softly told him.

Garon drove us past all the bright lights and excitement, straight to a secluded hotel entrance garage. Which unfortunately was our cue to stop fooling around and touching each other. I managed to stop sucking on Manuel's neck as we came to a stop and the lights slowly came on. I wanted to have some alone time with him tonight.

"What's happening tonight?" I asked him.

Everyone got up and out of the SUV as the concierge folks grabbed our luggage.

"Some last-minute shit came up and Chris needs me. I gotta run to the studio tonight, you're invited to come hang out, you can come with me if you want." Manuel told me as we were waiting for the elevator to open, it seemed like we were on the top floor. I noticed Garon shot Manuel a mean look when he invited me.

"No, I'm kinda tired," I lied so as not to cause any more friction between Manuel, myself, and *the rules* before I get a chance to learn them myself. I wasn't tired, I was pumped up just being around him again, I could have stayed up with Manuel all night.

"Okay, I figured you might be," he said understandably, "If you wake up, change your mind, or just miss me, text me. You promise?"

"Sure," I promised.

Tré and I had our own suite, Manuel walked us to our room first, then went with his crew to their own suite a couple yards down. Jenny hooked up our clothes for the weekend and even filled our fridge and cabinets with snacks.

As soon as our door closed Tré let out all his excitement, rummaging through his closet. Being in the private jet, riding in expensive cars, and most importantly meeting Swift meant the most to him. He went on about the itinerary Marcus gave him and some cool things we'd be doing tomorrow, but he was speaking football-gibberish to me.

"Mom, this is so insane! I'm gonna call Dad." Tré asked, looking through the expensive ass clothes and sneakers in his closet that I would never splurge on. "I want to tell him where we are! Do you know what kind of jeans these are? Three of these sneakers ain't even out till next month, Mom. I gotta show this to Dad."

"There's a time difference and it's late, do that tomorrow."

Truthfully, I didn't feel like arguing with his dad tonight, and that man will find something to argue about as soon as he found out what was going on.

I kissed Tré, goodnight and headed to my side of the suite to try to get some sleep. Tomorrow was going to be a big day between the boys dragging me to a bunch of football festivities in the morning, and Manuel trying to give me the whole world in one night.

But probably an hour later I got up to use the bathroom and had an urge to text Manuel. I missed him already, so I followed through with my promise.

Manuel	
	The view of the strip from my balcony is beautiful, thank u for the suite
Send me a picture	
	How about u come stand out here with me when your done working
I thought you were tired?	
	I just didn't want to be a distraction for u

Manuel video called me almost right after I pressed send.

Fuck.

I answered his call, not showing my face on the camera, but looking at him. He was in a mid-studio session, with the mic in front of him and headphones on.

"Show me the view from your balcony," he directed at me. "I can use a little inspiration."

I awkwardly chuckled at the spontaneity, facing the camera to show him the skyline. "Aren't you supposed to be working, sir?"

Somehow I was still managing to be a studio distraction. Were the Sweethearts going to lecture me again.

"I am working. I was calling you for a favor, since you're not tired." He spoke. "I need a female voice on this track, I need you to come down to where I'm at and say just three lines."

"Three lines?" I laughed nervously, showing my face so he could see my expression. "Okay, I will try. I don't like my voice."

206

"Don't talk negatively about yourself, you are stunning. I'm gonna send someone to come get you now," he told me. I nodded my head and couldn't get the smile off my face when he hung up. "Get dressed."

I quickly rummaged through the brand-new clothes and put an outfit together. During the time Manuel sent another message.

	Manuel	
YOU ARE THE GOAL. Never my distraction. Don't let anyone make you think like that		
		K. But if u feel like I start to distract u promise that you will tell me
Promise		

Garon was my very silent ride to Manuel at the studio, he always seemed to want to say something, but didn't. Even when I tried to speak and be cordial, I got nothing from him. When we got to the building we silently walked through the building, bypassing all the security guards who nodded at Garon respectfully when he passed.

"No women," the final security guard meekly told Garon, barely making eye contact.

"She's fine." Garon told him, but the man didn't move.

The security guard seemed new as he was timid trying to stand his ground on the rules, "Well she should at least be searched."

"Shut the fuck up," Garon told him as he pushed the security guard out of the way and let us in Manuel's session. Garon was apparently a *somebody* also.

Manuel had the lines I had to say written down and handed them to me after greeting me with a kiss and a big bear hug. There were three

207

other people in the room, they were working on the music as well, Buck was one of them. Another was Chris, who I was sure was the snitch who ratted me out to the Sweethearts for the last studio session I went to.

Manuel jumped right back into the booth and got back to work. I was glad he didn't waste too much time greeting me, I wanted to prove I wasn't a distraction. Watching Manuel work was an aphrodisiac, he was so confident in his musical vision that he delegated and made decisions so smoothly. He was a fine businessman, not only was he sexy to watch in control, but he could take the criticism and corrections too.

Chris came over to me and explained how I was to say the lines. He practiced the words with me until I felt comfortable enough to go into the booth.

"I'm gonna step out there, unless you need me to hold your hand," Manuel whispered to me once I was all geared up and had my professional tutorial on the studio equipment.

I loved that he was available to hold my hand, but I let him go. "I'm a big girl."

"I like babying you," he flirted and left me with a kiss on my cheek.

Buck surprisingly was better at working the equipment than he was at being security. His personality even matured with the job responsibility; he took it more seriously. He even spoke to me without sarcasm, gave me tips when I recorded my lines, and stayed kind!

Buck wasn't the only one that had begun to warm up to me, by the end of the studio session it seemed like even Corbin and Chris were a little more accepting of me than they had been before. They were engaging me in a little small talk, nothing too serious, but it felt nice to be treated like someone relevant.

I was glad I came to the studio after all, if I had to hear the Sweethearts mouths again then so be it. The men were starting to know me. Garon still hated me, he purposely walked away when I came around him.

208

After catching me do a few back-to-back yawns, Manuel took a break from his work to drive me back to my hotel. "Get some sleep, they'll call you for your breakfast order, but if you hungry before just call them. I'll be back."

I nodded and kissed him goodnight. Unsure of when he ever found time to sleep with his busy schedule.

I put Manuel's solo album on my phone before falling asleep soundly to dream intentionally about this man.

When the sun was up and our stomachs were full, Manuel was at my door with bright eyes and his welcoming smile. Beside him was Jenny and a beautiful makeup artist with a box of makeup and sexy-lady equipment.

"Let's get you pretty, Princess." Jenny came right in with a smile, I concluded that the confidence was genetic. She had that same charisma as her older cousin.

"Ain't nothing pretty, she wakes up gorgeous," Manuel kissed me, then went straight to Tré's room to compete in some video game they both claimed GOAT status in.

How is he not tired? I wondered to myself.

Jenny and the stylist quickly transformed my bathroom into a mini salon just like before with Stephanie. The stylist was much nicer to me though, she asked me questions about my preferences and explained why certain things complimented my tones and aura.

Once my face was lightly beat to perfection, Jenny had my outfit ready for a football day in the city. The long sage, floral dress was nothing I'd ever choose for myself, but saw I was exactly who it was made for once I had it on. My outfit complimented the sage accents on Manuel's outfit, I loved that for us.

"Please tell me you feel this chemistry as much as EmManuel?" Jenny asked cautiously.

I nodded my head yes with the smile that comes to my face when I hear his name, "As much as I keep telling myself that this whole thing is not real, I do feel a strong connection to him. It just feels too fast... I don't want it to be forced."

She nodded, "Time doesn't matter to him, if it weren't for Corbin his whole schedule would be shot. He lives *freely* like that, it's just Manuel's way of doing life. The chemistry is there, we can see it too."

I couldn't help, but to smile wide, of course I wanted his team to like me. "Even Garon?"

"Garon is so damn meticulous, is he giving you a hard time? We *all* agreed it's truly so good to see him happy again," she responded dryly with a side eye. "Everyone said it, even Ma and she's a bitch. You're his muse, he needed this."

"It's a little scary," I admitted, dropping to a whisper. "Manuel is pressure."

Jenny agreed with a nod. "He is a lot, his life is a lot, I get it. Nobody would fault you for leaving, not even him. I promise."

I reluctantly nodded back, "What would you do if you were me?"

Jenny looked at me for a moment with the face you make having to decide between a lie and the truth, then with a low whisper she said, "I'd run."

She flashed a smile and a wink; I believe there was a bit of truth. Even Jenny thinks I should run away from him?

Manuel knocked on the open door, stopping our girl talk. "How did you get finer. Are you ready?"

"Yes, yes," I confirmed, getting up to hug the stylist bye. "Thank you for everything, you were excellent." She'd gathered all her things and was waving goodbye at the door.

Jenny left with her to help escort her to the front.

"I can't stop staring at you, it looks like she did a good job." Manuel told me after I flashed him a smile upon catching him staring at me. "How was her interview?"

"Interview?"

"Yes, hair and makeup, personal artist, did you like her?" He asked, "Jenny liked her, and that's tough, but I want to make sure you like her too. She's even cool with traveling."

"Hiring a makeup and hair stylist? Manuel, how are you interviewing for me to have a personal anything for *travel* before you ask me if I want to be traveling? Why are we moving so quickly, can we go on our second date first?"

"Why are you counting dates? Who cares about how many dates. We can go on as many dates as you want," he played with my hair. "I'm with all of that, but you don't want to travel with me?"

"I have a career, a business, and a child." I reminded him.

"I'll hire you to work for me," he explained. "Corbin will do all the paperwork today."

"I'm not working *for* you." I side-eyed him. "Dating the boss won't work for me."

Manuel paused, with his lips pursed, he looked disappointed. Watching him hear no was almost sad, it was so unfamiliar to him.

"Why are you so difficult?" He asked. "What else do you need to see for me to convince you that you'll be happier with me."

"This is just too fast for me, quitting my job to travel with you is just not in my plan." I told him sharply. I grabbed his hand and kissed it as a truce. "I don't think we should start talking about this right now. Let's follow the plan for this weekend and have a good time."

"You're right, it's about Tré today." He nodded, killing the argument and moving forward, "And you are tonight."

"Nothing too crazy, nothing extravagant. Just dinner alone, getting to know each other." I reminded him, "Simple. Plus, I'm getting coffee in the morning with Jenny, so I don't want to stay out too late."

Manuel kissed me and we headed out to the football stadium for the big event.

The three of us; along with the occasional company of Marcus and Jenny, our incognito security, and sporadically different DeCreed members had a busy day. Tré had a great time, mostly just talking to Manuel, and others about football. Manuel didn't have to try very hard to win my son over, he's charismatic and everybody around us loved him. It was too easy.

My favorite part was getting the freebies. We had so many football souvenirs and got just about any snacks without standing in a single line. Vendors were giving Manuel their merch, just hoping he'd wear it and take a photo. Manuel gave Tré first dibs on any merch he was handed, my son was looking very festive in all the football gear..

We had club seats which meant we walked through a fancy upscale level with adult drinks and seductive women walking around in cheerleader outfits. We sat at a semi-circle booth with sleek, black leather seats.'

"This is how you are supposed to watch a football game," Tré leaned back with a smile. "Are we doing this for the Super Bowl too?"

"You'll have to ask your mother that," Manuel told him, not saying no. "I hear one day you will be watching it right on the field, right?"

Tré nodded sheepishly, "I want to."

"You can," Manuel told him, "Start claiming it now, get comfortable saying it, every day. Come up with a plan, discipline yourself with good habits, and stay true to both."

Tré nodded confidently and smiled at Manuel, then at me. Tré was sold.

The rest of the day continued much of the same. Manuel took us to a signing after the game, Tré got some of his favorite athletes to sign his limited edition, Pro Bowl jersey. There were mini events that we saw as well, but slowly everything was beginning to just be a big merge together for me.

212

Manuel and Tré were getting along so well, trash talking each other's favorite players, at times when I thought Manuel was a little harsh, Tré stepped up and matched his humor. I noticed a little more independence in Tré, no doubt from living with his dad half the time, and of course the natural teachings of high school.

I'm not sure if I was holding them back or if they were holding me back, but I was somehow excused from the festivities. The men were still having a great time, Jenny seemed to want to leave just like I did. Manuel forced Marcus to leave with me and Jenny, which he didn't seem too mad about, but he took us back to the hotel.

"Sorry Marcus, I just could not hang anymore." I apologized.

"It's okay, I kind of have some plans of my own tonight that I should be getting ready for." He told me with a wink.

As soon as I got back, I took a long warm shower, then walked through the spotless suite with just my little white towel on. I sat on the oversized balcony couch and relaxed with a pen and pad in hopes to get some work done.

However instead of working, I found myself drifting off into the daydream of being with Manuel. What he might feel like. I closed my eyes to think about it, but I kept jumping back to my ex's face in my mind!

Seeing that face just brought chills to foreshadow what I knew was going to happen tonight. It was just too good to be true, the curse was on its way to fruition! It was getting hard not to fall for Manuel, but I've been here before, this is how it happens. Everything seems to be going in the right direction then I give in, and everything turns out completely wrong!

I got up forcing my daydream to end and walked into the huge master bedroom closet. As I looked through the closet I began to play "fashion show" with the outfits, although my stylist already had specific items labeled with a location and time!

When the guys got back from their invite-only football festivities, Manuel got ready in his suite, and I hung out with Tré in his room for a while to pick his brain while he played video games.

"What do you think about him?" I asked my son.

He looked at me dumbfoundedly, "Mom, what do you expect? He's great. It's weird that you're not with dad, but he's good."

I sighed it was weird, "You think this is too weird?"

Tré shrugged, he didn't care about my dating life half as much as I expected him to. "Wanna get on this new system?"

"No, I have to finish getting dressed for this date. You'll be fine here alone right?"

"Yes Mom, I'm a teenager, I'm not a little kid. Dad leaves me home alone all the time."

I was wearing a Cousin Jenny original; a black dress featuring a lot of skin and see through material. In my son's room I kept my robe on, so he didn't see my lack of clothes. Although all the important parts were covered, I hoped it wasn't too risqué, but it was surely fierce and flattering!

As if saving himself from my thoughts, Manuel video called my phone. I excused myself from Tré's room, kissing him good night as he set up some gaming system.

15

"Cay, hurry up and come outside, you gotta hurry up and see this," he said with a huge smile on his face big enough to cover my whole phone screen. "You are going to love this."

Although his excitement through the screen was contagious, I could not find the right shoes Jenny told me to wear with this dress. "I can't remember what shoes she said to wear with this. Why do I even need this many shoes for a weekend? Barely two nights, she can be excessive."

Manuel looked annoyed, "Do I need to come carry you down here barefoot?"

"Why are you outside already?" I asked, finally focusing on him, he made an even more annoyed face. I rolled my eyes and laughed at how giddy he was at times. "Okay, okay, I'm coming down now, I got the shoes."

I hung up and rushed to the elevator, with the strappy black shoes with rhinestones and mesh that complimented the dress' mesh and rhinestone embellishments. I glanced at my phone to check an incoming notification.

Jenny	
Hey Princess change of plans I got an early flight out tomorrow. Send me 100 pictures of	

She canceled on me. Why would she cancel? *Manuel?*

As soon as I got to the huge glass rotary door and felt the cool outside air on my face, I heard the familiar voices of DavenPort, my all-time favorite group, singing an apology song of theirs. They were standing behind Manuel, outside the hotel beside the oversized hotel emblem statue.

Manuel was grinning from ear to ear and holding a shiny gift bag in his hand. He walked over and stood beside me as we watched and listened to them sing.

"They happened to be coming in, I told them their biggest fan was upstairs," he whispered with a shrug, handing me a travel pack of tissues from the gift bag he held.

We stood there holding hands. Me listening and trying to watch through my glassy eyes, ruin the makeup touch up, as the men sang! Manuel watched me, smiling at my joy.

The lead singer, my all-time favorite member, told me, "Keep him," pointing at Manuel.

I could feel the tears falling from my face as Manuel tried to blot them off with a tissue. I looked at Manuel in disbelief, "There's no way you didn't plan this?"

He held up the gift bag, "I didn't plan it, I was too busy trying to find this apology gift."

I made a skeptical face at him, I was arm's reach from the men of DavenPort, serenading me! As they were wrapping up their song the small audience that had gathered and were also cheering, although they were denied photos as DavenPort hurried on into the hotel.

216

"So do you accept my apology?" Manuel asked after scooping me up and carrying me to a white bench, handing me the shiny glitter gift bag.

"Are you serious? I've been listening to them since I was eleven!" I said once I was finally able to catch my breath and realize what just happened. "What am I supposed to say to that? Not only are you... you, but you just got DavenPort to sing to me?"

"Just say you accept my apology and won't be standing in line to meet anyone, then I'll be happy." He shrugged, trying to appear nonchalant. "Or maybe now you can believe that I am *that* Nigga? Put the walls down."

"I guess you really are *Him*." I laughed, admitting it as I wiped my nose and tears. "Not that I doubted it, but I'm in shock. Trying not to overthink anything."

"Owed me a little family favor, it wasn't even that big really, they are great. What's there to overthink?" He explained then spoke with a serious tone. "Why do I feel you keep pushing me away?"

Because I am, I thought to myself. I questioned why I had my walls up, he was everything that I had on my Dream Man vision board, why did I still have the resistance? I remember one of Hazel's soror's at the event telling us, 'If you don't feel you deserve this man to exist in your life, he will not'. Did I not feel I was even worthy of my dream man?

"I'm scared, I guess. I'm a busy person, I wasn't necessarily looking for a relationship so soon and you don't even want a *real* relationship. And I don't want to uproot my whole life for a situation like that." I told him with a friendly smile. "Your life seems amazing; I just don't see where I'd fit in."

"*Real,* is subjective." He looked into my eyes. "I get it, I got you. We'll find out where you fit in, I won't let you get hurt, won't put you in places you can't grow. And please don't ever wear Jenny's line unless you are with me, I should fire her for making that."

I shook my head, "No, she's my favorite person in your staff. I enjoy having her around."

"You would choose her," he said with sarcasm, kissing my hand.

217

I smiled at him, "Yes I chose her. Why don't you think she's ready for her own shop? Her designs are sexy, women will buy these."

"Because Jenny's not ready yet, her designs will sell but she won't be happy. Of course, I could give it to her, but until she is ready to change the way she thinks, I'd be doing her a disservice. Life is not only the day-to-day motions, how you really tell who a person is, how they handle the storms. Their actions during life's storms will show what they are ready for."

"Happiness is in the progress, not the finished product." I remembered a quote from my ivy league professor.

"And maturity comes with practice, she'll get it in time." He paused and looked at me quizzically, "You wouldn't keep a doctor that didn't seem mature enough for their position, right?"

I shook my head no, "Okay of course not, but you thought CoDéy wasn't ready and look at her. She blew up, she even won the best award the other night, she's successful right?"

"Ya bombs blow up one time and typically destroy shit. Being successful is a decision a person needs to make every day." He rationalized, "Anyone can have what they believe if they have faith in themselves, but wisdom to maintain and create something favorable that sustains over time, that's what makes the difference. I know what I'm talking about, that's why you should have at least the tiniest amount of faith in me."

"Okay, super tiny, like, that much." I pinched my fingers to show the tiniest amount of space. "Nowadays the more I hear, *trust me,* the more I worry. I've been hurt more by people that I trusted, than those I didn't."

"Understandable, I just need a little." He told me, pulling me up by my hands. "Now let's go for a ride. I'm going to take you to my favorite lounge in this city."

"I can." I kissed him on the cheek. Whether or not my skepticism got in the way, Manuel kept things interesting and fun for me. "And thank you for the best apology ever."

218

"Damn. You haven't even opened the bag yet." He led me to a sleek black coupe with racing stripes and held the door partially open, "So we're good now, right?"

I sighed and smiled at him; it was easy to forgive him. A light rain with just enough strength to destroy my hair for the night started to come down. "Yes, I accept your apology, let's get in."

"You sure?" He double-checked and after I nodded, let me into the car. "You look very fine in that dress."

"Thank you," I accepted his compliment.

While walking to his side of the vehicle he was approached by a small group of fans and stopped to take some photos with them in the drizzling rain.

At that time, I was able to peek in the gift bag he'd given me to see what it was. I cracked it open and saw an elite looking ring box, with a familiar sounding name etched on the box, but I closed the bag when I heard him opening the car door.

A ring box? And the more it came to me, the name on the gift bag looked very familiar. He was a famous jeweler, who made lots of pricey wedding jewelry for rich folks.

Manuel jumped right into the driver's seat when he finished speaking to his fans, he adjusted his mirrors and smiled at the open road. He looked like a young boy living out his racecar dreams in this vehicle.

"You are gonna love where I'm taking you, the vibe is good, but the view is what I want to show you." He peeled out the parking spot, pushing the speed limit immediately, and not missing a beat of the conversation. "A little nighttime romantic thing."

Who would hand someone a ring in a bag as a gift. I couldn't stop thinking about the gift he handed me. I tried to ignore the gift bag all together. Maybe it was not as serious as I was making it. Maybe it was an earring or belly ring... just put in a ring box. A very widely known engagement-wedding ring designer's box and bag.

"How long was your last relationship?" I asked him.

"Well, I guess I gotta explain to you a little more about her and me. We knew each other since we were kids, she was a friend of my older brother. We were off and on since I was a preteen, we had a very convenient relationship at one point." He explained.

I understood a little more now, "That's why she's still around?"

"Yes, she comes around when she wants to be, getting everything, she needs when she calls my people. I don't abandon anyone. People will tell you my love is my biggest fault, but that's how I was raised and so far it's gotten me this far."

"Did you pressure her to get an abortion?" I asked a question that had been plaguing me since the moment CoDéy blurted it out. Who'd do that to a lifelong friend?

Manuel loved kids, in every interview that I stealthily watched throughout the last week, he said he is from a big family and wants a big family. So, it didn't make sense to me why he would have her abort the baby.

"I don't pressure people." He said, clearing his name. "I gave my opinion when it was asked."

"Which, I'm sure, your opinion was to abort it, so she did it to make you happy," I muttered, I almost felt sad for CoDéy, no wonder she was so hurt.

"My opinion was she should go be with her unborn daughter's father" He told me.

"Okay, that wasn't you?" I tried to understand.

He shook his head no, "No way in hell I am able to give her a girl, I didn't love her like that."

"Wait, is this about that *curse* you told me about? She was having a girl?" I asked.

"It's more than that, can we talk about something else? And can you stop comparing yourself? Especially to her, she's irrelevant." He asked, as we zig-zagged through traffic, his right hand on my inner thigh.

220

I sighed, he was right, we should be having fun. "Okay."

"Just sit back and relax." He said as he squeezed my thigh. "I want you to know, you're gonna love falling in love with me Acacia."

I laughed out loud at his huge ego, he knows he's sexy, his confidence a constant aphrodisiac.

Through the opening of the gift bag, I peaked at the box again to get the spelling of the foreign designer's name. *Is that an actual engagement ring?* Having full faith in my privacy screen, I secretly searched for the designer on my phone.

The only thing on the designer's website was engagement rings. No earrings. No belly rings. Just engagement and wedding rings. I filtered the results to show the rings prices low to high, the lowest price ring was $500,000.

Shit.

"Falling in love." I repeated, "Manuel's definition of fun."

He shrugged, "It could be cute." Manuel told me. "I could see you beside me forever."

"Forever? We don't know each other."

"I like what I do know," he told me, letting his hand go up to the highest point of my thigh. "I love everything I'm finding out. It's hard not to keep my hands and eyes off you."

I agreed with him, putting my hand on top of my inner thigh. "Well keep your eyes on the road, your hands are fine."

I thought back to the file I found on his tablet. Did he truly think a list of random details on my life and small talk from a fake profile is enough to get me an engagement ring and be with me forever?

He gently rubbed his fingertips on the front of my panties, then applied a little pressure as he took a turn on the road. I felt myself getting wet, it was seeping through the underwear, I'm sure he felt it too.

I took a deep exhale wanting him inside of me, struggling to keep up with a conversation as he teased me. "I don't even know where you live. I know nothing about you other than random internet information, possibly misinformation?"

He chuckled, taking his hand off me and using it to drive. He somehow weaved effortlessly through the traffic. "You are such an overthinker! What does knowing things about me have to do with letting yourself have fun, maybe even falling in love?"

Manuel took my left hand in his right and weaved our fingers together, kissing the back of my hand. The ring finger specifically.

He appealed to me in every way, the way I imagined my dream man would. His style, his mindset, his smile, his confidence, the simplest mannerisms, the way he walked, talked, and apparently even the way he drove turned me on.

I struggled trying to be honest with myself, hoping that it was not his income that was somehow subconsciously winning me over, playing with my emotions. Maybe I am morally no better than those groupies I deduced to be less than because they were so willing to pimp themselves out to get through that long V.I.P. concert line, hoping for a room key and the chance to smell their musty DeCreed balls.

That's not me. Right?

I thought about all the things he did and new things he bought me, from my classroom to my closet just in the last week, the delicious food, the luxury transportation. The views alone from the jets could make a woman fall in love with him. The mini live performances by people who get paid hundreds of thousands to do such a show. Am I falling for him or the things he comes with?

Even more thought provoking, did it even matter? We were both having fun, enjoying the company.

"I guess you're right," I smiled at him. "We don't need to know everything right away."

"I can see your brain moving through your forehead, stop thinking so much for a change." He kissed my forehead. "Open the bag."
222

"Okay, but one last question, did you make Jenny cancel on me?" I asked.

"Is that what all this pressure is about?" He sighed, but made a sly grin, as he turned up the music. "Yeah I did. That's why you've been acting so funny?"

I shouted at him over the music. "Why would you do that?"

"You're so persistent." He pulled over into an empty parking lot and put the car in park, ironically singing his own song on the radio. "Because I know why you want to meet with her. You just want to ask all your questions, you're like a reporter."

"Is there something you don't want me to know?"

Manuel shook his head no, but he was thinking about that answer for sure. He *wants me to wear his ring, comfortably fall for him, but can't even trust me alone with his cousin.*

"What are you trying to find out? Why do you want to meet with her?" He asked,

"I don't know, it's just my intuition, I want to talk to her and get to know more about you." I told him. "I can tell she loves you and wouldn't want you to be hurt. She knows your heart, so I trust her to talk to me about you."

"Okay, I'll reschedule her flight. If it's that important to you."

"I enjoy learning about you and spending time with you. But everything is moving so fast for me right now." I told him, "Having a girl friend who I can talk to is important to me."

"Yeah my time moves differently." He spoke. "I get it."

Manuel leaned over and kissed my lips, then he came around to open my door. As soon as I put my feet on the ground I was mesmerized from the beautiful view. Manuel surely knows how to quickly shift my focus with aesthetically pleasing sights.

"This view is so wonderful!" I told Manuel as he put his arms around me from behind and I laid my head back against his chest, he knew he was making quite a big impression on me. "Spoiling me with a wonderful life when I'm bothered is a really convincing way of making me fall for you."

"I just want to spoil you with a wonderful life… you just often seem to be bothered," he joked. Then followed up with, "I'm playing, I'm playing. I know you been in some awkward positions since we've met, but each time made me want you more. I'll get it together for you though."

"You're good at apologizing, thanks for this weekend. It's wonderful, I have loved every minute of it. So did Tré, he was so happy." I thanked him, looking around at our current location. A partially paved parking lot.

"He's a good kid and you're a great mom. I'm glad you both came, it was fun." He played with my hair. "This last part, with you, is the part I've been waiting for."

"Yeah me too, I can't wait to see this *favorite* place," I told him looking around the lot and noticing there were no restaurants around at all. "I thought you said something about food. Is it another 5-star picnic, but by a mountain?"

"Not another picnic. We are just waiting on our ride." Manuel proudly pointed up at a helicopter that was slowly descending. "I knew I would make it on time."

"Are you serious? We're getting into that?" I hit him on the chest, and he pulled me into his arms with a hug. I felt tears swelling up in my eyes, for so long I wanted someone to show me something different, a surprise helicopter ride was surely different. "Why are you so extra for me? Please tell me if you do this for everyone?"

"Stop saying that shit." He kissed my lips, "I'm with you, don't overthink, don't be insecure, enjoy the moment… I need you to see you're worth it."

I nodded, taking my tissues out again. It's true that if your brain hears something enough times it will begin to believe it. Manuel was helping to build me up.

"It's like you really live in a whole other world from anyone I've ever known." I told him, as we stood back waiting for the landing.

"You ever been on a helicopter?" He asked, holding my hand, I shook my head then he gave me the basics. "Never approach a helicopter from the tail or even the front, the pilot will bring you to the side. Don't take pictures with the flash on and don't open the doors. We will put headphones on when we get in, so that way we can talk to each other."

I listened intently to his directions; I'd never flown in something so small before. "Will he be able to hear us talking?"

He smirked, "Yes, so don't be nasty."

I rolled my eyes, *me nasty?* Not yet, but as my comfort level rose I began to imagine a few things we could do after the date.

Although the sleek red helicopter looked expensive it was still no bigger than my small bathroom at home, nor did it look like a sturdy way to travel. I noticed that it slightly wobbled as it came down, but through the huge window I saw that the driver looked secure as he handled the machine. The propellers spun viciously quick in the air, nowadays I like to think I'm adventurous, but this would be quite a dare. I had to kick out the many intrusive thoughts.

I grabbed Manuel's forearm and let him lead us to the aircraft when the pilot fully landed and waved us over. Typically, the laws of nature are not the type of laws I tamper with, but the closer we got the bigger the helicopter looked, I decided it wouldn't be too bad. The pilot got out and greeted Manuel and I, then properly secured us for the flight. We put on our headphones with attached microphones, which we needed to talk through the loud noise.

The pilot greeted us both over our headset and began his spiel of the city tour.

The lights of the city would have probably been stunning just standing on the well-lit strip at night but seeing it from above was completely different. A sight that most people won't get to see in their lifetime. Hovering above the world was very Manuel.

The view reminded me of a drone, we could see everything. The way the lights glimmered against the various water fountains, from above it looked as if the world I knew to be real was so, so small. Everything, every person, every problem, was so little from up here.

We were practically floating above the earth. I felt elated that I was stepping outside of the many boxes I'd hidden in over the decades.

I took out my phone and recorded the scenery. When I took selfies I turned away from Manuel, he didn't complain, but I remained respectful not to get him in my pictures. However, to my surprise, he leaned over and took a selfie with me on his own phone.

Our first selfie, I watched him use the photo as the lock screen on his phone.

Maybe I'm not dreaming, I could be the woman he wants in his life? I fought to keep the tears from falling out of my eyes. We were connecting and things were going so well that it was a fight to get away from the self-sabotage. All of the insecurities I had were from my own thoughts, my own head.

Manuel held my hand and gave me that familiar comforting squeeze, with a smile. Be soft, I told myself, he's here with me and at the very least I will enjoy the moment.

The pilot tried to give us a tour, but it was hard to listen to him with Manuel beside me. We flirtatiously touched each other every chance we got, made vague sexual jokes on the headset whenever we could slide one in, and kissed anytime we locked eyes for more than 7 seconds.

"I'm guessing that this is young love?" The pilot suggested after he warned us we'd be descending to the restaurant.

"Yeah, maybe," I responded, stealing a glance of Manuel's big smile.

"Nice, I moved up to *maybe*?" Manuel asked, whispering in my ear after the pilot got us safely off the helicopter. We'd landed at the top of a roof; it was within walking distance of our destination.

"Okay, I would be lying if I didn't say I was *starting* to fall for you," I said putting my face in his shirt.

Not enough for a damn ring... I still thought.

Manuel led the way to the lounge, holding my hand, the way he finds any reason to touch me is appreciated. It was a constant reminder to be present in the moment.

We walked into a gently lit foyer with live music on the stage and a crowd full of circular tables with tall black stools. The vibe was elegant, and the people were down to earth and friendly, some even dancing. Manuel took me straight to the back exit of the lounge which led to stairs, they were sketchy, but I trusted his direction.

At the top of the stairs was a beautiful rooftop bar that overlooked the city's skyline from a distance. The lounge had canopies with expensive looking drapes intertwined with decorative sepia lights. The seating options were cozy booths surrounding a few sporadic fire pits or swings at the bar. The staff were dressed provocatively, but somehow the establishment was still very classy.

First, we sat on the swings at the bar and just had small talk, sharing life stories. The laughter between us was contagious, bouncing off of each other, it was as if we were sharing inside jokes that were old and deep.

Whenever Manuel was spotted, guests in the lounge acted a little differently, the staff sent more appetizers, so much that we only nibbled at the options, for the most part we talked. Folks were sending free drinks and desserts, as if he needed it. Only a few fans came over to speak to Manuel, which he spoke to briefly, but he respectfully declined to take any pictures with them while we were having dinner. I did notice a few people taking pictures from a distance.

The overstimulating atmosphere had me wanting to hide a little, I wanted Manuel to myself, he felt the same and we moved over to a private booth near a fire pit. When we were alone Manuel acted a little silly and less reserved. He began taking pictures of me with his phone, he used an Italian accent as he told me how beautiful I was and playfully coached me through poses while he took pictures. I pretended to be his model until I took his phone, and we took some selfies together, silly and serious ones.

"I love spending all this time with you." He said, using his much sexier normal voice and in between us kissing. "Did you open that bag I gave you?"

The ring. "I left it in the car, did you want me to bring it?"

"It's okay, I guess it's better if we open it later," he said. "Did you see what it was?"

"Not really," I started to lie, but responded truthfully, thanks to the liquor. "Kind of."

"Kind of? What do you kind of think it is?" He inquired with that mischievous smile that I'm not sure any of his mothers could punish.

"A ring box." I responded blankly.

"How did that make you feel?" He wanted to know.

"Manuel, what are you trying to ask me? How do I feel about marrying you or something?" I tried to whisper-yell at him. "You've known me for a week. You don't believe in relationships. Who are you trying to prove something to?"

He responded matter-of-factly, "I've known you for months, talked to you almost every day, and you know I can provide you with anything you want and need."

"Yeah we talked on a dummy account! And we barely talked about anything!"

"We still talked. Stop saying you don't know me and tell the truth, say you're not sure if you want happiness."

"I'm kinda crazy for not wanting to wear your ring?" I scoffed. "We're not having a conversation about a ring right now at all, Manuel,

228

this conversation is too much for even you." I insulted him. "We are not even in a relationship; you don't even *believe* in relationships! You're not just going to love-bomb me into wearing a ring."

"You were wearing one on the same finger and threw it to the ocean, what difference does it make," He casually compared a ring that was thousands of dollars less. "We don't need to talk right now, but I can tell you what it means to me and if you want it, you can wear it. If not, donate it."

"Do you hear yourself; you sound like a gameshow. Donate it," I mimicked him. "That ring is more than most people's salaries! What does that ring mean to you, Manuel?"

"I just want it to remind you that I am here, and you have me. Even if I'm not right where you need me physically," He explained, "Because I probably won't always be there right when you need me, but I will make sure you are good. Long as you keep me beside you."

"And by wearing it, what am I guaranteeing you?" I asked.

He shrugged, "Companionship."

"Companionship, a friend? We don't need a ring for that, I have plenty of friends." I told him.

He smirked, "You know I'll be more than any of them." He said after a long moment of keeping his eyes on mine, "I had the ring made for you. Use it to replace the one that got lost, it doesn't have to mean anything."

I really wanted to change the subject and stop talking about this ring stuff. We were in need of some fun and the music at the lounge was beyond fitting for the night. "I wanna go dance."

Without hesitation he led me on the small dance floor. We danced as the DJ played lots of old school R&B; the atmosphere was a good vibe. The drinks kicked in and I could have danced and winded all night against this man's body.

Our chemistry on the dance floor made me want him more, even knowing that he is probably too much for me, that none of this would be able to fit into my life realistically. It made him more enticing, knowing that I was only a visitor in his world.

Manuel pulled me back over to our booth taking a break, he leaned back as I kissed him, "You can come over to my room tonight when we get back if you want?"

"I had a feeling you were trying to get me in your room?" I flirted, he dropped his chin pretending to look shocked. "But it's good cause I'm 95% sure you will see me tonight in your hotel room."

"My dad would take a 95% chance as a locked bet," He told me, "I really like those odds."

"Me, too," I slowly mouthed to him, hoping the 5% chance of having to use *umbrella* or just that the baby daddy curse didn't win.

"You are feeling comfortable, I love this." He wrapped his arm around me. "No pressure though."

I covered my face, "How are you the most perfect person in the world?"

"I already told you; I'm just trying to bring you over to my world, but you won't let me." he told me casually raising up his shoulders and giving me a kiss on the cheek.

16

The beginning of the helicopter ride back was practically foreplay
for Manuel and me. The pilot didn't say a single word to us; he'd given up
on his mission as a tour guide. There was a little armrest between us, but
it didn't stand a chance, we couldn't stay apart from each other. We
touched and made eye contact constantly, I just knew it was going to be a
good night.

I was ready to break this curse. I was sure he was what I
needed… and if he wasn't, then at least I tried. No regrets. No umbrella. I
desperately wanted to be with someone else, someone I felt safe with.

We were almost at our destination when the helicopter pilot broke
up our kissing session. "Hey back there, you must be an important man, a
crowd of people found out where you are headed. My supervisor got a
nearby hotel to clear us for a landing and your security team is there
waiting. Guess they got that all squared away for you."

"Got ya Boss," Manuel agreed to the new plan easily, he was
hardly ever angered by anything which was different for me. A lot of men
I met while dating were so easily upset with minor things. Manuel handled
himself differently, he trusted himself to fix any problem, he didn't get
over stimulated with every little hindrance. Snapping and making others
walk on eggshells to avoid what could be a powerful wrath. "Guess we get
a longer ride."

"I have to say, I'm very impressed by how you handle things so
smoothly, you must have had very patient parents growing up."

"Can't waste time being upset about every obstacle and change,
not if you want to grow. You waste time wishing everything out here was
easier, you just have to motivate yourself to work harder and get better."

Withdrawing his hand down from my thigh. "Both my parents are gone, neither were patient."

"Sorry," I apologized for bringing it up, he didn't respond. "It's only because I wondered, where did it come from? I like to learn about people and families. Your upbringing, the parents, mothers, and brothers, it's an interesting upbringing."

"Is this the psychology side of you or the writer side of you? I don't want to talk about that right now." He told me, nonchalantly going back to kissing my ears. "I want us to get to know each other."

"It's just me. I am trying to get to know you, your family, childhood, anything other than just this superstar." I fussed, I could feel my guard and voice going up. "Okay then Manuel, when do I learn about you beyond this surface?"

"Are we about to argue again?" He mumbled, leaning back in his seat with his palms covering his forehead, we were arguing in a helicopter 1000 feet in the sky on a call center headset. "Are you just insistent on fighting tonight? I feel you have just been searching for red flags since your hotel. My father is the reason my biological mother is not here anymore, after that my brothers' moms raised me. He left not long after she died."

I cringed at the sensitive information and how his patience with me was slowly diminishing, "Okay, I didn't know, sorry for being so pushy. I do want to know *you*, I'm not trying to look for red flags, but I don't want you to hide things from me."

"Can you just stop trying to run away?" He tried to go back to kissing, but I resisted him. "What is it that you think I am hiding?"

"You tell me. Look at how you act with personal questions, so indirect. Then I tell you I'm meeting up with Jenny, who you know is the only one who talks to me about you, and you cancel my date with her. Send her on a fuckin' flight back *home*. Wherever the *home* is, because I don't even know where you live."

"You're right." He said surprisingly, taking my hand in his. "You keep telling me the same thing. I'll make sure you go out with Jenny, I'll get it setup when we land."

"You make it so forced, unauthentic," I said with an attitude. "I don't want to go out with her if you don't want me to."

"I just want you to be happy. We can just have fun together and go back to our separate lives. There's no pressure."

"Yeah no pressure," I sighed, the vibe was off.

I took my hand back from him and turned away from him, looking out my window. What was he saying? What was he asking me? I looked out the window at the lights below us, it was getting very late, but that just made the city look even more beautiful. Life with Manuel was filled with lots of beautiful stuff but seemed to be more trouble than just staying in my warm cozy comfort zone.

For the first time that night we had our hands to ourselves for more than two minutes. We sat in a loud silence filled with the spinning propellers.

Although it was only for two minutes of separation, I missed Manuel's breathing down the back of my neck, I missed his hand constantly reaching for mine. I wondered what he was thinking, sitting beside me, giving me space.

"Umbrella." Manuel whispered in my ear.

I sighed in relief, pleased to hear his voice, turning around to whisper back, "I thought safe words were for sex?"

He shook his head, "We can do whatever we want. I want to *umbrella* this fight."

I agreed. "Okay, I accept your request."

"Request?" Manuel scoffed, "Umbrella is immediate stopping of whatever is the problem. It doesn't matter if we're arguing over the color of the sky or if we are in a shootout, you hear me say *umbrella*, stop shooting. It's more of a kill switch."

233

"It can't work like that, it won't work." I told him. "Some things you can't say umbrella to!"

"Bull shit. Me and my brothers have been doing this for years, trust me, it works. There's nothing more important than us meeting at a compromise, respecting the kill switch before any emotions." He tried to convince me, "We're not meant to fight against each other. And for the record I wouldn't bring you to a shootout."

"Why wouldn't you bring me to a shootout?" I asked, raising my eyebrows at him.

"Can you shoot?" He asked me surprised, intrigued with my versatility. "I'll let you be my secret weapon if you want."

"Seriously, please teach me how to shoot, I learn fast," I assured him. "Recently I've really wanted to learn."

Manuel laughed, but I could tell he was happy to teach me, "You serious? I'll show you how to shoot tonight if you want. Just gotta make a phone call."

I shook my head at him with a grin, how was he this perfect? We held hands, sat back, and enjoyed the end of the ride.

When Manuel and I were finally back on the ground and cleared to exit the helicopter. We walked over to Garon and Buck who were parked side by side. Garon was standing at Manuel's sleek sports car that Buck must've driven to our new pickup location.

They were quite reliable, both working on their night off.

"How was your helicopter flight Princess," Buck asked me, getting out of Manuel's car. I only flashed him a smile, it never felt he was laughing *with* me, but always felt he was laughing at me.

"I told you don't talk to her," Manuel snapped at him. I wondered when and why that conversation happened.

"Yes sir." Buck said sarcastically, with a forehead salute in Manuel's direction. "Acacia, you wouldn't even be able to tell him I'm

234

older than him." Buck continued to talk to me casually, only to piss Manuel off from what it seems.

Manuel let go of my hand, changing his path and walking aggressively toward Buck, not scared or shaken. Nor was Buck scared, more understandably he is far more muscular and broader than Manuel, but I was a little intimidated for Manuel's sake by the match up. Not only is he bigger but Buck is a trained, and most likely an ex-felon, hopefully he gets paid enough to not hurt Manuel in a random fit of rage.

Manuel wasn't scared. "I'm not saying it again."

"Then don't, I found it unnecessary to be said all together, she's grown, we're grown. I brought your car, Golden Child. Be grateful always." Buck tossed Manuel his car keys, he caught the keys not losing his glare on his security guard. When Manuel got a little too close, Buck unzipped his man-purse and intentionally exposed part of his gun to Manuel, as if he'd need that for such a frivolous altercation. "If she's perfect, why are you worried?"

Perfect? Me? *I'm not.*

"On your Daddy's grave if you touch that, you better kill me." Manuel threatened him, partially seeming to be serious. "You won't ever sleep in peace again."

It was clear this argument was a continuation of something else, not sure how I got involved. I hoped this was just their weird way of male bonding or a new edgy form of employee team building.

"You're right, we'll wait." Buck nodded with a sneaky grin, looking down to adjust his shirt, checking that his weapon was concealed. He looked at me and winked, "It wouldn't have prospered."

Garon, who never seemed to be but a hop away from Manuel's rescue, pushed Buck in the direction of the SUV that they were to be riding in. Manuel opened the door of the fancy sports car for me to get in.

Then he went around the back of the car and had a few words with Garon, but I didn't care to listen. Both of them should be fired in my opinion. Buck shouldn't be starting fights and Garon should've intervened in the altercation.

Buck may have been drinking, I'm almost sure it was their night off. Maybe firing them was too harsh.

I looked back inside the gift bag, but the ring box was gone. I checked around on the floor, it was gone. I checked under the seat, the glove box, and it was nowhere to be found. I guess I cared about the ring more than I believed.

Nope! I wanted them both fired.

"Do you trust them?" I asked Manuel when he got into the car. "Really, really trust them?"

"With my whole life. As your boy Todd would say, they are in my 20 percent." He told me sincerely, "They would do anything for me."

"Ummm... yeah, especially that one that just brandished his gun at you," I added sarcastically, shaking my head, more baffled than impressed at his daily environment.

"When we were teenagers we used to take apples off my dad's tree, toss them up and try to shoot them in the backyard. We aren't good with the gun safety rules around each other, but we both have a lot of professionally trained experience. You don't have to worry, you are safe." Manuel laughed at my slightly shaken face. "A bad way of joking around, from the outside looking in."

"Well, not to cause problems with your shooting buddies, but one of them took your ring," I told him, making a nervous face.

"You mean your ring," he corrected me, not seeming surprised. "I'll get it back."

"You and Buck have an interesting relationship." I pointed out to him, curious as to why he'd keep staff with such an immature disposition. Plus, I assumed the ring was taken by him more than likely. "Interesting relationships with both of them really. How long have they worked for you?"

236

He clarified, "They work *with* me, not for me. Before day one, Buck was one year old when he was looking out for me, since birth. Garon came after me, some of our mothers did their maternity photo shoots together. Then Corbin joined the crew not too long within the year after."

That's a strong relationship to have to uphold. "So, your mothers were good friends?"

He shrugged, pulling out of the parking lot, holding my left hand. "They had some friendly moments."

I smiled, longing for those types of truly timeless friendships that at one point seemed so prevalent in my life but seemed to diminish more the older I got. "That's special, now I can see why you are so close, and why they are so protective of you. Perfect men for the job. I want to know deep things like that, thank you for sharing that with me, it's special."

"You're special."

"You don't think a thirty something year bond is amazing?" I questioned his sarcastic ability to change the subject anytime we talked about his personal life.

"Honestly, all I can think about is how amazing you are Acacia Ivy. Do we even need to talk about anything else?" He asked, rubbing my leg.

17

I rolled my eyes and moved his hand, "Here we go again."

"Yes, here we go again," he agreed condescendingly. "We're about ten minutes from my soft bed, with the big white hotel pillows. I set the room nice and cold just in case you came over and wanted me to hold you... and here you are asking me about my mother's friendships. Anything to throw off the connection."

Was he right? Am I blocking him?

I was sabotaging, my subconscious was trying to keep him out! He may be a little too private, but I was also being a little too much as well. I wanted to get to know more about him so badly that I wasn't letting him get to enjoy spending time with me. I wasn't making the best out of enjoying spending time with him either, I had to shake this bitchy attitude.

"I'm sorry," shamefully I covered my mouth and flirted my way out of it, taking his free hand, "I'm being horrible, let me make it up to you."

"It's okay, I'm starting to learn how you are, Cay. I'm not mad at it." Manuel interrupted my thoughts with a squeeze to my hand and kissed it with a warm smile. Although in the back of my mind I was just waiting for the moment that he loses patience, it felt nice to have it.

"Thank you for taking me out tonight, it was really fun. I haven't danced in a long time. The rooftop lounge, the helicopter ride... everything was beyond what I dreamt."

"I had fun with you, too," he told me.

I could hear Hazel in the back of my head, *he is not the practice squad.*

I wanted to do something for him, show him I am spontaneous. Something sexy to show my interest and appreciation to Manuel at the same time. Maybe it was for me, proving to myself that I too can have a hoe phase!

I moved myself in a position to get to his pants zipper, he smiled and helped me as I undid the button and unzipped his pants. Manuel was watching me eagerly, maybe a little more than the road, but I noticed his car practically drove itself, but occasionally he would look up.

Once I got it out, I used my hand to feel him getting hard whilst, sucking on his neck and nibbling on his ear to get him fully turned on.

I whispered in his ear, "I think it's ready."

"Mmmhhmmm," he mumbled, then paused while I bent over and kissed it. "Do you know what you're doing?"

I hit him, sitting back in my chair, playfully teasing him with a sexy look.

"Hush," I said bashfully, slowly sliding back over to him.

"Come back over here." He pulled my chin to his face for a sloppy kiss.

After kissing his mouth, I went down and kissed the top of his dick twice playfully before wrapping my lips around it and midway down. I wanted to watch his face for a reaction, but it was hard to see much other than the city lights, blurry through my watery eyes.

He stroked and gently rubbed my hair, as I tried not to choke too hard on him. I listened to his breaths get deeper and closer together, as his grip on my hair got a little harder. I wanted to make him cum, I sucked a little faster the more heavily he breathed and occasionally moaned.

It was working, the tips and tricks I read were pleasuring him!

"Acacia," He moaned my name again, before he came, I loved the way it sounded coming from him.

This time he came. It was warm and soft, but slightly thick like a disgustingly bland projectile shot of smooth cream of wheat. I really tried my best to put on my *big girl panties* and swallow it, trying to remember all the hints I learned from an advantageous oral sex book.

At first it felt like the cum was going to go down, but once I thought about it too hard I threw it up right in between his legs, along with some of the liquor from the lounge. Luckily it just about missed him, although some puke got on his pants. The car took the worst hit.

He said with a light howl, "Whoa!"

"Oh my god, gross, I am so sorry!" I put my hand over my face as I rummaged around for a napkin, Manuel took off his shirt and handed it to me to clean up with. He helped me get it out of a few hair strands.

"It's fine, you're fine. It was perfect… up until that last second." He said, trying not to laugh at me.

I hadn't even noticed we were already at the hotel. The valet was standing not too far at the front door waiting, but Manuel hadn't driven up to the entrance enough for them to come over yet.

"Oh no, your shoes too!" I said apologetically, sitting up in my chair as the valet now stood with Manuel's security waiting for our car to drive up. "This is so embarrassing."

"The tint is too dark, no one can see," he assured me, trying not to laugh. Taking off and using his shirt, Manuel fixed my messy face for me before fixing his own vomited-on-pants, then drove up to the valet. He grabbed his jacket from the back and put it around me. "You look good, but it's chilly."

"Sure," I mumbled, still embarrassed.

Manuel got out of the car very cool and casual, with just his undershirt on, he walked right around to my side of the car as the valet opened my door.

240

"Can you have this car cleaned tonight?" Manuel asked the valet driver who nodded as Manuel handed him a sum of cash that made him smile wide. We walked into the hotel, and although it was late, it looked just like it did in the movies. People were still roaming around; most were probably gambling and some just looking for someone to dance with them.

Buck and Garon were standing by the elevator waiting for us. I figured I better start learning to get along with them, since these lifelong friends weren't going anywhere and apparently they'd be around a lot. However, I couldn't help but wonder which one took the ring.

Manuel and I got in the next elevator with them and went straight to the corner, he whispered a little too loudly for me. "That's going to be a very funny story later."

I buried my face into his chest, knowing we most likely smelled like my puke. "Hush, we will not talk about that ever again."

"I kinda liked it," he flirted loudly. "Especially when we made eye contact."

"We can hear you. Y'all acting like some fuckin' horny ass teenagers," Garon judged, Manuel flipped him off, he didn't care. I was enjoying the puppy love feelings.

"I love being with you," I whispered to him as he held me in the elevator. Maybe I could fall for him... maybe I already am.

"I wanted to hear that from you." He sucked at whispering, he was always either too loud or too quiet. His eyes looking into mine were unlocking combinations to locks I had shut years ago. "I told you you'll have a good time with me. Just no more trying to swallow."

His presence was proving to be very comforting for me. Dare I even say, trusting. "Shut up, what was I supposed to do?"

"Not that," he joked. "Just spit it out."

Buck looked disgusted, "She threw up on you?"

"Yo!" Garon yelled, disgusted. "Can you please all shut up?"

We silently arrived at our floor, as the off-duty security friends went over to Manuel's family suite, he and I had to stop by mine. I wanted to grab a few things for our nightcap at his place. I also wanted to be sure that Tré had some sleep and hadn't stayed on his video system all night. We had a busy last day and plane ride ahead of us.

"Tré?" I called when I noticed he was not in his room nor his bathroom. "Tré?"

Manuel walked into the room after hearing me call for Tré, "He's not in your room either. Maybe he went downstairs."

"No, he wouldn't just leave like that without my knowledge, with no permission." I checked my phone for his location, "He turned it off three hours ago. He fuckin' turned off the damn location on his phone! He kept claiming it was bad service, back home, but now it's the same issue. He's *been* turning off the location *on purpose*."

Manuel rubbed my shoulders, "He'll be fine, he's probably just out living his life. Don't over shelter him."

I felt as if I was being judged. "He's a child, just recently a teen."

"Exactly." He said, then gave in, probably to appease me. "I'll get some people to find him Cay."

I raised my eyebrows at him, "You don't get what it's like to be a parent, having to raise a child is difficult. Simultaneously wanting the best for him, but not wanting to spoil him and knowing you can't do it for him. Having to discipline him when I want to play with him or laugh. Parenting is not easy."

"I do understand that you also have to realize he's growing up, and you have to let him be a man, too."

I rolled my eyes, "Can we go find him."

"I am going to go find him. I will get him." He said calmly, scrolling through his phone. "I was a little younger than that when my parents lost me for a lot longer than this, and my mom went crazy trying to find me. Meanwhile I was fine, better than fine, it was beneficial. Just try to chill out, he might be exactly where needs to be."

242

Manuel went out of the room, making phone calls, as I looked around the suite for any clues or a note of where Tré might have gone.

The more I looked around his hotel room I considered there were probably more digital clues than anything in this room. I sat on his bed and scrolled through what I was able to see on his social media, then local events that he might find interesting.

"Marcus and Jenny are looking for him in the hotel, and I'm going to ride with Garon to somewhere he might be. You stay here in case he comes back, call me." Manuel told me the team's plan when he got back to the room, he planted a goodbye kiss on my forehead. "He didn't leave that long ago. He may just be out with my youth football team."

"Can I go with you, I won't be able to sit here," I told him.

"And what if he comes back?" Manuel asked, "This is the first time he's done this; chances are he won't go too far."

I shook my head, "No, you're right, he's not that type of kid. He'll be back, I'll wait here."

Manuel's voice has a way of making you feel like everything was going to be okay, easily he convinced me it was better for me to wait.

I decided to brush my teeth and clean up while I waited for them to get back.

Tré and I weren't as close as we once were pre-high school, back when I was the primary parent for everything. Now, he is typically on the phone or playing video games, unless told to do otherwise. I require him to enjoy our weekly Wednesday date nights together distraction-less, and we try to get caught up on our lives in two hours. Being completely honest with myself, I felt he was growing distant from me.

Just not to the point he would run away from me.

When Tré was younger I used to get him out of school early every so often and go on a dollar store shopping spree, then end our day with lunch and ice cream. However, once he got into all his after-school sports, it just never seemed convenient for me to take him.

Plus, as he got older he didn't find it as entertaining, he'd rather be with his friends, and I understood that. Now apparently I'm the last person he can talk to.

Intermittently I called Tré's phone every five minutes in case he turned it back on, he did not. I considered calling his dad but did not want to cause a panic several states away.

As the clock continued to turn, so did my stomach. Manuel called twice, the first time was five minutes after he left, to just make sure I was calm and OK, not stressing out. The second call was to update me on some places they'd gone and were going, but that second call was 20 minutes ago.

I tried to remember what Manuel told me about his own experience of being away from his parents, how it was a positive experience. I trusted Tré's judgment, his father and I both did a fine job, Tré's being lost in a big city might be enriching for him.

I began to notice the sun would be coming up any minute now and my baby is still missing. I called Manuel, twice, he didn't answer. I hoped he found Tré.

After fifteen more minutes of growing simultaneously pissed and worried about both Manuel and Tré at this point, I heard a knock on my suite door.

I ran to the door at top speed, eagerly anticipating lecturing and yelling at a 14-year-old boy.

It was Buck.

He never looked particularly bad, but he was cleaned up very well for this time of night– or morning, I guess. He wore a tan suit, with a tan vest, tan shirt, and tan tie. The button-down shirt had gold chain link embellishments that matched the gold cufflinks with diamond accents. The plain tan pants were a compliment to the gold-spiked, tan flats with red bottoms. In his hand he held a rich leather coat. He cleans up well, maybe Hazel was on to something.

"Hey Buck, have you heard from Manuel or anything about Tré?" I asked him, although he didn't look like he was here to talk about Tré. "No one is picking up for me. Even Jenny's phone's dead."

"Call me Nate. I'm off the clock. Why the fuck do you look so worried," He said matter-of-factly. "I'm sure your son is fine, in some cultures he would have a career, wife, and children by now. Don't baby him." He told me. "Your boy left the spare key on the fridge and the valet misplaced his, can I come in? Gotta photoshoot to make."

"Okay, Nate, sure." I let him in the suite, wondering if I might get him to spare a few minutes to find my son. "I would've drove around to find Tré if I knew the keys were still here. I think I might know where he's at. He said something earlier, about a strip of video game arcades that we passed by earlier."

"That's probably why Manuel didn't tell you the spare key was here, it's an expensive vehicle and right now you're an irrational mother. Your son is okay." Nate walked in and grabbed the keys, then headed back towards me. "EmManuel got enough people looking."

I rolled my eyes, not surprised he didn't want to help.

"Fine, want me to take you?" He asked, stepping closer to me. I guess he does have some kind of heart after all.

Nate stood only a foot away from me, but it was the first time I saw a close-up look at him. He is taller than Manuel, although they had a similar physique, Nate is more muscular. However, he didn't have the same aura around his confidence that Manuel has, the one that makes Manuel charismatic and larger than *everything*.

Nate was more interesting tonight, something made him look more humane. I noticed he had a rich chocolate glow on his brown skin despite quite a few flaws and aged scars. The high number of imperfections made him appear more of an attractive art piece than an eye sore, however his personality and demeanor made him ugly. It was as if he was intentionally trying to come off as a jerk or pervert to me.

"Yes, thank you." I explained. "I don't remember the name of the place, but it was on the way here. Let me get my shoes," I quickly went and threw on some house shoes, no longer caring about what looked alluring with Jenny's hand sewn black dress.

Nate held the elevator for me in the lobby. "Let's go Princess, I got shit to do too."

"Thanks for doing this, I appreciate it," I thanked him as we waited for the elevator to close, maybe he isn't so horrible after all, hard to believe Manuel considered him one of his 20 percent.

"Did Jenny make that dress? It looks good on you," he complimented, but his eyes and the way he was looking at me, just screamed that he was in the 80 percent Todd talked about.

"Thanks," I told him softly with a smile, wishing I would have changed my clothes or kept on Manuel's jacket.

"Do you want my coat?" He asked, apparently reading my mind wasn't as hard to do as my ex used to say. I nodded as he came behind me to put the coat on my shoulders. "I'm not too bad, I know we got off on the wrong foot, I can tell you don't like me. My bros and I play around a lot, so you can't take it too personal." Nate said, then prematurely laughed at his own joke, going back to his side of the elevator. "Shit, I'm really no worse than EmManuel, and you seem to be comfortable enough bowing to him."

I wanted to pretend not to hear him, shitty-*jealous*-best-friend for sure. "You must be the comedian in the friend group?"

"No, most refer to me as the brains of the group. Corbin is somewhat the financial advisor and aspiring comedian, EmManuel is the face or voice, and I guess Garon is the strength, he protects the team. I'm more, future CEO." He clarified with somehow a look of truth; he believed it. "I get it, EmManuel has that lover boy thing going that bitches love, that stereotype. Y'all fall for that magical bullshit, a fairy tale when you could just enjoy what's here in reality, there's blessings literally all around us. I'm the real truth, the real package, flaws and all."

"Got ya." I conceded in hopes to end the awkward conversation.

Nate's sense of loyalty was shady at best, what a bad best friend, why was he talking negatively about Manuel to me? I wondered if Manuel knew what kind of person Nate really is behind his back.

"You don't have to be nervous around me," Nate said. I was impressed at his ability to read the room, because I seriously contemplated finding an excuse to just get off at the next floor. "Me and Manuel tell each other everything, so I know you, too. We share everything. Always have, since he was born, I even drank his mom's breastmilk."

I looked at him disgusted, as his eyes were surveying my body. Did he really think Manuel was going to share me with him? Did Manuel think that? The name Nate... was in that list of recipients in that list of notes he had about me, Nate does know about me.

"You're not serious right now, are you?"

"It's really not weird at all, what's his is mine and what's mine is his," He assured me, "We don't take it personal."

"You're really starting to make me want to leave," I told him, truly hoping Manuel was not as twisted as his security-friend was telling me.

Nate leaned back on the elevator wall. "Did EmManuel tell you he was conceived to be my friend, just for me. His mother loved me. My mother couldn't have children after my birth, and his mom didn't want any. She even will say that to this very day, he was born to play with me. So basically, he wouldn't be here if it weren't for me."

"I thought his parents were dead," I questioned, in hopes of receiving clarification.

"Is that what he told you?" Nate asked with a smirk. "Then, I guess they are dead. How did they die?

I sighed, exhausted from this game of detective with this man. Who the hell am I dating?

"I don't know, I'm sure you do." I shrugged sarcastically while playing along. "He shares everything with you, right."

"You're right. They are dead, truthfully, I technically got rid of the man who killed his mom." He admitted to me. "He knows I'd do anything for him."

"I see," I couldn't tell if he was serious or not, but it would make sense why he still has his job. Manuel probably feels like he owes him something for avenging his mother. "Even steal jewelry he bought out of his car?"

Nate laughed, "Is that what you think I do?"

I nodded yes, "I do think you would do that, but it's okay, I didn't want it anyway."

"Well lucky for both of us then." He shrugged, talking with a little more aggression in his voice. "I do other shit, big brother shit, vet the hoes, maybe give the pussy a test run if I see fit or throw her to one of the local security crews. He's too busy, he can't handle all the women he gets, are you serious? I keep the rotation smooth for him."

"You're sad," I told him. "But I'm glad you shared that with me."

"I'm happy. You think you're different, he thinks you're different... but you're not. Y'all types are just as easily impressed as the vocal hoes, you ain't different, with each little miracle he did for you. I peeped that." He played in his front pocket; I couldn't help but watch via my peripheral.

"It is what it is."

"He's shared a lot of money with you though," he winced, then winked, "Me and the boys were starting to wonder, how much do you cost exactly?" He bit his bottom lip as he eyed me. "You found out he stalked you, now he spent 2 million on a ring." Nate paused, then with a sly smile then handed me my ring box from the car! It was in his pocket. "I ain't hating, I wasn't going to steal your ring. Charge your worth, but maybe I can run a side bet, how much do you cost?"

I looked at him, unsure how to feel holding the ring box, "What are you trying to do? Push me away from him? You're his best friend, that's saying a lot."

248

"I just wanted to know how much it is going to cost and maybe even what's all included Acacia." He intentionally said my name very sexy, taking two steps closer to me, but not too close.

"I don't know if you think you're funny or if you are serious, but I am not CoDéy." I pressed the elevator button multiple times when I felt us come to a stop. "Whatever y'all might have been doing with her will never be what you can do with me. I'm good on the ride, I'll just wait."

He shrugged, "Of course, wait for your superman."

"You are the most hating, envious best friend I have ever met." I called him out, sick of him sabotaging his friend. I have had many of my exes' friends be sexually suggestive or flirtatious, but Buck seemed to be taunting me. "You think I won't tell him what you say?"

"Wait, am I really the bad guy? He pulled the oldest trick and you fell for it." Nate laughed loudly, "Ohhh no, think about it, Young Todd? EmManuel bursts your superstar fantasy crush into a fuckin' supernova, nothing but a beautiful sad artistic mess. Yet, I'm always the bad guy."

"Wow." Did Manuel purposely turn me off from Young Todd? I didn't even have a sexual desire for Young Todd, that was a little shady now that Nate broke it down. "You're an asshole."

"Feisty, too, I like that." Nate nodded his approval at me.

When the elevator door opened Tré, Jenny, Marcus, Manuel, Garon, and Corbin were on the other side. For almost five different reasons the situation was awkward.

Manuel glared at Nate. Tré was looking down, he knew he was in trouble. However, he just was not in more trouble than Manuel if everything his lifelong friend just told me about him is true..

"Marcus, take the women and Tré in another elevator." Manuel directed.

Marcus walked away with Tré, but I stayed put, staring at Manuel, who was staring at Nate. Jenny stayed with the men, and they all went onto the elevator with Nate and me.

No sooner than when the metal elevator doors clanked shut, Manuel plunged over to Nate and punched him right in his face!

Nate, as if he knew the punch was coming, leaned back and didn't get much of an impact. Nate shoved Manuel with a mighty force to the other side of the elevator. Manuel hit his back on the wall, but still jumped back up to punch Nate again.

"This is what y'all wanted?" Garon asked them. Stepping back against the elevator wall extending his arms out to protect Jenny and me.

"Don't let them fight," Jenny told Garon, but he only shrugged. He was not going to help her. "Ma is going to lose her shit!"

Nate shoved Manuel against the elevator wall even harder, it looked like a dent was in the elevator wall! Manuel got right back up to get another punch this time not even connecting with Nate at all, he was no match. He also seemed slightly dizzy.

I screamed out loud when I saw Manuel get pushed that hard, but he kind of deserved it. I didn't like seeing him get hurt, but he was so out of character. What else could Nate do to stop him? He could easily knock Manuel out in one punch.

Jenny screamed at Manuel repetitively, pulling his shirt to no avail because he kept charging at his own security! "Hey! Hey! Photoshoot! We have a damn photoshoot!"

Garon, who barely ever cracked a smile in my presence, just stood in front of Jenny and I, laughing at the men!

"Are you letting this happen?" Corbin asked Garon, although short, he was tough and stood his ground trying to stay in between the fighters, which helped Manuel tire himself out a little.

Garon lifted up his arms and with a shrug said, "You know the rule, they got til the doors open."

Nate stood shaking his head at Manuel's sad attempt to get to him. Nate's dress suit was disheveled, and he wiped blood from his lip on the shirt. He still had the asshole smirk on his face, appearing rather composed other than the fresh stain and slightly heavier breathing.

"I was just trying to help Acacia find her son." Nate told him, nonchalantly, Manuel stopped fighting to get to him. "You take everything with me so personal, EmManuel. What are you worried about me telling her?"

"Tell her whatever you think will make her leave me!" Manuel threw up his hands.

"Like, how much you share everything with your security-friends?" I asked Manuel, who stood three feet from me, he hadn't made eye contact with me yet.

"What do you think, Cay? I did all that to share you with anyone. *Him?*" Manuel responded, panting. "Why are you even *with him* right now? Wearing his fuckin' coat."

What? How was this being turned around on me?

Jenny pushed Manuel, "Shut up, EmManuel. What are you five up to?"

"Four," Corbin corrected her.

"Do you think I'm the type to run off with your security guard lifelong friend? He gave me the coat because I was cold. I've been calling you; you didn't pick up and I couldn't wait anymore." Although I was dressed up in my lacy black dress and runway makeup, with his best friend in an elevator holding keys to his $100,000 sports car, how dare he even accuse *me*. "Nate said he would drive me over to where my son might've been."

"Do not call him that!" Manuel snapped at me. Buck began to laugh at Manuel or maybe at me, wiping his bloody lip.

"What the hell is going on Manuel?" I asked, he was acting so differently, not the person I finally got to be soft with.

Their rivalry seemed very childish, beyond immature. I could not believe Buck's inside jokes and gestures had Manuel losing his cool.

Finally triggered up enough, Manuel charged past Corbin and definitely got a good connection on Buck's face with that last punch. That punch must've hurt Buck because he rubbed his jaw for a good second.

"Umbrella!" I yelled at Manuel, with frustrated tears in my eyes, everyone paused and looked at me. Maybe he did think I was just another groupie, if he felt I was that his friend was a threat to us. "Can you stop fighting and talk to me about whatever this is?"

Manuel finally looked at me for a second, and he looked like himself again and not a raging maniac.

Unfortunately, in the midst of my distraction Buck sucker punched Manuel right in the eye!

"Shit Buck!" Jenny yelled, "We got a fuckin' photo shoot in two hours, thanks a lot!"

"You saw he hit me first." Buck defended himself, as Manuel struggled to get sturdy on his feet. "It was self-defense."

"Umbrella?" Corbin repeated, looking at me than Manuel,

"He's stupid enough to give her a kill switch?" Garon put his hands up in disbelief, "Yeah, you deserved that punch, Idiot."

As the elevator doors chimed open, Garon grabbed Manuel and pushed him out the elevator doors, before he could do anymore damage to himself.

Garon and Corbin walked beside Manuel to their suite and Jenny walked with me to mine. Buck stayed in the elevator.

The childish elevator fight was scary, it'd been years since I saw two grown men fighting. I hated to admit that Manuel was kind of sexy when he was angered, that shouldn't have been on my mind, but I was so used to seeing him under complete control that it turned me on a little.

"What was that about?" Jenny asked once the boys were out of earshot, I could only shrug. "Then you just got my cousin punched on a performance and photo shoot day."

"Sorry, I was just trying to get him to stop." I told her.

"Yeah, learn from me, it's best to just try not to get into their shit." Jenny cautioned me. "They'll be fine, brothers fight, and half-brothers fight even more. Their dad would have flipped out seeing them do that in public. Just pray for me and this damn makeup job I'll have to pull off today with his eye, it'll be red before it turns black. I'm going to see you for brunch after the shoot, can you please try to stay out of trouble until then?"

"Half-brothers?" I asked. "They have the same father?"

She rolled her eyes at me, "Yes, only one actual kin to me is EmManuel, but you would never know. My uncle didn't play, we were all family."

"They are his brothers?" I asked, dumbfounded by the information.

Jenny rushed me along, helping me get the key card out just as I opened the door and Marcus came out as well, he was waiting until I got back to leave Tré.

"Tré was just exploring the area, everything was innocent, Manuel and myself already talked to him. He's fine." Marcus gave me a sympathy hug, "Plus, I'll be keeping an eye on him for you all day today while you're at brunch."

I nodded and smiled at him and Jenny politely, then closed the door.

I got in the shower and went to bed.

After tonight's activities, watching them fight in the elevator and finding out Manuel and Buck are brothers. I didn't have the energy to figure out what was going on with Tré, who'd shut his door before I even got in our suite.

18

I dreamt about Manuel… good dreams. Little talking in the dream, no umbrellas in the dream. I wanted him.

My phone's notification sound woke me up.

Manuel	
Hope I didn't scare u away. I let the situation get the best of me	

Putting everything to the side that Nate/Buck said to me before the fight, seeing him outside his normal character kind of had me crushing on him a little more.

But there were still so many loose ends, if not more than before.

Manuel	
	u thinking about me?
You're all I could think about for months	
	Are you okay?
Yes. I keep seeing myself together with you. A wife and kids.	
	Now you believe in relationships?

254

I could	
	U don't know what you want.
I got punched for you last night	
	You did it to yourself, is he your older brother?
Ya	
	I can't believe u didn't mention that all this time he's been here
Didn't want you to feel pressure. U mad?	
	I guess not, but it makes a lil more sense why he acted so strangely. I'll see u after the gym and brunch
Yes you will. What's the opposite of umbrella again?	
	Everything
I want that	

I decided to ignore the things his brother said about him, at least for now, as of 2020 I don't believe in stress. I had to see it for what it was, the men have a weird sibling rivalry that I refused to let get me all anxious!

Anxiety and fear do not come from the heart, they come from the brain's desire to keep up with outside demand. Our brain has the tendency to first treat every fear like a big deal, if we don't learn how to take control of our thoughts it could lead to real problems like high blood pressure, digestive issues, and immune system suppression!

Instead of getting worked up, I went to the gym with Tré. Positive action toward progress defeats anxiety.

It was hard for me not to harp on my child's runaway stunt last night but told me he went for a walk to clear his mind and I accepted it. We talked about the fun adventures of yesterday, he confirmed that he was in football heaven. Tré was also very excited about Manuel, the people they were meeting, and the attention that they were receiving wherever they went.

My son made it very clear that my new *situationship* had his blessing. Yet, I was still surprised when he asked, "Why are you giving him such a hard time? You could push him away."

"I want to make sure my next relationship is right before jumping into one." I assured him, unaware he was minding my business. "It can be a lot of stress, if it's with the wrong person."

"Like dad?"

I nodded, "I meant the wrong person for *you*. We're not right for each other."

"Dad asked me if you were dating anyone, I didn't know what to say." He told me, he looked a little sad for his father. "Should I say that I don't know?"

I shook my head and reminded him, "No, Tré, you know I do not do secrets. You can say whatever you feel comfortable talking with him about."

I was not necessarily excited for my ex to know that I was feeling *serious* about someone. I was not ready for his comments. However, we agreed that Tré should be able to talk to us freely, without an obligation to keep secrets for either parent.

"Good, because it feels weird not telling Dad stuff, we talk about everything. Anytime something happens to me, I tell him, and he tells me

256

stuff, too. He's changing a lot; I think he's really being more mature."
Tré informed me. "Plus, he's like my best friend for real."

"That's great, I'm glad you can talk to him," I told him, but Tré
still looked like he was trying to say more. "Are you sure that everything
else is okay?"

He nodded, but he was for sure not telling me something, I wasn't
going to pressure him. He had fun, but a busy day ahead of him.

Today once the photo shoot was over and the day got started, Tré,
Marcus, and Manuel were going to a private brunch with a few athletes as
special guests. Jenny and I would be having a celebrity brunch using
Manuel's invitation and tickets to an exclusive brunch pool party.

Then Tré and I were heading back home to relax for a week off
work.

When it was time to go, Garon drove Jenny and I to our brunch
location, which wasn't too far from our hotel at all and of course the view
was remarkable. The restaurant was a little quaint spot with a rich rustic
feel with modern furniture. It was set on an oversized patio that
overlooked a luxurious pool with a fountain.

There was hip hop music coming from the DJ booth at the pool,
and it was prime time for singles. There were women wearing string
bikinis and men in everything from Timberlands to thongs. Very grown
and sexy atmosphere at the brunch, even a few celebrities scattered about
minor and major.

Most people this weekend was just in town for the football event,
many men were dressed from a higher income bracket of people than I
typically mingle with. Socializing with them was giving me quite a view
on humanity. I never desired to socialize or get acquainted with the elite-
type, but that only assured me that my perspective was very biased. It was
nice being with them at these places.

"So, you're showing all the signs, how does it feel?" Jenny asked
me as we sat down in our seats that overlooked the pool's fountain.

"Signs?"

"That you're falling for my cousin's crazy lifestyle and ready to leave your world." She sighed jokingly, "You're glowing everywhere, you are feeling high on life, it's pouring out of you. Don't deny it."

"Scary *and crazy*," I told her honestly, "he's full of surprises, almost stressful keeping up. Plus, I like my life, I don't really want to necessarily change it. But you're right, I'm falling for him, he's so different."

"You can literally have just about anything you want, how can you not want *that* change?" Jenny sighed and nodded, smiling, "I get it, it's a lot. I don't know what spell you put on him, but he's hooked too."

I loved that for me. "So, he really doesn't have women often?"

She shook her head no. "No! You'd think I'd be helping him if he did this a lot? I'm not that girl, I'm a designer, stylist, I'm in my focused era."

"Can you tell me what yesterday on the elevator was about?" I figured Manuel would never give me as much background as Jenny would.

"Okay, so I don't know for sure. But this is what I think, Buck and Manuel deserved the punches they got. They've been betting on shit and with those two brothers, everything gets personal. It stems from their relationships with their father."

I looked at her intrigued, "Manuel told me they loved their father."

"Yeah, but he's very feared and the boys fought to be his number one forever." She sighed then took a pause, "So anyway, you know how the Eaton's are always in everything together, long story short the family rumor is CoDéy was carrying Buck's baby and not EmManuel's. She spent just as much time with Buck as EmManuel, maybe even more, so it made sense."

"Oh no!" I said, feeling bad for Manuel.

"Recently CoDéy insisted on a podcast that someone made her get an abortion, of course the world assumed it was EmManuel's baby. Now Buck is acting upset again, but he knew she wasn't keeping *his* baby."

"He killed Buck's daughter," I repeated to myself.

"They say it was a daughter, because he loves CoDéy, but she been in love with EmManuel. That was going to be another hardheaded boy. This is old news, years ago."

I nodded, shocked, I did not think CoDéy was the cheating type, nor did I think Buck would hurt Manuel like that. After all they are brothers, but that would explain a lot of the way they all acted at the vehicle after the award show after party. I had felt some tension between them.

Jenny and I ordered drinks and a few shareable items.

"You know, Manuel didn't even tell me that he and Buck were brothers. Is it weird he doesn't tell me anything?" I asked her.

She shrugged, "Not sure why they didn't tell you."

"No, not until I asked today," I told her, "He's so private with me."

"Garon and Corbin either?"

"Garon and Corbin are his brothers too?" I asked, dumbfounded. "He doesn't tell me anything, but he does these grand gestures to profess his feelings. Is Marcus his brother?"

"No child, my grown ass is fucking with Marcus!" She hollered, then covered her mouth at the slip up. "You couldn't tell?"

The more I thought about it, it did make sense. "I wasn't certain, since you said you were longtime friends."

"Good! Because he is terrified of my cousin. Our relationship grew so much, but lately we're both so busy that I'm not sure we have the time to focus on growing the relationship," she breathed a sigh of relief and flashed a smile. "Don't say anything though, I'm fine with everyone knowing, he isn't."

"I'm happy for you too," I congratulated her. "You have to find a way for you to be able to be open with it."

She shook her head, "Well they treat Marcus like Ryū's substitute, they would not appreciate our relationship. We spent every minute of the pandemic together, sneaking and hiding, it was fun then."

I nodded, understanding the awkwardness when family and friends begin to date. "You look good together."

"I know, right. Oh no, here comes CoDéy," Jenny muttered, halting our conversation and looking behind me with apathy.

"Is that my baby cousin-in-law?" A familiar voice called from the door.

CoDéy was sashaying over to Jenny and me with her hand up and two pretty girls with her. They had on lots of makeup, but that seemed to be the trend this weekend.

"It was nice seeing you and talking to you today at the photoshoot," CoDéy said to Jenny with a fake hug, "Sometimes family just needs to get things said and out the way. They are gonna be fine."

Jenny put on a smile to talk to CoDéy, but CoDéy didn't even have the decency to look my way for acknowledgement. Even after I greeted her and her minions, by saying hello, no one spoke to me or even waved.

"Anyway, the photoshoot went really well," Jenny agreed and glanced at CoDéy's friends. "Your ladies were looking beautiful."

"Yes, I was glad Manuel knew who to call, he knows what I bring to the table and that is a big deal for me. Starting the modeling agency has given me so much joy and today was exactly the dream he knew I envisioned." She glanced at me to be sure I was listening, her model companions hung onto her every word. "A few of us stayed behind late and talked about the good old' days."

"Yeah some of us had a great time *talking*," a model added with a giggle.

"And some of us had our mouthfuls and couldn't get much talking done" CoDéy winked at me, flipping her long weave ponytail.

Although I truly wanted to know why Manuel chose to work with CoDéy after how she acted last weekend. There was no way he would fool around with this woman after last weekend and asking me to marry him yesterday!

"Are you trying to make me jealous of you?" I asked CoDéy as if she were a child.

"I'm not trying to make you jealous, but I do want you to be aware, I *will* always be in Manuel's life." She informed me.

"I guess we'll try to find a place for you out back," I said over Jenny who sat uncomfortably between us.

CoDéy leaned in, but still spoke in her regular volume, "Oh I'm sure he'll make room, ask him, he will always make time for me when I call him. When you ask him, tell him thanks for letting me taste him today. His brother told me you're holding out."

I kept my poker face on, no way was she going to get the best of me. Unfortunately, she was correct about us not having sex, but Manuel and I seemed to never be on the same page or just have bad timing when it came to sex.

I wasn't purposely holding out; I knew him for less than a month!

"You are so pathetic, CoDéy, at first I felt bad for you, but now I see why he treats you the way he does." I stood up so that we were standing at the same eye level. "You should've tasted his tongue, you would've found me there."

She laughed, and quickly shot at me, "You don't get it, I'll always be here for him when he gets bored with whatever he is seeing in you. I'm his reminder of where he came from. And he knows that, he loves that. And he loves the way I feel."

I felt hot, I felt flustered. More because I believed her than anything else.

Jenny stood up and put her hands on CoDéy's shoulders, "You need to leave."

"You are right Cuz," She pulled Jenny in for a hug and smiled at me before turning to leave. "This world, his world... It might be better, but it ain't easier. And it ain't for everybody."

Jenny rolled her eyes as we both sat back down, she sighed, "You sure you want to deal with what comes with him right? Cause she ain't lying, she's always been around."

"You think they had sex?" I asked Jenny, then remembered I was not the one Jenny worked for. "Never mind. I really don't even care about her, maybe I should, but I still want to know more about Manuel."

"Wait, did you not sign his NDA?" Jenny asked with a long pause, I shook my head no. "I knew it, he is so damn stubborn. He didn't even talk to you about that yet, did he? Ma's going to kill him."

I raised my eyebrows, not realizing that I would be faced with having to sign paperwork just to date someone. "Whose Ma again?"

"Buck's biological mom, everybody knows she ran the house for real, *my* auntie's polar opposite. The brothers all have very different mothers, each mother talented in something, there were 5 brothers, all born about 4 years of each other." She explained, "Their dad was a real live playa' in the 80's, or was it the 70's? I hate history, but my uncle's is wild. My mom believes he has more children out there, girls too, but these brothers won't even acknowledge the thought. Raw-B believed it."

"Their father, was he some kind of pimp or was he with them all at the same time?" I asked shockingly. "They all lived together?"

"Yes and no, off and on. I don't know. The mothers had their independent relationships with him, from what I could tell, but his sons had to treat all the moms equally or they'd have to do push-ups. Even when their mothers would leave the house, my uncle kept his boys with him." She made a stern face, "My uncle did not play about his boys."

"Their mothers never tried to take them?" I asked.

"Tried? Maybe they tried, but it didn't happen. They were all doing well with their dad, there was no reason to." She scoffed, "Plus, it would never happen with the way their father was with his sons."

I gathered that their father must've been very structured, consistent, and powerful to get that many lucrative women to be in relationships with him and have babies for him. How interesting it was to me just considering the socialization of five young men, with five different mothers, being raised in the same house by their father. Yet, he seemingly taught the boys *some* pretty admirable qualities about life, family, charity, and community awareness.

"My uncle was very protective but didn't have to say much. He kept his family close, even me, since he had no girls." Jenny told me. "That's why they are all still living on top of each other. You gotta sign the NDA, Ma's never going to let you stay around without it. Manuel knows that that's probably why he doesn't tell you shit."

"I guess so," I nodded, understanding that that might be something that comes with the territory, but not so sure I was fully ready to sign anything to date someone. "He never even told me about it."

"Probably scared to make you feel uncomfortable, you know how you get." Jenny sighed, "I really shouldn't even be telling you anything Acacia. You shouldn't even be around him without signing it. For his sake."

"Can you tell me about the NDA?" I asked her, hopeful. "It doesn't seem normal to do, is it?"

"First off, nothing about the man you are dating is normal and you probably know way too much already. It's just to protect him." Jenny said to me as she began recording herself dancing the routine to the trending song that blared from the pool. "We are officially done talking, I get why the boys were so nervous about you. Wanna go dance?"

"Sure," my search for information was at a dead end. I would either need to sign the NDA or just walk away, otherwise I was trying to solve a never-ending puzzle.

19

Once we got back to the hotel Jenny snuck off with Marcus and I headed to check on my boys as well.

Manuel had texted me that he and Tré were playing video games in the living room area of my suite. Neither seemed to be invested in the game, in fact, when I walked in I felt that awkward feeling you get when you walk into a room of people that were just talking about you.

"Hey Mom," Tré greeted me, taking his eyes off the television to shoot a glance at Manuel.

"Hello Gorgeous," Manuel put the game controller down and leaned back in the recliner, the makeup job was amazing because I could barely see any bruising. "How was brunch?"

"Hello, hello. It was… educational." I kissed my son on the cheek, seeing them spending time together was nice, however Manuel and I had to talk. "Can we talk in private once you two finish this round or whatever?"

Tré stopped me, "Wait Mom, there was something I wanted to talk to you about."

"Okay, I'm listening." I glanced at Manuel, "Can you excuse us."

Manuel came and stood by me, "Tré asked me if I could stay while he talked to you."

"Yeah mom, I asked Manuel to stay. I want to tell you, or ask you, if it's okay, that I wanna move with Dad. No more switching." He managed to finally get out. "I've been trying to tell you, but I didn't want you to be upset."

"I told him you wouldn't be upset," Manuel tried to touch my hand, and I pulled back from him, he was not allowed to touch me just yet.

Tré noticed me pull my hand away and got more nervous, but it wasn't about him. Manuel wanted to tell me to be soft, but I didn't want him to touch me. All I could imagine was him using that same hand to hold CoDéy's fake ass ponytail when she was sucking him off this morning at the photoshoot.

"Mom, I'll still come see you. Just every other weekend and even on Wednesdays, but I don't want to live at home anymore. At your house. It's just a lot of going back and forth." He tried to explain. "Once I get a car I'll do more visits."

"You can't drive." I stated, imagining these futuristic visits with my son.

My house? I thought it was *our* house.

"Manuel's assistant found me driving classes back home."

I looked at Manuel who was trying to avoid my eye contact. "Tré, your dad is teaching you how to drive when you're ready. No one else."

"Okay well," he backtracked, "I just don't want you to think I won't come see you."

I paused, looking at my nervous son, "Sure, is this what your dad came up with or you?"

I could see that it was difficult for him to have this conversation with me, he looked at Manuel twice while trying to get the words out. I saw Manuel give him a reassuring look for confidence each time.

"Both. Dad treats me like a man, and every week when I come back home to your house I feel like I'm a little kid again. I just wanna live with Dad." He told me.

"OUR house. Tré, since when have you wanted to go live with Dad full-time?" I asked, still surprised, due to him usually wanting to be with me.

Tré looked at Manuel, then looked at me. "I've been wanting to tell you for a couple months."

"Is this coming from your father or your coaches? Is it about some girl?" I asked him.

"No mom. Dad knows I want to leave, but he said I have to man up and tell you myself." He had a baby face grin, "And no, there are no girls right now, just football and school."

My son leaving home was a conversation his dad and I battled quite a few times in our many break-ups over the last fourteen years, sometimes even the reason for a few reconciliations. We never wanted to have to make our child choose, but when we did, he always chose me in the past. It wasn't a contest, but I rested easy, always being able to peek in on him at night.

"Well, we can talk about it if you want to, but if you are sure you want to go, I won't make you rotate weeks for me."

"I'm sure," he told me. "It's that too, the back and forth every week, it's a lot. I like my school, I want to get settled, not leaving things at your house and his house. Having two of everything. I'm doing great in football, dad and I are having fun, and you seem happy too."

"I know you are doing so well, making me very proud." I nodded in agreement, sitting on the arm of the couch beside Tré and putting my arm around him, then teasing him. "Okay, go stay with Dad, I'm okay with that. Now that I did the fourteen years of hard work he can have you. You were worried about telling me?"

"I just didn't want you to be worried or upset." My overprotective son confessed; it was even visible that he'd just gotten a lot of weight off his shoulders. "I was also afraid of you being home alone all the time. I like that Manuel is around for you too, you're safer."

266

I laughed, "I will be okay, I will surely miss you, but I completely understand if you want to live with Dad. You can still come to *our* home anytime too, not just scheduled."

Manuel smiled at me, I was surprised Tré felt more comfortable telling Manuel about this than just telling me himself, they were in sync. Although it was nice to see them bonding, my son and this amazing man I am getting to know, I couldn't push back the thought that things were just moving too fast with Manuel and me. He and I really had to talk before things got deeper.

"Did you want to do anything else before your flight?" Manuel asked us. "I just want to play the game," Tré quickly announced, putting his headset on and unpausing the system. I kissed him on the forehead, my baby was growing into a man.

He looked at me, "There's somebody I need you to meet."

"We gotta talk before I meet anyone else." I told Manuel sternly.

He led the way as I followed him out of Tré's room, out of the suite, and into the hall. We walked not too far from the elevators. He stood tall, as always, seemingly never slouching and prepared for anything.

"So, there's an NDA?"

"Jenny is stupid. It's not a big deal to me," he told me calmly, as I made a face of disbelief. "That's them, they care, I don't care about it. I'm going to introduce you to Ma today, then tell you about it."

"Yes you do, because you are not telling me shit. You're vague and keep so many things suppressed from me. I want full disclosure from you so if that's what it comes with... I'll sign your paper, if it means you'll be more open with me."

He shook his head, "Because the things you want to know don't define me."

"Everybody else wants me to sign it, right? Your brothers? Your mothers?"

He nodded, pulling my hand to get me closer to him and wrapping me in his arms. "I don't care what they want. That kind of stuff changes the relationship."

"Changes in a bad way?" I asked.

He gave me an once overlook, then a shrug. "Maybe."

"Maybe it will be a good thing." I sighed, pulling a little away from him. "You can have some faith in me, too."

Just then, when we were gaining some moment of clarity, Buck was coming down the hall from Manuel's suite, he stood looking at us with his menacing smile.

I could possibly see him as the girlfriend stealing type, but from your own brother!

"Ma is asking about you," Buck told us.

"Okay." Manuel brushed him off.

Buck didn't leave, "Let's go."

"Go back inside so I can finish talking." Manuel told him, he was beginning to squeeze my hand. Buck stood at the door, eyeing me, seeming to piss off his younger brother. Manuel snapped at him. "Get in the fuckin' door!"

I pulled my hand back; he was gripping it too tight.

"Sorry," he held his hand back out apologetically, I shook my head *no*, I contemplated if I wanted to participate in his game anymore.

Garon came from down the hall behind Buck and pushed him aside. "What are you gonna do EmManuel?"

"We're coming." Manuel told them. "Just give me a minute to talk to her first."

Garon went back into Manuel's suite. Manuel was looking at me, but not talking.

"Say something because this is weird," I told him after the door closed and we were alone again.

"My family is more like a business than a family, but that's not bad, it just comes with a lot. We are close, very close. Buck, Garon, and Corbin are my brothers, their mothers are my mothers too. Ma runs the business, manager so-to-speak." Manuel explained, "My father set everything up and we played the roles."

"She's gonna tell me to sign it?" I asked him. "An NDA?"

"She's not going to tell you to do anything. Of course, she is going to want you to, but that's not what you are here for. I want you to meet her as Ma, one of my mothers, not my manager." He explained.

I nodded in agreement, "I think that's fine, let's go."

We stood up and went down to his suite to meet his Mom-ager together.

After Manuel greeted Ma with a hug and kiss as she sat on the rocking chair and then pointed to the couch for us to sit down across from her. We obliged, still Manuel held my hand… or was I holding his.

Ma wasn't as friendly as his other mothers I met, but she was just as dynamic. She got straight to the point, "Finally I get to meet the newest lady who has my sons fighting. I'm Dawn, Ma, CEO of…. Everything these five do."

"Hi, I'm Acacia, I'm a teacher… and a writer, I have a son too." I told her, committed to acting and appearing braver than I really felt, one of the best tips I've gotten. "Nice to meet you also."

"We're not fighting, Ma," Manuel clarified. "No one is fighting."

"Anymore. No one is fighting anymore. you punched *my* son for a reason, EmManuel, and I'm sure he sucker punched you for one as well from what your brother told me. Which I don't feel sorry for either of you because look at the number of rules you broke." She nodded then turned her body towards her other boys. "And I blame all of you for this because the four of you always stupidly follow behind him like you are still children and to find out your mothers knew and didn't tell me is not surprising. Which is why I will always be the favorite."

"I can't believe you are blaming this on anyone but Manuel, I was attacked," Buck was laughing from behind his mother, like a troubled adolescent he enjoyed her attention.

His mother looked at me, "Please excuse my biological child, he's socially stupid, he was alone in the world for a while."

"The fight was over money, Ma, it was not her fault, she was just collateral damage. The man fought me and still owes me." Buck explained, recusing me from any blame of the fight. "Dad said a man who doesn't pay his debts will suffer much more than those he owes. Anxiety is a killer when you fuck over people who care about you, think about it."

"You two don't fight over money, you were fighting over money?" Ma snapped and looked disgusted at Manuel, then looked at Corbin. "You were gambling? Was this a bet? You are your fathers' children!"

Corbin looked at both of his brothers and shrugged. He seemed only a little less innocent than his brothers.

"No, Ma. There was nothing that I owed him. There was no bet." Manuel tried to explain.

Buck taunted him, "EmManuel, you lost, you bet against the public. We all liked the teacher; we knew she wouldn't fall for it."

Garon intruded. "You should've paid when you lost."

"No, don't do that Garon, EmManuel called it off," Corbin said, they sounded like some grown teenagers.

"It was too late!" Buck laughed. "You can't call off a bet when you're losing a fuckin' bet! Ryu's dead and the odds are off. The bet was still on."

"I was not losing, I wasn't playing!" Manuel snapped at him, then looked at me. "I was not playing."

270

"What was the bet?" I asked him.

Manuel looked at me, "There wasn't a bet."

"If there was no bet, why did you pay me this cash?" Buck pulled out a stack of money from his pocket, it was in a bank envelope. "This your bank, right? It damn sure ain't who I bank with."

"I paid you so you would shut the fuck up." Manuel angrily shot at Buck. "There was no bet."

He was too angry, the way you only get at family because there was definitely some kind of bet.

Ma snapped at both of them, "After the way you two fools acted at that photo shoot! Pissed me off so bad, you set my immune system back 5 years. All of you are too damn grown to keep doing this outside gambling. You are not sixteen, we are not still in a pandemic! End this childish shit already, text him whatever is left of the money, and move forward."

I agreed with Ma, this behavior was definitely feeling like some teenage-boy drama. Although biased, she was well equipped to be the judge of her boys' argument, many years of practice, I'm sure.

"It's over." Manuel said, shooting a mean stare at his older brother. Ma looked at Buck to see if he agreed that the debt was paid.

Buck waved his hand back and forth, not in agreement, "She has her ring back, so how is it over if it's not fully paid EmManuel?"

Manuel sighed, Buck was for sure his rival sibling, they'd probably been competing for years to get their father's attention being so close in age.

"It's the principle," Manuel told him, "You're doing the wrong thing."

"Principle?" Buck repeated out loud, "When I sent you a digital money request you insisted on paying in cash," Buck looked at me to finish the story. "I got to this man's dressing room, and he was in there with CoDéy on her knees, just like when we were kids. Man pulled the same prank today as when we were in middle school, no upgrades on it."

Manuel wouldn't look at me, but I think all his brothers did.

"We were 12!" Manuel yelled at him, "Are you serious holding onto that right now?"

"Exactly! You pulled the same trick from when you were 12!" Buck sighed, "I was cheering for you to get you back with the hardheaded teacher, she doesn't listen good but at least she's nice."

"That was not planned like that," Manuel put his hand on his forehead as if it could've been accidental.

I wanted to get up and just run out the room, I was embarrassed, but couldn't move. Buck's mother stood up and smacked him in the face.

"Is this about the abortion you told me about?" Ma asked Buck. "Are you getting back at him?"

Corbin coughed, "You told *your* mother?"

"50," Ma snapped at Corbin, he sighed and got down on the floor and started doing push-ups. Ma looked at Buck and shouted. "Get over it!"

Manuel looked at Buck, "It would've ruined her career."

"Ya, sure. I'm over it," Buck lied, putting on a front for his mother. "I just thought that was some real Manuel shit to do, EmManuel."

I'd let Manuel's hand go as soon as I'd heard confirmation that CoDéy was in his dressing room, now my hands were being used to cover my face from screaming in front of these strangers.

"Don't start that stupid shit." Manuel said.

Buck sighed, "Okay well this meeting is over, she said she wasn't going to keep the ring. There's no need for any hard feelings."

I came from hiding behind my palms, although I didn't want to show my face. I felt beyond stupid. I knew there was no way he just genuinely fell in love with me without knowing me.

"That's what it was?" I asked him, searching in his eyes somewhere to make me believe it wasn't true, this couldn't have been fake, I felt something with him. "Tell me if that's what this all was? A bet with your brothers?"

"I wasn't betting on sleeping with you. I mean, I liked you before the game even came up," Manuel tried to explain, but it was all finally starting to make sense to me. "I guess I was joking around, before we met in person, but once I met you it wasn't like that."

"This is crazy," I mumbled.

Ma was upset at the boys, "It was a prank? Like when you were teenagers having to get pulled out of the malls. And there go your mothers hiding it trying to baby you grown fools. You are not children anymore, quarantine is over, your baby brother is gone, you can't keep pretending to be children, so he'll come back!"

"Ma," Manuel started to stop her, but she cut him off and he didn't persist.

"EmManuel, what would your father say? You all were so proud to tell me you ran a thorough screening without me, and completely dropped the ball. Your mothers found out and still dropped the ball! She's a damn writer and you're risking your reputation for what? A damn bet with your brothers on the teacher!" Ma instructed, pointing at the door. "And before the NDA, your geniuses, the five of you, get out."

"Four," Corbin corrected. "R.I.P. Ryū."

"Oh, he's just as guilty as you and your mothers. Goodbye." Ma dismissed them rudely.

It was very awkward watching a bunch of men in their thirties listening to this angry little businesswoman, but she was quite intimidating to me as well. I did not want to have to talk to her alone, I almost left with them, to get Tré and get back home.

Garon left the room, then Buck and Corbin followed close behind him. I glanced at Ma, she seemed to have a slight hint of a smile on her face helping her boys, but I couldn't tell if it was an evil smile or just years of Botox.

"It was not how it seems," Manuel held my face at the chin to force me to look at him. "We will talk later."

"What?" I hissed, snatching his hands off my face. "This is so wild; I am done being your joke."

"They bet on everything," Ma told me plainly. "EmManuel go outside with your brothers so I can speak to her alone, she doesn't want to talk to you."

He didn't stop talking, "I watched you, got to know you, and I liked you… as a person. I love getting to know you, Acacia, I just didn't know how to tell you the truth about how I met you."

There was a silent pause.

"EmManuel, excuse us, please," Ma asked. He obliged, leaving the suite and going out to the lobby. I didn't say anything nor look at him. "Do you need a tissue?"

I nodded and took a couple from the box she offered me. "Thank you."

"It's the least I can do, he's one of mine." She rolled her eyes, "I heard you met his mothers while he's been flying around the country, and I've been working on building the brand. I had a lot to be filled in on, in the last couple of hours. I'm his favorite mother, the one who handles everything, I own the company. Are you okay?"

"The whole experience has been kind of out-of-body for me, I kept trying to comprehend why he and I had such strong chemistry. You know why we were so in sync, but I guess it was just fake."

Ma sighed, "People are drawn to EmManuel because of his mastery, he's become a total magnet that attracts everything he wants. He's in a whole other world, it was always hard to parent him. Don't feel bad, it's not you. His father knew and that is why the rules exist, to avoid

274

any issues. Like this. It was his plan, as his mother I am supposed to be guiding him to do right by them. And now from what I understand, they have just been setting decoys in my way so he can avoid me and his mothers. Do you see my problem?"

"I do," I started to say as I have always been quite the rule follower myself.

"Acacia, my sons can be assholes, just like my late husband was the majority of the time, they are all similar to their dad in that way. Fortunately, you got the best one. I know he *really* likes you, despite this *bet* business. However, for my son's safety, I need you to get this signed and notarized."

"Safety? He said—," I started to tell her what Manuel and I spoke about, but she cut me off.

"This paperwork protects him, and if you care about him then I need you to take care of that and send it back to my office," she handed me a white envelope, prelabeled and stamped. "Put this in your bag."

The pre stamped envelope read, Sora Eaton, I took what I assume was the NDA paperwork and put it in my purse.

"Did he give you some kind of insurance? Do you need anything, money?" She asked me. "A safety net or umbrella?"

Hush money? Did she know about *umbrella*?

"No, thanks. I don't need anything," I stood up to leave, not giving a damn about an NDA after I was just fooled by these people.

"All of them got their daddy's gambling problem too, so take that bet with a grain of salt. There are some things that will continue to pull down people, and the one for the Eaton men has been gambling, they bet on any and everything, the overall need to fill their ego with a *win*. It ain't personal, nothing is ever personal, even when someone else wants it to be."

"I'm sure." I nodded at her, "Again, it was nice to meet you… and your family."

"Likewise, I'll text you so that you can lock my number in, you can let me know when you are sending the paperwork out." She extended her hand, and I gracefully shook it.

Ma wasn't a fan of me, I could tell she wasn't a fan of any women her sons ever brought home, but at least she was somewhat polite at surface level.

I turned and left the suite, walking into the lobby where Emmanuel and his three brothers sat, collectively looking like four grown children outside the principal's office. Bickering about who was most at fault until they heard the door open.

*   *   *

Talking to Ma and then seeing her grown boys sitting in the lobby brought me back a year, to the end of the pandemic's quarantine. I'd been hearing vague tidbits of information about these men for years; I knew about these uncles. It made sense now why things felt so familiar.

Back when the sky was prettier, the air felt cleaner, the grass was greener, there was truly an undeniable sense of calm in the air. It felt as if many things in nature were growing quite naturally and undisturbed. In all my decades, I've never breathed air fresher than the air we were breathing now. Locking people away from nature had its perks on the environment for sure.

Continuously we were hearing on the radio the term, *new normal...* and I did not mind, because the old normal wasn't working for most people. Maybe it was the Quarantine Education, but I fully embraced being optimistic about my life.

It took me some time to not feel guilty in admitting that the quarantine itself was a much-needed break... I needed to sit still and think.

May I remind you; people were losing their lives and freedoms for their political beliefs and as for me, I was losing 'friends' on social media left and right. We had celebrities leading street protests against brutal treatment, while on the other hand possibly the biggest riots were being led by highly trusted officials. Perspectives were being analyzed and folks we were really separated, as news reports gave daily death tolls by the city!

Times were tough and lots of people were lost trying to get back into the swing of things.

I still remained hopeful. I had more than enough vision and goal boards posted to keep me on track.

Despite the daily foolery because here I was hosting a virtual high school detention… just inviting the rule breaking fools into my home office.

I took out the latest book I'd been waiting for in the mail, although the country was opening back up I was still finding most of my joy in books. My library was growing, I constantly collected books from book recommendations that came from other books' recommendations. Today I planned to read whilst running a super silent detention today.

I waited right until it was time to open the digital detention classroom, praying no one would arrive and I could relax in bed with the book. However, I had one student to let in.

"You must be my only detainee showing up today," I told Garrett after waiting the required fifteen minutes for any late arrivals. "You know the drill, work on something and stay on the camera, I'll mark you as present as long as you stay thirty minutes. Please and thank you."

"I was gonna ask if I could stay the whole hour today, I was hoping you could help me write an essay. Please?" Garrett asked, after unmuting his microphone to speak to me, knowing this is not my tutoring hours. It'd been a long time since anyone had come and sat with me for lunch, the students were home now, they weren't knocking on my door telling me about their life concerns or seeking advice.

"I guess you can stay since you're here, how much help are we talking about?" I asked rhetorically. "Why do you even have detention?"

"Broke Mrs. Kingmore's dumbest rule, no eating on camera," he told me. "In my own house, my cousin dared me to do it. At least I won a bet for once."

"Well, the rules are the rules! Guess you get the consequences." I laughed and shrugged. "Love them or change them, the right way. Tell me about the essay."

"It's an essay for my history class, it's due Sunday night, but you know Mr. Putnam gonna take off points for every little thing, especially if it's late. I just need some help with the intro."

"Why are you just asking now?" I asked him while groaning, logging into my personal computer, with a larger screen than the school issued-pandemic laptops. My students know I will help them whenever I can, it was my weakness as well as my strength. "Grab whatever research you have, let me see what you have been doing so far."

"Honestly, I don't have anything on paper, I just been searching online a little bit." He admitted.

"Not even notes?" I sighed, putting my book completely away, "And what did I teach you about trusting your memory? Write everything down."

"Truthfully, I wasn't going to do it, I just wanted to go outside and play football with my uncle. I'm getting so much better, he could've gone pro, he's the one who taught my father. But your speech last period about trying to get the codfish from New English and California inspired me to do some work," he said proudly. "If you can't help, I understand. I know you getting ready for your weekend."

I was secretly proud too; the art of oral storytelling may have been one of my favorite new skills to use on my students.

"Oh, just stop the baby violin Garrett, I'm gonna help you, but you're doing the work. I'm just guiding you through an outline." Garrett nodded at the reminder, a student who continuously found ways to take my classes despite the tedious work and projects.

"Okay I'm gonna run to the kitchen and get my food, then we can start." He said triumphantly, he knew I would help, Garrett turned off his camera.

I muted myself and began to tidy up my office before I signed out for the day.

278

I could faintly hear grown masculine voices on the opposite side of the online classroom. Garrett was my only student in detention this afternoon, he still had not turned his camera on since he'd gone to the restroom. I was beginning to believe someone was watching me from my only detainee's home based on their conversation.

None of the voices sounded like my student.

"Look at them big things, even with the collared shirt on," I heard a male voice say when I turned around. I looked at myself in the camera, surely I was the one in the collared shirt!

The people in my student's home seemed to be under the impression that just because their video camera was off, their mic was off as well.

"Is this what you want to say you did during the pandemic? That you stalk your nephew's online high school teacher?" A voice said, then laughed. "What you gonna do if you do get her? Buy her an ass?"

Someone defended me, "No, her ass is good, she's been getting right."

"You know he be tuning in every third period to her class, laying right beside Garrett, taking notes like he's in the bitch's class." A second voice said with a laugh.

"She ain't a bitch, don't call the teachers that. Look at what they are going through with the pandemic."

I couldn't help but raise my eyebrows at the comment, the one main reason I was not very happy when we went to teaching from home via camera was because I did not want to be on camera in the first place. When my boss made the announcement we'd be teaching on camera, I looked for a new damn job! I didn't like the way I looked and knowing families were sitting at home rating me didn't make me feel any better.

Luckily in time Quarantine Education had me working on my body and physical appearance more, so by this time I was not too bothered by the camera. Sadly, they sounded like adults on the student's side of the internet but were talking like children. I questioned the ages of my mysterious classroom visitors.

I'm partially to blame, a more mature teacher probably would immediately confront and report the parental figures on the other end of the computer. Yet in the midst of quarantine where male attention was sparse, the shady compliments weren't completely unwelcomed.

"Don't tell me the high school teacher got your nose open, Lil Depression?" A voice taunted. "She makes like thirty dollars an hour. Maybe."

"He cares about her money?"

I got closer to my seat in front of the computer, pretending not to hear them, but wanting a closer listen as there were many voices at once.

From what my principal told me, as many students received accommodations for their living arrangements through the pandemic, Garon was currently living with his grandmother while his mother was working, saving lives. Fortunately, he was able to take his classes online until things went to the *new normal*, that way he didn't miss his classes.

Unfortunately, like many other students, even with online classes available and free tutoring, Garon still struggled in school and was possibly going to be ineligible to play sports when he returns home.

A groggy voice, that I immediately picked up as Lil Depression, said, "Every one of y'all shut the fuck up, because I really enjoy learning vocabulary."

"You're going to spend your free time learning high school level English? You are in a slump my brother."

"Do you also like learning detention? Is that what you are here for now? Why don't you just ask the teacher out?" Another said with a chuckle, teasing Lil Depression. "Maybe it'll help you get through this pandemic depression you're going through."

"Is she Miss or Mrs.?"

"She says Miss, but she wears a ring."

"She's wearing a ring and you ain't book smart. You barely passed school by yourself, and Mom was your teacher! Go find someone else."

"The ring doesn't matter." Some asshole said. "I'll put 10 on it, you fuck his teacher, I would even do 15. Hell, if she's married 20, you in?? Smash or Pass? You so scared to bet me."

The seemed to be a pro at applying pressure, although a very cheap bet maker. I was worth way more; this bet was insulting!

"Ain't no depression or slump?" The groggy voice sounded offended by the slander. "There's a pandemic outside! I'm just staying safe, masked up, and to my damn self. I'm not taking a chance of bringing that virus in this house."

"Lil' Depression, no excuses. Smash or Pass the high school teacher? I got 25."

Someone laughed, "That's how you caught the virus the last time, stop trying to smash these people are sick!"

"He can wear a mask."

"And take her where? Everywhere in the country is on lockdown." Lil Depression had a point, what respectable places could he take me? I tried to figure out how to casually lose the internet connection, just in case this miserable guy tried to ask me out.

"You know what state she is in, my boy? They don't give a shit about a damn pandemic down there. Go ask the damn teacher out, fly down there, and see what's she on. Bet she ain't saying no." One of the voices coached.

Another voice interjected, "No, y'all stop playing now, leave Garrett's damn teacher out of y'all's bull shit, for real. That's a grown woman."

"Teachers need love too. Maybe if you get a good wife she'll kick that little depression right out of you!" The antagonizing voice sang, "Smash or Pass?"

Lil' Depression seemed to pause, then he replied responsibly. "I'm not taking nobody out during a pandemic, I pass, I'm not playing."

"He stays afraid of the smart hoes; I knew you were going to Pass."

"I'm scared of smart ones. When?" Lil Depression did sound a little scared. "You know what kind of women I'm capable of pulling, don't try me."

"So? I'll ask again, smash or pass the high school teacher? You've been watching her over Garrett's shoulder since he got here weeks ago! You damn near in the class and I'm pretty sure you are doing his work to get brownie points, too."

"How much you got on it?" Lil Depression asked the instigator.

Someone laughed and I felt saddened in humanity that the depressed man would be willing to even consider such a bet.

"Well shit, sounds like a sweet bet."

"How do I turn this shit on, you talking to this lady today." Another voice threatened. "Just invite her to a later show or something, say hi."

"Garrett said she doesn't date her students' parents; he knows some that tried." A man explained, I struggled not to giggle.

"He has no kids."

"Just drop it. Keep the games for the internet models, leave the pandemic-heroes, people who are actually going to work in this shit, alone. You got me?" Someone scolded them.

I heard someone shuffling with keys on Garon's computer. Then a few curse words were thrown around.

"I'm sure we can find her on the 'net, too."

I struggled to keep a straight face and not show my nerves, remaining casual as I eavesdropped, and the guests watched me in the camera. I'd spent the whole half of the school year prior working from home and found humor in a lot of accidental camera or mic slip ups. However, this was appearing to be a slightly epic mic slip.

"No, get off his computer."

I heard more shuffling and tussling around on the computer. "Oh shit, I don't think that his mic was off."

"Nooo, what the fuck did you do! Did she hear us? Could she hear us?" A sharp voice, maybe Lil Depression, snapped at them, the mic clicked off then on while they tried to determine if they were caught. Then the mic gets turned on again.

"Did she hear us or not?" The sound turned off again. Holding a natural facial expression, I casually walked to the side of my office playing coy as I had to turn around for a quick laugh.

I heard the exit notification as Garrett's laptop had exited the online classroom detention. I waited five minutes just chuckling to myself off-and-on as I looked back on what just took place, waiting for Garrett to come back so I could tell my class guests that I heard them and was not interested!

However, I was the only one that remained in my digital classroom for the remainder of my teacher duty. My one detainee did not return to finish his detention time nor to work on his essay, which meant it was just about safe to clock out for the day. I even decided I would not report Garret for missing detention, it probably wasn't his fault.

I looked at myself on the computer screen checking myself out before logging off, proud the positive changes and self-discipline were paying off.

As always, the first thing I did is run and tell my bestie, she was my favorite person to share these male encounter stories with. We bounced our experiences and advice off each other since I can remember dating. She had just as many crazy interactions as I did, maybe more.

We say we will write books of horrible experiences in the past, as an inside joke we give them chapters.

Hazel

I meet all the weirdos I swear!
Chapter 74 ☐

Lol. Aren't you at work? Why are u adding chapters

I AM at work!
GROWN men at my students'
houses betting fifty dollars that
one could smash me!
Didn't know the mic was on

Dead. 50 a piece?
Let them, don't be a victim of
the drought or are you and your
curse still having silent rough
sex in the middle of the night
when the baby's asleep???

Bitch BYE
U don't want me to be great
Books coming soon!!!

Manuel stood up as soon as I walked into the lobby, he was as far from Buck as possible, but with Corbin and Garon in the middle I suppose their threat to one another was over at this stage in the game. Manuel walked over to me, we stood face-to-face, neither of us spoke for a little while. The brothers were silent as well, I didn't hear a thing, but his breathing.

"You know, nothing I said to you was a game to me," Manuel told me, breaking the silence. "You know I care about you."

Silence. He deserved no words from me.

Manuel tried to make sense of what happened to me. "It's just a game me and my brothers used to play sometimes when we were growing up, then during the pandemic we somehow were playing with women on

284

the internet. But I promise I wasn't playing when I was getting to know you in person."

"I don't believe shit you say anymore," I told Manuel. "So, you just found my social page and tried to have sex with me by sending me some tickets?"

"Okay, so no. They couldn't find anyone for me online." He paused and took a breath, "You are my nephew's teacher, he stayed with us during the pandemic because his mom is a doctor and my brother died just before she was sent away. I watched you teach your class damn near every day; I really loved your personality and the way you talk. My nephew talked to me about you, how you are with him and other students."

"I don't meet women like you every day, Acacia, I meet fans." He tried to touch me, but I slapped his hand, his brothers defensively looked up at me, but Manuel waved his hand at them. "You can't think this was just a bet with my brothers, I spent more than the bet was worth, I told you I wouldn't try to have sex with you the whole first weekend which was the entire bet."

I wanted to listen to him, but I couldn't tell what was real anymore.

"What do you want me to do to prove I'm not playing with you?" He asked.

"There's nothing to prove, I'm glad you lost your bet." I said, then I turned to Garon, and I realized why he didn't like me so much, he was against the bet. "Can you take me and Tré to the airport?"

"Thought you'd never ask," Garon nodded happily, getting up and walking past me to get into their family's suite to hopefully grab his keys.

I touched Garon's arm, and he looked at me long enough for me to see why he'd looked so familiar. Since the moment he ushered Hazel and I out of the concert, I kept thinking I recognized him from somewhere. "Wow, Garrett is your little twin."

Garon finally gave me a real smile. "He means everything to me, I'm his godfather."

I smiled, "You are lucky, he is a great person."

"He looks just like me, I for sure thought you'd figure it out sooner. He loves you." Garon sucked his teeth, then paused. "No one can know he's related to EmManuel, his mom can't find out, the school can't find out, you can't say shit to anyone. His mother will take him back, he wants to stay with our family."

"I would never put him in this shit, I promise." I promised Garon as he walked off to get the keys.

"Can we talk alone?" Manuel asked me softly.

"How about we never talk again, you *are* too much for me." I confirmed my earlier suspicion.

He tried to reach for my hands, but I stepped back. He whispered, "Umbrella."

I shook my head, no, "I'm not with *this* Manuel, at all. You could have said *something*. I was a joke to you, a bet. My feelings were worth fifty bucks to you?"

"Thousand," Buck corrected me with a dumb look on his face, he was still getting a kick out of this. "But he only paid me ten thousand. He really owes me forty more. He finally loses a bet and won't pay."

I took the ring box out of my jacket and tossed it to Buck. "Pawn it, you won."

Disappointed at another failed attempt at love, I headed back into my suite to get myself and my son's things together for the flight home.

@AcaciaIvy2020

Free yourself. Become the person you desire to be. As many times as you need to.

20

Epilogue

"You're late as fuck." Buck pointed out impatiently, sitting down sporting his usual man bag and mischievous grin.

"I wasn't going to come at all, and the line was long," I reminded him, taking a seat at the small round coffee table. "But let's be grateful I'm here, you said fifteen minutes."

"I already know it's impossible to hate him, so let's start with letting all that pride go." Buck sat across from me looking friendlier, but I wasn't falling for the nice guy act. Nevertheless, this was a short coffee date that I accepted, so I would hear him out as promised.

"What pride?" I asked him, looking out the window at all the greenery. "I never took you as the coffee and botanical garden type?"

"I'm not, that was to convince you to come," he stood up and motioned for me to join him. "Thought we could go for a walk. Pick flowers."

I smiled as I got up and followed behind him, now with my coffee. "I'm up for a walk around the garden."

Buck picked up two envelopes that were between us, on the table and put them in his large hoodie pocket. We walked out the back door of the coffee house into a rich garden of flowers, grouped together throughout long windy paths. As I read the labels looking for my favorites.

"So, I know you've been hearing all the new music, right? You're a whole muse out here Acacia. Even hate turns into beautiful love songs for EmManuel, you must admit."

"Oh, don't say that. I don't hate anyone, y'all were trying to play *me*!" I told him, taking pictures and recording videos of the exotic flowers as we walked through the garden. He casually lit up a thick blunt. "I don't think you can smoke out here."

Occasionally I wondered if Manuel was going to cook up some elaborate scheme to get back on my good side. But it seemed we were really done. He made a couple of recent songs that surely have been about me or us, but other than that there was nothing. There was no hate or hard feelings, I listened to his music more now than before.

It'd been a couple months since I last heard, or been accessible to many, including Manuel or any of his family. My social media was off, and my phone number was brand new, I wanted to escape for a while. Disconnecting from people and spending some time with my own thoughts, I even had to take some time away from Hazel and other friends, to question who I was becoming through the friendship.

The only social platform I was feeling qualified to give advice for these days was on SchoolSpace, my virtual classroom component!

I thankfully didn't find myself back on the kitchen floor crying about this breakup, but instead chose to be grateful and learn from my time with Manuel. I appreciated the experience we had.

The reason why we stopped wasn't relevant, simply a childish joke between him and his brothers that went too far. As I see it, he tried to play me, but I won. I had fun and got spoiled, time well spent. Even the things I left behind, he made sure got sent to me… except the ring. Part of me was hoping that Buck might come with it to give it back, but I was okay if he didn't, afterall I advised him to pawn it.

At first I talked to myself a lot. Then I reread a lot of my library, for more clarity and clarification. I wrote notes and more notes, until I felt I was truly grasping those ideals I'd previously learned in my quarantine education. Then my thoughts were finally flowing onto the blank pages of my journals again, like they did in younger days.

My writer's block has been cured since Manuel, maybe to his merit for softening me back up so that I could feel again. It's hard to fully experience life with a hard shell. Although I felt cured, I was still intrigued when Buck reached out to me through my work email.

"How'd you find me Buck?" I asked him as we walked along the trails.

"You're not a ninja Acacia, you were a little too easy to find if you ask me, I'm telling my brother we gotta fix that. I would've found you anyway, I own a security company, I have ways when I need to." He told me, he wasn't the same as when I first met him, less mischievous looking for sure. "I came to apologize, in person. Things went too far back in February, and you didn't deserve that, really."

"I appreciate that, but trust me, you have made up for it. No need for any more apologies from you or your family. Your mothers have been beyond generous since you four disappointed them. We don't even need to bring the situation up, please." I bowed to him jokingly.

He went on anyway. "Seriously everybody knew Manuel liked you before the bet when you were just Garrett's teacher. I knew he wouldn't say Pass, he was interested, and responding is mandatory. We've been playing since we were young."

I couldn't hold back my disgusted facial expressions, but I remained silent as he explained the game.

"So, I pushed him, but he really cared about you before that! Garon was against it from the start; he shut it down because of Garon. Corbin was kinda against it, but we saw how you were helping him get through his depression. As much as I didn't even want to admit he was going through something. The more my brother learned about you the more we all knew he was going to make it happen whether we did or not. We were trying to help."

"So here you are, because he always gets what he wants." I retorted.

He nodded yes, "Yes, you can say that. You've been around him; you can't tell the world is his? It is his, could've been mine, but I got too smart. Fucked it up."

"What did you do to fuck it up?" I asked Buck.

"I got entrapped, set up with a decoy really, but a real man takes accountability for where he lacked. It was my fault; I did what I did. EmManuel is better for the position; he listens, he's compassionate, and other qualities that I choose not to possess. He is innocent."

"It doesn't matter anymore."

"Everything matters. I brought you to the dressing room and y'all fell in love ever since!" Buck said, picking a flower for me straight from the garden.

"Stop picking the flowers here, you're not supposed to do that." I told him.

"Urgh! You really do follow the rules." Buck laughed with a nod, "I brought you to him. He *had* to meet you, I know him, meeting you was good. You helped him get out of the bed. You've seen how tight Corbin is with EmManuel's money and even he wanted to see Manuel happy, by meeting you." He told me. "Although the budget pissed Corbin off."

I admired the way Buck "big brothered", over-explaining and taking majority blame. Years of practice and with so many younger siblings.

I promised I'd hear Buck out at this meeting as long as he didn't bring Manuel, since Buck was the one who told me the truth at the hotel and a small part of me wanted to tie up the loose ends.

I cleared my throat, "And how much did he have to pay you for losing the bet on me?"

"That wasn't a real bet," Buck told me with a chuckle. "EmManuel only paid me after the elevator, because he didn't want you to know. He knew you would leave if you found out."

"No, he paid you, so you could see his ex was sucking him off." I reminded him. "I was sitting at the hotel waiting for him to finish a photoshoot, thinking we were going to get to the *next level* with a ring, and he was getting a blowjob by the woman who goes out of her way to harass me at an awards show. You think I'm signing up for that."

"Everything isn't so serious," he said with a smile. "My brother is a great man, Acacia. You seem okay, too. I never heard him talk about no one like he talks about you. I told you already, I am my brother's keeper, and *I* went too far, I was wrong, not him. I need you to give him another chance, you know you want to."

I rolled my eyes and started back in the direction of the coffee house, "Thanks for your apology, but I'm not interested anymore. I'm honestly not mad at anyone about it either, I get it, it was a joke– a game. I'm dating someone else."

"Cap!" Buck accused me of lying, and laughed a forced laugh, he seemed almost offended to think I would move on. "Who are you *dating* after my brother Acacia? Who, the fuck, is measuring up to the 5-star resorts, jets flying you to dinner, meeting your idols, views that only knowing the right people can buy, shutting down expensive ass restaurants so they can concentrate on you, and partying in palaces?

"Acacia, I handpick and employ about 400 men at any given time over the last decades in the family business, and I don't even know a man better than my brother. Other than myself, but you are not my type, you gonna downgrade? Stay comfortable?

"You just like to talk, there are other great guys out in the world." I remark, I see why Manuel was such a good listener with him as an older brother. He liked to hear himself.

He laughed coyly, "I know this world very well, they not comparing to my brother."

Buck was right, so far none were comparing now, and no one really had before either.

About it all, plus I was somewhat lying, there was no one new. My dating life hadn't been crazy exciting before, but the dates I've been on in the past month since Manuel have been embarrassingly lame in comparison! No disrespect because the men before Manuel were not clicking much better with me either.

"I've met some decent people," I cracked a smile at Buck, he smiled back at me, deciding if I was being honest. I saw how he could be charming, in an annoying future brother-in-law way.

"You're such a liar." He accused, "I feel bad for the men that y'all have to date after us. You probably got a couple on your phone right now, negotiating with you to meet them halfway somewhere, while my brother is sending luxury flights and paid drivers. Didn't he have a new car delivered to you? Be for real Acacia, you're gonna play *yourself*? You marry a king and you become a queen, you marry a jester and you too, are a clown. You know you miss him."

"Of course, I think about *him* a lot, I was having a great time with him, but he also is a lot. I'm still skeptical about how he fits in my life or how I'll fit in with y'all." I admitted.

"He'll make sure you fit in, he gave you a damn kill switch, that's only some brother-shit, we don't even do that with women!" Buck said with a wink and laughed at himself, "You know he's just trying to enjoy life *with* you, there's no scam or catch. Stop over analyzing it."

I nodded. Buck reminded me of every car salesman who sold me a car.

"You heard the newest song with Todd?"

"I definitely listen to it almost… every single morning and all day." I admitted. "I cry to that song. I do care about your brother, Buck. I never said I didn't."

He smiled, pleased. "Did you hear your name in it?"

I looked at him quizzically, "My name is not in that song."

"Listen for it the next time you hear it. I know you care about him. You love him." He asked, making a quizzical face. "Your ego is so big that you ain't even making good financial decisions at this point."

"This has nothing to do with *my* finances. I didn't say I love him, of course I do miss him, too, but…" I tried to say.

"But nothing," Buck cut me off. "Go be with him, have fun and be corny together again kissing with your matching outfits on. Go vomit on some $600 pants again, fuck up the interior of some more rentals, he'll pay for it. Money brings security, opportunities, and satisfaction with life, you should get comfortable talking about it."

I rolled my eyes. Buck's way of handling things was too blunt for me, he was definitely the unrefined version of Manuel. "Well, the way you say it, it sounds like you are saying to use him."

"Mutually be an asset to each other, what's wrong with that? We're all adults. Just go take these." Buck handed the two envelopes to me, "This one is from Ma, just in case you lost the first one. This other one here, is the ticket information for an all-inclusive summer vacation. My last apology gift to you and EmManuel. I also put some money in here to get you home first class if you decide you want to leave early too, because I know how you are."

"The NDA." I mumbled, seeing the similar envelope addressed to Raven Eaton. "What does that even mean? It just puts me in a box. I can't be myself."

Buck shrugged, "He's not going to make you sign it. But you should, can't get into the chateau without it, it's worth it and no one wants to hear the truth anyway. They want the magical bullshit, the fairytale, give them that and the media cap that they want. Keep the real you private." He paused, looking at me with a little disbelief. "Don't say you act like you don't know these people just want to be sold a dream? Sell one. What are you selling?"

"Sincerity, I thought. What happened to meeting people and just being yourself?" I let out a sigh, maybe he was right. *Does* the truth still sell anymore? Did it ever? I shifted the focus, "What did you do during the time we were quarantined, Buck?"

Buck slowly smiled with a smirk reminiscing of mischief. "Spent a lot of time with my family, Ryū had just passed, so the bonding was needed. It was like the good old days with the moms and my little brothers, getting into bullshit trouble to pass the time. Played cards, gambled, fished, and taught the next generation of Eaton men a few things. Made a lot of bets."

"Smash or pass?"

He chuckled with a little smidgen of embarrassment, "Yes, we played a little Smash or Pass with internet girls, not many there's like 90% chance it's a PASS, for EmManuel it's a 99.999%!"

"And on your nephew's teacher." I sassed him.

"Yes, unfortunately we did include an unsuspecting, but understanding sweet teacher," he said with a serious face. "One who does not date family members of her students, so really we had no choice but to trick you. Just take the vacation!"

Of course, I wanted to accept the vacation right away, but I needed to measure out the pros and cons. Was I ready to take on a whole new life, no matter how much they believed I would "fit in", I would always just be Manuel's (insert owned title here).

"Speaking of sweet," I decided to see how much info I could get from Buck since he was a little vulnerable. "Are the Suite Hearts real? S-u-i-t-e?"

Buck did a nice belly laugh for more than thirty seconds. "That depends on the person."

"Answer the fucking question, Buck." I shot at him.

"Some people say they can see angels or demons, others just see a bunch of folks walking around an open city garden. Look around, tell me what you see?"

I nodded my head, "So they are real."

"*You* would be the type to see them," Buck shook his head at me, then checked his watch. "He doesn't know I'm here, but I know he will say yes to seeing you."

"He's mad at you, huh?"

"Yes, my protégé little brother who is incapable of hate, hates me right now. And he doesn't even know how to hate correctly, so it's horrible." He nodded with exaggeration, it's sad, but I could tell he missed his best friend.

I put the other envelopes in my purse. "I will consider going away *alone* with your brother. None of *y'all*. No DeCreed. None of his exes. No mothers. I'll let you know."

"Damn, is my family that bad?"

I coughed accidentally, but the timing was comically impeccable, "A man with five mothers, who are all competing to be his favorite. The stupid sibling rivalry fighting, pranks, and gambling all the time with his three brothers, who are just always fuckin'.... right there and don't play about him."

"We really don't," he smiled.

"More rules to learn and follow, only to watch everyone else break them around me? No, I'm not a huge fan and I think I've given up on following rules."

Buck shook his head at me, disappointed. "How are you so smart and dumb at the same time? The rules, the laws, they all work for you when you know them. Acacia, you know them. Knowing the laws is the key to attracting everything you ever dream of freedom, health, wealth, and happiness. Look at your predicament right now, aren't you living proof that the laws work."

I somehow get a flash of memories, making vision and dream boards for my goals. The dozens of mini notebooks for journaling daily thoughts of gratitude and aspirations that live in my top drawer, hoping never to be read by anyone but me for memories in my old age. I'd aligned everything to those aspirations, I followed what the law said.

Buck was right, in a variety of ways I'd been asking for an enchanting adventure with a spellbinding man. The universal laws were only responding to me.

"My family isn't that bad." Buck continued, "And how can you even call that fighting! I thought you were on my side! Who uses a kill switch in the middle of a fight, what were you thinking? Ryu might've done some stupid shit like that."

"You cheated in that fight! That was bad." I laughed, pointing at him, "I can't believe you did that to your brother."

He shrugged it off, "He's my little brother, we fight. Don't you know anything about family?"

"Yes," I smiled, "I come from a big family, we were close growing up."

"Well either way, when you helped me in that fight, that was the moment that I agreed you could be my sister-in-law. I always wanted a sister." He winked, "Did you finish any of those books you started in the quarantine or are you still being a procrastinator?"

I smiled, "I prefer when Garon calls me a perfectionist. But yes I am almost done with one of them, it'll be soon."

He clapped for me, genuinely happy. "What's the genre? What's it about?"

"I guess it falls under Romance," I said, then watched Buck roll his eyes. "Not a typical romance, a combination of lifetime romances thus far. I've been struggling to summarize it. I think it's just about the author leaving this invisible comfort zone, freeing herself from who she thought she had to be due to life experiences and expectations of others. Falling in love with who she is becoming."

"Got ya. I'll wait to hear the reviews. I'm not much of a reader," Then after a blank stare he told me, "The vacation is going to be the best you ever had, don't worry about anything, just show up. Okay?"

I shrugged, "Not sure, but I gotta get out of here and pick up Tre from practice."

"That's fine, I'm actually going to stick around here, I have a business meeting starting soon."

We walked back through the flower-filled arbor back into the coffee shop and he gave me another friendly hug goodbye. Then he

296

walked toward a table in the back where Chris and a B.R.O.S. security guard sat looking at us. I smiled hello, then headed out the door.

I got a much better perception of Buck this time, he was a lot less bitter than when I first met him. Dare I say I might even like Buck as a brother-in-law-type… one day. Chris on the other hand gave me sketchy vibes.

As I was opening the door to exit the restaurant I bumped into Hazel, she was headed in with a few of her sorority sisters from college, I'd noticed she'd been hanging with them more on her internet posts. I was happy she had them.

"Hey, very long time no see, you look great!" She told me with a hug, checking me out with a big smile.

I smiled, "Same to you Haze, it's good to see you."

"I bet you're glad the school year is almost over, get to take some summer vacation time. Are you going anywhere special this summer?"

I smiled, "Maybe. Not sure yet."

"Well let's catch up one day, maybe go grab a drink." She shrugged, probably knowing it won't happen. "You know where I live, you have my number. I'm here and it doesn't have to be awkward. If you ever want to get together, just give me a call."

I nodded, with a smile and gave Hazel a hug. "Thanks, I appreciate that."

We'd always have great memories, and I loved Hazel, but we'd grown apart. The step back from the friendship helped me see life from a more preferred view, the view of the person I was becoming and not who I was when we were young. We weren't who we used to be, I surely wasn't the same, but I 100% loved her and appreciated the friendship that we once had.

We hugged goodbye, with much love, then I headed out.

*   *   *

SchoolSpace	
Upcoming Assignments:	*Live a great life that someday in the future people might read about!* *Have a great summer!* Those of you who are taking me next year make sure you have your summer journal ready on Day 1! I will be keeping one too! Let's have a great summer and fill our journals with awesome adventures to share in the fall! **Summer Journal Requirements:** Mini composition book Minimum two sentences per day (**new** thoughts/things you learned/reflection on your day) 1min- something you are grateful for (cannot repeat any, but can be the smallest thing) 1min- person who loves you (can repeat)

The ride from the airport to destination was a little sketchy, the entire drive felt like we were in a Jurassic forest. But once at the private oceanside location I felt like a queen amongst the people. They treated me as if they'd known me all their lives.

The staff introduced themselves by name and their occupation in case I should need them for anything. From the maids to the chef, everyone called me by name, they were expecting me. I admired the crystal-clear ocean water as the concierge escorted me to a quaint overwater bungalow. She opened the door and we walked into a glass floor living room; we were literally standing on top of water.

I walked into the master bedroom, eager to find EmManuel. His bags were on the floor. Buck surely picked an extremely romantic home for us. All the furniture decor was set for two. The soft lighting. Candles. Flower petals just strewn strategically throughout.

"EmManuel?" I called out, he walked out of the master bathroom with his swim trunks on.

"My Acacia, you came," he said softly, with a proud smile. I ran and hugged him, it was nice to see his face again, my heart smiled. He lifted me off the ground as we stood holding each other in silence for about a whole minute. "I didn't think you were going to make it. I really missed you."

"I heard," I said, taking my earbud off and letting his newest single play from my phone out loud. I danced around him playfully, singing every lyric to his latest 'I miss her' song.

"That's not even about you, so don't get so happy," he joked and tackled me onto the bed. "Don't be laughing at my feelings."

"Never," I told him seriously, looking into his eyes. "I wish I could share my feelings the way you do. I missed you too."

"You do, in your writing. My people loved your work that you sent." He said proudly, I'd forgotten about the short story once it was sent. "They will meet with you."

"You never stop, do you?" I got chills knowing I was moving closer to my dream career as a writer, but was I ready to just up and change everything in my life? "My writer's block is gone, I'm able to think more freely now."

"Free Acacia. You're worth it," he said with a laugh, "Oh, and speaking of Free Acacia, let me show you something I made for you. With some help from a painting instructor, a new potential business endeavor I'm considering." EmManuel walked over to a tripod and turned around a painting of an acacia flower on top of a piece of wood, floating in water. "It's called Free Acacia."

"You made that?" I asked, choked up, trying to hold back tears for just one moment before I let go and cried. Urgh! "Thank you."

"Don't cry, it's a thank you present to you!" He told me with a laugh, putting the large canvas down and giving me a hug as we sat on the bed.

"No, thank *you* for making me feel again EmManuel." I said, "Getting me to soften up enough to get close to you, feeling the ups and down, and emotions again. I felt like I used to before I let myself get so caught up in other people's shit. Opening myself up again was worth it. I can now admit I was a little scared."

He squinted his eyes, "You are telling me I fixed you?"

I laughed, "I won't say that I just thought I'd never connect with anyone for real. That eventually I'd have to settle into the system like everyone else who wants to afford a nice middle-class status."

"You connect with people everyday Acacia, my nephew told me when my brother died, and he was going through a hard time, he would come to your class, and you looked out for him when he needed a minute. You have no idea the impact you had on him, sometimes he'd wake up and go to class just so you wouldn't be disappointed," He told me.

I was grateful to have made an impact. I felt myself grow emotional, reminiscing upon my relationship with his nephew. I didn't know how to help him when he told me his dad was killed, we'd just met. I felt so useless as I had no words of wisdom to say and no comparable personal experience, but I still wanted to help. So instead, I just kept my classroom door open for him to sit in the back of the room with his head down every day at lunch.

After the first week of him coming in about twice a day and sitting in the back, I gave him one of my empty journals. On the inside I wrote a simple note, 'May these pages be the friend you need during this time.' That second week he wrote in the journal nonstop while he'd sit back there. By the fourth week I noticed he had to buy himself a new journal because he was writing so much.

"Can you write that same note as you did before in the front of my book, Ms. Anaiah." I recall him saying.

I was so proud I could help, a few times a week at lunch he'd stop in to share with me a bit of his journaling. He only shared the clean, poetic pieces with me as he was too respectful to curse in front of me, but I saw other thoughts he'd written as he flipped through the pages. I was just happy he had an outlet.

Not too long after that we went into a nationwide shutdown and only would barely see each other outside of a small square box on my laptop.

"Well yeah, that's my job. I meant that I don't connect the way I did with you." I took a sigh of relief, "I was done looking for a real connection outside of myself by the time we met."

"I get it, but all those connections matter," EmManuel told me. "We are all connected."

"I'm a teacher, I'd do that for all of them." I humbly told him, "They just need a safe place to express themselves without being discouraged, shut down, or ignored. I try to be the person that I needed when I was a teenager."

"I know that you would do it for anybody, I talked to a couple of his close friends, they had good things to say about you too." He informed me, I couldn't help but smile. "It's the kind of person you are, hearing that from young people really made me want to learn more about you."

"Glad my name is good out in the street," I played down the sweet words from my former students, which literally makes my career worthwhile. "I have met some of the most interesting, entertaining, and innovative people inside of my classrooms. I've witnessed great debates, art, conversations, and ideas."

"You sound like you would teach forever."

I quickly shook my head, "No, I love it, but that's not the forever plan."

"I wanna be in the forever plan, so you have to stop blocking me and changing your number, I don't like that type of shit Acacia. So yes, I'll go get DavenPort to get on a hook and make sure you hear my message, but I shouldn't have to do that. I'll go all out to show you my love, but you can't quit, ignore, and shut down on me anytime things don't go your ideal way." He wiped my hot, tear-stained face with his thumbs, "Don't cry, you missed me for real?"

"Of course, I missed you, I missed your energy." I blinked the unexpected tears out of my eyes. "Missed how you make me feel, I like being in this world you created for yourself. You make me feel sublime, and that's scary for me because I have been through a lot, and I know what happens when I get that feeling. I've worked hard Manuel, I've changed so much, grown so much… I can't go back to who I was before."

"Trust yourself and trust me I am not *them* or *him*. I know you can see that. You didn't grow to go backwards did you? Don't get scared and run back to an artificial comfort zone." He gave me a seductive smile, "Have faith in me, I know the plan."

"You aren't the easiest person for me to trust."

"Stop that," he told me. "For real, I want a relationship as strong as the ones with my brothers. And I want you to wear my ring as a reminder."

"You think it is so simple, huh?"

"No, but it doesn't have to be hard." He shrugged, reaching in his pocket and holding out the burgundy ring box out to me. "We can talk through anything, make our own rules, I don't care what anyone else says. Can you just hold this? I'm not into pillow talk, but I can let you in my mind give you more of my truth."

I wanted to tell him my truth. I wanted to say what was on my mind, *'Manuel, I fell back into comfort, I mean, the curse with my ex, a little while after our football weekend. I was sick of crying and gave in to my most dangerous midnight snack, responding to his pointless late-night text. Hayden came over to fill out some paperwork, that was an excuse, he just wanted to see me. I knew why he wanted to come over. He asked about life and some flowers he sent me, then he touched all my mental and physical triggers, next thing we're in bed and he's playing that broken record he replays promises to make everything better, his new achievements, and how he will give me the life I deserve if I give him just one more chance. We know each other so well that my eyes call out his lies, but it doesn't matter, we both wanted the same thing. Comfort. Then I slept in my comfort zone all night.'*

"Okay," I couldn't tell him the truth, it was too messy, besides I didn't owe him anything right now. I picked up the burgundy ring box, tempted to see the ring, but put it down on the nearby countertop.

302

EmManuel held his hand out for me to take and picked the ring box up with his other hand. "No rush, no time limit. Let's just enjoy the vacation."

"I like that." I agreed. "Enjoying each other, not forcing anything or any ring."

"Well, Stubborn, you just put it on when you ready for the fairytale." He guided me out the room, with our fingers interlocked, out onto the see through deck that put us right on top of the ocean again. The sun glistened against the water; the view could've been a postcard.

I wanted the fairytale, I looked at him and smiled with my hand out to him.

He opened the, unveiling my 2-million-dollar gift. It sparkled and shined remarkably; it reflected every bit of light around us. I smiled whilst he put it on my finger. And EmManuel smiled just as big as he watched me model it.

"Oh my, this is gorgeous," I told him, breathlessly. "I cannot seriously accept this! Your world is ideal for you, you worked hard for it and I'm happy for you. This really is two million dollars; I don't want to take this from you."

He held my hand admiring the ring on my ring finger, "Just take the ring, there's no commitment. And especially if your resistance is about the money, I made more than triple that on just the first three songs you inspired. No, it should never be about the money, it's always about who you are becoming. Who you help others become."

I gave him an impressed look. He's made over six million dollars just writing three songs in the last year.

"Since it's not an engagement ring, in that case, I will wear it," I couldn't stop blushing at the fruits of my inspiration.

"It looks exactly how I imagined it would on you, like a little umbrella. In case it rains."

"Thank you, for the umbrella." I told him.

"Of course, you deserve it, you owe me nothing. I think we've been looking for each other, both doing work." He told me, kissing my hand. "Just remember the work never ends."

What we focus on, what our goals are aligned to, and what we give will be the majority of what we get. That is what I learned from my informal interviews whether it was love, live, learn, or just to leave a legacy; the folks who were consistent in effort got their sense of fulfillment. Who knows if, in this lifetime, we'll have another year like 2020. That's why it's important to prioritize time for ourselves.

We gotta do the work, EmManuel is right. Gather knowledge, embrace the daily lessons, give time for introspection.

Everything pointed to this is, to take some huge leap of faith and believing in yourself. This was my *sign* to finally take the jump, to sow and grow.